WAR BOY

WAR BOY

A NOVEL

KIEF HILLSBERY

Perennial

An Imprint of HarperCollinsPublishers

A hardcover edition of this
book was published in 2000 by
William Morrow, an imprint of HarperCollins Publishers.

HarperCollins books may be purchased for educational,
business, or sales promotional use. For information please write:
Special Markets Department, HarperCollins Publishers Inc.,
10 East 53rd Street, New York, NY 10022.

First Perennial edition published 2001.

Designed by Nicola Ferguson

The Library of Congress has catalogued the hardcover edition as follows:

Hillsbery, Kief.
War boy : a novel / by Kief Hillsbery.—1st ed.
p.   cm.
ISBN 0-688-17141-9 (acid-free paper)
I. Title.
PS3558.14534W37   2000
813'.54—dc21   99-39527

ISBN 0-06-093501-4 (pbk.)

01 02 03 04 05 WB/RRD 10 9 8 7 6 5 4 3 2 1

FOR JASON HAYES
FROM THE HEART

The truth is the best part of a man is a boy.

—MAXWELL PERKINS

WAR BOY

ONE

'm Rad I'm deaf I don't talk I'm fourteen I'm telling the
story. And storytellers lie so why bother you ask.

Because just the way any white boy would tell it there's a
place where I knew there would be a story and a story like
none in my life or anyone's and it was in the light at the end
of the General Douglas MacArthur Tunnel.

On the Green Tortoise bus.

When I woke up suddenly seeing two things at once: a
huge truck loaded with redwood logs headed the opposite direction out of the sun and into the tunnel and also the hairs
on Jonnyboy's legs glowing brighter than gold like they were
fiber optics lit from inside and his skin was a solar collector.

And I asked myself one why were the logs going north

across the Golden Gate Bridge where they already had red-woods to cut of their own and two where to the south did they come from anywayz unless Big Sur which was practically a national park and three was it the way kweerboyz feel the way the light on Jonnyboy's legs touched something inside me that also seemed new like being in San Francisco for the first time really that I could remember even though I was born there.

All these thoughts in the time it takes to strike a match. And now it seems like signs and portents in more ways than three but then I just knew somehow it was the beginning of everything changing and would dead sure be a scene to scroll the screen when I breathed my last. So I made a promise to myself when the truck passed by and the rumble of the logs moved the air and Jonnyboy shifted his leg against mine that I'd try like a trooper to keep track of what happened so some-day I'd read it and know who I was when I left home for good and made my life mine.

Storytellers lie was right up there at the top of Jonnyboy's rules-to-live-by list with *Ignore heroes* and *Never make decisions based on fear*. It was how he'd buck me up in the old days when I was head down kicking dirt while people around me grooved on someone talking and I mean fully with their eyes and the moves of their faces and it was just like music before I found punk rock. Because I couldn't be part of it no way never nohow and there I was unwashed and alone in the won-derful modern world. And is it lame to wish you're what you're not and even worse something you know less than zero about. So Jonnyboy could have read me hard on that but never did. He just smiled and eyed me and moved his lips and it was me who did the reading.

—Storytellers lie.

As in don't worry get happy. As in happy you don't have to listen. As in most people's stories are your basic commercial on TV that's maybe interesting to watch but nothing to pump up the volume about.

And since he was the storyteller nine times out of ten that's really film at eleven on Jonnyboy. It wasn't so much lying as entertaining the way he saw it. But he was proud he never lied about the big things. Big things like being a full-blooded kweer-boy he took seriously the way some people take religion or politics or dressing in black seriously. Once he told this bigtime homo in Monterey he didn't like old movies and the guy asked what kind of kweer he thought he was and Jonnyboy worried for a week I swear.

Because he thought he was a good kweer. Just not a good S.F. kweer was what he finally decided.

Since he came from down south.

Since he listened to the unheard music.

As in *do U know about the Germs?*

Which is the first thing he ever asked me way back when at the Electric Light Arcade on Lighthouse Avenue in New Monterey. He saw me before I saw him and is it blushing material because I had full long hair in a surfer cut and worse curse an upside-down KLOS visor cap. I rode my sk8board hella fast through the open doors the way I always did and braked with my skidplate to stop hard in front of the pinball game I was shredding then which was *Mars Attacks*. And Jonnyboy didn't waste time he just walked right up.

He slid two quarters across the glass so we started playing doubles and did we rock that machine more than twice around the clock. And it was almost three hours later I swear after multiple new high scores when he finally realized I wasn't just

the silent type and popped the question with the one-inch yellow pencil stub complete with pink eraser he pulled from the
piercing in his left ear.

And is it surprising I didn't know about the Germs or any
other bands really except for Kiss and I only knew them because when I was little I had a cheesy old notebook with their
stickers on it. But Jonnyboy wouldn't take no for an answer.
The way he saw it was that I knew inside and he knew I knew
from the way I shredded my way into the arcade and the way
he put it as in read my lips was:

—You're a punk when you're born.

Meaning there's more to it than music and fashion. Which
may be how it started with the New York Dolls and the Sex
store in London but really the look is just a package to get
attention for what's inside. The look tells everybody you don't
blend in and you won't blend in. And that was Jonnyboy hands
down your pants no doubt about it. He blended in nowhere
and it wasn't just his hair whether it was purple or shaved or
piled in a greasy high pompadour or his glow-in-the-dark nail
polish or his jewelry made from old computer parts and other
machines he scavenged from the trash in alleys behind stores
and offices late at night. He was only regular-sized but everything about him seemed big from the way he smiled to the
way he moved to the way he looked at you sometimes like the
two of you just got the punch line of a rad-ass joke no one else
would ever understand.

And I mean no way never nohow. By the end of that first
time we hung out he was calling me Radboy and I knew it was
curtains for the name I used to have. Because it just felt right
and walking out into the parking lot beside him afterwards I
looked at our shadows on the pavement and mine seemed taller
and badder than ever before and I knew it was goodbye forever

to the generic deaf and dumb kid who never got in anybody's way except sometimes on a sk8board.

So Jonnyboy was like this real live hero to me from genesis ground zero. Especially because after my mom died all I had was trouble with my dad and my brothers and sisters and what Jonnyboy called the question authorities namely the cops and courts and smiley face do-gooders buying me hamburgers and patting my back and predicting I'll go far against all odds because I know how to read and my complexion is clear and I can set the time on a VCR. And was that trouble sure to be continued in our very next issue with Tommy getting out of Chino and swearing to kill my dad in revenge for my mom. Only calling Jonnyboy a hero breaks one of his own A-list rules so I guess he was more like a sun to me with a warmth I could feel. And remember I lived my whole life where it's foggy for weeks at a time.

Or at least I did until my dad tried to kill me or maybe just scare me worse than ever before which is saying a lot.

What happened was he had Mateus Rosé bottles lined up in front of him dead soldier style on the coffee table in our house on Grace Street the way a normal dewd might have a few Bud longnecks. It was like four in the afternoon and he was sitting there in his wife-beater undershirt peeling off the labels with my brother Terry's eight-inch Buck knife when my sister Rita walked in and said something to him and suddenly the knife was flashing fast in her direction but not quite fast enough.

I jumped up to run too but the power cord connected to the portable TV got in the way and when I tripped on it my dad nabbed me by the neck in an iron grip. And to tell it longer than it took to happen he had the knife at my throat and my sisters and my little brother Timmy going crazy in the doorway in front of us and I could feel him yelling and smell the wine so hard I couldn't help but thinking if I only had a match.

Naturally this didn't just happen out of the blue and though we never had what you would call a father knows best kind of situation in our family things really started going downhill when my dad got acquitted of killing my mom on grounds of insufficient evidence and came home from jail in Salinas to live in happy harmony with the main witnesses against him.

Namely my sisters number one Rita number two but only by seven minutes Rose and number three Rachel. And they'd been set on putting him away for life so they wanted me to testify to things I didn't know for sure and it was a turning point in the trial because I was the only person who could have seen my dad push my mom down the back stairs if he did it and I didn't see him do it and I wouldn't say I did. I thought he probably did do it but it's also true she was even drunker than usual and the steps were definitely slippery from fog and she could have fallen and broken her neck with no help from anybody else.

Which is what my dad's lawyer told the jury without even putting him on the stand.

So my sisters thought I was covering for him out of fear I'd end up in a boys' home if he got locked up for good and did they hate me for it and try to turn my brothers against me too. But I wrote letters to Tommy in Chino and to Terry in the Coast Guard in Florida explaining just how it was and that if I saw him do it I would have said so but I didn't want to have perjury on me for the rest of my life. Especially not against my own dad. And they were kewl with a k about it as far as I was concerned and wrote back all *Don't worry get happy* but let me know it would be a big mistake to get too attached to the guy if I got their drift.

Which I definitely did.

But thinking my dad might be counting his own days in the double digits didn't exactly make it feel all better now did it.

Meaning the cold flat of the blade pressed hard into the skin of my throat with the edge about a millimeter from my jugular vein. I could feel his hand shaking then realized it was his whole body and this weird light-headed feeling started building inside me that was almost like it wasn't happening to me but someone I was watching from a distance and from above like a floating angel and then I was me again smelling the wine and feeling the cold steel but still I felt the angel looking down on me making sounds that somehow I could hear and the sounds turned out to be words in a whisper saying *Oh pretty boy can't you show me nothing but surrender?*

And I thought it was the voice of God I swear.

Telling me to fight back and win.

But before I could do anything my dad yanked my head up with my mohawk so he was in my face and started yelling and when I closed my eyes he did this clockwork orange thing jamming one eyelid up with his thumb so I could see his lips. Which made me feel pretty sick because what he was saying over and over was:

—I did it! I did it!

Meaning he killed my mom.

Why did he have to tell me whether he meant to kill me or not. Maybe he finally figured out that living with my sisters and waiting for my brothers to show up was worse than prison and he blamed me for ruining his life or something. And when you've already killed your wife I guess that killing your son doesn't seem like such a big deal and in fact might even later be seen as proof you're crazy considering the son basically got you off the hook the first time.

But he had to be a jerk about it the way he was a jerk about everything and he got what he always got out of it which was grief because in looking at me and yelling at me he wasn't seeing or hearing Jonnyboy come charging in like a mad-ass bull.

I didn't see the flying leap or the boot between the legs but I watched him break my dad's arm so it hung limp and crooked like a broken crank and then twist it behind him wrestling him headfirst to the floor. Jonnyboy sat on his shoulders still twisting his arm and pounded his head on the carpet until he wasn't moving and there was blood coming out of his nose and then he jumped up and stepped back and kicked the side of my dad's chest so hard with his steel-toed boot that even through his shirt you could see it cave in a little.

My sisters meanwhile had fled the scene but little Timmy who's eight was still there and he went up to my dad and kicked him too but in the side of the leg where it wouldn't have done much damage even with weight behind it. Then he ran away too. And Jonnyboy looked at me all sprawled on the floor and his face went white I swear. There was blood dripping from biting my lip I guess to stop from shaking when my dad was holding me but I didn't realize I was bleeding at the time and I just tried to smile at him so he'd know I was all right.

Except halfway into the smile something happened and I started crying and then Jonnyboy was kneeling beside me pressing his face next to mine and holding me tight in his arms. He was breathing hard and felt hot but not like hot on the surface from laying in the sun more like hot from inside from blood flowing so fast it made friction or something. I closed my eyes and could feel him talking to me while he ran his hand back and forth through my hair so I put my fingers lightly on his lips like I was listening and suddenly wanted for the first time ever to kiss another guy and did I.

So I ended up tasting my own blood which will probably scar me psychologically for life but did serve the useful purpose of dragging me back from dreamland to reality bites. And did it hard because the first thing I thought of was the question authorities and all their words of grown-up wisdom.

—Look at Helen Keller.

—Look at Stephen Hawking.

—They could do it and so can you.

Never mind Hellen Killer as Jonnyboy always called her coming from some rich-ass southern slaveowner-type family or that Stephen Hawking is like the second coming of Einstein and wasn't born the way he is besides. And he isn't deaf and I'm not blind.

Not that my own family isn't pretty much welcome to my nightmare material except for Terry and who knows about Timmy but if my sisters are raising him I don't need Magic 8-Ball to tell me the escalator isn't headed up. Like for example the next thing that hit me while Jonnyboy was wiping my blood from his lips with the sleeve of his jacket was that by then the twins had 911 on the line from the neighbors next door and except for Dunkin' Donuts there was no address the cops knew better in all New Monterey.

So it wouldn't be long before the domestic disturbance detail was on the scene. Thinking of the cops I looked over at my dad and could see he was still breathing and the only reason I told myself fortunately was for Jonnyboy's sake. Because I didn't really care if he was dead or alive anymore and the truth is I preferred him dead.

Jonnyboy saw me looking at my dad and misunderstood I

guess because he turned my head back with his hand so we were face-to-face and mouthed:

—Don't worry. I won't leave you here.

And I just drew a *K* in the air as in kewl with a k.

Then Jonnyboy reached over and pulled my dad's wallet out of his back pocket and fanned it open. My dad is the old-fashioned kind of guy who doesn't write checks or qualify for credit cards so he carries cash and lots of it for incidental expenses like buying rounds for his fishing buddies at the Portuguese Hall and betting on the 49ers. So there were two franklins and three grants that Jonnyboy gave to me plus a few jacksons he kept for himself then suddenly he jumped to his feet looking wild-eyed at all the windows and doors and the way he smelled changed just like that to a strong almost animal smell.

I didn't need a help file for that one. I ran to the kitchen for my backpack and sk8board with Jonnyboy close behind me and practically pushing me out the back door because if he was hearing sirens it meant we had maybe thirty seconds over Tokyo to get out of their way.

Our backyard slopes down steep from the house and we took the steps three and four at a time. I started running for the back fence to get over it and out of sight then stopped Roadrunner style treading air when I didn't feel the ground vibration from Jonnyboy running too. Looking over my shoulder I caught him playing statues at the bottom of the steps and then he saw me and pointed to my sk8board and I realized he left his out front when he came in from the street. And we're talking getaway vehicles here not toys so it wasn't like autopilot to just leave it behind. But then I could tell from Jonnyboy's face that he heard the sirens getting closer and he just shook his head hard and fast like he was waking up after falling asleep doing something important like driving and then he started running too and we vaulted blindly over a redwood fence taller than I am and ended up tangled in the strings holding up the bean plants in the Presteras' garden.

And were we crazed we just picked ourselves up and kept running flailing our arms and dragging string and poles and beans behind us until we got out to the sidewalk on McKinley Street and pulled all the wreckage off each other and Jonnyboy looked at me mouthing:

—You're the homeboy. You decide.

I knew the way to go farthest fastest was to head down McKinley a block and sk8 down David Avenue all the way to Cannery Row so my instinct took over and I just ran that way without thinking about how long and steep the hill is and how much traffic there'd be at that time of day and whether my trucks and wheels and deck could handle the weight of both of us besides. But as soon as we got to the intersection and looked down the hill I knew that run would be stories for the grandkids.

It was so clear you could see all the way across Monterey Bay. And David Avenue goes straight down to the water so for a second I saw this movie where I couldn't stop and shot out airborne over the bay and I told myself *Dewd there's sharks out there!* But closer at hand and more like real jaws of hell was the traffic on Lighthouse Avenue maybe fifteen blocks below. Because we could run the stops and lights before that with some fisherman's luck but we needed the green on Lighthouse or we'd get hit by a car or at least cause an accident because we dead sure couldn't stop.

Looking down David you could see there wasn't room for nice wide slalom turns for speed control and with two people on board we couldn't exactly count on the skid plate in a pinch now could we so there was only one way to do it and that was fast and dirty. Get down low on the board and weave in and out of cars if we had to and hang on Snoopy when the speed wobbles started.

Which is exactly what we did after I pulled the sk8 wrench out of the cargo pocket of my army pants and tightened my trucks and looked at Jonnyboy who shook his head from side to side all *Maybe I'm amazed* but held his thumb sky high anywayz and motioned me forward so his weight was in back.

I wish I enjoyed it the way I should have especially since Jonnyboy who was in all the sk8 mags and won a million contests back when they still had sk8parks later told this dewd in San Francisco it was the raddest thing he'd ever done on a sk8board. But at the time it was like jumping out of an airplane and sketching on the scenery and the rush of the free fall because all you can think about is whether the chute will open.

Every part of me was vibing green green green to the universe at large and I was thinking green cheese green party green apple green eyed green onions green kryptonite green hand green thumb green lantern green house green land green tea green goddess green green grass of home and finally green eggs and ham when the light came into view and it was green all right and that green light is mostly all I remember about that sk8 run really except for passing a car going down with another car coming up the hill head-on and I mean coming up fast.

After Lighthouse David flattens out and widens and there's no cross traffic until just above Cannery Row. So we carved back and forth to slow down and bailed just before the train tracks but relax your mind they haven't been a hazard to speeding wheeled vehicles since the sardines split for South America. My sk8board shot off toward Jupiter space but a switchbox got in the way and it came to rest wheels not so much spinning

as smoking from the grease in the bearings burning abso-
fucking-lutely up and my trucks oh heavens to Betsy oh suburban lawns oh kitchens of distinction my trucks were looser
than the nasty girls in the *Titty Titty Gang Bang* video my
brother Tommy sent me and wanted me watching regularly on
a preventive basis I guess when he found out I was hanging
with a homo.

Jonnyboy took my sk8board from me and held it up sighting down the deck to see how warped and trashed it was then
flipped it sideways and held it by the trucks like a machine
gun and started rat-tat-tatting in every direction like Sgt. Sands
of Iwō Jima. He bobbed and feinted right then charged left
spinning in the air. He landed in a stance looking both ways
ready for action and threw himself down on the ties. Then he
propped the deck on the rail and ducked his head low while
he panned a 180-degree field of fire. Finally he grabbed me by
the wrist and pulled me running and tripping down the middle
of the ties toward Pacific Grove with my sk8board aimed skyward in his other hand like he was leading the charge of the
rad-ass light brigade.

We kept running for a half mile only slowing down once
when Jonnyboy heard a helicopter from the Coast Guard station and being from L.A. where the cops have a bigger air force
than most countries in Europe he couldn't waste a chance to
draw a bead even if *To Protect and To Serve* wasn't stenciled
on the sides. Only this time my sk8 was a mortar and I had to
help him hold it and we dug our feet into the ballast rocks to
brace for the recoil which knocked me head over heels anywayz
with a slight assist from Jonnyboy who'd managed it all so that
by the time he helped me up the chopper was nowhere in sight
and he could claim a kill and pound his chest like Tarzan
Terminator Rambo.

We finally stopped out past the Coast Guard station where there's a place in the rocks we knew really well which is also the farthest we could be from a road in either direction. It's a ledge like a giant couch with a backrest right over the foaming water fifteen feet below and big enough for three or four people to sit and watch the waves and I mean in style because the ledge faces south and a little east so there's no wind and the overhanging bulge of rock you have to climb down to get there makes a roof to keep you dry. And it also keeps tourists and power walkers and amateur artists out of sight and up on deck where they can groove on local scenic wonders like the big fake smokestacks of Monterey Bay Aquarium and the shiny fleets of tour buses in the parking lot at Lovers Point. Which comes off all be my valentine unless you know that back in the days before birth control and rock and roll the full john hancock was Lovers of Jesus Point.

We sat there a long time catching our breath and thinking and checking out the otters swimming in the kelp. Then Jonnyboy made our sign for *I have seen the future* which is eyes downcast on fingers of both hands locked together in a crystal ball at belly button level. It's something we made up between us like a lot of the signing we did so it was like our own private channel to go along with our eyes and our lips and just moving a certain way plus of course my notepad and by then too it seemed we read each other's minds I swear.

I passed him my notebook and he pulled the old No. 2 stub out of his earlobe and started writing.

U know what i think? we should go down south.

Kewl with a k.

I didn't need to ask why L.A. because I knew it was all about Roarke who was sort of Jonnyboy's boyfriend and who also had a band. Still we couldn't just go buy bus tickets and play hopscotch with the stars on Hollywood Boulevard by sunup now could we. No cops are lazier than the bullet boyz in Monterey but it only takes a phone call to put the hound as in grey on alert as in red leaving one hand free to hold a donut. And with Jonnyboy's warrants outstanding for trashing motel rooms on sk8 trips and me being a juvenile in flight or whatever it was they had against me it would be stupid risking getting nabbed before we even got started.

Though was I pissed because I was the one on the brink of getting snuffed and Jonnyboy was the rescuing white hat white boy out of a million movies and who ends up on the run from john law. Still in my mind I harshed more on my sisters than on the cops themselves since after all their job is to be on the other side while my sisters should have known the score and looked out for me and Jonnyboy.

Yeah right.

The thing with Rita and Rose was they were born again and converted to this little storefront church in Seaside about three years ago when they were sixteen. And right off they got down hard not only on drinking which didn't exactly require divine inspiration in our house but on everything else from dancing to drugs to dyed hair not to mention immorality in the form of Jonnyboy in his black leather jacket with *Buttfuck the Majority* painted on the back in big dripping red letters. Every time they saw him they asked him why somebody his age was hanging out with a kid my age as if he was some dirty old creepoid with a bag of candy in the bushes by St. Anthony's Elementary instead of just ten years older than me and a sk8boarder besides.

Plus they turned Rachel against him too same wayz they got her joined up with their church. Sometimes I'd be laying awake early in the mornings when Jonnyboy stayed over and

I'd feel the draft from the door opening and watch Rose through my eyelashes checking out the sleeping arrangements which were always Jonnyboy in my dad's old sea hammock and me in my bed and then scanning the whole room and I mean hard for slimy used Trojans I guess and probably signs of devil worship too.

The truth is Jonnyboy never tried anything with me even though a couple of times I admit it I kind of wanted him to just to see what it was like. I mean after all at my age you do think about sex almost constantly and is it surprising since you want it so bad and it's so hard to get it with anybody but yourself.

But I knew about kweer stuff generally going all the way back to the summer I was seven or eight and Tommy came running into the backyard all out of breath and dragged me up the stairs and we ran three blocks to the alley behind Garfield Street and stopped at a high wood fence where he showed me where to look through a space between the boards at two grrls sitting side by side in lounge chairs naked. One was reading a book but she had a hand over the other's crotch and the other grrl was rubbing her own tits. Tommy pushed me away and watched for a while and when I looked again they were kissing. After that we made so much noise I guess fighting to see that they must have heard us and went inside.

I was in a daze because I never thought of anything like that before. We went back home and Tommy wrote out for me that they were dykes or as he put it dikes. And they must have been nudists too because we went back that night and sneaked around to the side patio and looked right in through the windows where they were careless with the curtains and there they were stark raving nude. Except for nipples and pubic hair we didn't see anything we couldn't see on a sunny day at Lovers

Point and they weren't even lipstick lesbians or anything glamorous like that but what Jonnyboy called lezzie boredoms when I first ran it by him. I mean instead of diving on each other they were just ironing and watching TV and eating potato chips. But it was way more exciting than any porno and especially for a little kid like me.

We stayed there spying on them an hour I swear until the wind blew the curtains together and Tommy reached in to pull them aside a little and I guess one of them saw his hand moving because suddenly I was standing there by myself with Tommy making smoke for Grace Street after a scream that was probably the loudest thing since Krakatoa east of Java. I ran too but not fast enough to miss being seen by people looking out the windows of every house in the neighborhood and the next morning bright and early those dykes were at our door.

And was I scared at first but my mom was already drinking and they could tell and once they found out about me the mad look left their eyes and I saw they were actually pretty nervous too and they never called the cops or anything. So a few months later at Halloween when Tommy wanted to spray paint their house and hassle them hard in costume so they wouldn't know who it was I flat out just said No which was really the first time I stood up to him on something important and made it stick.

The second time had to do with Jonnyboy which pegs me I guess as a big defender of kweerz but the truth is hella plenty need no defending from me or anybody else. I mean as many a moron learns too late just because a guy sucks dick don't mean he can't kick your ass.

Ok so Jonnyboy's an extreme example but he took my dad who weighs 250 down just like that and afterwards he wasn't even touched except for one chipped knuckle and a floor burn on his knee. While I felt like my ribs were broken just from being grabbed by my dad so it was more than kewl with me if we laid low until we found a safe way out of town. Though our hangout options were pretty limited since even though Jonnyboy's dad lived in Marina they were on strictly yelling terms with each other over Jonnyboy being kweer and also a tweeker. So he decided to go home by himself after dark and collect his stuff and hook up with me again later at my dad's fishing boat in the harbor where we could sleep in the berths and no one would bother us.

We watched the sunset together and it was one of those bloodred heart drop into the water sets you see in early summer before it heats up in the Salinas Valley and the big fog bank sits on the bay like the lid of a coffin closing forever. We looked for the green flash and high-five palm-slap wristlock fingerpull there it was and I leaned back against the rock with Jonnyboy's arm around me and my head on his shoulder thinking *Oh swell maps another gorgeous green light* and the next thing I knew I was waking up with a start alone in the dark looking up at the stars with my lips still quivering from my little kid dream that comes back again and again where I'm sitting at the kitchen table with my mom and I understand what she's saying and she understands me and it just goes on that way fully casual till she stops mid-sentence realizing with her mouth wide open and jumps up from her chair spilling her coffee and that breaks the spell and I'm reading her lips instead of hearing the words.

—Call the doctor call the doctor call the doctor call the doctor call the doctor call the doctor call the doctor.

I never slept anymore that night or the next. When I met Jonnyboy at the harbor he was all cracked on as in the snap crackle pop of crystals of meth and he wanted to get his sk8 back and I mean wanted hard and single-mindedly in true blue tweeker style though how could I blame him since it was an original Jay Adams Santa Monica Airlines board he got flowed out the back door of Rip City Skates and to any sk8er who knew anything it was basically the neutron bomb. Plus he'd been thinking about money and how we needed more cash to be styling like white men once we got down south and wham bam thank you man bright before my inner eyes was my dad's coin collection on the top shelf of his bedroom closet.

Which my sisters hardly knew about and might never be missed if something happened to my dad. There was one penny with the year struck twice by mistake that was worth at least $200 and the way everything was organized in navy-blue fold-out pages with labels and slots for the coins made it easy to snag and easy to carry and bet on it easy to sell. Just not in Monterey because sure we were punks but we weren't stupid.

So we went back up the hill to check things out and got Jonnyboy's sk8 back easy since it was on the front porch right where he left it and if you're thinking storytellers lie in crime-ridden America remember my family has a reputation which is better than a starving rottweiler for making sure that homeboyz just walk on by with their hands in their pockets. But even though it was three A.M. there were mass lights on including the light in my dad's bedroom and Jonnyboy heard voices inside.

Not just my sisters either. There was a man's voice too though definitely not my dad's. And it kind of crazed me for a while because somehow I got the idea it was my brother Terry and I wanted to see him and the idea wouldn't go away. So I made Jonnyboy try to listen outside for like half an hour which shows you what Jonnyboy was made of since Terry couldn't have gotten there from Florida that soon if Rita called him right after 911 and he shipped himself FedEx.

I guess it kind of creeped me out going back and hiding in the dark. Not so much because I thought it was wrong to lift the coin collection. More because I felt superstitious about going back in there again after I got away once. As in don't tempt fate. It was this waitress Dolley at Eddie's coffee shop in downtown Monterey who helped relax my mind afterwards and made it easy by telling Jonnyboy a story. And was it a coincidence because she didn't mean it that way of course but it was all the inspiration we needed to take action and I mean right away.

We were the only customers there who weren't counting down the early morning minutes until six when the bars on Fremont Street came back online and she was sitting in the booth with us filing her nails and flirting with Jonnyboy the way she'd flirted with scruffyboyz there in the same booth with the same kewl little jukebox on the wall and the same food on the menu for like thirty years. She always wore lots of little charms pinned to her blouse that her regular boyz had sent her from all over the world and she was always telling Jonnyboy he looked like Errol Flynn who was an actor in movies with Reagan I think. Everybody reminded Dolley of somebody in show business. I was a dead ringer for the older kid in *Flipper* which I think had a lot to do with me being blond and taking my shirt off whenever it got hot.

But it worked the other way too and the soap opera hunk on the front page of the *Star* she had spread open on the table was mistaken identity material for some guy she and her best girlfriend had teenage crushes on but who didn't even know they existed. So they found out where he lived and dressed up with clipboards in hand and knocked on the door pretending to be taking a survey about high-school student attitudes toward world government which they knew this guy was big on from being president of the civics club or something. And he fell for it totally and ended up asking her girlfriend out who reported back that he never tried anything nasty so they both lost interest and I mean immediately.

Even before Jonnyboy finished running this by me on a page of my notebook I could see him connecting dot after dot after dot in his mind's eyes and at the end he asked me what rooms in my house had phones and were any of them cordless and which of my sisters would likely be home at what times on that day of the week. Because he wanted to call up when only one of them would be there. Preferably Rita or Rose. Then disguise his voice and say he was a polltaker on subjects of prayer in school and abortion and Christian values in the home and really get her going while I sneaked inside and snagged the coins.

And it seemed like a plan to me since there was some church youth fellowship deal that Rose took Rachel to every Thursday night dragging Timmy along and I could either slip in through the front if Rita answered the phone in the kitchen or up the back stairs if she was talking in the living room. So Jonnyboy went in the bathroom to do a bump of speed for inspiration and together we wrote up lots of white boy sounding questions at Eddie's then spent the morning sk8ing Custom House Plaza and the afternoon as usual playing pinball. Just not at E.L.A. where everybody knew us but incognito with all the geeky tourist boyz around the indoor carousel at the Edgewater Packing Company on Cannery Row.

Around seven we split up with Jonnyboy going to the pay phone in the back of the entrance lobby because it was quiet there and me heading back up the hill one more time where sure enough Rita was jabbering away in the kitchen. So I took off my shoes and went through the front door and down the hall and opened the door to my dad's room feeling cocky as Big John Holmes.

Until I saw my dad sitting bolt upright in bed staring straight at me with his head wrapped in bandages and his arm in a cast.

And was I Bambi with brights in my eyes. I couldn't move. I stood there like a statue in the middle of taking a step with one foot off the floor and my arm in midair. My dad didn't move either and it was too dark in the room to see if his eyes were moving. I couldn't even tell if he was breathing.

After the total shock wave crested my first insane thought was to touch his hand on top of the blanket to see if it was warm. I finished my step but aimed it toward the bed without thinking at all. I took another step starting to think and one more which brought me to the end of the bed before I stopped again. Even though I had my senses back finally and knew I should get the H E double L out of there my arm was on autopilot and I started reaching out.

Then my hand froze. I looked him right in the eye and didn't see him blink. But he might have blinked his eyes when I blinked mine. I drew my arm back still watching his eyes. And I thought to myself *Maybe he's blind now*.

Which I admit it made me smile.

It took maybe half a minute to get the coin books out of the closet and into my backpack. I didn't really look at my dad again. Though I would have noticed if he moved or anything. And for the first time in my life I wished I smoked because if I did I would have sat down in the chair next to the bed I swear and made it a real father and son farewell jamboree. One last cigarette with Dad.

Back down at the Edgewater Packing Company Jonnyboy was still on the phone with my sister and upholding a tweeker

tradition by doing most of the talking. And when Rita did manage to get a word in edgewise he passed me little notes and
held his hand over his mouth to keep from busting up.

have U heard the news?

disabilities R a test from god.

read all about it, Radboy.

the holocaust came from jews disrespecting jesus.

I just yawned and watched the horses on the carousel go
round and round. I guess I got kind of hypnotized. Eyes closed
or open the view was the same.

I saw horses.

All directions.

And I remember wishing we could go back to the boat and
the big berth in the bow and get rocked to sleep like little
babies but it just wasn't in the deck of cards and the next time
it was rise and shine for your boy Radboy was coming out of
the General Douglas MacArthur Tunnel in San Francisco
which like I said is where the story really begins.

TWO

K ewl with a k is the word for the day even though this bus smells like incense which I hate. And there aren't any regular seats but beanbags and cushions covered with tapestries and tie-dyes. But you know what they say about going to San Francisco.

Be sure to wear some flowers in your hair.

If you've got any hair. Which I don't anymore since Jonnyboy chopped my mohawk off in Monterey to better travel incognito.

Of course San Francisco isn't exactly on the road to L.A. from Monterey now is it. So maybe you're thinking I must be at least a little retarded which is a common reaction that comes from misunderstanding the expression deaf and dumb.

I don't mind really since it gives me a little edge. When you're deaf and you don't say anything it makes hearing people nervous at first and sometimes you get special attention that bites if you're shy but once the novelty is gone you might as well be the Invisible Man. And the end result is you get to find out a lot of things that nobody realizes you know because they either forget about you or don't even notice you in the first place.

Like these two other boyz on the bus for example. Who Jonnyboy's been making friends with ever since the Bay Bridge being shut down for earthquake repairs forced us up to Oregon practically just to get to San Francisco. He didn't even notice them until I passed him a note and pointed them out. Just by watching them awhile I pegged them for tweekerboyz first and kweerboyz second. Or actually it was the other way around because there was something about the way the boy with the shaved head looked at me when we first got on the bus in Monterey. It sent a message to my body with a cc. to my brain instead of the other way around.

Almost a thrill. Like the way I felt yesterday when I was waiting for Jonnyboy to score at the old lobster grotto on Cannery Row and I noticed the Green Tortoise flyer for the Tibetan Freedom Concert in Golden Gate Park and right there on the list of performers just before the names got down to *no bottles cans or cameras* size was Roarke's band Chaotic Stature.

I checked the date to make sure it wasn't history already and then the pages of my brain calendar were flying off hurricane style the way they do in old movies until the freeze-frame close-up on December 25. Because did I feel like a kid again with reindeer on the roof and presents under the tree. Plus on the true-meaning-of-Christmas level the flyer seemed to bless our journey the way the Portuguese priest blessed my dad's boat and the rest of the Monterey fishing fleet every year on Saint Somebody's day.

The thrill part came from knowing for sure that something would happen and I mean something kewl. And is it scary in a way to have the same feeling about a total stranger who looks at you one-seventh of a second on a smelly old hippie bus. But he's not a total stranger anymore. His name is Finn short for Finnegan and he's half-English and half-Irish and full skinhead. His boyfriend who's more of a generic alternative type with piercings and bleach blond hair and black fingernail polish is Critter. They're around Jonnyboy's age and they've been down south somewherez at Critter's dad's funeral but they live in San Francisco. Which is the photo-op backdrop when we all hang out together at the rest stop overlook on Highway 101 before we cross the Golden Gate Bridge.

By skinhead I don't just mean Finn's #1 cropped hair but the tight Sta-Prest Levi's rolled halfway up his fourteen-hole Grinders and the narrow red spaghetti-strap braces over his black-and-white checked Ben Sherman long sleeve shirt. I recognized the look right off thanks to all the punk stuff Jonnyboy flowed me the first time he left Monterey and went back to L.A. He promised he'd keep me up on the scene and did he with big envelopes filled with record sleeves and articles and pictures ripped from zines and crazy long letters written in different colored pencils with all the things he said that came from songs in red. I taped the kewlest of the kewl to the walls of my room and seeing Finn for the first time brought it all back because at least three or four pictures of skinheads ended up on the back of my bedroom door despite their bonehead reputation.

I guess because I like their style. Which is weird because it's the total opposite of punk rock *DIY* as in *Do It Yourself*.

You have to look a certain way and even wear certain brands of clothes. It's been that way for like thirty years. There's none of this *It's what's inside that counts* crap. A skinhead's always in your face as in 24/7. And I like that. I'm kind of the opposite and I wish I wasn't.

His clothes aren't the only reason Finn stands out from the rest of the crowd when we get off the bus. Here we are in the shadow of the skyscraping red tower of the Golden Gate Bridge with all San Francisco spilling over its hills across the glittering blue bay and Finn stands leaning back with one leg bent at the knee so the sole of his boot is planted flush against the rock wall of the overlook and what's he looking at. The sloping parking lot and the bumper-to-bumper traffic snaking down toward the bridge from the twin tunnel mouths on the highway above. He's the only person not facing San Francisco.

The only person facing me.

I can see the city and the bay and the bridge and sure it's pretty but I stay back from the edge so I can look at Finn. Because now I've got this idea he actually is one of the skin-heads on my bedroom door. And I watch him nonstop hoping he'll hold his head a certain way with one eyebrow kind of cocked and prove it beyond reasonable doubt. Only I probably keep it from happening at all by staring too much and making him nervous. Because he mostly just looks down and when I start a notepad conversation he takes his time responding to everything I write and I mean takes his time saying next to nothing.

I never met a true skin before.

Fancy that.

It must be hard to find those clothes over here.

'Tis.

Do you like any punk bands?

Is Bedlam Ago Go punk?

I don't know them. What do you mostly listen to?

Trad ska.

Trad?

Traditional.

Anything else?

Northern soul.

That's it?

ABBA.

??

Critter plays it at home. Techno at work, as well.

You like techno?

Despise it.

You boyz are pretty good friends?

The best of.

Ever sk8board?

Never.

Know any deaf boyz?

Now I do.

Which he definitely scribbles with a smile. Still it isn't quite the gabfest Jonnyboy and Critter are having a few feet away. I can't read their lips in profile but it's obvious they're spinning at 45 instead of 33⅓ and interrupting each other so often I couldn't have followed even head-on fullface. Though I really don't need to. I know Jonnyboy and how his mind works and as soon as I proved to his satisfaction on the bus that Finn and Critter had to be tweekers based on their runny noses and dead giveaway fascination with every detail on every page of a Dremel power tool manual he was on the case and looking for an opening to make fast friends and I mean fast as in go-fast.

Because in Monterey he only scored a sixteenth or what's

called a teenager and he wants an eightball which is twice that much for partying with Roarke. It's a matter of pride with Jonnyboy due to Roarke's family the Lovejoys who are hella rich and own a newspaper plus half of L.A. and want him to reform so he can help take things over when the time comes. Meanwhile he's got unlimited funds for unlimited supply and plenty opportunities for company based on it and Jonnyboy won't go that route no way never nohow. Because the worst thing he can think of to call someone is *bag whore*.

Likewise Jonnyboy would no way never count on Roarke for a place to stay without an invite first. So I figure that a roof over our heads in San Francisco is most likely behind door number two in the overlook episode of *Let's Make a Deal* with special guest tweekerboy Critter and from the Grammy Award–winning air scribbles complete with flourishes for his adoring fans that Jonnyboy starts making when we got back on the bus I know he got the word to come on down. When we settle onto our cushions and I pass him my notepad he pulls me next to him so I can see what he writes when he writes it and even the space around us seems full of his pulse like Jonnyboy's whole body is one big heart beating wikked fast.

o skinny puppy do i ♡ U my o my. who needs ears when U got eyes. hell yeah they're tweekerboyz & bigtime 2. Critter deals & he gave me a taste. the word's vintage as in Shard-onnay, the supply's unlimited as in EMI.

You did some out there?

hee hee. guess U don't notice everything. C palmed me his inhaler.

Did you find out if they're boyfriends?

U called it, i believe it, that settles it. appy polly oggies 2 jesus & thanx 2 rose & rita. hell yeah 2 the 10th. We're invited 2 their little love nest in some back alley somewherez.

Suddenly Jonnyboy looks up then puts two fingers under my chin and tilts my head up too so I can see the bus driver aka Jerry Garcia on steroids standing front and center announcing something. Then all the passengers who are mostly twentysomething Europeans in American university sweatshirts and brand-new Levi's stand up collecting their backpacks and camera bags and Jonnyboy does bored to tears for all these years and turns fullface mouthing:

—Flat tire.

I give him a rebel look instead of a yell and spin one of my sk8 wheels with thumb and forefinger and puff my chest out all superior as in *The turtle's dead but sk8ers still shred.* Which is all it takes to get him into *Heeere's Jonny* mode and the next thing you know we're airborne off the lip of the bus stairs and performing for a crowd.

We've got momentum with us from the downgrade to the overlook wall and gravity too until we catch air off the lip of a storm drain bank and even then it puts us down right where we want which is sideways railsliding on the steel pipe barrier that tops off the waist-high rock wall. But as soon as we get up here I realize the feature presentation isn't going to be *Easy Rider* because the metal braces supporting the pipe clamp over the top of the railing itself and that means an ollie every dozen feet or so to keep from hurtling ahead while your board stays behind. And since hurtling ahead means launching into Jupiter space over a cliff that drops all the way down to the birdshit-stained rocks on the edge of the bay it isn't what you'd call the default choice on the options menu.

Ahead of me Jonnyboy clears the first clamp smooth as greenglass surf on a summer morning without a ripple of muscle to show it's work and lands back on the rail scattering the ranks of the Instamatic Army along the next section like a fox gliding sleek and sudden through a henhouse door. And then it all goes slo-mo for me as I clench my teeth and crouch for the grab feeling the sharp chill of the salt air between my spread fingers and there's the shining city and the surging gray-green water and the perfect arc of cables thick as boxcars sweeping toward the sun and there I am too in the Polaroid Finn took the moment I was airborne and hands me three clamps later when friction gets the best of me and the speed isn't there for the fourth so I bail.

Jonnyboy's weight takes him farther down the barrier and he jumps off to applause from the same scared tourists who fled the scene when showtime started. I guess most of them are foreigners. Because your average American hates sk8boarders. I'm surprised there weren't spikes on top of the barrier next to the pipe just to keep us away. Maybe they figured the sheer drop-off was discouragement enough. And the truth is I would have just watched Jonnyboy myself like everybody else if I realized what a cliff it was. But was I clueless because all I paid attention to earlier was Finn.

Who stays next to me while I stand looking at the Polaroid and Critter moves on toward the knot of people around Jonnyboy. Next to me and close to me. He smells like smoke from wood mixed with eucalyptus leaves when it rains. It's like inhaling a drug. One that makes you feel different right away. Gets your blood going like speed I guess.

He looks right at me with the darkest eyes.

I'm holding the edges of the Polaroid as tight as the rails of my sk8 when I ollied. I have to. Otherwise my hands would be shaking like Northridge and Loma Prieta put together. Slowly and straight-on fullface so I can read his lips he says:

—I always wanted to be like you.

Which completely confuses me because talk about *No way*

San Jose. All I can think to do is scratch a *Y* on the ground with the toe of my shoe.

—Because you're beautiful.

And I'm all *Yeah right*. I mean the mirror works for me just like it does for you and yours. I may be deaf. I may be dumb. But I'm not blind. And I'm not beautiful.

So I jerk my thumb toward this older babewatch type perched on the overlook wall who's looking in Jonnyboy's direction. I noticed her earlier on the bus because she was reading a book called *The Society of the Spectacle* instead of one with cable cars on the cover like everyone else. But she'd be a lot more noticeable to your average Joe on Main Street USA for her long blond hair with real streaks from real sun and tits that are big without looking like they came on order from General Hospital and legs that remind you why those oldschool pinup girls didn't need to show anything else. And when Finn has her in his sights too I nod up and down approvingly as in *She's* beautiful then flip my thumb backwards to my own scrawny chest while my head wags slowly side-to-side sad-but-true *I'm* not beautiful.

Finn just rolls his eyes. Then Jonnyboy swoops up and grabs the Polaroid and checks it out all *Isn't that amazing it slices it dices* until Critter moves in with his thumbs and forefingers framing the scene and we strike a pose with our fists in the air *Rocky*-style while Finn gets ready with the real camera.

With Jonnyboy next to me holding his arm up like that I breathe in his smell and talk about another drug. Don't get me wrong though he always smells good like tobacco without smoking more than two cigarettes a day. And like leather. And like spices. And it's his natural smell that he never covers up and besides he likes it too. But it affects me the opposite of Finn. It doesn't get me going. I haven't slept for two whole days and smelling Jonnyboy and feeling him warm next to me makes me want to close my eyes this very second and wake up next to him in San Francisco.

Which is basically what happens after a slight delay while Jonnyboy burns off the rest of the surplus energy provided by Critter. As soon as Finn snaps the second Polaroid this fatass oldboy in golfer Ray•Bans wearing a Greek fisherman's cap and a shiny silk scarf tied just so around his neck and I mean just so Hollywood waddles up and does the you-boyz-ought-to-be-in-pictures number while eyeing Jonnyboy's crotch and exercising every bit of self-control he has to keep from licking his lard-laden lips. Finally he fishes out his wallet and hands Jonnyboy a business card reading *Nick Vogue—Photographer.*

Which busts Finn and Critter up and I mean totally. But Jonnyboy just looks thoughtful until a slyboy grin lights his face watching them and he says something to the dewd then turns to me and pulls the pencil stub out of his ear.

fatman's got em laffing but i wanna show these boyz an even better time as in showtime. so i tell him yr a genius like hellen killer and can C the future. so U B the oracle & tell our fortunes. start w/ me & go all trancelike building it up that mine's connected w/ fatman's & U gotta do us 2gether. rite out only that i've got instructions from God & make mumbo jumbo sign 4 the rest then just U wait it's Heeere's Jonny to the 10th i swear.

So I write back all cocky smartass:

Kewl with a k but if I'm supposed to tell fortunes WTF's my crystal ball?

As in *Where the fuck's.*

And talk about signs and portents. Because right after I pass Jonnyboy the note a shiny domed hubcap shoots spinning across the parking lot and stops two inches from my feet. It's big and solid and chromed like something off a sixties American car. Or make that a sixties American bus. Because up the hill the Green Tortoise driver is looking our way and breathing easier through the fur on his face since at least it landed by people who won't be driving away with it.

Meanwhile Jonnyboy's stomping and yelling and shoving what I wrote in everybody's faces and he practically topples Fatman over squatting him down Indian style with both hands on his shoulders. Then he pulls Fatman's fancy scarf over his head and starts polishing the hubcap dome. When he spits on the chrome for good measure you can see this involuntary jelly quiver of excitement running up Fatman's body which almost sets Finn and Critter off again but one hard look from Jonnyboy as he squats beside me and hands over the hubcap like it's on a red velvet cushion gets them sitting white-man solemn in our perfect reflected circle of distorted Gumby people with the top of the bridge tower bloodred blurry and mixing like oil and water with the blue sky overhead.

Critter's on my left so I take his hand in mine and try to ignore him tickling my palm while I bend over almost touching my nose to the chrome and unfocusing my eyes. Then I snap my head back up and my other hand goes zombielike for the notepad. Jonnyboy puts the pencil in my hand and guides it over the paper while I stare glassy-eyed at nothing then slump exhausted after tracing out that the destinies of Jonnyboy and the stranger are bound as if by ropes and chains and Jonnyboy must now obey instructions from the Higher Powers. And does Fatman respond to the ropes and chains revelation and does Jonnyboy work it holding Fatman's arm in an iron grip and whispering in his ear every now and then until his eyes are glazed and beads of sweat ran down his forehead into his eyebrows.

Then Jonnyboy gives me a wink and I fall back exhausted

at the same time he hoists Fatman to his feet and starts pushing him toward the parking area and yelling at the top of his lungs.

Your chariot! Your chariot! Take me to your chariot!

After Finn captions it for me we jump up to watch the action which starts out with the two of them lurching across the pavement toward one of those slime-green seventies Cadillac convertibles with the top down and room in the back for options like patio furniture and a hot tub. A real Fatmobile in other words and Jonnyboy turns Robin's evil twin with a vengeance after he courteously opens the door and settles Fatman behind the huge upholstered steering wheel. Because instead of jumping over the passenger door and cheering him on to Gotham Jonnyboy dives onto the hood then spread-eagles grabbing the frame of the windshield and pops his face over the top just inches from Fatman's.

Jonnyboy snarls and whatever he yells makes Fatman cringe and cower and look like he'll be shopping for economy-size Attends the first chance he gets. He bends down and either keys the ignition or releases the parking brake because the Fatmobile starts rolling with Jonnyboy hanging tight practically foaming at the mouth while Fatman just stares up at him in horror mixed with obvious fascination that slows his stubby sausage finger moving toward the dashboard and pauses it there before finally connecting with the panic button. Then Jonnyboy rolls off catlike landing feet-first on the driver's side just as the ragtop fully extends and Fatman remembers the mechanics of the accelerator pedal.

With the Fatmobile speeding uphill toward the exit Jonnyboy jumps onto a low retaining wall and does some final grandstand shouting with his arms spread wide and his head swiveling round to take in all the overlook. Then he shrugs his shoulders and hops down to the pavement walking back toward us with his hands in his pockets like just another day in the life. Only halfway across the parking lot he stops and turns toward the blonde I pointed out to Finn who's still sitting on the overlook wall.

Jonnyboy stands listening to whatever she has to say which isn't much and just hangs there motionless afterwards looking at her without answering back. Then he turns toward us again and when he sees Finn and Critter still bent double next to me laughing with tears running down their cheeks he sprints back and they pound one another on the back and whoop it up bigtime until Jonnyboy stops to catch his breath and fill me in on the audio track which sets me off like a bottle rocket on the Glorious Fourth myself because what he yelled over and over spread-eagled on the windshield of the Fatmobile was *Jesus told me to skin you alive!*

After we calm down and stand waiting with everyone else to get back on the bus I notice the blonde and ask Jonnyboy what she said to him and he just shrugs and rolls his eyes. But when we're inside next to each other on the cushions again right before I finally fall asleep he motions for my notepad and writes:

after Fatman revved the engine & i bailed i yelled WHY ARE YOU LEAVING? COME BACK! LOOK AROUND YOU! THIS IS PARADISE! & U know what blondie said afterwards? This isn't paradise. This is where the jumpers park their cars.

As in bridge jumpers. As in suicide.

We read each other's minds in real time and we both trace the same letters in the air.

D.

As in *Damn!*

F.

As in *Fuck!*

I only sleep maybe twenty minutes before I wake up coming out of the tunnel but I'm wide-awake and I guess it's the city energy as in the city never sleeps. Everywhere around there's mass people and buses and streetcars going all directions and without a millimeter of space between the buildings the only way to see any sky is by looking straight up and even that depends on the neighborhood you're in. I've been to L.A. before on the way to visit Tommy in Chino with my dad and I know it's a lot bigger but San Francisco feels like a city's supposed to. Like it's constantly looking over your shoulder instead of off in the distance somewherez else. Plus here there's so many shadows you don't even need sunglasses on a clear summer day.

Unless you're a tweekerboy that is. Jonnyboy's got his wraparounds on and so do Finn and Critter. They're sitting a few cushions back on the opposite side of the bus leaning into one another with heads and shoulders touching when we make a turn or go into a curve so they're like a mutual support system. Which is how I picked up on the boyfriend thing when I was watching them earlier. Because Critter split for the closet bathroom not too long after I first noticed them and while he was gone Finn kind of went 2-D like he was in suspended animation or something and then revitalized when Critter came back. It wasn't like they were all touchy-feely or anything but it hit me like a smack upside the head that who they are is who they are together.

The blonde is sitting right behind them. She's not reading her book anymore. She's looking out the window and good for her. Because most of the cable-car book-club members are still turning pages like there's no tomorrow or actually like there is tomorrow and you'll be quizzed on the material students so

don't waste your time in class. I swear if I could talk I'd get
on the intercom and tell everybody they can stop reading about
San Francisco now because WE ARE IN SAN FRANCISCO
as in *It's the real thing* as in *This is paradise*.

Well not really. Too many poor and crazy patheticals beg-
ging on the streets for one thing and the streets themselves
aren't exactly paved with 49er gold now are they. More like
trash and little bindle Ziploc bags and flyers for raver clubs and
squashed Starbucks coffee cups. And all those clenched-jaw
people jammed standing on the dirty white buses with orange
worms on the sides. Not quite your happy campers in the
promised land.

But fuck em. I like San Francisco already. There's two or
three sk8erboyz on every block. There's black people and
brown people and yellow people and kweer people and just
plain weird people but hardly any old people. And face it most
old people are just beyond the valley of the fucktards.

I mean they pay their taxes.

Salute the flag.

Call cops on sk8boarders.

And worse play golf.

At last we roll up to Golden Gate Park. As far as you can
see in both directions the sidewalk looks like an assembly line
conveyer belt delivering an unlimited supply of boyz and grrls
aged sixteen to twenty-five to the mouth of a long green tunnel of leafy trees. In the original recipe before the bus lived
up to its name so well thanks to the detour around the bay
and the flat tire we were supposed to stop first at some hostel
also run by the Green Tortoise incense and patchouli empire.
So everyone could freshen up and ditch their carry-on bags
and made-in-China-by-slave-labor sneakers before cruising on
to the opening ceremonies of the Tibetan Freedom Concert.

But the concert's about to start any minute and Uncle Jerry's dropping the passengers off then hauling their luggage to the hostel.

Not all the passengers though. Some just bought tickets for transportation and not the concert. Such as Finn and Critter. Not to mention Jonnyboy and me. Only we're going to the concert and they're not. Getting free drugs from Roarke is one thing but Jonnyboy didn't think twice about making the right phone calls yesterday to get us on the guest list. Which is kewl with a k because the tickets cost $20 a day for three days. I don't think Finn and Critter care much about the concert anywayz. But they offered to take my backpack and Jonnyboy's duffel bag home with them and we've got full instructions on how to find their place later thanks to Finn's true blue tweeker devils-in-the-details hand-drawn map complete with street key compass rose and miles/kilometers conversion bar.

They see us off outside the bus and Critter catches me catching him palm his inhaler to Jonnyboy and makes an A-OK sign with his hand that shows off this little homemade pin-and-ink Playboy bunny head tattoo on the outside edge of the first joint of his thumb. He doesn't flash it in the air just does it on the side of his jeans so it's between the two of us. I don't know if he means just say Yes to drugs or that it's kewl with a k to do them more or less publicly here in San Francisco or what. I wonder if he thinks I'm a tweekerboy.

I wonder if he thinks that Jonnyboy and me.

NFW. As in No Fucking Way.

Though does it matter and if it does why. I mean I try not to care what other people think and this is religion I'm serious about it.

But still. After Jonnyboy pretends to have a coughing fit

that requires covering his mouth and nose with his closed fist three or four times and palms back the inhaler and we all do later daze I'm watching Finn and Critter climb the steps into the bus and this thought suddenly hits me and I mean upside the head.

They go inside each other's bodies.

And it does seem kind of weird. It makes me wonder if I really am prejudiced deep down. Then I remember how I felt when I first found out my mom and dad did that and talk about weird.

It's impossible to stand still very long on the sidewalk because the crowd is like two rivers converging and going suddenly into rapids on the pathway through the trees. There's a current that carries you along and we're already moving with it when the bus pulls away but I can't help turning back to scan the windows in case Finn and Critter switched sides. They didn't but the blonde did and now she's sitting where I was and looking right at me or actually a little over my head which means she's looking at Jonnyboy.

Who's looking noplace but straight ahead and charging forward with one hand locked around my wrist and the other clenched above his head and I can't see his lips but I know what they're saying which is vintage Johnny Rotten.

As in *Follow Me!*

Where the trees stop and the open field starts the sudden heat from the people and the sun is like an airlock into another world. Everyone slows down and there's room to move apart a little and head for the different ticket kiosks. There's portable chain-link fencing between them topped with blue and yellow helium balloons instead of barbed wire and most of the people taking tickets are Asian types in robes the color of those crushed velvet ropes you see outside restaurants with valet parking. We're at one end of a huge long grassy space too narrow to really be an oval that slopes uphill toward a giant stage built on scaffolding maybe three stories high. Bright colored boxy tents with streamers and flags around the edges make it seem like the midway of a carnival.

Before the semis hauling the rides get there that is. Before the drivers discover there's no room for any rides with all the people. Who knows how many but all of Monterey has like 25,000 total and there must be twice that here. With more than half of them boyz with their shirts off or else taking them off right now the way Jonnyboy is because the field is completely surrounded by trees that shut down the natural San Francisco air-conditioning from water on three sides and since it's the middle of June the sun is twelve o'clock high in the sky even though it's more like three. The film of sweat on Jonnyboy's chest just emphasizes how built he is in a natural way from surfing and sk8boarding and the letters of the *Team Pain* tattoo on his left upper arm are distorted from climbing up the swell of his biceps and it almost shames me into keeping my own shirt on but I just figure what the hey and tie mine around my waist too.

We aim for the kiosk labeled *Invited Guests* where we're greeted by this Buddhist nun I guess who looks Chinese to me but is it the Chinese Freedom Concert or is it not so she must be Tibetan. She's a foot shorter than me and looks about the same age though it's hard to tell since her hair's about as long as mine and Finn's. She doesn't read English too well and Jonnyboy has to point to our names on the computer printout which she carefully checks off without asking for ID or anything and then she motions for us to bend down and drapes one nylon cord with a laminated red card reading *Access All Areas* around Jonnyboy's neck and then another around mine. When I straighten back up she's grinning ear to ear and points a finger first at my chest then reverses direction pointing at her own and follows it locking the fingers of both hands together doing this is the church this is the steeple. So I guess the message is *We're all one* or whatever which must be the Buddhist version of the Golden Rule or the Ten Commandments.

The next thing she does is rub her palm in a circle on her shaved head and then on mine while she laughs till her eyes water. And I'm thinking she has it all over the sisters at St. Anthony's in Monterey who always made me feel like a worm in the mud being punished by God when some fur-faced neanderthal hands me a flyer with big black letters saying:

Read the Labels!
Don't Buy Chinese!

And I admit it my first thought is *What about takeout?* But then I slap myself interior upside since I don't know exactly what happened in Tibet but I know it wasn't pretty and you can bet on it being done with help from America one way or another. So I read myself and I mean hard for following the family tradition of wise-guy ignorance that makes my dad such an appealing role model. I mean you learn or you burn and being fourteen is no excuse for being stupid. Because you're only fourteen once but you're stupid forever if you don't watch out.

Not to overworry though considering what's happening up on the stage which isn't even some plaidshirt grunge rockers tuning up their guitars. Instead four men who look like samurai warriors in wild multicolored robes with golden peaked helmets are parading around followed by Asian skinhead boyz in plain red robes like the nun's carrying weird thin brown and silver horns that are ten feet long I swear with two boyz to a horn.

They get in formation and say some kind of prayer while we hurry down to the foot of the stage where the security guards give us hard looks at first and square their shoulders but turn into doormen at a fancy hotel when they see our passes. They hold the chain across the stairs up the scaffolding aside for us just like we're headed for the rich-ass presidential suite and give us plastic packages with earplugs which Jonny-boy makes a little ceremony out of putting in for me. And it's not quite the killing joke you'd think because the horn players start up right when I grab the handrail and it snaps my head back like someone slugged me in the stomach. Because that's where the vibration hits. In the guts and I mean hard like it's coming out of me instead of the PA.

Which pretty much goes double quadruple for the hearing masses. I look out at the crowd and everyone's standing with their mouths open staring and feeling this incredible rumble that seems to thicken the air itself and slow everything down from your blood to your breath and even your blinking eyelids into slo-mo curtains that rise and fall with a rhythm you realize was always there but you never noticed before. At first it seems like a drug to me. But then I realize it's more like mass hypnosis with all of us vibrating to the same frequency.

It even mellows Jonnyboy who's naturally hyper plus fully amped on go-fast and the special coming attraction of seeing Roarke again besides. When we get up to the level of the stage itself he scouts around with his eyes in case Roarke is around then sits down cross-legged at the base of one of the PA towers and holds his chin in his hand. Sometimes his eyes open but mostly they're closed and I've never seen him still so long I swear. Even sleeping his body twitches all night long.

I try closing my eyes too but it's too much black hole beyond Jupiter space and I end up focusing on the long slow rhythmic rising and falling of Jonnyboy's chest which continues even after the musicians stop playing and leave the stage. The vibrations from the horns still hang heavy in the air when I realize he's watching me watching him and our eyes meet and he takes my hand in both of his and moves his lips.

—I love you skinny puppy.

Suddenly huge banners drop down from the tops of the PA towers with bright complicated pictures of Buddhas sitting meditating I guess and holding their hands and fingers in different positions that look just like sign but don't translate at all. Then some actor who obviously registers in the red zone of the fox-o-meters of most of the females present but who Jonnyboy doesn't recognize comes out and talks for thirty seconds max before stepping back away from the center microphone doing praying hands in front of his chest and bowing his head toward someone walking out.

It's the Dalai Lama. This smiling middle-aged moon-faced man with hair like mine wearing wire-frame glasses and one of those red-and-yellow robes showing one bare shoulder that must be the height of Tibetan fashion. And it's hard to explain but there's this feeling that replaces the sound of the horns and seems to radiate out from him like a ripple on water and touches everyone. This feeling that gets stronger like a river grows until it might be a physical force keeping everything still with no Frisbees in the air no hacky sacks no one even putting soda or water bottles to their lips just sitting listening.

This feeling that's familiar.

Not common but I've had it before.

Those times when everything seems sharper and softer all at once.

Colors.

Smells.

The touch of the wind on my skin.

There has to be a word for it but I can't think of one and I understand why after he finishes talking and everyone stands applauding and the feeling is gone and Jonnyboy passes me a note.

i can't believe how quiet it was.

So now I know.

I finally know what quiet is.

It's like surfing.

The green room we call it. Where you're in the wave instead of on it with the water curling over like an endless tunnel and the light all soft and spooky. And the speed and the sound too I guess is like a runaway freight train but the feeling is the opposite.

The feeling is a quiet.

That you never want to end.

Though all things must come to an. And do they now with Jonnyboy springing forward and yelling out so loud to someone walking toward us that his words move the air.

You know he's a star right off the first time you see him. He looks like somebody should be taking his picture. Except he isn't really a star as in Hollywood or MTV. Not a big one. More a star the way the sun's a star and planets move around it and some even rotate like the moon with the earth so one side's always got the heat and light and the other's dead dark wikked cold and might as well not be there at all. And that's Roarke with Jonnyboy circling him watching him. Never looking away. Never turning his back. But the opposite of paranoid. Whatever the word is.

Roarke gives me a look when he shakes my hand that says *Do I know about you boy*. And I shoot right back with my own look to him and fast back to Jonnyboy doing *Storytellers lie*.

Which Jonnyboy translates so Roarke laughs big time. Up close I can see that the smile lines around his mouth and the corners of his eyes are the kind that stay there when he isn't smiling and so much for imagining him about Jonnyboy's age from the photos on the record sleeves. Because think about it Stephen Radboy Hawking those pictures were probably taken when they still used flashcubes.

And though he doesn't look old enough to play daddy or anything Roarke in his black leather motor jacket and greased back outlaw rocker hair definitely puts bold on the boy in Jonnyboy. Who looks a lot more like a kid beside him and probably always will. I mean you can see the boy in his eyes and look away then back and see it again. While with Roarke you see someone different every time you look it seems but never a kid. It's weird. He's probably never had a regular job and still has that eight-to-five tiredness in his face you see in clerks at blue light discount stores. Which is pretty scary since he's been a rebel all his life.

At least in the world according to Jonnyboy.

Though Jonnyboy always says it takes work to be hip. And Roarke's on the time clock right now. He's headed for the only kewl place to see and be seen at this day date and time which is watching some unknown opening band on the second stage in the no-commercial-potential zone at the far end of the field that we didn't even notice coming in. He doesn't want to miss them because nobody knows them now but just you wait. And would we like to join him because this will be like catching the Pistols at the Babalu Club or the Clash at the 101.

As if Jonnyboy isn't joined to him already and I mean Siamese style as in heart-to-heart soul-to-soul. Which kind of leaves me by my lonesome and I admit it I feel jealous. Though not romantically at all. When Jonnyboy mouthed *I love you skinny puppy* he didn't mean it that way. Of course not. I'm just greedy I guess for Jonnyboy. And I tell myself *Buck up fuckup* because greed is one of the seven deadly sins.

Besides I could do hella worse than tag along behind two boyz who squeeze out sparks from the multitudes from one end of the concert to the other. This crowd's a little too cool with a self-conscious c for anyone to ask for an autograph but Roarke is definitely recognized and I don't see any obvious oldschool sk8er types so Jonnyboy probably isn't recognized but he's definitely admired.

Plus he's on the receiving end of the only real outbreak of fandom. Halfway to the second stage this geeky-looking pasty-faced guy with bad blue-black hair dye and pen in hand frantically worms his way past a dozen people to jam a little diary book in Jonnyboy's face and starts jabbering away. I'm behind so I don't catch anything other than the hostile vibe that fills the air around Jonnyboy and I mean fast and then Roarke puts a finger through one of his belt loops and leaves gothboy in our dust doing confusion to the tenth.

I tap Jonnyboy's shoulder a minute later all *Hey remember me?* and he turns around and apologizes with his eyes then scribbles on my notepad:

fucker thought i was a BOXER. hell he KNEW i was. star of some moovee called broken noses. wouldn't take no for an answer. i'm all i'm a SURFER, i'm a SK8BOARDER, boxers are STOOPID, boxing is STOOPID, people who like boxing are STOOPID. tho maybe i said lame kunts not people.

Then he turns and doubletimes it after Roarke like a scared

little kid losing track of his dad in the biggest toy store in town on the day after Thanksgiving.

The small stage has about 500 people in front of it instead of 50,000 and it's three feet high instead of thirty. After we stake out prime standing space on the sidelines at the base of the stacked wooden pallets holding the PA speakers thanks to *Access All Areas* Roarke and Jonnyboy get lost in head-down conversation that I can't follow so I just look out over the audience. People are so much closer than at the main stage. They're mostly dressed thrift store style or sidewalk sale punk instead of blacks and boots antifashion fashion and another really noticeable difference from the main crowd is that way more than half are grrls.

Some of whom are obviously into each other. And since in the world according to Roarke the grrls in the group are rumored to be dykes I get my chance to suss out whether it's a lezzie band or not when this stagehand grrl dressed in slacks and a geoduck clam t-shirt walks by carrying a big stack of lyric sheets. I motion for one with a question in my eyes and she stops and hands it over. There's something about her and the way she looks at me very straight-on and smart. She's not pretty in a glamorous way and actually kind of plain but I like the way her lips curve. I wish we could talk so I could just keep watching her.

But she's gone. I skim over the lyric sheet she gave me for juicy drippy lesbian love odes but don't find any. Though some of the songs are definitely addressed to shes not hes. Then I look up and see her again.

Standing upstage to the side with two other grrlz. Only now she's holding a guitar. And she's holding it like it's part of her so I know right off she isn't holding it for somebody else. When she sees me watching her and smiles I finally get it.

She isn't working for the band.

She isn't a fan of the band.

She's in the band.

And is she. The PA is nothing like those monster towers at the other end of the field but it rocks me like never before and I get my wish after all I get to watch her. She's the lead singer and it's like watching a volcano erupting and there's a fleeing villager inside me afraid of the lava but hypnotized by it too and waiting for the burn the steam the sizzle. Because I can read her lips enough to figure out which song is which and she's singing words that seem to be for me alone.

I sign I sign I sign anonymous.

I'm no monster I'm just like you.

These words are all I have these words are who I am.

But it isn't words moving me like a wave to the shore even *I'm tired I'm hurt I'm fine.* It isn't words but her face and the way she tears at the air with her hands like she's fighting for something fighting to finish the songs fighting the fucked-up crazy world fighting for life.

And winning.

Because when they finish she walks offstage looking taller than she did before with her head held higher and her shoulders thrown back and I want almost fiercer than anything to run after her and dot dot dot I know not what. Just not quite as fierce as I want Jonnyboy and Roarke to find words for the sound of her voice but they can't. Not really. It doesn't translate. And I guess how could it.

They're mostly impressed with how hard those three grrls rocked without a bass player.

I fold the lyric sheet into an envelope for the Polaroid of me sk8ing at the overlook and before I stash it in my cargo pocket Jonnyboy motions me to pass the photo to Roarke. He's all smiles and thumbs up *You rule dewd* and checks it out longer than he has to just being polite and from the far-off way he looks at Jonnyboy after handing it back I'm pretty sure he didn't see me in it but Jonnyboy as in the Jonnyboy he first knew. But he doesn't look at anyone very long before looking away. And when he looks at Jonnyboy again it's as opposite from far-off as up close and personal can be.

It's one thing tagging along to go watch a band. But I feel weird going back to Roarke's hotel room. I know Jonnyboy's nervous about it from the way he mouths twice and writes down once that I must be really tired. As in drop-dead Rip Van Winkle mode. As in *Seven seconds after we get there you're out like a light. Am I right?*

Roarke though is fully casual. While we're waiting to flag down a taxi outside the concert entrance he makes a point of letting me know it's not just a room with a bed and an easy chair but what he calls a hospital-fatality suite. Paid for by the record company. Living room dining room wet bar microwave everything. On the twenty-sixth floor.

I've never even been that high off the ground. From the outside Roarke's hotel looks like a giant jukebox made of mirrors and the lobby floor is marble so polished we can see our reflections walking to the elevators. Jonnyboy's still got his shirt off which seems almost obscene in here somehow with all the fountains and flowers and look-but-don't-touch furniture but all the boyz on the hotel staff have that light-in-their-loafers look and don't seem to mind at all. Roarke and Jonnyboy start laughing as soon as the elevator doors close and I know it has something to do with the way a couple of the onlookers checked them out first then did double takes on me but I just file it in the don't ask don't tell category because I've got enough to worry about already.

Roarke's rooms must be meant for entertaining both A- and B-list guests at the same time without any embarrassing overlaps. You walk into a living room area that's got a couple of fake leather sofas and four boxy fake leather armchairs arranged in a square around a big low coffee table. There's a kitchen alcove to one side separated by a fake wood wet bar complete with half a dozen padded swivel stools. Everything's brown and beige. The wall opposite the door is all windows but they're covered by heavy dark drapes. You turn left where the drapes end into a passage with doors to a bathroom then a bedroom and the window wall starts up again but uncovered this time with a view south to Salinas practically and east to the Erector set towers of the Bay Bridge and the hazy gold hills above Oakland beyond. Then you look ahead and realize the corner of the building's coming up and the ceiling goes fifteen feet high and you're sighting down this polished conference table as long as a full stretch limo toward a wall-to-wall and floor-to-ceiling view of the top floors of every high-rise in downtown San Francisco.

Which distracts your attention at first from the one large and two small crystal chandeliers and the gray-and-black-veined marble fireplace and the seriously old glass-front wooden cabinets with prisms edging every pane and brass keyhole locks on the drawers complete with skeleton keys that look like they're fresh from some blacksmith's forge at Plymouth Rock. Plus the highback reclining armchairs surrounding the table are so soft to the touch they must be upholstered in doeskin I swear and the Confederate gray carpet is so dense and deep you have to pick your feet up vertically to walk without tripping.

I don't think Chaotic Stature is a big enough band for the record company to spring for all this. When Roarke throws down his leather jacket on the table alongside a basket filled with picture-perfect fruit and picks up the phone to check his messages I try to signal Jonnyboy as in *Storytellers lie* but the frequency's jammed or something and he doesn't get it so I just end up all *No way never you mind* and wander over to the windows and look maybe ten stories down to the spire of the steeple of an old red-brick church next door.

I look back at Roarke and Jonnyboy moving closer together standing talking by the fireplace and touching each other's arms and shoulders sometimes the way you do with friends but for longer and longer until their hands just stay on each other and their eyes do the talking and then their hands are moving. Not below the waist or anything though which is definitely shout of relief material to your boy Radboy.

For about seven seconds.

Until they kiss.

And am I like a virgin thinking what makes things sexual or not is where your hands are. Because this isn't a movie star kiss or a health class documentary on understanding gay people kiss. This is a kiss like I've never seen between people in person before and it scares me knowing it leads to more than kissing.

It has to.

It has to and it does.

At first I admit it I'm all *I'm outta here.* But then I realize I'd just be calling attention leaving when I'm already off the screen again and this time for the duration. So I just do my deaf boy thing and shuffle back to the B-list zone where I sit in a chair nowhere near as comfortable as it looks and take out the lyric sheet from the grrl band at the concert and practically memorize all the songs I swear until I'm just sitting here staring at the paper with my thoughts 2,000 light-years from home when I feel a hand on my shoulder and I'm all *Damn you.*

Meaning me.

Because I've got a sense about people close to me who I can't see as in this is religion nobody gets the drop on me. So it creeps me out at first. But I relax my mind because the hand is Roarke's and he bends down forward with his arms around me to take the lyric sheet in his hands. Then suddenly from behind come arms bracketing his and Jonnyboy's fingers circle Roarke's wrists like handcuffs. Jonnyboy slowly raises Roarke's arms with all the blue-black tats standing out like patterned giant lizard skins or something and they're so close I can see a few old track marks but nothing fresh or even recent.

I wonder if he's hitting between his toes the way some runnerboyz do in the world according to Jonnyboy.

Which always seems heinous to me when I think of it and do I try not to. Because when I was five or six I stepped on a nail that came out the top of my foot almost. And it still shrinks my nuts to acorns just remembering.

With Roarke's arms all the way up over his head I can feel the heat radiating out from his armpits and I close my eyes and breathe in deep his sweet strong smell with a tang like rock salt baking in a cast-iron skillet before you add the giant prawns. I keep them closed when he pulls away to follow Jonnyboy back down the passage toward the bedroom. I mean I already feel like I'm spying on them even though they know I'm here.

I don't know why.

It just seems wrong.

Though I expected something different and that's why my first thought when the real kissing started was to bail. Because it's no secret males are basically animals and is it *Fright Night* the director's cut imagining two boyz all glassy-eyed and panting for the finish line doing the selfish things that women complain about to the sex advisers in magazines only doing them to each other in worse and rougher ways.

But maybe it's just my imagination.

Running away with me.

They're gone now but with my eyes closed I can still see the way Jonnyboy first took Roarke's hands then took all of him away from me.

Not at all hard.

But not exactly soft.

Maybe the word that's opposite isn't soft.

Maybe it's tender.

Maybe it's not spying on Jonnyboy at all.

It's not secrets he's keeping.

It's something he's sharing.

Still it makes my head hurt.

So I open my eyes. Which focus on two drawer pulls on the side of the coffee table. I wonder if the drawer is real. Or is it Memorex. With the money for the baby formula and next month's mortgage payment riding on Memorex. So of course when I reach down and pull it's old Hella Fitzgerald after all.

There's nothing in the drawer but a tourist map of the city and a black covered booklet with white letters reading *Narcotics Anonymous Northern California Meetings 1996*. Which I don't think hotels are flowing to guests alongside Gideon Bibles even in San Francisco so it must be Roarke's. I reach for it thinking I'll page through and see if any dates are marked or anything but then my hand goes into freeze frame. Because is it private or is it not something in a closed drawer in a room belonging to a friend not foe and another punk besides. And I ask myself why am I sitting here watching the detective when defective's more like it and I don't just mean physically.

I mean morally. Though I wonder if it's in my genes coming at me both directions. I mean look at my family's track record at making the right decisions about important things. Tommy in the Men's Correctional in Chino is just the flipside of the twins in the New Monterey First Protestant Church of God in Christ. You don't have to live behind bars to be in prison. Just ask my dad.

Yeah right. For laughs. There's gotta be a joke in there somewhere. About the other kind of bars.

Heh heh heh.

It's thinking of my dad that unfreezes my hand and closes the drawer. The same hand that played statues reaching out to touch his own still hand on top of the blanket on the bed.

The day before yesterday.

Though it seems like a long time ago in a galaxy far far away.

I don't decide to walk down the hallway to the bedroom.

I just do it.

The door is open.

The lights are off.

The blinds are drawn.

The room is lit from a candle inside a blue glass shade.

The bed is empty. They're on the sofa against the wall at the end of the room. There's an easy chair blocking my view of their heads but I can see the Ritchie Dagger tattoo on Jonnyboy's tanned leg standing out against Roarke's pale shoulder with the clown crying tears of red white and blue.

They're moving of course but in slo-mo I swear. Roarke's muscles ripple from his shoulders down his back like water. Jonnyboy's hands follow the ripples.

His fingers wide apart.

His legs relaxing when Roarke pulls away.

Then tightening into a chokehold almost with Roarke pressed back hard close against him.

Every part of Jonnyboy strains to hold Roarke there and they rock in one motion.

Roarke pushing down.

Jonnyboy up.

Jonnyboy lets go just a little but arches his back to follow Roarke until Roarke levers up and forward from his feet like a sprinter off the blocks and puts space between them for a moment that seems to last forever while they hang there in the air.

They must be holding their breath.

I know I am.

Then Roarke's head snaps up and back and I can see his mouth wide open eyes wide shut and they slam down together and the slowness and smoothness are gone and there's panic in their bodies until suddenly they're still.

Again.

And I can breathe.

Again.

I remember Jonnyboy's arm around me on the rocks by the Coast Guard station and the rhythm of his breathing on the back of my neck.

There's something big and physical about it.

The memory.

Like something I'm actually carrying with me walking back down the hallway to the fake leather living room.

Something heavy.

So heavy it drains my strength getting there and pushes me hard back against the cushions when I try to sit on the edge of one of the sofas. Which ends up rocking me to sleep.

But still I can feel it.

The rhythm of his breathing.

Hear it.

The beating of his heart.

In my dream the sound is loud enough to move the air around me.

I wake up. I smell fake leather.

The air still vibrates. It doesn't fade away and I sit bolt upright thinking *Quake!* and I don't mean the computer game because this is San Francisco after all.

What is that vibration.

That sound.

It's like a panic reflex that stands me up and sends me almost running past the closed door of the bedroom and the length of the limo table to the wall of windows where the vibration tears the air again and I press my forehead to the shivering glass.

In the corner of the belfry beneath the steeple of the church below a rope runs slack and loose over the guidewheel of a giant pulley. And far far down like the wrong way through binoculars the wedding cake figures of a bride and groom move slowly into the sunlight on the wide brick stairs.

The earth does not move.

THREE

I pick up Jonnyboy's shirt off the back of one of the Who-killed-Bambi chairs and put it to my face. The map Finn made is in the pocket. I reach for it but stop then ask myself why. It's different than Roarke's Narcotics Anonymous book. It isn't private. Finn made it for both of us.

I guess I'm afraid to look at the map because it's the first step towards going to Finn and Critter's on my own. Which is what I'm really afraid of. Because Finn might be there alone.

I'm not scared of him.

I'm scared of myself.

I've never done it in capitals with anyone before.

Finn could be the first.

It's up to me.

Am I scared.

To be that different.

Am I scared.

I am that different.

I don't know.

But I know one thing.

Never make decisions based on fear is always Jonnyboy's advice.

Comparing Finn's map with the street map from the other room makes it easy to connect the dots from *You Are Here* as in this hotel at Fifth and Mission to *They Are There* at 99 Sumner Street. Sumner is really an L-shaped alley connecting Howard Street and Eighth Street. Howard runs parallel to Mission and one block east. So Finn and Critter live like three and a half blocks away.

I write Jonnyboy a note saying if no one's home on Sumner Street I'll sk8 for an hour and come back here but otherwise find me there. I snag an apple from the fruit basket and eat half in one bite then grab a banana too and stash it in my pants pocket in case it comes in handy later for one of those or-are-you-just-glad-to-see-me jokes.

Outside there's too many people in a hurry to sk8 on the sidewalk and too many cars to make it sane on the street. This neighborhood isn't jammed with two- and three-story wooden houses marching up and down the hills bay window to bay window like we mostly saw yesterday. It's flat and kind of industrial. Not as in factories and railyards but more along the lines of auto body shops and paint stores and lots of brick warehouse-type buildings with covered windows and steel roll-up doors. It doesn't look like anybody lives around here period until you check out the narrow alleys that break up the middle of the blocks and see all the old houses and apartments. Even a few trees.

Not on Sumner Street though. Or any other sign of life which is fine with me because that includes cars and I finally get to sk8. Past lots of trash along the curbs and metal bars over even second-story windows and locked gates with buzzers and intercom grates in front of most doorways. When the numbers hit three digits and I realize I've gone too far and put my foot down to turn I almost plant it sole to departed soul on a bloated dead rat.

Number 99 is just a doorframe and door built into a high painted fence flush with the edge of the sidewalk. It leads into a narrow outdoor space between the buildings on either side. I guess it's a path leading back to Finn and Critter's. And probably not a long one because there's no buzzer or bell or even knocker on the door to get their attention.

I could just pound on it battering-ram style. Of course if you're a drug dealer and someone's pounding on your door and you don't know who it is and you're not expecting anyone you might assume the worst. As in the police. And react accordingly. As in destroy the evidence.

The last thing I want to do is push anybody's manic panic button. And that includes the neighbors because this doesn't look like Neighborhood Watch territory but you never know. They might let their fingers do the walking and bring on real boyz in blue.

So I'm staring at the painted-over metal nines nailed to the door and wondering should I stay or should I go when the knob starts turning and the door opens. This twentysomething boy wearing a bright yellow Skippy dog food t-shirt and baggy brown pants charges out looking down without seeing me and I jump aside to save us from a head-on. Which gets his attention and he snaps his head up looking almost scared. He's a little taller than me with light brown cropped hair that's bleached on top and our faces are so close I can tell his eyes are that rare kewl color called hazel that has flecks of brown and gold that squeeze out sparks in the sunshine and shine like fireflies at night. His lips move making two or three words I don't catch then he reaches into a pocket for his shades and after shoving them into place he heads toward Howard Street without another glance in my direction.

I wonder if he's kweer.

He didn't look at me the way Finn first did on the bus yesterday in Monterey.

I wonder if I looked at him the way Finn looked at me.

Inside the door a rough paved path runs downhill between a dirty stucco wall spotted with the outlines of long-dead ivy and the unpainted wooden shingle siding of the building Finn and Critter live in. Or live under actually because the path descends in five terraced steps to a daylight basement with small head-high curtained windows on either side of a dark green Dutch sailor's door. The open top half of the door frames Critter who's leaning back at a forty-five-degree angle with his hands gripping the edge of the closed bottom half. His shirt is off and is he smiling.

His arm muscles look too big for his skinny tweeker chest and torso. Unless he's flexing them just for me. I try not to stare at the small gold rings piercing both his nipples. Which is easy because there's a big blacked-in tattoo of a dog's paw right next to one of them. He follows my eyes and explains with gestures that it's a tracing of the real live paw of the dog he grew up with back in Nowhere Town. Then he aims a finger up the path behind me wondering with his eyes *Wherrre's Jonny?*

I do rock-a-bye baby with praying hands next to my ear and all I get back is a sly knowing smile as in *I just bet he's asleep.*

I aim my thumb and trigger finger inside and raise my eyebrows asking *Finn?*

His eyes go mock sad for a seventh of a second. He lets go of the door with one hand and fingerspells *W-O-R-K* and am I stoked he knows enough to spell it backwards from his point of view. Because I'm nervous and it puts me more at ease somehow. He opens the bottom of the door walking backwards behind it and waves me in then pushes both halves forward and latches them closed. Now all I can see in the weird glowing darkness is the searchlight white of my shoelaces and the even brighter blinding glare like sun on snow of Critter's boxer briefs.

Which are all he has on besides a tan the *Baywatch* cast would kill for and the radio for all I know. And which draw my eyes like magnets in spite of myself. Which in turn makes me blush so hard I must look like the bare-butt grrl in the Coppertone ads I swear.

But I don't. My eyes adjust enough to see myself in a full-length mirror a few feet away and I've got the same magic blacklight tan as Critter. Then first in the mirror and then with my heart in my throat looking straight down I see this shining white shape the size of a football but soft-edged like Casper-the-you-know-what glide fast across the floor in front of me and disappear.

I jump in the air then trip over my own two feet when I touch back down. Critter holds his arms out to catch me if I fall.

I think I've got my balance back and lean the other way.

Or else I'm afraid.

Of what might happen. With his arms and the heat from his body around me.

Critter's.

Not Finn's.

Break Jonnyboy's rules and see where it gets you. I fall backwards into something that's crusty and prickly and dusty with grasping petrified tentacle arms. Something bigger than me.

An old flocked fake Christmas tree. I'm not hurt or anything. Just covered head to toe with what looks like dirty Styrofoam. Critter reaches down with both hands to help me up doing everything he can do to keep from laughing. But when I'm on deck again I rub my fingers on my pants then hold them out in front of me and we both go off together because they look like hand transplants from Frosty the Snowman I swear.

When we finally stop laughing I draw a ? in the air and look down at the carpet all *WTF was that anywayz* and Critter just points to the *Playboy* bunny head tattoo on the outside of his thumb all casual as if every homeboy's got a rabbit running loose in his crib. Then he pulls off my black Sk8 Ragz t-shirt and with both hands rolls it into a rope and holding the ends flips it over my head and around my neck like a scarf and walks backwards pulling me through a kitchen area barely lit by a night-light somewherez and around a corner past what smells like a bedroom and down a narrow walkway next to a long clothes rack to the bathroom. He points to a towel hanging on a peg next to the shower stall and looks at me kind of expectantly.

Expecting what.

I can feel the blood rising to my face and he must see it because his eyes shift gears to apologetic almost and he points to himself and acts out putting clothes on and before I know it he's out the door and closing it behind him.

When I finish my shower my clothes aren't where I left them in a heap on the floor so I wrap the towel around me and head out looking for substitutes. Outside the bathroom there's an overhead light on now and I can see that Finn and Critter's bedroom isn't really a room but a wide hallway on the way to the bathroom with curtains at the far end separating it from the kitchen. Their bed is supported by furniture and boxes stacked neck high so there's space underneath for a desk and one end of a pipe jammed with shirts and jackets on hangers that walls off the passage to the bathroom. Without any windows back here it seems like a cave or closer really to an animal den with smells from the bed and laundry and cigarette butts and empty soda cans. It doesn't smell bad or anything because these boyz are clean boyz but there's a bleachy part of it that's like a sex smell to me or else maybe it's a drug smell. Because after my shower I noticed fresh drops of blood in the bathroom sink and a sharp safe on the shelf above and thanks to Nirvana everybody knows that bleach is used for disinfecting needles.

I push through the curtains into the kitchen where another light's on now too and which isn't a room of its own either. It's just an alcove walled off by a breakfast bar that's stand-up-only because stools would block the way into the bedroom. There's still no sign of Critter. I turn toward the living room and feel something furry creepy-crawl against my ankles but this time I only jump enough to lose the towel and look down at a big white rabbit foraging in the two-tone green and brighter green yarn of the longest shag carpet I've ever seen. The kind you have to rake instead of vacuum. In my head the rabbits and the rug and my bare legs split apart in geometric shapes doubling and tripling and sliding past one another kaleidoscope style and at the same time I'm remembering the Christmas tree and thinking these boyz have got Easter covered too I'm forgetting I'm standing here stark raving naked with nothing but breeze between my knees and no idea where my clothes are.

And I'm still forgetting it when I look back up at Finn standing ten feet away inside the open door of the apartment. He's staring at me and is he smiling. He starts walking toward me and I just stand frozen playing statues as in *David*.

Yeah right.

When he's right in front of me he tips my chin up with his hand and time-travels back to the overlook.

His darkest eyes.

His smoke and rain-slicked eucalyptus smell.

His lips forming words.

Again.

—You are so beautiful.

He unclips the sliders on his narrow braces and shrugs them off his shoulders so they fall to his sides. He unbuttons the cuffs of his long-sleeve blue-and-yellow checked shirt then tugs out the tails from the waist of his jeans and starting at the collar his blunt fingers move down freeing the rest of the buttons which are oversized and bone-colored and imprinted with *The Original Ben Sherman*. He pulls the sleeves off his arms then lifts the shirt over my head and holds it behind me while he guides my arms into the sleeves. The stiff cotton makes my skin tingle. Plus the pressure of his fingers through the fabric working buttons into buttonholes gets my pulse going and am I thanking Jesus Mary and Joseph the shirttails hang to my knees almost.

When he's finished Finn squares the shoulder seams then stands back looking me over with his arms folded across his white ribbed wife-beater. He slowly raises one hand to point to his mouth.

—Just say the word.

He grins and his tongue darts across his lower lip.

—If you want it done.

His head tilts sideways just like the skinhead in the picture on my bedroom door.

Which excites me even more.

I reach without thinking for my notepad and not only remember my jeans are missing in action but suddenly remember Critter who I blanked from my mind and I mean fully when Finn started taking off his shirt.

And who's standing in the doorway now himself but with the door closed behind him. He's all spiffed out in hella polished oxblood creeper-style shoes and black drainpipe trousers. No shirt yet though. He's holding a plastic jug of detergent in one hand with his other hand pressing a cotton ball against the inside of his arm and he's got this dreamy smile going that turns into a laugh when he points to the ruins of the Christmas tree on the carpet at his feet and behind him.

But my eyes don't stay on the tree very long. Because now that it's not a room divider I can see this huge aquarium against the far wall of the living room that's filled with jungly-green plants and nothing but eels and fish that are all or mostly black with little accents of the brightest Day-Glo colors this side of the X-Ray Spex album sleeve. Which are highlighted by black light tubes in the concealed fixtures above and below that also luminize the coral backdrop. The aquarium takes up most of the wall and since the ceiling is low and there's hardly any natural light it's basically Our Mr. Sun giving everything a liquid glow. Including the funky green shag carpet which I now realize goes halfway up the walls so you almost feel like the whole room's underwater and you're inside a glass bubble. Plus facing the aquarium there's a sofa covered with olive-green velvet that looks like the moss you see in tide pools and at either end of the long low table in front of the sofa are two chairs covered in the same material. Even the plastic milk crates holding the vinyl below the audio shelf on the wall by the door are spray-painted pippin-apple green.

So it takes me seven seconds to nick this place the Greenery in memory of this hippie health food store where I used to shoplift fig bars in Monterey called the Granary. And the name fits with the rabbit factor too since they're vegetarians. At least Bugs Bunny's always munching on a carrot. I've never known any real rabbits before. It's nowhere in sight now but next to the milk crates full of records there's a cube of brushed aluminum the size of a small footstool with a carry handle on top and jail-style bars over little windows on the sides and a wide-open barred door.

Critter says something to Finn and points first to me then at the detergent he's holding and I nod to show him that now I know where my clothes are. Then he points at his own bare chest and holds up his wrist pretending to check an air wristwatch and hurries by us on his way to the bedroom. When he passes he winks at me and is it blushing material but I'm not sure why.

Finn leads me into the living room and sits me down beside him on the sofa. The coffee table is actually a big wood-framed mirror with screw-on legs attached and mounded on the glass next to lengths of Pyrex laboratory tubing and a black butane mini-torch is enough crystal meth to turn a geriatric ward into a mob of hyperactive hooligans I swear.

We call it crack to confuse normal people and also because that's what happens to the crystals when you roll them with a weight through the flat side of a plastic phone card or credit card before you chop them with the edge. Which is what Finn

I look back at Finn right when he raises his eyelids and I draw bunny ears in the air over my head followed by a question mark while I scan the room with my other hand shading my eyes. He jumps up suddenly looking like he just woke up with the mother of all toothaches and peers around doing Lewis to my Clark then gets down on hands and knees and checks under the sofa. Standing again he says something I can't lip-read before he turns and runs out slamming the door behind him so hard it shakes the floor.

Which brings Critter out from the back buttoning a plain white shirt that smells freshly ironed and though he smiles when he first sees me as soon as I do instant replay of the rabbit ears he's frowning and out the door with another slam.

The sudden draft of air reminds me I'm covered but not exactly decent so I decide to check out the clothes rack in the bedroom for some grubby wash pants or something. By the time I find a pair of old bleach-spotted camos Finn and Critter are back in the living room having some kind of domestic dispute and I don't need audio to make the call. You can always tell from the predatory stances people take without realizing it and face muscles you never notice otherwise working overtime and the way their eyes dilate and contract without changes in the light. And just like I was always glad I couldn't hear my parents I'm glad I can't hear Finn and Critter.

Though of course it's strictly minor league compared to what went on in my house. Critter's standing by the sofa looking disgusted arguing back and forth with Finn who's searching behind and under everything larger than a toaster oven. But Finn's not moving carefully and deliberately the way he usually does. He's doing what he's doing because of Critter and not because he cares. And if I know it so must Critter.

is up to right now using a small carved jade dragon with a square pedestal base for the weight.

I like watching his hands crush and chop and form the crack into three long jagged lightning-streak lines. It's almost a ritual with all his physical and mental attention focused on doing what he's doing and doing it just so. Same with the way he put this shirt on me. Most people get sloppy and distracted doing familiar things. I guess because they're bored. But one of the first things I learned from Jonnyboy was if you try to do everything with style you'll never get bored.

Even the angle Finn's holding the foot-long glass straw he's heating with the mini-torch seems calculated to the tenth degree. The straw is shaped with two right-angle bends in the middle that form a step so you can hold the upper tube with your fingers while getting the lower tube so hot that most of the crack is vaporized the moment it enters the glass when you vacuum up the line with your nostril at the other end. Which is called doing a hot rail.

Finn offers me the straw when it's almost cherry red and I put my face and eyes into saying *No* without saying *No you're an asshole for doing that and a double asshole for asking me.* Or *No I'm scared of that shit.* Or *No I'm too young.* Or *No I'm Mormon have you heard the news we don't drink coffee either.* I mean Bush's wife really missed the connecting flight with *Just say no to drugs.*

Because you don't JUST say no.

It's not polite.

Finn gets it I can tell. Then he returns the straw to the torch a few seconds to make up for it cooling when he offered it to me and leans over vanishing the line from beginning to end without a single wasted move of any muscle and sits back with his fists on his knees and his eyes closed.

I wonder how much crack has to do with it.

I wonder how much I have to do with it.

I wonder what time it is and WTF is Jonnyboy.

It's time for Critter to be at *W-O-R-K*. After he spells it out again for me he cocks a trigger-finger gun to his head to show me what he's under. Behind him and strictly for my eyes only Finn draws the same weapon but aims it at the aluminum cube by the door as in *Guns don't kill rabbits people kill rabbits*. Critter catches my grin and starts to turn around but gets interrupted by the telephone and it turns out that right when I was wondering where Jonnyboy was he was pulling into Sumner Street in a long black limousine with Roarke.

Critter invites himself along for a lift to work to the tune of *Your chariot! Take me to your chariot!* and after I lace my Van's up Finn follows us out to the street and rubs his head on mine as Critter opens the door. On the street Critter kisses Finn goodbye and I want to kiss him too but I just wink and Finn winks back.

The limo's a stretch job with Jonnyboy and Roarke sprawled across the back dressed all in black wearing matching wraparound shades. Roarke's facing forward with his legs fully extended crossed at the ankles and his arms folded across his chest. Jonnyboy's slumped sideways on the seat with his knees bent and his boots planted on the tufted ivory upholstery a few inches from Roarke. As soon as we climb in and sit in the folddown seats across from them Critter's on the car phone alerting his coworkers to his arrival in style and a little crowd is gathering in the corner doorway of what looks like a run-down pool hall when we pull over just a block away at Ninth and Howard. They're all wearing sunglasses even though they're indoors and one of them is the Skippy t-shirt guy who almost ran into me earlier. He's directly in my line of sight when the driver in full black tie opens the door for Critter and I nod at him but I can't tell if he notices me or not.

After Critter bails Jonnyboy motions for my notepad.

so what's up w/ the big timez?

They've got a rabbit.

a live rabbit?

A white rabbit.

Which starts Jonnyboy strumming air guitar and singing and pretty soon Roarke's trading lyrics with him and by the time we cross what looks like the main street of San Francisco and cruise past the big green dome of City Hall they're scream-ing in stereo out the two back windows until Roarke finally settles back and massages his throat. But Jonnyboy's all little-boy excited and can't sit still. He pulls the pencil stub out of his ear again.

Roarke wrote a song 4 me w/ my name in it & everything & they're doing it 2day 4 the 1st time ever.

Have you seen the words?

no it's a surprise.

And though I'm all *Kewl with a capital K* I know it doesn't do justice let alone truth or the American way and thinking about it I finally understand how Jonnyboy gets around his *Ignore heroes* rule with Roarke. It's because Roarke isn't so much a hero to him as a god. He totally changed his life be-cause of Roarke before he even knew him. After the first time he saw Roarke onstage at the old Cuckoo's Nest in Orange County Jonnyboy followed Chaotic Stature wherever they played down south wearing Wayfarer shades exactly like Roarke and rolling the cuffs of his jeans exactly like Roarke and smoking Players cigarettes like Roarke for the same reason as Roarke which was they're numero uno on the cancer-causing hit parade.

And Jonnyboy wanted to shoot drugs like Roarke right off too. But his friends were still mostly just sk8erboyz and he didn't have a chance until he was sixteen and his mom moved to Hawaii when she found out she could get welfare sent over there. He didn't even know his dad was alive then let alone chilling in the army at Fort Ord so he ended up squatting on the piers of this old abandoned amusement park in Santa Monica. One morning sk8ing home in the hood by the Venice boardwalk he watched a homeboy lose a bindle when some cops drove up and he circled around the block and swooped it up off the pavement like a pelican chowing smelt off Monterey Bay. Then he went back to the ruins of this roller coaster he'd claimed for his own and tried smoking some of the powder on the end of a cigarette which made him sick. So he decided to go hang with his friend Red Dog whose mom was a diabetic and dot dot dot he learned how to use it like a white boy.

On his own. He won't say he started using to be like Roarke. But look at before and after. In the first place before he was afraid to even talk to Roarke. In the second place after he couldn't wait to start the conversation. Except Chaotic Stature did a disappearing act right then and it was months later when Jonnyboy finally got the chance and by then he was using big time and living in Hollywood. Where he used to walk every day past the old punk club Cathey de Grande on his way to score on Hollywood Boulevard. The club was closed but he kept hearing muffled Chaotic Stature songs coming out of the basement and I mean every afternoon until finally on the hottest day of the year he realized it wasn't haunted and it wasn't Memorex. So he just sat on the steps with his shirt off listening and sweating and waiting. There was no shade not even palm-tree shade but even that Big Gulp machine shimmering oas-islike inside the windows of the AM-PM down the street couldn't tempt him.

Which all worked out for the best when Roarke finally came out the door because as soon as Jonnyboy stood up to say Hey he blacked out from dehydration and the next thing he knew he was laying on the tiles inside with Roarke giving him mouth-to-mouth.

So what could a kweer boy do. He started sucking on his tongue.

And Roarke sucked back.

Which was probably the kewlest thing that ever happened to Jonnyboy.

Outside the limo the long hill we've been climbing since we passed City Hall tops out in the wide green sloping lawns of this park called Alamo Square with a view of San Francisco you already know by heart even if you've never left Nowhere Town. In the foreground is a row of seven oldschool three-story houses with bay windows and spires and curlicues all painted in different pastel colors just so. Behind and beyond across a wide flat valley filled with houses and apartments the clustered rockets of the buildings downtown launch into the sky all the way from the monster mirrored jukebox of Roarke's hotel past the vertical whiter-than-white acreage of a church shaped like a washing machine agitator to the spike on God's desktop of the pyramid. It's this jam-packed supercity shooting up out of an older city that's jam-packed too covering hill after hill and hollow after hollow but lower and lighter-colored. And where the buildings stop the water starts. Framing everything in liquid blue and setting off Alcatraz and the other islands and the Bay Bridge and the far-off rolling country the color of sun on wheat.

I've seen it on postcards and jigsaw puzzles and there's even a TV series set in the pale green house at one end on the corner. So it's fully déjà vu all over again and I'm pointing back openmouthed for the benefit of Jonnyboy and Roarke who missed the Kodak moment since they're facing forward. Once they check it out Roarke has the driver pull over but he grabs me by the wrist when I go for the door handle and makes me wait for the driver to open it the way he did for Critter.

It's a lot colder and windier here than down below and it's obvious why looking west because a huge thick fog bank sits about ten blocks away on top of the last hill between us and the ocean. But it's just a climb up a few steps from the street to get out of the wind in the lee of a bush at the top of the grass rolling down toward the houses and the city. As soon as we sit down Roarke has Jonnyboy ask me for my notepad and writes:

The door & driver—sorry about that but it's his job & we don't show respect doing it for him. We make him look bad in his mind. Treat people the way they want to be treated & they'll do the same for you.

And I just write back:

Kewl. Thanx. I didn't know.

Because I thought it was some poshboy thing and the punk rock way is to rebel against shit like that. I wouldn't have seen it the way Roarke does on my own.

Speak of the devil though because who's hovering over us seven seconds later but the driver with the car phone in his hand. And after stalling at first Roarke decides to take the call in the limo but tells Jonnyboy he'll be right back.

I write Jonnyboy a note while he pulls out the Altoids tin he uses for crack supplies and opens it shielding what's inside with his hand.

Roarke is kewl with a k. And wise but not as in wise guy. You boyz are a good team.

He grins then holds up a miniature Ziploc and tilts some crack crystals into one corner of the bottom of the bag then crushes them through the plastic between the nails of his right thumb and left index finger. He dips a key into the bag and fills the groove above the teeth with powder and slowly withdraws it flat side up cupped in his other hand on the way to his nostril. Repeat rewind play times three. Disappear the tin. Pluck pencil stub from ear.

i saw U watching us last nite.

Knock wind out of Radboy.

I'd be speechless if I wasn't already. It's like the opposite of blushing material. I can feel the blood draining from my face till I'm as white as Our Lady of St. Maytag in the distance below us.

He puts his hand on my knee.

it's ok. i'm not mad.

I feel like crawling under the bush behind us.

i didn't tell Roarke.

All I can think of is when did he notice. If it was right when I first looked in. And what if it was.

i glanced that way rite after we finished.

Don't ask me how long I was there. If God's in heaven don't ask how long.

He writes fast and big ripping the paper.

IT'S ALL RIGHT.

I finally look up at him and he's swallowing hard. He searches my eyes. I can tell he's expecting me to answer and all I can do is draw a *Y* in the air. Not as in why it's all right but as in why he told me.

*i wanted U 2 know Bcause it was the best time ever 4 me. it was
really making love.*

He stops writing and wipes his jacket sleeve across his eyes
then takes a deep breath.

*and i wanted U 2 know I'm glad U were there. 2 see me like that &
feel that love. 2 know it. U being there makes it more real 2 me. i'll never
look back & wonder if it was just a dream. it wasn't. it was love. true love.*

Two big drops fall on the paper and smudge the words
before he's finished writing.

there's hardly been any 4 me ever xcept in dreams.

He covers his face with his hands and I put my arm around
him and remember watching the two of them kiss in the hotel
yesterday and wondering if it wasn't secrets he was keeping but
something he was sharing.

He turns away and rubs his sleeve across his face again
then reaches for the pad.

*1 more thing then I'm done. I don't want U feeling U owe me Bcause
i stopped yr dad. it's more like we're even & this is Y. when i 1st went 2
my dad's B4 i met U i was lo as i could go. Roarke and me tried cracking
off together & it worked 4 him 4 awhile but 4 me only a week (less really)
& he kicked me out & vanished me from his life till he started using again.
& i wanted 2 end it all. i thought about wayz 2 do it every day, i surfed
storms when no 1 else would go out, i ran so much crack, even dry hits, i
didn't care. i had nothing & no 1. going 2 my dad's made it worse. then i
met U & it was like making friends w/ myself when i was yr age. (only yr
smarter.) U were such a smartass radical animal. i couldn't let U down. i
knew U'd kick my ass 2 Xmas mass in the afterlife if i did. U saved me,
Radboy.*

He watches me read it and right off I'm shaking my head
from side to side and when I finish I look up and Jonnyboy's
smiling nodding up and down decisively in time with me and

we're having a little head war when Roarke gets back. He says something to Jonnyboy and points toward a grove of Monterey cypress a little below us that borders the path on the edge of the lawn. And just like that Jonnyboy's up in a flash with Roarke in hot pursuit behind him down the hill though they both turn to make sure I'm following when they disappear into the trees.

I do the walk don't run thing to give them some time alone together. I wonder what Roarke's doing after the concert and when he's going back to L.A. What Jonnyboy wrote gets me thinking about the Narcotics Anonymous book in Roarke's hotel room and the fast efficient way Jonnyboy packed his nose the moment Roarke walked away. I can't help wondering if Roarke is clean and what that means for Jonnyboy. The insides of Roarke's arms were inches from my eyes and there weren't any holes. His nose isn't runny. I haven't seen him bite into a single Krackel candy bar.

But I saw him and Jonnyboy.

As close as two people can be.

I see them now.

Climbing up the lookout tower of a log fort in a small oval playground fenced with chain link tucked below a ridge of ragged trees so it's sheltered from the wind. Squatting down to lean against the kid-high railing on top and starting up a spitting contest as fast as any little boyz would. Running down the express exit slide and kicking sand up all the way to the swings and the start of the who-can-go-highest-soonest event. Looking at each other and arching their backs for more leverage and talking back and forth while their legs pump the air.

I'm not the only one watching them. On the other side of the playground but on the same level there's a paved terrace with two wooden benches facing another steep lawn dropping down to the sidewalk on the street with the row of houses. A woman's sitting alone on one with her arm draped over the back and her head turned sideways toward the swings.

It's the blonde from the Green Tortoise bus.

And I don't waste time I just walk right down. Because I'm curious about her. I remember what she said to Jonnyboy at the overlook and it doesn't fit the way she looks. Most guys would have answered back anyplace was paradise if she was in it. Even dressed the way she is right now in a black beret and navy-blue turtleneck and plain khaki stretch pants she might be lounging between takes on the set of a movie. But not the kind they make in Hollywood. The kind they make in the Valley.

Nordic Nurses.

Stilettos over Stockholm.

She smiles big time after she hears me coming toward her and turns to look my way. She beams her china blues on me like a long-lost friend and it's obvious she's already got my number because she lets her fingers do the talking as soon as I join her on the bench. After we get the small world chitchat out of the way she starts telling me about herself and it turns out she is a nurse. And she is Swedish. Though her mother's American. Her name is Ula and after she noticed me on the bus with Jonnyboy she almost came up to me at the overlook for a chance to practice her sign. Which she's forgetting now that her boyfriend is.

—Dead.

She pauses and articulates with emphasis like she's convincing herself as in *repeat after me*. And I know exactly how she feels because did it take a while for my mom to sink in.

Her boyfriend was a Russian who lost his hearing from a bomb when he was in the army and they had big plans for a honeymoon in Spain and a house back home with reindeer in the yard and a dock on the fjord or whatever the Swedish version of the white picket fence deal is and then one day the dewd got diagnosed with leukemia thanks to some nuclear-plant disaster in the bad old daze over there. And just a week after that he went to sleep and never woke up.

This happened like a month ago. And he had always wanted to travel in America especially California and she was already on leave from her job to get married so Ula decided instead of taking his body back to Siberia where his family lived she'd send it air freight and fly herself to New York and take the Green Tortoise bus across the country in memory of him and their life together. Plus she wanted to see her sister who lives just two blocks from this park.

When she asks so how is it I ended up on this exact bench at this exact moment in time I give her the news of the week in review as in the *Reader's Digest* condensed version. Excluding the details of the boy-on-boy and white-punx-on-crack stuff but including the fact that Jonnyboy on swing A is in love with Roarke on swing B which results in a thoughtful nod of her head but not *Shock! Horror!* or anything like that. And I also let her know that I cruised down here because Jonnyboy copied me on what she said at the overlook and I wanted to find out if she was really a goth in disguise.

Which makes her throw back her head and laugh so hard it vibrates the bench. She guesses it wasn't a very good pickup line. But she was kind of down and it was all she could think of at the time.

So Ula thought Jonnyboy. I don't know why I'm surprised. I guess I'm still too young to understand what attracts people to one another beyond the basic biology-class level of different body parts. And that doesn't account for kweerboyz at all. Though Jonnyboy doesn't exactly float around in public on a lavender cloud with his wrist just so. I mean how would Ula know.

Still and all.

How did I know about Finn.

I guess it could be that way with Ula and Jonnyboy. I can tell she sees more than most people do. And she knows how to connect with someone like me which takes a long attention span more than anything else.

She probably knows how to connect with most anybody. When Roarke and Jonnyboy notice us together on the sidelines they abandon the swings with knowing smiles and their eyes dancing in my direction all hubba-hubba for scoring with the babe. So I sign to Ula to let me make the introductions and I write a note for Roarke and Jonnyboy.

If you're tired of playing with each other how'd you like to play doctor with a real nurse?

The way she laughs when they show it to her makes everybody instant friends. And watching the two of them get acquainted with Ula I realize the difference between Jonnyboy and Roarke is that Jonnyboy seems bigger than life 24/7 while Roarke is only that way with an audience. One-on-one he's basically shy and a little nervous. But with even a couple of other people and I mean normal hearing talking people he projects himself out and takes center stage. Not in a king of the jungle chest thumping way but easily and naturally like it's where he belongs. It doesn't look like work at all but it must be.

Maybe Jonnyboy couldn't keep it up 24/7 without go-fast. And he knows it. So he's afraid he wouldn't seem like himself even to himself anymore if he stopped using.

Nah. No way never nohow. As in *Never make decisions
based on fear.* Which is the first of Jonnyboy's rules to live by
that Ula learns after they talk her into going with us to the
concert. Because when she sees the limo she stops dead in her
tracks and shakes her head in disbelief.

—I can't do this. I'm practically a communist.

So Jonnyboy takes her by the hand and tells her she's just
afraid of the unknown and gives her the word on fear. He puts
her hand in mine and tells her I'm her copilot. If she follows
my orders no one gets hurt.

So I have Ula close her eyes when the driver gets out to
let us in and escort her no peeking through the open door
without a glimpse of black tie to gun her guilt engines. And
once we're moving I warn her that the seatbelt sign has been
turned off and smoking is allowed but passengers are prohib-
ited by federal law from touching any door handles at any time
and violaters will be imprisoned for life without possibility of
parole.

Roarke and Jonnyboy approve. But not necessarily improve.
They make up Swedish Blond Communist jokes all the way to
Golden Gate Park.

It's not quite arriving at the concert on the Green Tortoise
bus this time and we're waved through a maze of gates on
unmarked security roads by rent-a-cops instead of Buddhist
nuns until we pull into a reserved parking slot that's directly
underneath the girders of the main stage. As soon as the driver
lets us out Roarke's sprinting toward the stairs going up top
without much of a goodbye for any of us including Jonnyboy
and by the time we're on deck too the rest of his band are
already setting up.

The best part of watching Chaotic Stature is watching Jonnyboy watch the band. To me Roarke looks a little over it and the others just look old but after all I'm fourteen and most people do I guess. Plus I've got fingerprints on my imagination from those grrls yesterday and especially the singer who made me wonder sometimes if they'd get through to the end of the song and there was that thrill of danger like dancing on the edge of a cliff and seeing how close you could come and suspecting not quite knowing that the cliff is crumbling or an earthquake's due. Chaotic Stature seems a lot more professional and a lot less punk but are they loud and does Jonnyboy bop around our access-all-areas corner of the stage with his elbows pumping pistons like a 2-Tone boy in the *Dance Craze* movie. His face is one big smile and he's surrounded by sweat-drop comets colliding with each other but never with him since he's too much a moving target.

And then the best part turns into the worst. When Roarke announces a new song about a friend Jonnyboy grabs me around the shoulders after gesturing so I understand and holds on to me listening not dancing but vibrating with energy so awesome it could light Los Angeles. And the first time Roarke sings his name he shudders like one of those Apollo rockets on the launchpad and grips me harder I swear like I'm the only thing keeping him from going into orbit. After that though the light dims fast fading to blackout and I can feel whatever filled him slip away escaping like your soul the very moment that you draw your last breath or so says the priest.

Which creeps me out to the tenth because when the song is over and Jonnyboy zombie-walks away slower than I've ever seen him move without saying anything or looking at anybody just staring straight ahead I ask Ula what Roarke sang and she couldn't make out most of it but one thing definitely is the song talks about Jonnyboy as if he's dead.

I want to run after him and nobody stops me but myself. It paralyzes me not knowing any words to make things good again and the only ones I can think of watching him cross the back of the stage are *I love you* which just aren't enough and I mean no way never nohow.

It's easy telling.

It's showing that counts.

And I ask myself *So what can I do?* until I realize the answer is nothing because Jonnyboy's gone.

I keep my eyes on Roarke for the rest of the set and he never looks in our direction not even once. I try to work up hate for him for hurting Jonnyboy but it's a tough sell since he's never been anything to me but a symbol of the kewlest of the kewl and besides I don't know the details as in the lyrics of the song. What keeps flashing through my mind S-O-S style is *Ignore Heroes Ignore Heroes Ignore Heroes* and I guess it's a message to myself as much as Jonnyboy.

It's not so bad hanging around afterwards in case Jonnyboy comes back because in all directions it's one big bottleneck with everyone leaving at once. But as the fog gets thicker and thicker and the people fewer and fewer I start feeling abandoned like all the trash that was hidden by bodies before and covers the entire field.

There's nothing I can do except go back to Finn and Critter's. Ula invites me over to her sister's but I don't want to be somewherez else when Jonnyboy shows up. Which reminds me how he appeared like magic just when I was wishing he'd rescue me from Finn and Critter arguing. And that brings on this wave of almost panic. Because I hardly know those boyz and their place is really small.

Now we're talking real panic. Jonnyboy's advice is always put the worst-case scenario front and center so you stare it down and not let it spook you and this is it:

A boys' home.

A Catholic boys' home.

My sisters hate me. I don't even want to think about my dad. And there's not much chance the question authorities would turn me over to Tommy when he gets out of Chino. He won't be outside for long anywayz because he's dead as in call-the-coroner serious about going eye-for-an-eye with my dad.

A foster home would be just as bad. That's what the social workers were pushing along with adoption when my dad was in jail. And I mean pushing hard. As a lemon-into-lemonade chance to start a new life as they put it with nice parents who have clean-hand jobs and who really want children as if mine didn't. These white picket fence parents-in-waiting just put off having kids because they were too busy making money and then one day on the tennis court they noticed it was too late. And reading between the lines I realized they all have something in common besides color-coordinated Nike warm-ups made in slave-labor China namely they want blond & blue-eyed boyz and grrls.

Who are in hella short supply compared to surplus black and brown ones.

Which makes me a pretty hot property in the kid market-place despite being say it in a whisper damaged goods.

Still the county people got all offended when I wanted to know if they worked on commission and if they got paid extra for placing someone like me and even more for a spazz or a tard. And one of them was like this televangelist type with teeth so white you needed shades to cut the glare who shook his head from side to side looking me right in the eye for about a minute then signed that it would be a shame and a waste to add a chip on the shoulder to my other physical handicaps.

This from a guy telling me I should start a new life that really just amounts to mass new things and new trouble with new people when my idea of a new life is hearing the waves break on the rocks and talking to my friends and knowing their voices and if that's not part of the deal I'm sticking with what I've got.

Jonnyboy's right. Face the worst and be your best. Fuck that weak shit. I ain't going to no boys' home. So let's get the show on the road.

I ask Ula to call Finn and Critter's just to make sure they're home and kind of explain the situation. And I figure if there's any problem it's easy it's easy it's easy for them to break the news to someone else. She's on the phone so long I start wondering if that's what's up but I guess she reads my mind or more likely the hang of my head because while she's still on the line she signs that everything's kewl but Critter's very talkative.

Nobody wants me going back there by myself at night so Ula's invited too and besides she talked to Finn and Critter on the bus for quite a while after they came aboard at Bakersfield which means she's actually known them longer than I have. I don't know how much she knows about them though and right after we hail a taxi I think of that miniature white volcano glittering on the living-room table and ask her how she feels about drugs. Because she is a nurse after all.

—What drugs?

I spell out *Crack* without thinking and are my fingers flying clearing up the confusion when she's immediately all *Shock!*

Horror! Then it turns out speed doesn't bother her too much. Though she looks a little relieved when she asks if I'm a user and I come back with *I don't take drugs. I am drugs.* Which originally was said by some wild artist guy and then by Jonnyboy to me.

Finn and Critter are so glassy-eyed when we show up that they could probably say the same themselves. Maybe that's why Mount Crack-atoa's nowhere in sight.

No way. That much crack would blast them into Jupiter space. They're definitely spinning at 78 though and I can tell Ula likes being in on the secret without them knowing she knows. Then the same kind of contact high I sometimes get from Jonnyboy kicks in and Ula starts acting pretty tweeked herself after my investigation of the vinyl supply yields a couple of Abba LPs.

I didn't even know they were Swedish. I just remember Finn writing Critter liked them when we first hung out at the overlook. But for Ula it must be like someone handing you a Western bacon cheeseburger in Outer Mongolia if you're an American. She lights up like a Lotto winner on Slywitness News and signs *Have you listened to them?* and looks at me beaming like she expects me to fire back *Oh heavens to Betsy oh suburban lawns oh kitchens of distinction why yes indeed.*

I just pause for a second then make a moron poker face and start slowly shaking my head from side to side. Then she realizes what she asked me and in sign no less and we both bust up so hard we're still pointing at each other making faces and laughing two minutes later when Critter finally tells Ula he didn't quite hear the punch line.

Which she passes on to me and that gets us going again to the point of rolling on the floor while Critter looks back and forth between us and the Abba sleeves like he's a teacher on the first day of kindergarten and the records are the lesson plan which he's just discovered is written in Swahili. Meanwhile Finn's all past-tense disgusted present-tense amused until it evolves into *guess-you-had-to-be-there* when Ula catches her breath and shakes her hair out of her eyes and explains our little dialogue. And once Abba's coming out of the speakers it's like the Pied Piper to the seventies for Critter and he chatters nonstop to Ula for half an hour while keeping me more or less on the frequency by flowing me books like a disco dance-step manual and one about Elton John showing him the year he was named the world's worst-dressed woman.

The whole time Finn sits at one end of the mirror table leaning back in the chair with his upper lip curled ready to sneer. And every so often he says something. As in the same thing.

—It's all rubbish.

Then he looks at me.

—Innit.

Which makes Critter laugh harder every time he says it.

But even though he was just a baby when the world came down with Saturday Night Fever Critter's got a serious case of nostalgia and it's definitely not in the realm of something so bad it's good like *Plan 9 from Outer Space*. He likes Abba as much as Ula who's old enough to remember them in all their glory.

When Finn and Critter bend over the table to inhale a couple of massive bumps I decide it's my cue for some shut-eye since it doesn't look like they'll be occupuying their bed anytime before sunup. Finn reaches out for my wrist though when I stand up to bail and keeps me on the scene while he says something to Ula who translates it into sign. And it turns out the haircuts on the Abba sleeve or more like the desperate need for them reminded Finn that Critter promised to shave his head tonight. Only Critter in turn reminded Finn that HE promised to find the fugitive bunny tonight. As in tit for tat.

If Ula will pardon the expression.

So it's up to me to shave the day and I fetch the cordless clippers from my backpack which is stashed under Finn and Critter's bed and warm up for action pretending to trim the shag carpet on the walls. Which helps keep me from staring too hard when Finn takes off his shirt.

The whole top half of his body is solid compact muscle like you see on a gymnast. And except for a dark trail of hair below his belly button his skin is totally smooth so the definition shows up clear as boldface in *Webster's Unabridged*. He's got thick coarse tough hair on his head though and since he wants it fully skinhead shaved with no guide at all I have to press harder than usual and besides I don't know the curves of his skull like I do Jonnyboy's. So when he coughs and moves his head a little I give him a rat bite which at first looks hella worse than it really is because the scalp bleeds faster and harder than any other skin on your body.

Finn's blood starts running down his neck and for a second I wonder what kind of nurse Ula could be because I see instant freakout in her eyes. So I dip my finger in it and hold it up to my lips thinking I'll do *Interview with a Vampire* and lick it to show her this time it'll be all right this time it'll be ok. But then she shakes her head all *No means No* real seriously and Critter jumps up moving fast toward me.

At first I think he must be playing along with the vampire deal because he holds his fingers together to make a cross shape. Though he isn't smiling at all. Then Ula who's been playing statues just staring signs plus for *positive* which I still don't get until she fingerspells A-I-D-S.

For a second I stare at Finn's bright red blood smeared on my finger.

Understanding.

But still.

Not really believing.

The same way I felt beside my mom at the bottom of the stairs.

And say the same thing to myself.

No way.

Finn turns around and I don't want to look at him. But I feel the warmth of his bare chest radiating up.

I breathe his sun on tree bark smell.

Now the difference hits me and I feel ashamed.

It isn't like my mom at all.

He's still alive.

I hug Finn as hard as I can as long as I can and nobody besides the two of us knows that I kiss him on his shoulder and nobody but me knows the force of the lightning inside me and hurricane winds and thirty-foot waves blasting sheets of spray like nails from a nailgun and me in a dinghy taking water spinning senseless in a whirlpool sucking deeper darker blue to green to black dead calm in the eye of the storm where no light shines but I know there's something there and another sense tells me another sense shows me what my eyes can't see and at last I recognize it.

Recognize her.

The singer in the band yesterday.

Broken pieces.

I know exactly what she sounds like.

Try and make it good again.

For the first time ever I know a sound.

Is it worth it.

Not an idea of one or words about one but the sound itself.

Will it make me sick today.

I know a sound.

She sounds the way I feel.

FOUR

Leave it to the Swedish Blond Communist to sound an equal opportunity wake-up call that does the job even if you can't change the factory setting on your mute button. I don't know where Mickey's big and little hands are when I open my eyes alone in Finn and Critter's bed but I know exactly what time it is thanks to the international aromatic language of hot brewed coffee and fresh-baked dairy-case cinnamon rolls. And I don't waste any either jumping down to the floor and pulling a Kill Rock Stars t-shirt out of my pack to replace the Ben Sherman Finn put on me yesterday and someone must have taken off me last night because now it's hanging at the end of the clothes rack underneath the bed. When I pull aside the curtain walling off the kitchen Ula's sliding hot rolls onto four plates lined up on the breakfast bar with a steaming mug of java next to each and in the spirit of workers of the world unite as in you have nothing to lose but your names I immediately nick her Mrs. Olsen after the coffee lady in the commercials.

She's got her hair tied back and though her eyes are a little bloodshot she doesn't look tired at all. There's natural color in her cheeks and her smile when she sees me does hella more to light the room than the grimy airshaft window.

She asks me how I slept and when I come back with *Fine I guess* she seconds the emotion except for when I kicked her and I have to add two and two a couple of times before I figure out we must have slept together. Which means I guessed right about Finn and Critter and not only have they not slept since Memorial Day probably according to Ula they haven't eaten either since before she first met them on the Green Tortoise bus. And whether they feel hungry or not their bodies are hungry in the considered professional opinion of Ula Katerina Magnusson Registered Nurse. Who was scandalized when she asked how long since their last meal and they looked at each other wondering *Two? Three? Four?* and instead of hours which is what she thought at first they meant days.

Critter and Finn are sitting on the sofa bent over the mirror table. But the crack paraphernalia's nowhere in sight. Instead the table's covered with different-colored sheets of art paper and clippings from magazines and pages of press-on type. Scissors and tape and glue and pencils and pens spill out of a big red wooden box with a hinged domed lid. There's a clear space at one end where Finn's writing on a pad of paper while Critter dictates. When I turn the corner of the sofa I can read the big black letters at the top of the page.

Have You Seen My Lost Bunny?

Finn finishes lettering the flyer while Critter makes room on the table. When he moves a half cylinder of contact paper patterned with shiny 3-D silver cubes he points to a small laminating machine that was hidden underneath and then to a stack of newly minted crack cards in the middle of the table. They stayed up all night making them out of club passes and kewl little pictures and drawings from zines. The cards all have elaborate borders and backgrounds and layers of artwork like miniature collages and no two are alike. Some are business cards for Critter to give out with his name and pager number and nothing else but the words *For speediest response between 4 pm and midnite.*

I look through them while we eat and it takes a while. They're so detailed. I ask Ula to say I think they should put the cards on sale in a paraphernalia store and Finn wastes no time getting across with gestures that most of the credit goes to Critter. Who looks at me all *Really?* and I can tell he's stoked because he has Ula ask me again after he slowly licks all the orange frosting off a cinnamon roll like it's an ice cream cone on a lazy summer afternoon. Unlike Finn who tears his rolls in half and wolfs them down the way you eat fresh silver grunion hot off the grill on a foggy beach morning. He's only got one roll left out of six apiece and that compares to four for Critter. And remembering Finn's body when he took off his shirt last night I can't help thinking *He looks really healthy.*

Which bites even harder than reality usually does and makes me reach for coffee in hopes of charging up my memory banks because until now I forgot all about last night. I've got the mug to my lips when Critter slides his hand across the top the way you tell a waitress in a diner you don't want a refill. And I'm all *What?* with last night on instant replay now while I try to remember if you can get AIDS from drinking out of someone's glass or cup but all I remember for sure is you can't get it from toilet seats. Then I tell myself no way did Finn drink from this anywayz. He's at the other end of the table. And when I sneak a look down there just to check on the whereabouts of his coffee cup I can tell he knows exactly what I'm doing and I'm red as Rudolph's nose in seven seconds flat.

The coffee in my hand is Critter's. And he's acting out a little one-lump-or-two scene using a couple of micro Ziplocs he pulls out of his shirt pocket. As in one quarter or two. I was so busy looking at his crack cards I didn't notice what he was doing with his crack.

Then I hold my palm up flat out as in *Wait.* I take one of the bindles out of his hand and I'm all *I can't believe you dumped the whole thing.*

But he sure did and I guess Critter isn't one of those wise guyz who jokes about yuppies and their three-dollar cappuccinos. Not when he's sweetening his own cup of mountain-grown Folgers with $25 to $30 worth of crack.

Of course he's not paying that much for it. But he could charge that much for that amount. And realizing it brings my Mrs. Olsen moment back with a vengeance and I'm all *Extra! Extra! Give me a piece of paper and you'll read all about it.* So Finn passes down the pad of drawing paper with the bunny flyer on top and I flip it over to the back of the last page and sketch out two side-by-side cartoon panels. I draw one of those lemonade-stand-style booths like Lucy uses for psychiatric counseling in *Peanuts* in one panel and duplicate it next door.

On the overhead signs across the top of both booths I write HOT COFFEE. Then I draw a Lucy-style version of Ula sitting in one booth holding a steaming cup. She's recognizable by her hair and smile and especially her cleavage. In the other panel there's a Linus-style Critter in the same pose who's mostly recognizable because I keep looking at him while I draw it. Then I hold the pad up so they can't see the finishing touches and draw a sign on the front of Ula's booth that reads $1 and one on Critter's reading $30. The captions below just say *Mrs. Olsen* and *Mr. Critter*.

They all think it's kewl with a k especially Critter who asks me to sign it for him and in return gives me one of the crack cards which is actually a pass to a club called Rehab at a place called the Pit at Ninth and Howard with a DJ named Jason on Monday mornings from 6:00 A.M. to high noon. Which means it's going on right now. And which also means it must be where Critter works because that's the address where we dropped him off yesterday.

When I ask about it through Ula it turns out Finn works at the Pit too and in fact they're both headed there this morning and they invite Ula and me to come along. But Ula's all *Thanks but no thanks* since her sister's in the hospital and the daytime visiting hours start pretty soon. And then she drops a bomb and I mean literally when I ask why her sister's in the hospital. Because the reason is that a bomb exploded in her car and according to the FBI it was a bomb her sister made.

My first thought is Ula must not be the only blond communist in the Magnusson family but the way Ula tells it the FBI put the bomb there to either frame her sister or kill her or preferably both. Because her sister's an environmental activist and a pretty radical one I guess though in the world according to Ula she's never gone around preaching violence against the developers and polluters. But other people have been practicing if not preaching it and the goal was to link Ula's sister to them. So the official story is that she was taking the bomb to some oil company's office to plant in a wastebasket or something and it went off by mistake. And now there's a security guard with a submachine gun at the foot of the bed in the hospital room that Ula's family is paying for to keep her sister from being transferred to the hospital in the county jail. Because she's under arrest and being held without bail for terrorism. Even though she was the victim and got hurt really bad.

No wonder Ula wasn't buying paradise that day at the overlook. The Russians got her boyfriend and the Americans almost got her sister. It's so hard-core. And Ula looks like she's going to cry. So I figure the least I can do is offer to walk her to the subway station a few blocks away and hook up with Finn and Critter later. Which is just what the nurse ordered I guess because she lights up like we're going to breakfast at Tiffany's or something and leans over to give me a kiss on the cheek.

I haven't been this close to Ula before at least not awake and the way she smells reminds me of something but I can't think what. It's a little lemony but not the tangy part of lemon more the fresh clean part that's almost sweet. With something green in it like new-mown grass.

I know.

The smell of the green leaves you pull away from corn on the cob.

Exactly.

Which fits because she's like the poster girl for every farmer's-daughter joke ever told. Only it's no laughing matter for her which I get to see firsthand after I write out a note for

Jonnyboy in case he shows while I'm gone and we start walking through dense damp fog toward Market Street. At every inter-section where we wait for the light she gets stares from men in cars. And not just in passing or semidiscreetly. Blatantly openly totally. And not just from the neanderthal minority ei-ther. From about 90 percent of the US males.

There's something creepy about the way they look at her too. Like they're undressing her with their eyes. And like they have a constitutional right to or something. Like there's nothing wrong with it.

Which there definitely is. She can't help it. Her hair is really blond. Her tits are really big. I mean what can a poor girl do. Get a dye job and surgery so she doesn't look like herself anymore in hopes the cavemen crew will leave her alone?

It pisses me off. On the corner of Seventh and Mission I even try to stand in front of her to block the view.

Ula just shrugs.

—I'm used to it. Men always look at me that way.

You mean everybody? All the time? Like the checkout clerk at the market? Dewds at gas stations?

—Yes.

Do they say things? Or just look?

—Usually nothing is said. But it isn't JUST look. You can rape a woman with your eyes.

Do you ever like it?

—If it's the right person.

How do you know it's the right person?

—It usually isn't.

I wonder for a second if it's men more than anything that turns women into dykes and then realize how stupid that is because the way I'm starting to feel about boyz doesn't have anything at all to do with the way I feel about grrls. Which is basically neutral.

Except for my sisters.

Plus Ula isn't even a dyke anywayz. So I sign back *No wonder so many women hate men.* And she laughs but tells me she doesn't hate men like that so much as she feels sorry for them.

—They've been duped. Into wanting something they can't have. Ever. Because it isn't real. It's an image. But they want it instead of something they can have.

Duped by who?

—The forces of control.

As in advertising and business and government and churches. The usual suspects in the world according to hardcore. I sign back that whether she knows it or not she's a punk rocker. But she's all *No way not even.*

—I'm just another Swedish Blond Communist.

And too much of an Abba fan besides.

I've been carrying my sk8board but not riding it because after all Ula asked me to walk her to Market Street not lead the way on wheels. But when we get to Market with everything in motion in every direction from the escalator dropping to the subway across from us to the kewl antique streetcars pulling up to islands in the middle of the street to the mass people on the sidewalk swirling around us it's contagious and I give in to the urge to move too and I mean seriously and I mean fast. I pull an ollie to fakie over a planter box then a ten-foot railslide down a low bus-stop barrier with an acid drop to the curb which I grind till there's no tomorrow or more accurately until a turning streetcar cuts me off. But thanks to God's gift to sk8boarders the disabilties act I'm able to make the transition back onto the sidewalk because they've recently lowered the

curb at the corner just like everywhere else in my country 'tis
of thee sweet land of liberty.

When I started grinding that curb I knew it was the full
Toto moment for me in San Francisco. As soon as my trucks
bit the edge I could tell it was granite not concrete and I definitely wasn't in Kansas anymore. I've seen granite curbs mentioned in sk8 mags before but never ground one myself and
it's smooth and fast and almost frictionless like the difference
between ice sk8ing and Rollerblading I guess but make no
mistake I've never been a blader boy and don't you ever forget
it. Plus granite doesn't wear and chip and crumble fast like
concrete so there's no rough spots to trip you up when you're
hurtling hella hard and sparks are flying and I mean literally
because that's the other thing about granite. You get nice fat
sparks off crete sometimes but I read in *Thrasher* that granite
curbs are like the Glorious Fourth meets the Disneyland Electrical Parade and is it fierce to look down Market Street and
see it edged with wide dark granite all the way to the bay.

So I make myself a solemn promise that I'll come back
with Jonnyboy on a dark and stormy night and we'll watch each
other squeeze out sparks for miles I swear.

Ula's applauding when I roll back up to her and kickflip
my sk8board into my hands. It reminds her of the way I shredded at the overlook. And I'm all double thumbs-up *Watch me
bud 'cause I'm a stud watch me babe 'cause do I rage*. But talk
about storytellers lie. Because at the overlook she was watching
nobody but Jonnyboy. Same wayz I was watching nobody but
Finn. And just like with Roarke and the Polaroid at the concert
in the park I get the feeling she's looking at me but seeing
Jonnyboy.

At the top of the escalator I volunteer to go on to the
hospital with her. But it turns out visitors are limited to the

immediate family and anywayz I guess it's pretty depressing with the guard and everything. Plus I'd bet my virginity while I still have it that her sister's in even worse shape than she let on earlier and it's all she can do to force herself to go. Which is more or less confirmed by her willingness to put it off a little longer when we get distracted by a sudden parade of maybe thirty people dressed like trees and bushes who look like overgrown first graders doing dress rehearsal for the scenery in *Winnie & the Honey Tree.*

Only they're carrying signs reading REDWOOD NOT DEADWOOD and SAVE THE HEADWATERS FOREST which Ula knows her sister is interested in so we follow them about a block to a paved open area near City Hall where about two hundred people are already gathered next to a big fountain. First the tree people one by one go down for the count and then wannabe hippie types make chalk murder victim outlines around their bodies. Finally a villain with slicked-back hair and waxed handlebar mustache wearing a green see-through eyeshade visor and a shirt made out of newspapers appears carrying a little potted palm tree and sets it down in the middle of all the corpses.

He mops his forehead and collapses exhausted into a redwood patio chair decorated like a throne until a blond beach babe complete with bikini and the granny of all goose bumps from the cold brings him a giant drinking glass labeled *Owens Valley H$_2$0.* Which charges him up like he just mainlined vintage shard-onnay crack and he unrolls a big map of California and starts jabbing pins through it hysterically until paramedics come and buckle him up and lead him away.

Act two is a serious dewd in wire frames with a gray-streaked ponytail halfway to his butt crack making a speech that I guess explains the true facts behind the little melodrama.

There's no interpreter and I can't get a play-by-play from Ula because she might as well be watching an Abba reunion concert on pay-per-view. She's nodding her head and shaking her fist and answering back *No!* and *Yes!* aloud like quite a few other people when the speaker really gets going though he stands stock-still never gesturing and the only visual clue is his glasses steaming up a little around the edges.

And I admit it I'm thinking these eco-freaks won't save a patch of iceplant let alone a redwood forest until they at least get sweaty talking about it. But then this flyer gets passed out while the dewd's still at the mike that puts a different spin on things because one side of it's basically his résumé and maybe he comes up short on talking the talk but he walks the walk and I mean on the wild side. Considering he just got out of Leavenworth last year for get this trying to shut down a nuclear power plant. And not with petitions either.

With plastic. And I don't mean Visa. I mean plastique. Unfortunately for him the FBI had him in their sights from genesis ground zero. They got to some of his old friends and basically surrounded him with people cheering him on and even helping him make the plans until they had enough on tape to nab him for conspiracy. The only reason he's outside again after only twenty-four for such a serious crime is that there was only one other person in the conspiracy who wasn't a paid informer. And she turned state's evidence.

So he didn't really DO anything. He was just punished for freedom of speech. Because the way the law is I guess you tell somebody you feel like bombing the Pentagon and they say *Right on let's do it* you've already done the deed. That's conspiracy and the sentence is the same as if you're caught with a fuse in one hand and an Ohio Blue Tip in the other.

And that is so wrong. But when you think about it the only

way to fight a wrong like that is to ignore it. Don't let it get you down. That way at least you inspire other people even if the nuke stays on-line and the chainsaw massacre starts right on schedule.

The way this dewd's inspiring me. Because I don't much care for the details of politics. I'd rather put it on the one-to-one level. Like with Tibet. I didn't need any long-winded speeches to figure out which' way was up on that one. Just getting up close and personal with a couple of flesh-and-blood people in real time. One was the Dalai Lama. He said all the Tibetans want is to live their lives in peace in Tibet and not spread Buddhism to China or anyplace else and in fact people here should follow their own traditions and not adopt ones from far-off places. Which isn't exactly "Onward Christian Soldiers" now is it and makes me believe him right off because the way people are with cults in this country he could be rich-ass living highstyle the rest of his life just by saying *Give me your money and I'll save your soul*.

The other was that grrl who gave us our passes. She was just an ordinary Tibetan. The kind the Chinese claim is so much better off with them in charge. And just think about it. Think about her joking with me about our shaved heads and think about the picture of the Chinese tank facing down the lone student protester in that big Chow Mein square where they killed all those people. I mean it's a no-brainer to decide which side you're on.

Same with this dewd. He gets out of prison for trying to shut down something poisoning nature and according to the flyer what does he do. He goes after the same family that turned a huge part of the state into a desert by diverting all the water to L.A. and specifically to all the formerly worthless land in L.A. owned by them and their rich friends. And now they own the last big old redwood trees left in the world and they're counting the days until they can turn them into patio furniture and hot tubs. I mean they're already billionaires. Enough is enough.

There's nothing in it for this dewd. No money and no thanks. But here he is with probably half a dozen FBI boyz recording every word he says. And why. So some dumb-ass kid can dis him for not coming across like Jesse Jackson?

I'm starting to get it.

I'm starting to figure it out.

There's a reason he isn't ranting and raving.

And I know what it is.

Actions speak louder than words.

He's here to inspire people to take action.

The way he took action.

Because what he can do now himself is limited.

He's known.

I'm sure most of the people listening aren't known.

I'm not known.

I'm anonymous.

And the best way to stay that way is to keep quiet. So there's another reason he isn't ranting and raving. He's setting another kind of example.

And is he.

When the speaker's finished Ula looks like she had a little taste of crack herself. I guess the dewd's pretty famous in Sweden among the Greens anywayz and Ula's one of their supporters. Plus he mentioned her sister as an example of a political prisoner here at home and that gives her some good news to take to the hospital. Walking over to the subway en-trance she apologizes for not interpreting anything in real time but I show her the flyer and let her know I learned a lot just by reading and watching. And she looks back at me nodding with this light in her eyes that makes me feel important somehow. Then she turns me into the envy of all the winos and junkies propped up against the flagpoles of United Nations Plaza by giving me a goodbye kiss and this time I mean a wet one.

I'm supposed to hook up with Finn and Critter at the Pit and either get the key or else hang out if I feel like it until one of them is ready to leave. Riding my sk8board back South of Market I start getting curious about what the Pit will be like and cross my fingers it won't remind me of the Halfway House Saloon in New Monterey where my mom and dad used to be regulars. But when I get to Ninth and Howard and stand waiting for the light to change I notice that there's no sign at all for the place except an old rusty one hanging from the second floor and it says COCKTAILS so I pretty much prepare myself for the worst.

All the windows are blacked so you can't see inside from the sidewalk and once you're through the door on the corner you have to stop moving it's so hella dark. Then your eyes start to adjust and the first thing on the screen is the glow of pinball machines. Lots of them. Then dim shapes of pool tables in a room to the side lit only on top by low-hanging shaded lamps. Finally this long bar with one end just two steps away and the other as far as the pins in a bowling alley.

With a mirror behind it that you don't even notice at first because after all reflection takes light. Plus there's no one sitting at the bar to see double anywayz. Actually there's no one anywherez it seems which surprises me because I know Finn is a bouncer here and usually they're somewhere near the entrance. But I feel a bass vibration so there's definitely music and I smell fresh not stale cigarette smoke so I know there's somebody somewherez and then at the far end of the bar I make out two head-and-shoulder shapes blocking the light from a pinball machine and am I stoked.

Because I recognize Critter's back from the row of black-and-white knit diamonds across the shoulders on this vintage golf shirt I saw on a hanger in the bedroom. And there's something about the slouch and the hand on the hip of the other shape that tells me it's Jonnyboy but in disguise I guess since he never wears a baseball cap. And suddenly I understand the deal with hearts on valentines for the first time ever because the feeling I get starts in a definite place and it's right there in my chest before it migrates to my brain.

Walking toward them is one of those times I wish I could yell *Hey faggots!* or *Hey punks!* the way Jonnyboy does to his unsuspecting friends sometimes and watch them spin around amped and ready to kick ass. The closer I get the stronger I feel the vibration so I know all they hear is the music and just when I think they'll be jumping eight miles high when I sneak up and goose their butts Critter turns sideways and sees me.

He walks up and gives me a real kiss on the lips and a long one the way kweerboyz do when they see their friends anyplace in San Francisco and especially on the street. And that and being in the bar I guess make me feel grown-up and at home and does that feeling shred. Because sometimes I admit it I just want to be like everybody else. Not the universe of everyone no way never nohow just the world of everyone kewl.

Like Jonnyboy.

Who's not Jonnyboy after all and though he's wearing wrap-around shades and dark ones which make me wonder for a second if he's blind there's no doubt he sees me and more because he's checking me out in a way that makes me feel like a wanted poster in a post office where the line goes out the door and there's nothing else to read.

He isn't smiling. Or frowning. His lips don't move at all. It's like he already knows it would be a waste so he's just waiting watching and I'm wishing his shades had mirror lenses so I could see what he sees because for a second I want more than anything in the world to know what I look like to him. I mean before he gets the news from Critter. Which he's starting to get right now. But unlike a lot of people he doesn't go Hallmark on me.

As in his face a sympathy card.

Instead he reaches into the neck of his t-shirt which isn't fashion baggy but muscle tight and pulls out the necklace he's wearing so I can see the little silver single letter cubes like blocks for kids on a leather cord. The room is so dark and the letters so small I have to bend forward to read them and what they spell out is F-E-A-R.

Then I feel a hand on my shoulder and turn to Critter who gets the word across that Finn's downstairs and I should head that direction in case any by-the-bookers wander in from the street and decide I look a few months shy of twenty-one. And I'm all *Lead the way* because I don't see any stairs and he just points back toward Fear who isn't there anymore and then I see a narrow doorway on the black painted wall behind the pinball machine and realize the sound vibrations are coming through it like a funnel so I just do Johnny Rotten *Follow Me!* and lead the way myself.

The stairs are pitch-black at first but there's luminous tape on the edges of the steps and then a landing where the staircase turns and the weird purple shine of black lights rises up from below and everything white like the lint on the flannel

I'm wearing over Kill Rock Stars glows brighter and brighter the closer we get to the bass and the heat which more and more fill every molecule in the narrow space until I wonder how there's room for oxygen and how I'll ever breathe and especially deep enough to climb back up. But there's a draft of cooler air at the bottom and I gulp it by instinct and what a waste because the lungs are quicker than the eye and what I see right after takes my breath away and keeps it.

I don't know how big the room is but the walls are old bricks and the ceiling is low and I don't know how many people are suddenly in front of me but I know there's more than I could ever try to count and I know they all move crazy wikked kewl and fast. Arms waving hips pumping boyz with shirts off grrls in stop-sign lipstick Day-Glo tops and miniskirts. Everyone everything lit by hanging strips of crumpled foil blown by oscillating fans in front of projectors and flashing Xmas bulbs racing the beat and TV screens suspended in the corners showing kweerboy porno.

A big black guy with rasta dreads and rings in both nipples gets down boogying on the floor and what really hits me for some reason is that he's wearing shades. And I ask myself how can he possibly see to dance like that then smack myself upside and I mean hard considering two-thirds of the people are wearing them and wake up Radboy.

Because the last time THEY woke up wasn't this morning.

Or even yesterday morning.

It was probably Wednesday and this is Monday and it ain't spilled beer on the floor so deep their feet kick up sheets of spray it's Day 6 tweeker sweat from dancing all week with only bumps or hits for breaks. And it's one thing knowing about places like this in L.A. from Jonnyboy but high-voltage culture shock being here in person and am I Whistler's mother in line for Free Fall at Great America. As in oh most definitely weak in the knees.

The black guy bops back up and I start scanning the crowd for Finn and find him in a corner on the far side of the dance floor with his shirt off talking to the Skippy t-shirt boy. He doesn't see me yet and I realize to get over there I'll have to follow the walls around the room because the dance floor's way too packed to cross. So I turn around and the first thing I notice in an alcove next to where the stairs come down is a men's-room sign and I decide to hit it now while it's right in front of me.

Inside I'm standing at the urinal thinking it should smell like beer and piss in here and wondering why it doesn't when I feel the draft of the door opening. I button up and turn around and it's Fear.

He's leaning against the door staring at me and his hand goes into the pocket of his jeans and I fall backwards against the urinal when he pulls out the knife. I can't scream and who could hear me if I could.

—No no no.

I read his lips. He drops the knife. He holds both hands in the air then turns and latches the door with a hook I didn't notice. I'm slumped on the worn tiled floor. He walks over and touches my wrist. I'm shaking. His hand is warm and soft. Softer than a sk8er's. Softer than a fisherman's. The floor is cold and hard. Who is he. Fear. He pulls me toward him. What does he do. Drugs. He pulls from his pocket a little Ziploc with prepowdered crack. He points to the knife. Points to me. Points to the bag. Points to my nose.

Then touches it. Lightly softly two fingers over my cheek behind my ear down my neck back up my throat over my chin around my lips. He sits beside me on the floor. There's barely room. His leg presses mine. He's warm all over. With his eyes on me he reaches for the knife. It's big and silver. It's not his fault it looks the same as Terry's knife.

The knife my dad.

Fear doesn't know. He pinches open the bag and dips the blade point in then pulls it out flat up and holds the mound of crack under one nostril closing off the other with his thumb. It doesn't look like very much. He sniffs and it's gone.

Rewind. Repeat other nostril. Rewind. My turn. He holds the blade at my nose level so I can just lean forward. I'm not shaking anymore just my head *No*.

But inside I'm wondering why.

He starts to talk then bites his lip. He looks around like the words must be on the walls somewherez but there's nothing not the words of the prophets or even here-I-sit poetry or pen-drawn pussies filled with teeth. Then he points to his lips and mouths very slowly:

—I want you to fuck me,

It scares me worse than the knife and I jump up panicked lunging for the door. But something stops me when my hand's on the latch.

The look in his eyes.

The question in my mind.

He's still sitting on the floor. I bend forward and draw on his jeans with my finger pressing hard feeling muscle underneath a letter *Y*.

His finger tracing the air between us draws a *B*. His moves his lips.

—'Cause.

He draws a *U*. Then an *R*. His eyes meet mine.

—Beautiful.

Déjà vu all over again.

He rises on his knees.

Leans toward me.

His lips brush mine.

His hand still holds the knife and crack. The other moves toward my jeans. I stand back up and open the door just wide enough to slide through sideways and close it softly behind me.

Finn's in the corner by himself now standing at a bar that's really just a card table on high legs with rows of Evian squeeze bottles on top and instead of a cash register a plastic kid's sandbox bucket filled with bills and coins. Two coolers on the floor underneath hold mostly sodas and a few beers plus Snickers and Krackel bars on a paper plate so the ice underneath keeps them solid. There was ventilation I guess in the bathroom and I forgot how hot it was out here. Finn's chest shines with sweat and his teeth shine black light bright when he spots me. I go behind the table and after he hugs me I kiss him the way Critter kissed me upstairs.

We stand here with our arms over each other's shoulders watching the dancers who aren't just boyz which kind of surprises me. Because of Finn and Critter I just guessed this was a kweerboy place but there's lots of grrls too. Almost half and half. And I can't really tell because no one's dancing with partners but they can't all be dykes. At least they don't look like the only dykes I've ever seen for sure which are those lezzie boredoms we spied on in Monterey and some of the grrlz watching the band in the park. So I write Finn a note asking and he writes back:

Ever heard of lipstick lesbians?

Then he makes a big X through **heard** and writes:

Go ahead, have at me.

So I kiss him again but just a peck on the cheek. Then I nod my head and he writes:

All right then, these are black nail polish lesbians.

Which instantly fills my mind with Jonnyboy. The folded worn-out picture ripped from a book that goes with him everywhere. Lou Reed. Black nail polish. Yellow hair. Wraparound shades. Seeing that picture when he was a kid made him want to be a punk or at least made him realize he was born one and there was no turning back. It meant the music and it meant the drugs and it meant Roarke as soon as he saw Chaotic Stature. Because Lou Reed was like a god and far away and old but Roarke was real. Roarke he could touch.

Just think if Jonnyboy never saw that picture. It changed his life and changed mine too. I mean I wouldn't be here. I might be dead. I might not be.

What.

Kweer.

No.

It's still too intimidating. Still too mysterious. Not the physical details of course or the drive that makes it happen but the way it fits into the rest of your life. And that's something you learn for yourself or not at all I guess because they don't teach it in health class and I don't think you'll find it on the Internet either.

But I know one thing. I owe Finn an appy polly oggy that I wanted to make as soon as just the two of us were together.

I'm really sorry I looked over at you the way I did earlier when Critter stopped me from drinking out of the coffee cup. It was like a reflex not something I thought through.

He rubs my head with his hand and writes:

Shag it. I didn't take it personally.

And talk about not thinking. Because what do I come back with.

Do you know how you got it?

Like it truly fucking matters Radboy. Like why not just ask *Was it your own fucking fault?*

But Finn's on Court TV. No emotion. He just turns to me fullface so I can read his lips.

—I don't know how I got it.

He puts his arm around my shoulders again.

—But I wish I didn't have it.

We watch the dancers. I wonder how many are sick the same or will be.

I'm cold now and there's goose bumps on my arms. Even in the magic tanning black light next to Finn's they're pale. And smooth and small with hairs you don't see and veins that don't show.

Somewhere I read that blood is mostly just like seawater.

Yeah right.

FIVE

Life at the Greenery with Finn and Critter cracking off while I wait for Jonnyboy is the closest I've come so far to living like a white man as in when I grow up to be a. Because as soon as we got back here from the Pit that day they both cracked off and conked out and there's things I have to do every day to keep the trains running on time. I can't just take off on my sk8board whenever I want for as long as I want without leaving any clues where I might be.

First off there's looking out for the boyz while they sleep and flowing them food when they're awake. The food's almost as important as the sleep in recovering their bodies from the last few weeks of crack and it probably helps even more than sleep in reducing their tolerance. Which is the other reason to crack off now and then if you don't want to go all psycho killer. Because if you keep using without stopping you just use more and more and more to get the same effect. And mass amounts of crystal meth are lovely to look at and lovely to hold but once they're inside you your blood runs cold.

Right now they're both sleeping about 23/7 but that doesn't mean they're both awake at the same time for one full hour. Finn usually wakes up a couple times a day for a half hour at a stretch. Critter's up twice as often but never longer than fifteen minutes. And am I glad Critter's the restless one because it's his pager the important calls come to or will come to in the case of Jonnyboy and if I bring him a big bowl of Fruity Pebbles with milk as soon as he opens his eyes it's guaranteed he'll check his messages before he drifts back into dreamland. I'm actually the keeper of his pager while he's cracking off and I wear it clipped inside the waist of my jeans set on vibrate. He gets so many calls he'd end up with memory overload if I didn't write all the numbers down in my notebook as they come in and clear them off the display. Then every time Critter wakes up I give him the latest list of numbers and he looks it over and writes the date and time at the top and folds it in half and puts it in the pocket of his black book. There's only four people out of the dozens who call every day wanting crack that he'll actually get back to while he's cracking off and I've already memorized their numbers and if they call I circle them in red.

Plus I'm on the lookout for Ula's sister's number and the code for Jonnyboy. Both mean there's a message for me on Finn and Critter's home-phone voice mail which they won't check for any other reason until they crack on again. Before they started sleeping last week Critter recorded a greeting tell-

ing Jonnyboy to call the pager number and punch in his birthday digits for a speedy response and at least a couple of times
a day impostors try to fake it. You can always tell because the
prefixes are strange and the last two numbers are in the low
seventies. I guess there's a crack drought right now and people
are desperate.

They both told me to wake them up when Jonnyboy calls
and I guess I'll try but I'm not too optimistic based on what
I've seen. When they're out they're out and I mean out. About
a week ago after they'd been sleeping for two or three days one
of Critter's chosen four left his number and the next time Critter woke up he called back and told the guy sure he could stop
by for some go-fast if he could get here in the next ten minutes.
Which shouldn't have been a problem since the dewd lives at
Fifth and Folsom. But tweekers make potheads look like on-
the-dotters and he showed up in twenty. Critter was still awake
to let him in and they sat down talking in the living room while
he reached for the lockbox under the mirror table. Only he fell
asleep before he got his hands that far and slumped back
against the sofa. I watched the dewd try to wake Critter up for
almost an hour before he passed me a note asking how long I
thought he'd be sleeping.

I wrote back five or six hours thinking he'd split. But NFW.
He was a tall skinny nervous twentysomething boy named
Ziggy in a red cowboy shirt and black jeans who seemed like
one big itch with a giant invisible fingernail poised to scratch
just millimeters away in space but paralyzed in time. He sat
there watching the tropical fish while I watched him. No way
would I leave that lockbox full of cash and crack unguarded.
One thing I learned secondhand from Jonnyboy who learned
it up close and personal is that you don't tempt even your

closest friends with large amounts of hard drugs and easy money because a drug addict's best friend of all is the monkey on his back.

Finally around four in the morning Critter's eyelids fluttered and though they never went higher than half-mast the two of us propped him up on either side and walked him through opening the lockbox and weighing and bagging the crack. Then he fell asleep again with the Ziploc still in his hand and Ziggy's hand full of money frozen in midair between them. And did I feel sorry for the dewd because the itch was raging poison ivy by then and he didn't need it scratched anymore he needed calamine lotion and could he smell it and could he almost feel the blessed soothing coolness on his skin. Only was he wary of me and flat-out convinced I'd pocket the bills if he left them on the table and took the crack and bailed. So he sat there looking mournful another half an hour I swear until I got the point across through charades that if Critter trusted me with the lockbox I could probably be trusted with his cash and Ziggy's face lit up gratefully as in *Why didn't I think of that?* and he left a note for Critter and was out the door in sixty seconds flat.

I covered Critter with a blanket and slept next to him on the sofa until he woke up again in the morning. I pointed out the money on the table but I don't know if he even saw it or remembered why it was there. After I fed him a quart of chocolate milk and a whole box of raspberry Pop-Tarts I walked him back to the bedroom and he hasn't been out farther than the kitchen since.

Finn has though. Three days ago around noontime he wandered out in a wife-beater and boxer shorts eating an Eggo toaster waffle smeared with grape jelly. He sat down and pointed at the *Have You Seen My Lost Bunny?* flyer still unfinished on the mirror table more than a week after the bunny disappeared and did air scribbles so I had to look around for my notepad because I haven't had much use for it lately except for sketching the characters for this comic I want to do called *Greenheads vs. Greedheads* where the heroes are punk rock nature boyz with green mohawks and rad tattoos of birds and lizards who wear nothing but loin-cloths. Which means I've been practicing drawing muscles for the first time really using guess which sleeping beauties as models.

They can live two weeks without food. I'm nackered, but I reckon I should have a go at copying these notices and posting them about the neighborhood before I doss out again. I did leave the door open. It's the least I can do.

So I was all *I'm with you mate* and Finn put most of his visible energy into looking lively for seven seconds and count-ing. He had big black circles under his eyes and with the thick dark stubble on his face the same length as his hair his whole head seemed shrouded. When he stood up to get dressed I put long odds against him staying on his feet much longer than his ETA at the clothes rack. I don't know where he found the strength to lace his Grinders. Let alone fully deck himself out in tight black high-cuffed Levi's and narrow black braces over an electric-blue Fred Perry polo shirt with red laurel leaves on the chest.

I don't know where but I know why. The gear was like armor. It took the weak out of tweeker. It made him stand tall instead of not at all. He still looked hungover but hungover and mean not hungover and green. Like the very last man in the last gang in town.

I put two fingers to my lips and spoofed a wolf whistle. Finn thumped his chest Tarzan style.

I bet you miss being in a crew of boyz dressed like that and putting fear in the hearts of men.

And lust in the hearts of lad[d]ies.

Really? The laddies I mean.

Not the laddies I fancied, not the ones in the crew. Why d'you think I came out here?

To meet kweer skinz?

I'd met them already, on the internet. The QSF, Queer Skinhead Firm, Bay Area chapter, men's men, not fetishists, not white power, not boneheads. Aye, they talked a good game, except the only game that matters, football, and that troubled me a bit but I made allowances for Americans. Though how lads can claim skin and not follow English football is beyond me. It's part of the cult like the music and the gear. You can't adopt the one and the two but not the three.

There's no English group like that?

Not really. Not embracing the traditional skin life. They're all leathermen looking for a shag.

So what did the kweer skinz here turn out to be like?

Leathermen looking for a shag.

No way. You came all the way from England for the same old same old?

From Ulster. Northern Ireland. Belfast.

And I can't even count the levels of outcast Finn turns out to be. Because as everyone knows it's like a war zone there between the Catholics and Protestants. Though the way Finn put it was between the haves and have-nots with most of the haves English Protestants and the have-nots Irish Catholics. And his mother was an English Catholic so it's the worst of both worlds. Nobody trusts them. Plus he's kweer. And a skinhead. Which I thought would be especially gnarly over there but not necessarily.

There's pressure on Catholic boys to join the IRA, though a lot join on their own. Claiming skin's sort of a way out, since everyone knows we're not political. You find Catholic and Protestant boys together in the same crews. My uncle stayed out of the troubles back in the 70s by claiming skin.

Your UNCLE was a skinhead?

From the early days. My mum was a mod, actually.

No wonder he ended up disappointed in the so-called skinz out here. I mean back there it's a tradition passed down from another generation and here it's just another teenage fad taken up by especially stupid people who don't even know what the real thing's about. Like the bonehead Nazi skins thinking it's all about white power when the whole skinhead scene was originally based on music made by black people. Or the older kweerboyz thinking it's all bootlicking and peeing on one another and chains up the butt.

And did that crowd have the pedal to their metal when Finn showed up at a bar just a couple of doors down from Eighth and Sumner to meet some of his Internet skinhead buddies in person for the very first time. But after this cigar-smoking fortysomething ex-marine tried to use Finn's mouth for an ashtray he was definitely merging back into the slow lane thank you as in the first alley he saw after he walked out the door. The alley made a ninety-degree turn and a cute thin pierced and tattooed boy with no shirt on standing in a doorway smiled at him and said he had something inside that would lift his spirits.

Which turned out to be a bunny. As in *Have You Seen My Lost Bunny?*

I Just Want To Know What Happened to Her
She is black and white and has normal bunny ears and
weighs about THREE pounds.
REWARD for Info.
She is VERY important to me.
841-8075 Critter

Waiting to copy the flyer we were standing in a cheesy storefront on Folsom Street surrounded by greeting cards and rental mailboxes and teddy bears dressed in leather vests holding rainbow flags when Finn clapped one hand over his eyes and started shaking his head *No*. As in nobody. Which is who was on the duty roster at the Greenery answering the phone and checking messages for the next several days.

Unless Hellen Killer's miracle worker showed up unexpectedly to slay the cat that got yours truly's tongue. Meaning the flyers weren't exactly guaranteed to produce immediate results. So Finn and me held an emergency strategy conference.

I care sweet FA for that filthy rabbit. I reckon we could have a go at posting notices as planned, and if Critter mentions it later say it slipped our minds.

FA?

Football Association. Fanny Adams. Fuck All. Except it didn't slip our minds, so it'd be lying. And that won't do. He might not notice, so it's not dead certain we'd end up lying, but it's possible.

It made me think of Jonnyboy and *storytellers lie* and lies about big things versus little things. Jonnyboy wouldn't think twice about a lie like that. I guess the way Finn sees it any lie told to your boyfriend is automatically in the big category. Which probably saves a lot of time and grief in the long run. I wondered which category hiding how much crack you're doing from your boyfriend fits in. Or if Jonnyboy considers that a lie at all. And how long it took him to decide.

Which reminded me of the special pager code for Jonnyboy. Along with Ula's sister's number that I'm on red alert for too.

Why not call Ula and ask if you can put her sister's number on the flyer? Then she can call Critter's pager if anyone calls.

Finn jabbed his index finger into my chest and mouthed:
—Clever boy.

We found a pay phone on the street and while Finn was talking to Ula I wrote out a message for her.

Tell Mrs. Olsen if she wants to hook up for java she should name the day date and time and I'll be there trailing smoke behind me.

Finn held the receiver in place with his shoulder so he could write back while he talked.

She says yes. She'll drop by Thursday. Given up on finding excitement in our house, have you?

Back in the storefront Finn borrowed some Wite-Out and changed the phone numbers on the flyer then made a hundred copies. The cashier was this husky look-alike for that Janet Reno lady on the Supreme Court. In a denim skirt. A lezzie boredom if I ever saw one. After Finn paid her he started going over the flyer asking her to keep her eyes peeled and while he was talking she kept looking back and forth skeptically from the flyer to Finn and me and also in the distance behind us for the hidden *Candid Camera* TV crew or something. But finally she decided we were serious after all and let Finn pin one up on the corkboard by the mailboxes.

We got pretty much the same reaction from all the business people Finn approached whether they were Arab storekeepers or auto-body greasemonkeys or the Balloon Lady a couple doors down from the Pit. Disbelief then suspicion then benefit of the doubt and finally a hint of concern. Nobody kicked us out or refused a flyer and I don't think they were just humoring us and throwing them away later either. Which kind of surprised me and when we switched to posting-on-utility-poles mode I asked Finn if it was what he expected.

Critter's very clever. He told me what to write, and it's meant to get exactly what we want. First: sympathy. Second: help. And I've given everyone we've approached today another reason to help.

What's that?

Finn looked at me with his lips going into the kind of tight closemouthed grin you make to keep from busting up someplace where it might cause big trouble like during Holy Communion or on the witness stand in a murder trial. On either side of his smile the dimples went deep as Carlsbad Caverns and even clogged with whisker stalactites they made him look about five years old.

Can't you guess?

In my mind I started replaying the way people looked at the two of us and realized that after a certain point they always looked at just me.

Damn!

Fuck!

You told them it's MY bunny!!!

I started chasing Finn down the sidewalk and he ducked into an alley and fell back breathing hard against a rolled-down steel door. As he slid down the door to sit on the pavement he pulled the notepad out of my back pocket and the pen out of the ring binding.

All for the greater good.

You didn't want to lie to Critter. What about me?

I didn't lie to you.

You lied about me.

To people who don't the least bit matter.

They matter to me.

Why?

Because bunnies are lame that's why! And I don't want people thinking I'm a lamer!

Finn just laughed and promised he wouldn't tell anyone else. Not that there was anyone else to tell. There were cars on the main streets but nobody on the sidewalks and there weren't any cars or people in the alleys where we mostly put up flyers. By then it was around two in the afternoon and the sun was out and bright and hot. I could tell it hurt Finn's eyes even with shades on. He was pretty much running on empty after our little half-block chase. But he wanted to tell Critter we actually searched for the bunny too so we took our time in every alley looking under parked cars and in the narrow spaces between buildings and especially around Dumpsters and trash cans for signs of bunny shit. I don't think I've ever in my life been so convinced that something I was doing was such a total waste of time.

That bunny was dead. I knew it. It was like looking for a dolphin on Mars. Everywhere we could see in every direction was a completely alien environment for a bunny. Not a blade of grass or trickle of water. The air smelled like roofing tar and human piss and car exhaust. Broken glass sparkled everywhere. Stains from motor oil and battery acid made monster outlines on the pavement. Just imagining a white soft living creature there reminded me of that painter who plopped an apple in the middle of a human face.

But then I remembered the way I felt right after the concert with Jonnyboy gone. All alone in a strange city full of even stranger people. And did I start rooting for that bunny then.

We were back at their door on Sumner Street when Finn remembered he was supposed to drop something off at the Pit. And though it's not much more than a block away I had serious doubts he'd make it there and back under his own power. So I offered to do it for him and I could tell he didn't want to go himself but he was all *No. No. No.* And I figured it was some kind of drug delivery and he didn't trust me completely so when we got back inside I wrote out the story of Ziggy from the other night just to reassure him. But I could tell it upset him when he read it and he looked down motionless for so long afterwards that I was sure he was sleeping again until he slowly started writing back.

It's not that I don't trust you. I just want you to stay the way you are. I don't want to be responsible for making you part of that scene. I know you're not afraid of it, but you should be.

And since I never passed on what happened with that Fear dewd I could see how Finn might think I was still all starry-eyed. So I answered back:

That's kewl. I'll just hand it off to whoever and bail. No pinball or nothing. I'll come right back. I promise. Besides I gotta take care of you boyz.

And Finn looked at me almost crying I swear. He started to say something but stopped. Then he took a folded manila-colored envelope out of one of his back pockets and handed it to me. Written on the outside was *Jason.*

I knew if I left him sitting there on the sofa he'd be there when I came back with his hands in exactly the same position on the knot of his right boot laces. So I kneeled on the carpet in front of the sofa and untied both sets of laces then loosened them all the way to the last four holes so I could pull his boots off without any help from him besides holding his legs up. Which used up all his remaining energy and afterwards he dropped them slamming his heels on the table like free weights after one too many repetitions. I unbuttoned the fly of his Levi's. They clung to his legs and when I pulled them off his boxer briefs slid down too as far as his ankles. It was the first time I saw him naked below the waist and I looked at him for a long time breathing in the sweet humid forest smell and feeling the heat rising up. I wanted to lay my head down and sleep with my face buried there and open my eyes in the morning to his warm pink perfect skin.

Finally I leaned in and kissed him once softly and quickly then pulled his boxers up and wrapped my arms around his chest and stood him up. I walked him to the bedroom supporting one shoulder on me and the other against the wall. After I pulled his shirt off I kissed him again on his chest and his brain waves flickered enough for his muscles to understand how to help me lift him up into sitting position on the loft bed. Once I let go he fell back on the mattress with his legs still hanging over the edge and his ankles draped over my shoulders. Then his muscles tensed for maybe a minute locking my head between his calves and the pressure of his firm hot flesh against my neck and cheeks and jaw and the silky touch of hair from his legs on my lips made me wish that minute would never end.

But Finn relaxed and I folded the rest of him up onto the bed. Then I walked back into the living room and put the envelope he gave me in the left cargo pocket of my army jeans and rode my sk8board to the Pit. I stood just inside the door until my eyes adjusted and I could see a pretty grrl with blue-and-blond-streaked shoulder-length hair and a heart-shaped face behind the bar talking to a couple of tweekerboyz I remembered seeing downstairs. She smiled like she knew who I was and pushed a pad of notepaper and a pencil toward me when I walked up to the bar.

Hi. I have something for Jason from Finn.

She checked the time on a mini alarm clock behind her and picked up the pencil.

He should be finishing up right now. I'll tell him you're here if you just want to stay put.

I didn't want to admit that I didn't even know who he was let alone what he was finishing so I just nodded and wrote *Thanx*. After she left the two boyz at the bar kind of turned their attention toward me in a casual way without saying anything and it made me a little nervous. I started wondering if it was a good idea to hand the envelope over in front of other people and decided that since I didn't know if it was or not I should act like it wasn't. There was no one at the far end of the bar by the stairs and I don't know why but walking down the bar and climbing onto a stool started this movie in my head.

But not a Hollywood one.

Instead of slick as seagrass everything looked like those oldstyle home movies before video. All bleached out and jerky as if the sprocket holes in the film didn't quite match the projector. And the people in it were me and my older brothers when they were around my age now or a little older and I was really little. Plus these two old ladies who ran this run-down dive called the PassTime Tavern out in Sand City on the other side of Monterey.

They probably didn't have anything else to do and just kept the place open. They were older than my grandmas and were supposed to be almost blind even with their glasses on and that's how kids got the courage to go in there and order beers in phony deep voices and hang out playing pool and shuffleboard. Because the legend was they didn't notice all their customers were under twenty-one and even if they suspected they never asked for ID because they couldn't read the birthdays anywayz their eyes were so bad.

Tommy wanted to find out just how blind the ladies were before he tried to tap the register. And he figured if they'd serve a squirt like me it was definitely a go. But when he clued me in and I found out I might have to drink beer I made the First Lady proud and just said no because it was the last thing in the world I wanted to put in my mouth except for maybe brussels sprouts. So he bribed me with a Snickers bar and promised he'd drink it for me and flow me a root beer instead.

There was no sign of life when we walked in except for a couple of flies doing figure eights over the long shuffleboard running parallel to the bar. I sat down according to plan on the farthest bar stool from the taps and on top of my backpack filled with comic books to make me taller in the saddle. Plus I was wearing one of those old Michelin Man–style down jackets to look burlier and a Giants cap pulled so low over my eyes I had serious tunnel vision and couldn't even see myself in the big Budweiser mirror behind the bar unless I craned my neck.

The old ladies came out and one drew three beers and walked them down to us. And did Tommy figure bingo on the blindness meter when she pushed it toward me and looked right at me without my number coming up as in eighty-six. Which led to hard luck and trouble for him later since it was robbing the PassTime and thinking he wouldn't be identified that earned him his first vacation with the California Youth Authority and I mean all expenses paid. But we had fun that day and except for Terry slugging me when they got me a fountain root beer on the side and I wanted ice cream to make it a float I played my part to make my brothers proud.

Maybe that's why it came back to me like it was projected on a sheet tacked to our living-room wall on Grace Street in New Monterey. Because after a while you forget a lot of things about your family and it's all home movies. I mean the camera's for the good things not the ugly and the bad.

I felt the floor move from someone heavy climbing the last

couple of steps behind me and turned my head. And just like that I was face-to-face with Mr. Skippy dog-food t-shirt. Which didn't quite compute because if I weigh 115 he weighs 120. So I glanced around in search of his burly buddy but drew a blank until I noticed a big black steel-reinforced box two feet square on the floor beside him.

He drew a circle in the air.

Records.

Jason.

The name on the crack card Critter made from the pass for the club called Rehab.

A DJ.

And young. Our faces were so close that even in the dim light I could see how smooth his skin is. No wrinkles or lines. Even his sideburns and little goatee that looked scraggly and whiskery when I saw them from a distance turned out to be soft peach fuzz up close. I could tell that he's trying to look older. The cloth workman's cap he wears pulled low over his eyes is part of the disguise. And it works. Before I would have guessed he was older than Jonnyboy. Maybe Ula's age which is twenty-eight. But no way is Jason that old.

That's probably why he's so shy. Every time I met his eyes he looked away. And I could tell it wasn't the usual normal's nervousness.

Just like I could tell he's smart and I mean way.

Just like I could tell there's something shared between us.

Already.

I don't know what it is.

I don't mean the envelope. When I reached in my pocket for it my thumb and forefinger pinched the contents for the first time and there was no mistaking the skittering shards of a hella thick bindle of crack. I wondered if he sold it. Or if it was all just for him.

His body language told me he didn't know what to do after I handed it over. He obviously didn't know I could read his lips. Though you can't read the lips of people who won't look at you. Finally he pointed first down the bar and made a drinking motion then second at me with a momentary question in his eyes before they shifted away.

And I turn down drinks on autopilot it's just the way I am. So I started to with Jason but stopped short remembering that when tweekers drink it's almost always bottled water. Or soda. Plus I was thirsty anywayz. Plus I knew he'd stay there with me at least a couple of minutes if he bought me a drink. And did I want him to.

Hand it off and bail. No pinball or nothing.

But Finn was fast asleep.

I'll come right back.

A promise is a promise.

I thanks anywayzed him maybe a little too gratefully and stood up gesturing I was running late as in Roadrunner treading air.

He grinned.

I wanted to kiss him.

More than anyone ever.

It didn't seem like so much of a sex deal as with Finn.

It didn't seem like anything I've ever felt before.

I pulled my notepad out and wrote *I'm Rad* and ripped the page off and gave it to him then turned and walked down the bar and into the glare outside without looking back.

I thought about Jason all the way to the Greenery where I couldn't sit still but couldn't think of anything to do either until

I started looking through the records in the spray-painted milk crates. They're all Critter's of course and a lot of them are punk rock dating back to his days in Pumpkin Center which is where he grew up. It's got like 300 people and in the word according to Finn about 299 of them including Critter's entire family are dead ringers for extras in the movie *Deliverance*.

Critter figured out he was kweer by the time he turned sixteen even though he'd never done anything and didn't want to with anybody there. But he had to do something. So he became the only punk in town. Which meant he could stop going out with grrlz and stop playing football and his parents and everyone else could blame it on something that made him a weirdo and caused him hella trouble wherever he went but was nothing compared to what the truth would bring. It was just to throw them all off guard. And it worked. But he didn't actually like the music.

So a lot of his records are basically unplayed. Or at least they were until last night. Because even looking at the vinyl I couldn't get Jason off my mind more than a millisecond at a time and I ended up putting headphones on and playing record after record pretending I was a DJ too until I finally fell asleep with the turntable spinning and the phones still hugging my useless ears.

Now I'm waiting on Ula. The last time I saw her was when she came by last week for a few hours and was she stoked to find out Finn and Critter were in Rip Van Winkle mode and that I was making sure they ate something whenever they woke up. Though she wrinkled her nose when she inspected the stash of sugared cereals and Mother's cookies and Snackin' Cakes and Pop-Tarts and Eggos and Häagen-Dazs and chocolate milk that the something always comes from.

Her advice was cut back on the sweet stuff and go with

mass quantities of rice and beans. Because she sees a lot of malnutrition in her job which is with a group called Doctors Without Frontiers except the words are in French. They specialize in helping out refugees and other poor people in places no other doctors and nurses will go like Afghanistan and Iraq and some of those African countries where everyone's dying of AIDS and Ebola. And she's big on rice and beans as a strength-and-stamina builder. But rice and beans won't do the Wonder Bread thing unless they're actually ingested and I know how Finn and Critter would respond if I flowed them rice and beans instead of Cap'n Crunch or Fruit Loops or Sugar Frosted Flakes when they wake up grouchy as grizzlies after a long winter's nap. They'd kick my ass to Christmas mass and feed the rice and beans to the Disposall.

I guess the grrl can't help it. When she shows up she's got a coffee-can-size container of protein powder concealed in a Virgin Megastore bag and after making sure that Finn and Critter are asleep she spikes glass after glass of chocolate milk with increasing amounts and enlists me in a taste test to determine when the difference is noticeable. Actually it's noticeable right off if you're familiar with the texture of chocolate milk out of the carton but in the world according to Ula that's only because my taste buds are overdeveloped to compensate for lacking another sense and she pretty much decides on her own that I should start dumping a third of a cup of protein powder in every twelve-ounce glass of chocolate milk. Yeah right. But I promise I'll start flowing them as much as I can and that puts a smile on her lips.

And am I glad because she hasn't had much to smile about lately. Her sister's condition isn't improving anymore and though the doctors say it's stable Ula thinks it's getting worse. Plus now her sister is talking about dying for the first time. In fact she asked Ula to find some books for her today about the right-to-die movement and Ula invites me along so the errand won't be so reaper grim.

Walking toward the subway station on Market Street Ula's all stoked about how sunny it is and how I must be glad I'm not in school when it hits her for the first time that maybe I'm not just out of school for the summer. So she asks about it and I tell her I pretty much quit going when my mom died and were the teachers glad to get me out of their hair because I'd do things like bring up Madonna when they were patiently explaining the ways of the world as in you can't succeed in life with just one name.

Which makes her laugh but then she gets serious telling me about alternative-type schools the rest of the way to the station and while we're underground waiting for a train. She knows a lot about them because her parents sent her and her sister to what they call a Summerhill school in England because it was the only kind of education that lived up to their ideals which were pretty much anarchist/communist I guess because the kids at the school had a lot of say in running the show. Even in choosing the teachers and deciding what to do every day.

Thinking of the schools in Monterey I can hardly believe it but after we board the train I'm all *I guess it could work with really smart kids from good families* and is Ula on me for that all *Shock! Horror!* and fingerspelling *elitist* as in *You're an!* when I don't understand the sign.

I'm all *Realist is more like it.*

—You're thinking the way They want you to think.

And I know right off *They* is capitalized and who *They* are.

As in the bloody-handed brainwash boyz like Bush. So I'm all *Hand me the white flag* and *You're right.*

She laughs and shakes her head.

—No. I'm left. Far left.

Which doesn't keep us from leaving the subway on the right side platform of the Montgomery Street Station even though we've got a choice. Riding up the escalator to street level I realize I'm in the midst of all those high-rises near the foot of Market Street for the first time ever. The same buildings that reminded me of rockets shooting into the sky when I saw them from the park on the hill with Jonnyboy and Roarke. But up close they don't seem like rockets at all. They're not the least bit thrilling. They just look boring.

The bookstore fronts on the sidewalk right next to us at the top of the escalator. It's a big open multilevel place with armies of suit-and-tie customers called Stacey's. I follow Ula up the stairs but stop on the mezzanine to check out magazines for a while then wander over to the seafaring section to look at the books on pirates which usually have kewl illustrations and lots of kweer overtones when you start reading the fine print. Then I check out a guide to Portugal to learn a little more about my roots because basically all I know about the Portuguese or at least the Portuguese who fish is they like to drink and they like to fight and they just say no to going halfway with either one.

When I track down Ula she's in the environmental section holding the books her sister wanted and reading another one titled *Green Rage.* Her face lights up when she sees me and she thumbs through the book to a photo section and shows me a picture of the dewd we saw speaking at the redwood-trees rally. He's standing in front of a bulldozer with one hand holding a bullhorn and the other handcuffed to a big chain that's padlocked around the steel arm holding the blade of the bull-dozer. Behind him two cops are hunched together trying to cut the chain with a giant pair of bolt cutters. And there's something about the expression on his face. I'll never forget it. He's got this Mona Lisa smile and this calmness in his eyes. Like a saint I guess. Or an angel. It makes me think of Jonnyboy and his rule about ignoring heroes. Which he broke himself with Roarke. And it's a good thing too even though it turned out the way it did. Because if any rule's made to be broken it's that one.

You can't ignore all heroes. Or else you'll be head down kicking dirt from cradle to grave.

You just have to watch out for the wrong ones.

Back out on the sidewalk Ula points to one of the relic antique streetcars coming up Market in our direction and we decide to shine the subway going back and cross the street to catch it. The stop is directly in front of the entrance to this kewl-looking oldschool brown-and-cream-colored stone and brick high-rise called the Hobart Building. It's maybe twenty stories max and dwarfed by the massive blue-gray steel-and-glass curtain of one of the tallest buildings in the city directly behind it. Looking up you can see a couple of different terrace levels with green plantings and wide carved parapets where the building narrows in two big steps near the top. But what catches my eye and holds it is down at street level in the lobby.

Inside in big raised letters attached to what looks like marble on a curving wall opposite the double-wide glass doors where a security guard stands with his back to the street are the names of the five companies that must be the bigtime tenants. They mostly seem to be law firms or accountants or whatever with lots of last names strung together but one stands out because it's short and also because it's familiar.

TEJON HOLDINGS, INC.

I don't remember where from though and I guess my memory is semiphotographic because when I can't place something written down I start piecing together a picture of where I saw it. Like whether it was on the right or left side of the page in a book or magazine. What color the paper was if it was a flyer. What the type looked like. If there were illustrations or photos. And usually I figure it out if my mind works on it awhile.

But this is different.

What comes back to me isn't 2-D as in paper but 3-D as in the log truck going into the General Douglas MacArthur Tunnel when we first got into San Francisco. And I'm dead sure *Tejon Holdings* wasn't written on the truck or anyplace else. The only words in sight were the sign with name of the tunnel and *Team Pain* tattooed on Jonnyboy's arm. Then I get this feeling when I remember how big the logs were.

The feeling when they moved the air.

Redwood logs.

And suddenly the paper's in front of me inside my brain. The flyer from the rally in United Nations Plaza. With the quote from Reagan at the top.

You've seen one redwood you've seen them all.

The Headwaters Forest.

And the company that's set to chop it down.

The flyer that's in my left front cargo pocket right now folded in quarters. I unbutton the pocket and pull the flyer out unfolding it to the side with the nuke-bomber guy's biography. I turn it over.

Check.

Tejon Holdings, Inc.

Mate.

I look back up and see a face.

My face.

Reflected.

Her face.

Singing.

I hear a voice that sounds the way I feel.

It's me if you want but it's not what I want

I want to burn up the place

Set it on fire.

Ula's hand shakes my shoulder. I turn around and the streetcar's pulling away.

—Did you see a ghost?

I sign that I just remembered some song lyrics. Then Critter's pager goes off and I do a double take to make sure I'm not imagining the magic numbers 5221972 as in *Heeere's Jonny*.

I'm not. And Ula thinks it calls for a celebration as in a fast taxi home. So when we get to the Greenery I show Ula the codes for playing and replaying voice mail and feed the fish while she copies Jonnyboy's message down. It's a long one and I end up doing the dishes too before she's finished.

OK boy I'm a hell bound fucking asshole for doing what I did, saying nothing and just taking off. It wasn't that I didn't think of you, or I forgot I said I'd look out for you. I didn't forget, I remember every day. And it's no alibi, I stand accused and I'm guilty, but I wouldn't have if I didn't know you'd be ok awhile with those boyz because I know they really like you and wouldn't put you on the street even if your feet smelled bad and you farted in your sleep. And I knew you had some money, too. I knew you'd be ok, because you're smart and don't let shit get you down. I'm the opposite and Roarke fucked with my head so bad I couldn't see straight, I didn't know what was happening, I was in a daze, I wanted to end it all. I had to figure things out, on my own, and with Roarke, too, we had this communication meltdown, I can't believe he sang "If only Jonny would have opened up his heart," I still can't believe it. But he took me back to

L.A., I'm here now, and I've been hanging with my boyz in Venice. And the funny thing is, Roarke's going back up north to live for awhile, and I'm coming with him, and I mean pretty soon. We're cruising up in this old car he's giving me, from the sixties, it's full surf wheels, guess I'll have to get my license back, hee hee. Don't worry though, I won't be living with him or anything. It'll just be you and me and what we decide to do. Maybe go someplace totally different like Seattle if you want, wear flannel, anything, I'm burned out on L.A., it's an evil place. Hawaii would be cool with a k if we could get the cash to go there, I could see my mom again, you'd be halfway to your south sea island dreamland, how does that sound? Not at all, right? Fuck, I miss your quiet smartassness. I'm sorry I didn't call till now, I've been crashing different places, pretty cracked on. I've been skating some, kinda like old times with Red Dog and Mad Dog, and we heard about this pool, over by the Fruit Bowl we used to rage when we were your age, and we skated it but it wasn't like before, seems once you ride a perfect pool you ride something worse and it doesn't seem that fun anymore, now does it?

So anyways, I'm coming back soon, don't want to say a day because I don't know yet, just take care of yourself, ok? And oh yeah, I heard this record the other day by those dykes we saw in the park, and it's totally killer, they shred the shit outa Chaotic Stature anyday. It makes me want to have a band again and write songs, be creative. Plus it's kind of embarrassing, there's no good kweerboy punk bands. All the kickass kweer punk music's being made by girls. Fuck, if I was in Pansy Division or Xtra Fancy I wouldn't show my face on a stage knowing there's bands like the one we saw. Course I suck too so I shouldn't dis. HELL YEAH I SHOULD. THEY'RE THE WORST AND THAT XTRA FANCY SINGER IS A ROLLINS WANNABE FROM HELL. Maybe I'll start a band that does all songs about Roarke. Yeah, right. Anyways, so when I heard that record, I was actually sketching real hard, and I go "Who is this?" and get handed

the record, and remember you showed me the lyric sheet? So I recognized the words but sketched on the fact I actually saw them, at
first I mean, before I remembered, and just connected them with you.
So I go, "Oh yeah, I heard of them. I heard they kicked ass." And my
friend's all "Who told you?" And I said, "This deaf kid I know." He
didn't believe me. That fits though cause you're unbelievable. And I
love you Radboy, so don't give up on me. Stay where you are and I'll
be there with bells of St. Marys on before you know it. I promise.

And it's not like I had any doubt really but the last two
words make all the difference. Because talk about *This is religion*. I mean a promise to Jonnyboy is like the Ten Commandments to the Pope. It means more than anything. He
hardly ever makes a promise and he always keeps it when he
does. Like that first time he left Monterey after we made
friends he promised one he'd come back and two he'd stay in
touch. And I thought Sure he will I'm just this kid who maybe
plays pinball ok and sk8s a little better than ok and he's this
wild man with a million friends and a kewl reputation to people
who don't even know him in places like Iowa and I don't blame
him for it there's just no way I can matter in his life any
more than shark chum matter to those old great whites in
Monterey Bay.

And I admit it was I bummed because nothing was the
same right after Jonnyboy left and I wasn't the same and just
going back to reading books again and sk8boarding by myself
didn't make it all better.

It only made it worse.

Then I got that first care package full of punk stuff and it
was Christmas Thanksgiving Easter the Glorious Fourth and
Hellen Killer's birthday all rolled into one and it was only the
beginning. The hits kept on coming after that including this
giant Day-Glo movie poster for *Sid & Nancy* until the walls of

my room were covered solid. And when Jonnyboy kept promise number one with no advance notice just showed up and walked right in he looked around and stood there with his mouth wide open then he almost cried I swear.

I'm so wrapped up in reading Jonnyboy's message over and over I forget about Ula and jump sky-high when she touches my shoulder. Then I'm all fall-down-on-my-knees apologizing but she cuts me off all *Don't worry get happy* and is she happy for me I can tell. She has to bail for hospital visiting hours but promises to come by Sunday and that word promises reminds her.

—One third of a cup. Trust me. They'll never notice.

Cut to Critter three hours later standing in the kitchen in his underwear and checking out the date on the chocolate milk carton after downing a glass spiked with just one spoonful. Though he doesn't complain or anything. Just walks back toward the bedroom eating Häagen-Dazs from the carton with a spoon. When I look in ten minutes later he's asleep on the bed with one hand still holding the carton but the ice cream gone.

I'm asleep myself almost before I know it. I decide to read for a while and kick back on the sofa with this book Ula bought for me today after I signed that the *Green Rage* dewd was my kind of hero. It's called *Desert Solitaire* and there's a picture on the cover of those weird bloodred rock formations you see on Utah license plates. I open it hoping there's more pictures inside but I don't get any farther than the first three pages because there at the end of the introduction chapter are words that really rock my world and I mean twice around the clock.

You're holding a tombstone in your hands. A bloody rock. Don't drop it on your foot—throw it at something big and glassy. What do you have to lose?

Definitely not my place in the book because it's still in my hand when I wake up in the morning and the words *big and glassy* are still on my mind when I'm giving myself the twice over in the bathroom mirror after attending to the usual wake-up call of nature and I mean the one you can stay in bed to answer. Though what they remind me of right now standing here naked looking at myself is Jonnyboy thinking he was the first guy in history to splatter-paint his own reflection and how he got the idea from some punk rock singer saying in an interview that she jerked off to her own picture. Which is hilarious but also kind of heartbreaking to me.

I don't know why.

I guess because I miss him.

It gets me thinking of the ways we're different and I kind of space out looking at myself but almost seeing Jonnyboy for I don't know how long until I connect back with real time realizing one of the biggest differences between the two of us is right in front of me. Because Jonnyboy would have checked out the medicine cabinet behind the mirror the first time he came in here to take a leak. Just to acquaint himself with the house pharmaceuticals. But I've been here ages now and I still haven't.

I bet it would have taken his breath away too since I'm no druggie but it sucks out most of mine when I pull open the mirror to see what's inside. No Band-Aids or mouthwash or Q-Tips or even childproof Tylenol just row upon row stack upon stack of brown prescription bottles and not the little quarter-size diameter ones either. They're all industrial-strength jumbos and every one has Finn's name on the label.

Finnegan Francis Tierney.

FFT.

Find Fellow Toughs.

Ketoconazole.

It's amazing how they make up words like this for medicine names.

Didanosine.

They're totally unreadable. Totally meaningless. Like a monkey's at the keyboard getting his revenge for drug testing on his buddies.

Fling Foreign Terms.

Mycobutin.

I've never seen these drugs before anywherez and Jonnyboy taught me all the ones that shred and get you high.

Feed Frenzied Tweekers.

Zidovudine.

Fools Fear Trouble.

Fluconazole.

Fight For Tomorrow.

Crixivan.

I can't read anymore and I can't explain why I just want to knock them all off the shelves into the sink onto the floor down the toilet.

He doesn't look sick. Not at all. Though I guess he's had to stay in the hospital twice.

What good is all this fucking medicine anywayz.

Good for doctors hospitals drugstores insurance companies there you have it big and glassy. Good for big and glassy. No good for Finn. I'm seeing red and my hand is shaking.

Will I actually slam the bottles into smithereens.

Is it worth it.

Do I really know anything about this.

Will it make me sick today.

I know in my feelings. Not the details maybe. Though I read a lot about the AIDS racket in a punk zine called *Awaken Humankind!* But go pick on Stephen Jerkoff Hawking if you need a genius to tell you there's money in AIDS like there's money in bombs and there's power in making different people suffer like there's innocent blood on every page of every history book. And maybe it's thinking Mr. Genius Mathematician then blood then book that gets me distracted working out my own equation which equals bloody rock.

As in throw it.

As in at something.

As in big and glassy.

Whatever and whyever my hand isn't shaking anymore and I'm just seeing black-and-white *Finnegan Francis Tierney* one last time before I push the mirror back and look myself in the eyes and do I smile.

I can't help it.

I'm reading my mind one word at a time.

Fireworks.

For.

Tejon.

SIX

So I don't waste time I borrow Finn's white Fred Perry polo shirt to look employably preppy and ride my sk8board downtown to the corner of Market and Montgomery. I push open one of the Hobart Building's heavy glass doors wondering if it's bulletproof and walk right into an elevator that opens immediately for me signs and portents like I blinked an invisible electric eye.

The entrance to Tejon Holdings is directly opposite the fifteenth-floor elevator doors and you can see into the outer office as soon as you step out because the walls are all glass from waist-high up. It's the kind of glass with wire embedded in it so you need cutters to get through even if you break it. Half a dozen thirty- to fortysomething women sit at terminals inside and everyone looks very calm. Of course it's only the receptionist and secretary types with desks and cubicles out in the open like that but overall it doesn't seem like a place where voices get raised even behind closed doors.

Plus everything is color-coordinated as in fruits and flowers with the fruits ripe peaches and apricots and the flowers roses as in yellow of Texas. Which means marmalade skies on the walls and ceiling and flower power everywhere there's fabric whether it's the carpet or cubicle dividers or the sofa in the reception area. Not to mention the outfits of the receptionist and all her coworkers down to their panties probably.

I walk though the open double doors holding my sk8board deck out so all the punk rock stickers don't show and when the receptionist peers up at me through lenses thick as bottle glass in oval tortoiseshell frames I do my best to look young and innocent. Which amounts to playing along with the retard expectation once she figures out why I'm waving my fingers around instead of talking. I do waiter check please and she passes me a notepad but forgets a pen or pencil and I'm afraid the grin I flash is both noninnocent and nonretarded because I'm thinking *Too bad Jonnyboy's not here to whip the little No. 2 out of his ear and give her stories for the grandkids* and the result is she thinks I'm laughing at her and gets so flustered that when she pulls open the sliding plastic tray under the countertop it comes out all the way and morphs the neatly compartmentalized contents into chaos on the carpet.

And am I courteous and helpful as in around the counter in a flash and down on my hands and knees next to her when I notice the key ring mixed in with the pushpins and Post-it notes and plastic Day-Glo paper clips. But the keys are in the middle of the mess directly in her line of sight so there's no way to nab them unnoticed which is a close encounter of the torturous kind because I can read the *Do Not Duplicate*s on two of them and two more are miniature clamgun-style alarm keys. Still I just kind of freeze there tempted anywayz wishing and hoping the phone will ring or the boss will buzz until I notice two miniature manila envelopes right next to my shoe with something bulky inside. One is laying front side down overlapping the other and obscuring part of a label written in the kind of perfect handwriting they put on posters over the chalkboard in elementary school but I can read the words *Spare* and the letter *K* and I don't need a help file to figure out the rest.

I lean forward to scoop up some paper clips so my arm blocks her view and lift my foot up and plant it back down sideways over both envelopes. The next trick is to palm one of them then move so she'll pick up the other one herself. Because there's no point getting greedy. It's why Tommy's chilling in Chino for sticking up two AM-PM's on his twenty-first birthday and pulling off number one so easy he figured number two was licking icing off the candles.

Plus two sets of keys missing would probably lead to locks being changed while one set MAYBE missing depending on whether she remembered two sets plus the loose keys or two sets including the loose keys would likely get the benefit of the doubt since she'd just look bad and possibly for no reason if she said anything about it. And in an office like this where everything looks so good the last thing anybody wants is to look the opposite.

I get one envelope in my hand and step away from the other in a move slick as seagrass then help pick up the rest of the stuff one-handed and slip the envelope down inside my shoe when I retie it before I stand back up once we're finished. She's all *Thanks* then bites her lip looking rattled when she remembers how all this started and hands me a company-issue pencil when I step back around the counter and it's back to business as usual.

I smile slightly slackjaw retard style and point to myself all *It's my fault* then write down what I planned out earlier.

I'm deaf and my dad killed my mom and good people are taking care of me but I need to make extra money to buy a palmtop computer so I can communicate better with hearing people who don't know sign and buy other things too and I'm too young to get a regular job so I was wondering if you need somebody to empty the wastebaskets every couple of days any time day or night I'll do it really cheap and I'm reliable give me a chance.

Sk8ing down here I argued back and forth with myself about whether to put in the part about my dad since the mass of people stay out of trouble with the law and don't want any contact even secondhand with people who don't and especially when the trouble's murder. Even some of my so-called friends in deaf classes in Monterey started shining me on after they found out what happened but I'm not even touched by it. I mean they weren't really my friends anywayz in the world according to Jonnyboy and he said it I believe it that settles it.

Her face definitely goes Hallmark after she reads my note. And am I glad to see it under the circumstances because as much as I hate it sympathy can be pretty high octane stuff when you're a differently-abled orphan with gory details straight from tabloid TV and I just figure *Hey take advantage boy*.

But when her forehead wrinkles up and her index finger starts tapping on her chin while she looks at the notepad instead of back at me I realize she probably has to answer autopilot *No* on company-policy grounds and so much for sympathy for the rebel. Still she hesitates so long I hang on to hope and try to make what Jonnyboy calls the puppydog look in my eyes without going overboard into sit and beg mode because the only thing I know about psychology is that the best way to get what you want is to pretend you don't care if you get it or not. There's a drive in most everyone that makes them want to be liked by indifferent people while the flipside is the power drive that dominates hard when someone's fully craving and you just think *Fuckit I'm above this Nowhere Man* and that's where I'm staying and the way to guarantee it is *Just say No.*

Finally she chills the finger tapping and holds it up in the air *Wait one minute* style instead and takes a couple of steps back. But I guess the puppy magic works a little after all because she pauses after looking me in the eyes again and writes me a note before disappearing into the cubicle maze behind her.

We have a service that cleans this floor of the building on Tues. and Fri. eves and takes care of everything. And we don't need extra help because so much is on computers these days that we don't ~~gener~~make the kind of paper mess we used to! But let me ask my supervisor if she has any ideas.

Alice

And outside I'm all Groovy eager white boy smile *You can count on me* while inside I'm busting up naming her *As in Blunderland.*

Because first the keys.

Now the nights to cross off the calendar.

I mean what's next an engraved invitation?

Like the one I'm already composing in my mind for Finn and Critter and Ula and Jonnyboy once he's back.

The pleasure of your company is requested in destroying theirs.

Which has me patting myself on the back for a pretty good

joke but only for a seventh of a second because suddenly there's thrills running up and down my spine and finally it hits me as in *this ain't no* and you pay your money and you take your choice.

Party.

Disco.

Fooling around.

Whatever it ain't I know what it is.

Your boy Radboy living large.

As.

Life.

During.

Wartime.

Rat tat tat.

Hee hee hee.

Alice is gone about five minutes which gives me time to notice all sorts of things and I don't just mean the Garfield paperweight on her desk and the note from *Eileen* reading *Let's take our lunches up to the Promenade on the roof again, ok?* because even without a phone booth I've done the Clark Kent thing and now I'm your own Private Radboy reporting for duty SIR! So I'm checking off items like no visible security cameras and blinds that must be drawn over the glass entrance walls at night and the kind of acoustical grid ceiling panels you can push right up to find catwalks usually for working on the light fixtures and a/c and utilities. Plus most importantly there's no keypad for a password alarm system right inside the door and there's no place to conceal one either.

If I was Tommy I'd just high-five myself as in *Home free*. But though blood may be thicker than water brains are thicker than blood and by that standard we're not even distant cousins. I might as well have been adopted. And my gray matter's reminding me that this is a big office with at least one more entrance in case of fires earthquakes Rodney King rebellion whatever and it's totally possible that the first person in the morning and the last person out at night use that entrance and let their fingers do the talking there.

Or make that possible sure but hold the totally since there's at least one clamgun key digging into the side of my foot right now and I mean hard. And clamguns are more for the old-school predigital alarms that went off when a door was opened either by key or by force without the key first turning the cylinder that breaks the circuit flowing juice to the alarm. And in a building like this with nothing of value in the office to steal besides computers which are hella easier to nab on ground level in bad neighborhoods they probably don't feel like springing for a modern world system that will just cost bucks and go off false a lot from human error.

So it's a good bet passwords aren't included with the price of admission but not a sure one since I guess there might be valuable trade secrets here or something and they want full protection. How there could be anything fresh in chopping down redwood trees is beyond me though and I'm almost willing to go with my gut feeling.

I'd just like to see that other entrance. Which thinking of gut feelings was right by the employee bathrooms in the offices of both the Monterey County District Attorney and the Central California Health and Social Services.

Ms. Blunderland comes back with a Post-it in her hand and my first thought is she's gonna hand me the phone number for the teen jobline then realize what she's doing and this time she'll knock over the vase with the peach-colored rose next to her computer and get water in the keyboard and black out the entire Hobart Building and I can roam the halls at will looking for hinks in armor and Achilles' heels. But when she sticks it on the notepad and starts writing I relax my mind because I can read upside down the letters TTYD as in Teletypewriter for the Deaf.

We can't think of anything, I'm so sorry. Everything has to go through HR (Human Resources) in the L.A. (Los Angeles) HQ (Headquarters). It's a pain! But Stella (my supervisor) found these contacts for the Deaf Club here in The City. It's ~~orient~~ centered on young people, and they have job ~~referr~~ lists. So keep trying! You're doing the right thing! So many kids these days just hang out on the street and turn to drugs. ☹ Good luck! ☺

I pause after reading the note without looking back up to perfect my disappointed down-but-not-out look then flash her the puppydog eyes but only for a second because scamming is like sk8boarding as in timing is all. Then I write:

It's ok. I understand. Thanx. Excuse me though is there a bathroom here?

And psychology isn't exactly rocket science is it because I'm giving her a chance to say a little *Yes* after saying a big *No* to a harmless kid who's eager to please and even feel a little wikked about it if there's a customers-only rule or something. So once again it's Johnny Rotten *Follow Me!* and I mean into the belly of the beast this time because the men's room is back where the offices aren't cubicles but wood-paneled suites with polished nameplates on the doors. Some of which are open so I get to see huge leather chairs I can smell this far away behind massive carved desks and in one office there's even a fireplace where I bet they stoke the flames with redwood logs while they plan out the traditional whale-meat barbecue at the company picnic on the Glorious Fourth.

There's no sign of any people though until half a dozen

suits file out of what must be a conference room on the corner of the building just as Alice is pointing to a door up ahead with sure enough another hallway turning off to the right and a green *Exit* sign suspended from the ceiling. And talk about body language Alice is suddenly one big run-on sentence. Neck muscles tensing posture straightening butt in chest out fingers on one hand tapping her hip while the other smoothes her skirt adjusts her necklace pats her hair.

Which looks wind-tunnel safe from Aqua Net anywayz.

And I almost feel sorry for her because would it suck to get that uptight around people you have to work with every day. I mean I'd rather get dirty and greasy in some beat garage in Seaside where at least you can pop a cool one with the boss sometimes and even tell him to fuck off as long as you say it with a smile. Then I feel the slightest bit guilty because no doubt about it this bathroom must be RESTRICTED ACCESS in red letter capitals in some policy manual somewherez and Alice is shaking in her color-coordinated sensible shoes because is she busted. She can't exactly pass me off as some visiting exec from HR at HQ in L.A. now can she.

But I can't see her getting fired for it considering the circumstances unless this place is even worse than I thought in which case she's better off outta here anywayz. And sure enough the suits are all smiles when we cross their path and don't even look that curious about me except for one who's younger than the others and better looking and tanned. His clothes are direct express no connecting flights from the pages of magazines you smell before you see and that combined with him staring makes me wonder if he's kweer but I really don't get that vibe at all. Plus he's focused on my sk8board more than me.

Which I realize I'm carrying by the trucks bottom side out again the white boy way. So this guy's getting an eyeful of ANARCHY and DESTROY and KING MOB.

And across it all CHAOTIC STATURE in letters three inches high.

I'm all *Damn you* to myself but at least Alice's bad example keeps me from flipping the deck over and drawing even more attention by showing my true colors as in caught commie-red-handed. Still I'm rattled enough that I go into the bathroom without looking down the exit hall for the telltale magic keypad. Then when I open the door Fashion Boy is just turning away from Alice and though he looks at me he only glances this time and walks back into the conference room. Alice takes her cue from him ignoring me and following him with her eyes so I let my own wander exitward past drinking fountain bulletin board fire extinguisher to the bar release door labeled *In Case of Fire Use Stairs Not Elevators.*

And I'm thinking not to mention earthquake flood and drought but those aren't the only signs I don't see oh heavens to Betsy oh suburban lawns oh kitchens of distinction no sign of a keypad and I mean anywherez. Plus it's kewl with a k when Alice notices me looking that direction because she figures I'm wondering if it's a shortcut out and I guess I've been too hard on her. I mean she learns fast. She does waiter check please herself and with a flourish yet.

So I hand her my notepad and while she's writing I can tell she's all better now. No more girl with perpetual nervousness. Her cheeks are actually kind of rosy. She almost looks pretty.

Turn right for the elevators, left for the stairs. I'm glad we took the walk down here! I got to talk with the future head of our company! (The handsome one!) He's a race car driver & very nice.

And does that throw me. I mean what could days of thunder possibly have to do with trees of wonder. So I start harshing on myself for thinking *You May Already Be a Winner* in the IQ sweepstakes over Tommy when it didn't even occur to me that there might be more than one Tejon Holdings in the wonderful modern world. But Alice reads the confusion on my face and takes back the pad.

It's his hobby. (An expen$ive one!) He's the owners' son. We're not a racing company—too bad! Good luck!

The flesh-and-blood happy face I flash her back isn't Oscar material it's real as steel wheels and the green light in the exit sign takes me back to David Avenue with Jonnyboy onboard and the traffic on Lighthouse getting closer by the nanosecond and I feel like dropping my sk8 and bailing in a blaze of wheeled glory. But I don't cut loose yet just walk past the employee bulletin board and through the solid thick door that's totally anonymous on the outside. No name. No number. Just the telltale switch plate on the wall beside it with the raised round slot for a clamgun key.

There's nobody in sight and I touch it like a blind boy reading braille and even close my eyes thinking Jonnyboy wouldn't say blind boy he'd say Hellen Killer. When I open them I look down the long dim empty corridor and I don't even need to think about what Jonnyboy would do now. I just jump on my sk8board and feel like a senator because do I have the floor. And the floor's so smooth the friction's fiction. The floor's so polished it's like a mirror. And in the mirror is a boy with no fear.

Especially not after I check out the contents of the key envelope at the trolley stop on Market Street and find not one but two neatly labeled clamgun keys as well as three regular Masterguard *Do Not Duplicate* sawtooths. Because one of the

clamgun labels reads *Offc.* and the other reads *Mtgmry entr*
and when I skate around the corner of the Hobart Building
onto Montgomery Street I don't need X-ray spex to find the
unmarked doorway in an alcove with shiny silver clamgun slot
number 2 on a steel plate bolted to the bricks. I mean talk
about it's easy it's easy it's easy.

To celebrate I stay downtown and session for a while in
this plaza at the foot of Market Street with some local
sk8erboyz I meet who aren't all that friendly once they find out
first I'm deaf and second I'm a better sk8er. But nobody gives
me shit or anything the way they would down south at least in
the world of Lost Angels according to Jonnyboy. In fact I'm
the big bad aggro dude and snake a few runs on new arrivals.
Not really trying to start anything so much as just seeing how
they react. Which is hardly at all. They're all mellow boyz up
here I guess. And even if they're too young and amped to be
mellow they wannabe mellow and the way I see it wanting to
be mellow is like wanting to be dead.

So I'm not even touched when they shrug their shoulders
and shine me on. I just don't care. Not even when I eat heavy
lunch trying a flashy stale-to-fish off the side of an advertising
kiosk with a giant poster of the latest calvinboy's face and arm-
pit. I'm getting ready to pivot when Critter's pager starts vibrating below my belly button and tickles just enough that I
take reflex evasive action and end up obeying the law of gravity
with nothing between me and a faceplant but my skinny bare
forearm.

Which gets burgered as in ground beef bigtime and when
I stand back up the blood drips down to the pavement in fat
splatters with corrugated edges that remind me of drops of
summer squall rain pattering onto the grime of the wheel housing on my dad's fishing boat. But I'm spared any road rash

above the neck except a scrape underneath my chin so I feel like luck's still with me today and I just walk over to the free-form fountain in the center of the plaza and submerge my arm until the cold water shuts down the broken blood vessels and the numbness cuts the sting. When I finally look down at the pager display it turns out Ula's responsible for my fall from grace and am I surprised because I wasn't expecting to see her sister's number for a couple more days. And partly because she is responsible and partly because she's a nurse I decide to just head up to her sister's instead of back to the Greenery where I'd have to wait for Finn or Critter to wake up to return the call anywayz and where there definitely aren't any first-aid supplies in the medicine cabinet.

When my arm starts bleeding again after I pull it out of the water I'm all *Damn! Fuck!* because the way people are about blood these dayz I'll never get allowed on a bus. So I decide to sacrifice part of my flannel for a bandage and after I start the rips with my teeth I first dismember one sleeve then tear it long ways forming a rectangle. I wind it around my lower arm mummy style and there's no problem keeping it in place with the blood soaking through the first layers and sticking to what's left of my skin. Plus fortunately the flannel's a dark maroon-and-purple plaid so it camos the blood when it does start to show through and by then I've already got a window seat on a number-five Fulton bus anywayz.

The bus heads toward the same long hill behind City Hall that we cruised in Roarke's limo but on a street a few blocks to the north through what seems like a mile of housing projects that remind me of the CYA dorms when I visited Tommy before he went to Chino. Kind of fake cheery clean and bright on the surface but no hiding the heavy hand of the question authorities underneath. Finally near the top of the hill we get into the old tall gingerbread-style houses again and when I see the big green square of the park where I first hooked up with Ula I pull the cord for the next stop even though the directions she wrote out for me that first night after the concert say to ride the number-five a couple more blocks to Broderick Street. I just figure I'll check out the view again and maybe rebandage my arm with the other sleeve so she doesn't think I've lost too much blood and rush me to the hospital for a transfusion or something. Because the bandage I made is pretty much sopping now and though I could just wring it out I'd get blood all over my hands and there's no fountain or even bathrooms here to wash it off.

I climb a steep paved path up a grassy slope and suddenly I'm all by my lonesome at the benches where Ula and I sat watching Roarke and Jonnyboy on the swings. I sit down and try to pick out where the Hobart Building fits into the downtown skyline and I think I see a piece of it but with so many buildings jumbled together and overlapping one another I can't be sure. I mean talk about big and glassy. And I guess I should hate it all and wanna destroy but instead it seems beautiful to me and mysterious almost like an alien city or something.

I'm glad the trash can's right next to the bench and after I make a new bandage with the other sleeve I'm glad Ula's sister lives as close as she does because do I feel tired now and even a little dizzy. Too dizzy to take a chance on sk8ing there and falling again so I do it just the way any white boy would one foot in front of the other repeat rewind forever it seems until I'm standing at the metal gate in front of four doors on the porch of a pretty run-down example of oldschool San Francisco architecture. Then one moment I'm watching my finger move slo-mo toward the button labeled 4 and the next moment I'm feeling my whole body moving with it and the next moment after that it's dark outside but I'm inside and Ula's got me sipping this hot drink called Bovril with mass pillows behind me at the end of a sofa.

Which are hella softer on the sensitive parts of your boy Radboy than the cement steps where I was slumped when Ula came down to open the gate. And did her *Shock!* morph into *Horror!* when she raised my arms up to lift me and one of her hands went red and wet and I mean instantly. But she got me upstairs without calling 911 and involving the question authorities and I came to all cleaned and bandaged and even stitched a total of eleven big ones because a gouge from the raised edge of a paving stone I guess was hidden in the hamburger.

After getting the Bovril down I don't feel groggy anymore so much as weak. Which is exactly what I sign to Ula when she asks and she signs right back that what I need now is food and lots of it. And I guess my face keeps no secrets after her diagnosis because she's quick to add she doesn't mean rice and beans either. She's thinking more along the lines of steak and potatoes followed by ice cream for dessert and I'm all *Bring it on Mrs. Olsen* with my fists clenched around imaginary utensils and pounding an air table. But first she has to go to the market. Which means leaving a phone message in case Finn or Critter call back while she's out.

When I read Finn on her lips this little pang of guilt shoots through me and at first I tell myself it's because I was all *I gotta take care of you boyz* the last time I saw him and here I am far from the home front missing in action and wounded besides. But talk about storytellers lie. Because the real reason I feel guilty is I've hardly thought of Finn at all since the last time I saw him.

Though I've thought of Jason plenty.

And I feel even guiltier when I find out Ula phoned the Greenery after she finished with my arm and Finn was awake and answered. When she told him what happened he was practically out the door before she finished the sentence and she had to beg him to hold off jetting up here until I got a few hours' sleep.

It almost makes me cry I swear. But not as in *He likes me he really likes me.* More as in *It's just too much feel the weight crushing down on my face.*

Knowing someone wants you.

Wanting someone else more.

But talk about crying. There's no almost for Ula. She's been crying. I can see it in her red-rimmed eyes. And in the wastebasket half-filled with crumpled tissues next to the armchair across from me. It must be over her sister. I know it's not over me. She could fix what's wrong with me. But she can't fix what's wrong with her sister. She can't do anything.

She can't even pray because she doesn't believe in God.

I motion her over after she puts on her coat and ask about her sister. Then I take one of her hands and hold it between both of mine.

—There is good news and bad news. The good news is from the FBI. They have ended their prosecution. In the interest of justice as they say. This morning two agents returned a box of books they seized as evidence. It's right over there. You can see for yourself how ridiculous it is. The agents didn't even apologize. The bad news is from her physician. He says a week.

She doesn't start crying again. Maybe she's all cried out. Maybe she's starting to accept it.

No.

I remember how long it took to accept what happened to

my mom. And I don't mean when it happened and I don't mean at the funeral. I mean like weeks later when I'd be picking up newspapers off the furniture on autopilot because it was one of those things that drove her crazy. To have to move anything when she wanted to sit down after going out shopping or whatever. And I'd stop and tell myself *Whoa boy it don't matter anymore.* Or I'd be ditching deaf school sk8ing down Lighthouse Avenue toward E.L.A. and go out of my way to sk8 the alley on the block of the Halfway House Saloon because anytime after noon on the sidewalk I might run into her coming or going. Same deal. Screeching weasel wheels. Halt.

Big Mother isn't watching.

And times like that were when I'd cry. Not for my mom so much as for part of my life that would never be the same that really wasn't there anymore but seemed alive anywayz like the words to a song that just won't go away.

All I can think to answer back is *The doctor might be wrong.*

And she smiles and slowly frees her hand from mine and rubs it on my head.

I get up to use the bathroom after she's gone and looking around the apartment I don't think I've ever seen so many books in such a small space. The two narrow dark rooms downstairs are completely lined with overflowing bookshelves and the stairway to what must be a bedroom above is basically a library annex with stacked books marching up the steps on either side. At the bottom of the stairs is the box the FBI returned and it's full of subversive literature all right.

On Civil Disobedience by Henry David Thoreau.

A Sand County Almanac by Aldo Leopold.

The Selected Poetry of Robinson Jeffers.

The Collected Letters, Journalism, and Essays of George Orwell.

The Octopus by Frank Norris.

Wilderness and the American Mind by Roderick Nash.

The Revolution of Everyday Life by Raoul Vaneigem.

The Communist Manifesto by Karl Marx.

The last one's got *Hilke Magnusson POLSCI 204* written inside the cover and the margins are filled with asterisks and notes that are pretty obviously related to exam questions but no doubt the G-men were popping champagne corks all *We found the smoking gun all right* once this turned up. The only book in the box that doesn't look all serious and intellectual is a ratty paperback novel titled *The Monkey Wrench Gang* by Edward Abbey. His name is kind of familiar to me but I don't know why until I check out the list of his other books inside and discover he's the same dewd who wrote the bloody rock desert book. The cover looks like a movie poster for some stupid action comedy with a crazed-looking bearded guy in full camo at the wheel of a Jeep out in Marlboro Country somewherez and a slutty-looking big-tit blonde beside him and in the back this balding older geezer type next to this full-on cowboy holding on to all ten gallons and I mean hard. I guess it made the blacklist or maybe it's the redlist because the characters are chopping down billboards almost as soon as Chapter 1 gets under way. But you can tell from the way it's written that it's all in fun.

I take the book back to the sofa with me and doze off without reading a word. What wakes me is a smell that clenches my fists around the imaginary knife and fork again but this time they're replaced by the genuine articles in seven seconds flat followed by a wooden tray that Ula deposits on my lap containing a dinner plate completely covered by a T-bone steak smothered in grilled onions and a smaller plate devoted to a sizzling golden inch-thick cake made from shredded fried potatoes. And if this is what they mean by comfort food I finally understand the expression. By the time I'm wiping my lips with the napkin and Ula's busing the dishes back to the kitchen I can't think of too many things that could possibly make me feel any better.

And then I think of Jason. I don't know what it is about him that ties me in knots inside. With Finn there was that look he gave me on the bus and then my mind started working overtime connecting him with that skinhead in the picture on my bedroom door and the next thing you know I was practically molesting him while he was asleep.

I know what I want from Finn.

I don't know what I want from Jason.

How could I.

Unless.

Thinking of the pictures on my bedroom door connects with something.

Someone.

Her.

I reach into the cargo pocket of my camos for the lyric sheet wrapped around the Polaroid of me skating that Finn took at the overlook.

I wanna be your Joey Ramone

Pictures of me on your bedroom door.

Pictures of ME.

On YOUR bedroom door.

As in it's boring going after the dewd in the photo. That's what everybody does. What rules is BEING the dewd in the photo.

Though I am the dewd in the photo. This photo. But Finn didn't keep it. He gave it to me.

I know.

I'll give it to Jason.

This is all so complicated.

I wanna be his Joey Ramone. And I don't even know if he likes punk rock.

When I fold the lyrics around the Polaroid again I start to put them away in my right-side cargo pocket instead of the left and for a seventh of a second wonder WTF the bulky little package in there is and then realize it isn't only Finn I haven't been thinking about when I fish it out.

So I'm shaking my head back and forth thinking *Damn have I got it bad for this boy* and just staring at the envelope when Ula walks back in and naturally asks what it is.

At first she's got this almost dazed expression on her face when I explain what I did like she can't even believe it but it fades pretty fast when I sign that we should do something to fuck them over and get revenge for her sister. And she's nodding her head with her eyes getting brighter by the nanosecond when I sign that I mean something big enough to get on the news like torching the place so people realize it's not just Hollywood actors blocking traffic with banners on the Golden Gate Bridge. It's not just playacting violence. It's real violence to match their violence against nature.

It's war.

And I already declared it by stealing the keys to the place.

When I'm finished she just stares at me signing nothing back and I suddenly feel hot from head to foot and realize I must have it pretty bad for more than Jason when politics makes me blush as much as sex does. And do I wish I could talk because I know exactly what I'd say and I wish Jonnyboy was here because he'd understand it perfectly.

I mean it man!

As in *We mean it man!*

Which cards on the table four aces take all are the greatest words in all punk rock hands down your pants and squeeze it twice 'cause it's so nice no doubt about it. Because they say *No* and *Yes* at once and for all.

No not music.

No not fashion.

No not even wake-up call.

Just *Yes* in bold and capitals **CHARGE!**

I guess Ula's staring like this because she's looking at me and seeing somebody she never saw before and didn't know was there. And for seven seconds I wonder if she's just humoring the patient and figuring I hit my head a little harder than I let on but when I read the first word on her lips I know the conspiracy's on the tracks and it's too late to stop now.

—We need at least four people. What about Finn and Critter?

I nod my head and smile settling back against the pillows again and hold up my hands to start signing but instead they end up covering a yawn and I guess it's all the food hitting me combined with getting my blood pressure up over Tejon Holdings that sends me FedEx to dreamland for fourteen hours straight. And when I wake up at high noon according to the clock on one of the bookshelves my arm is sore and stiff but the dizzy brain-dead feeling's gone so I guess my blood count's back where it belongs. Which is exactly where I want to be too so I decide to write Ula a note and bail for the Greenery only to find one from her on the coffee table saying she left for the hospital at 9:00 A.M. and she'll stop by Finn and Critter's this afternoon to make sure I made it back in one piece since she's absolutely sure I can't stay off my sk8board more than twenty-four hours.

And do I get a grin out of that but not too big of one

because if she went to see her sister outside of regular visiting
hours the escalator can't be headed up which definitely puts
the reaper in the back of my mind sk8ing back to the Greenery
and the weather ain't exactly cheery either. The fog's in and I
get so cold just wearing a t-shirt and my flannel that's now a
vest I've got hot water running in the shower to warm me up
seven seconds and counting after I open the front door and
read the *Get well soon or we'll kiekss your ass* note from Finn
and Critter who are cracked back on and working at the Pit.

I'm naked with my clothes in a heap on the floor trying to
figure out how to keep the bandages dry when I realize Ula
might show up before Finn and Critter get home and I don't
want her chilling on the sidewalk and I mean literally as in
reliving her girlhood days in reindeer land. So I grab a towel
and go back outside to unbolt the lock. And on the return trip
I look up at the hazy pale disk in the sky behind the fog and
realize we're past the first day of summer already and is it
irritating because I always watch for the longest day in the year
and then miss it.

Not that I'd notice in here since there's so little natural
light anywayz. I mean forget the Greenery. It's more like the
Twilight Zone. And it's soaping up in the shower with my arm
wrapped in a plastic grocery bag from the kitchen and thinking
of those creepy reruns I guess that brings on showtime again
only not home movies this time but strictly Hollywood.

As in Hitchcock.

As in *Psycho*.

And forget seven seconds one-seventh of a second is all
recorded history under the circumstances.

Which include this neighborhhood being the kind of place
where the people two doors down called the cops when shots
were fired into their apartment and it's such a common com-

plaint around here they just wanted to take the report over the
phone until they got it through their Hormel heads that the
bullets didn't come through windows but through brick and
solid board walls and richocheted off the ceiling and went
through another inside wall to exit about two feet above the
pillows on the bed so it had to be an AK47 or something which
did warrant an officer on the scene but only during business
hours the following day.

So here I am leaving both the outside gate and the front
door unlocked just inviting any passing boombox homeboyz in
for both crack unlimited and an easy crack at a defenseless
white boy and while the lady at the Bates Motel at least had
the sound of running water to blame I've got no excuse not
even 17. I stand accused and I'm guilty.

Plus hella creeped even when the water stops and with it
the movie and I'm outta there standing dripping on my clothes.

Because there's something about the air. It's different.
Cooler. Like more fresh air came in like through the open door.
It isn't just me steaming from the shower.

There's someone else here.

And my goddamn sweaty clothes trick my nose since otherwise I'd know right off if it was Ula. Or Finn. Or Critter.

I wait.

If it was Critter or Finn they'd probably come right in.

The feeling gets stronger.

I try to tell myself it's stupid. I mean there's five or six
steps to get into the kitchen where I can see everyplace else
in the apartment and most likely Ula sitting on the sofa or bent
over the turntable spinning Abba.

THAT'S WHY YOU LEFT THE DOOR UNLOCKED IN
THE FIRST PLACE BOY.

So I wrap the towel around my waist but I still don't move.

I ask myself *Are you that scared?* and the honest answer is *I am*. It doesn't feel right. It doesn't feel like Ula.

It feels like a stranger.

Still the closest place to find something to defend myself is the kitchen and more than anything else it's not wanting to be trapped in a corner with no chance of fighting back or running away that puts one foot in front of the other with the noise I must be making scaring me more than ever because the worst fear of all is fear of the unknown. And sure I remember understanding quiet in the park thanks to the Dalai Lama but understanding it and being it are two different things.

So what really though. Since if anyone's here he heard the shower. Heard it stop. Knows he's not alone.

Somehow I'm sure it's a he and halfway to the kitchen I sort of pick up a smell but it's confused with my own bad scared smell and Finn and Critter's clothes behind the curtains. I take the mother of all deep breaths before the step I know will let me see into the living room if I crane my neck forward far enough and am I glad because first the good news nobody here but us phosphorescent fishies boss then the opposite that vacuums every bit of oxygen from the air because I'm staring at the door and is it locked.

As in somebody locked it.

Somebody I smelled.

Somebody behind the curtains.

It's my pure adrenaline spinning me around and his perfect timing pulling the curtains apart to frame his wild eyes killer smile moving lips.

Heeerrre's Jonny!

If it wasn't for the air in my lungs I know I'd black out. I feel suffocated. No more like drowning when you get slammed by a wave that's got the whole ocean to Hawaii behind it and it's thrashing you around like clothes in a washer only triple time and bouncing you off the bottom and you're trying to swim but you don't know which way is up and it's too turbulent to see your bubbles or the surface light and there's a second when you just let go of everything or else you fight.

So I'm paralyzed inside but not exactly motionless. I'm shaking and sweat is running rivers down my neck and back and chest. I tell myself *Calm down it's Jonnyboy* but I can't be calm and when the shock starts fading I realize why I'm getting mad. It's something you can't help when you're different like me. The way you feel about people taking advantage.

Because in some wayz it's the story of your life and always will be. And it's why lots of deaf boyz just live silent days silent nights with no hearing friends and hardly anything to do with hearing people.

They just don't trust them.

They'd rather be around someone they don't have anything in common with who's deaf than their fucking soul mate who's hearing.

Plenty kweerboyz are like that too actually and it's stupid and it's wrong but I understand how it happens. You always wonder what normals REALLY think and what they're RE-ALLY saying about you to each other and it's just too much feel the weight crushing down on your face so you turn away and never turn back.

I'm not turning away from Jonnyboy though and he's racing toward me arms open looking serious now while I'm admitting to myself he couldn't have known what movie I was screening in the shower.

And so what if cruel is the only word for pulling a real live HelIen Killer joke on somebody you care about. He'd never hurt me on purpose. He's been hurt too many times himself by other people. More I bet than he ever lets on. So Jonnyboy can't read my lips when I finally start to smile but it's only because my head's against his neck and we're hugging so tight I can feel his shoulder blades sharp and his chest hard against mine but not from muscle.

From his ribs.

He's thinner.

And there's another difference.

His skin.

His breath.

His hair.

The way they smell.

Like chemicals.

Not lotion though.

Not mouthwash.

Not gel.

From somewhere inside his body.

Though it's not sickening or anything just a faint edge in the air like being out in the middle of Monterey Bay when the PG&E plant at Moss Landing is powered up and the breeze blows onshore. I remember he smelled a little like this the last time he came back from L.A. But a lot less noticeable. Though maybe he hasn't been changing his clothes very much so it builds up.

It's all the crack no doubt about it.

I wonder why Finn and Critter don't smell this way too since they do it all the time. Except really they don't. Neither one of them did any at all for almost two weeks. Then I remember who else had this smell.

Jason.

The only kweerboy I've connected with on my own. In any way. I mean it was Jonnyboy who made friends with Finn and Critter.

What am I thinking. Here I am with Jonnyboy's arms around me and I'm telling myself someone who's pretty much a stranger is the only kweerboy I've connected with on my own. I mean what about Jonnyboy.

Just because he smells like a stranger.

Doesn't make him a stranger.

Now does it.

SEVEN

I have to pull away from Jonnyboy when my arm can't take the squeezing anymore. I show him the stitches and he's all *Shock! Horror!* but doesn't even have to ask just makes our sign for *Sk8 or Die* and shrugs his shoulders. Then he makes air scribbles and when I reach back for my notepad on autopilot my thumb hooks over the towel around my waist and the next thing you know it's around my ankles instead. I'm not so much embarrassed as reminded of what's happened since I last saw Jonnyboy and it flusters me realizing is it time for news of the week in review and I just don't know where to begin.

After covering myself back up I mean. Which is a little longer than seven seconds later. The first time I retie the towel it comes undone as soon as I let go of it. The second time I take two steps toward the bathroom before gravity wins again. The third time I pick it up I look over my shoulder at Jonnyboy who's trying not to laugh too hard and though it's definitely one of those laugh-with-you-not-at-you laughs the trouble is I'm not laughing at all which I know I should be.

Finally I just spin around so he won't notice and drape the towel over my shoulders where I know it'll stay put and book into the bathroom free and easy for my pants and my notebook. When I come back out Jonnyboy's standing at the kitchen breakfast bar which is where I think I'm leaning my elbow when I pull out the pen from the notebook binding and get ready to write. Only actually I'm leaning on the edge of a pane of glass that flips up in the air snowing speed all over the place.

Because there were bumps lined up that I didn't even see thanks to the record jacket on the counter underneath the glass which is that white album by the Beatles. And do I freak because there's no salvaging spilled go-fast from shag carpet. So it's my turn to do *Shock! Horror!* but instead it suddenly makes me smile my first real white boy smile since Jonnyboy got here.

The way the crack powdered the shag around the table like it sifted down from someone juggling sugar donuts.

Pause.

Insert disk labeled *Class Clown.*

Spinning beachball.

Did you hear the one about the needle and the haystack?

Jonnyboy grins and rubs my head and everything's just like it used to be. He locks one arm around my neck to spare my stitches then leads me out to the sofa in the living room and holds his hand out for the notebook.

so what's up w/ the bigtimez?

And I figure I'd better account for the war wounds first

since they're already on display. Though I don't spend much time on the sk8 session but lots of it on the next step back down memory lane as in Tejon Holdings as in go blast Alice and I run it all by him saving the best for last.

Exhibit A.

The envelope with keys.

When I'm finished it's just like last night with Ula. He's looking right at me and seeing somebody he never saw before I swear.

Then he writes:

i can't fuckin believe it boy.

Me neither.

i mean U just went down there like the CIA or something & shredded their security 2 shit.

I was lucky.

NFW, talk about signs & portents. we're meant 2 do this, this is religion.

So you want to?

is JP2 a pollack? hell yeah!

And am I stoked because though Ula seemed pretty gung ho last night I don't know if Finn and Critter will feel the same and especially Finn since he's big on skinheads being nonpolitical. But with Jonnyboy aboard it means we can move on this even if it's only him and me and Ula because one Jonnyboy's worth at least two regular people and that brings us up to Ula's minimum four. When he asks for the Headwaters Forest flyer to check out the details on the nuke-bomber dewd I fish it out of my pocket and after he reads all about it he turns it over and does he do a double quadruple take. Then he turns his head up to me slo-mo style with eyes wide real not eyes wide joke.

He points to *Tejon Holdings* and just stares at the page

with his eyes unfocused like he's really seeing something else.
Finally he starts writing again.

it's roarke's family's company.

And even while I'm noticing one he didn't capitalize Roarke
and he always did before I'm thinking two so the plot thickens
and we're talking honey from the squeeze bear stashed in the
refrigerator door. Then I'm asking myself whether it's good or
bad. Because maybe it means Roarke could just step in and
stop the logging somehow. And if he did then what. I mean
this is all about the bloody rock and how to throw it and right
now we've got a standstill sitting-duck target.

So in a selfish way I hope it doesn't make any difference
but that just proves I haven't thought this through very well since
the main thing should be what happens to the trees not me.

Jonnyboy's thinking hard though.

they're involved in so much shit, i wonder if he even knows about this.
Could he just say No to it?

*Fuck, it's more like just no say, as in no say in anything. he's like exiled
up here now 2 get fully clean & stay outa trouble w/ the law. he's going
along w/ it, 2. reporting in 2 his brother & shit. who's Bhind the whole
thing in a way Bcause after all these years of doing the good boy things
he's rebelling 2 but in a different direction & becoming a race car driver.
& the family's scared he'll end up a ball of fire @ the indy 500 so roarke
has 2 clean up his act 2 help take things over if the time comes. & that
means goodbye Like an Outlaw hello Like an In-Law.*

Since "Like an Outlaw" is Jonnyboy's all-time favorite Chaotic Stature song I guess he's serious about living up to his
ideals and ignoring heroes finally and it's a good thing but sad
somehow too and I can't help feeling sorry for him which
breaks one of my own rules of never feeling that way about
anybody. Because I've been on the receiving end of sorry since
one million B.C. and I hate it worse than anything.

Maybe he could help somehow.

help as in torch the place? i dunno, he's never been political about causes just a rebel without. how were U thinking of doing it, anywayz?

Some kind of bomb.

Not that I'm the mad scientist Unabomber type or anything. The closest I ever got to making a bomb was a capped-off wine bottle filled with jelly from one of the Sterno cans my dad had stashed in the garage for emergency rations if all the liquor stores burned down I guess. I used my mom's knitting yarn for a fuse. When it went off in front of the house of this older kid who grabbed my ears and called me a retard on the school bus every fucking day of fifth grade it shot a piece of glass all the way across the street and sliced through my double layer Skate Ragz shorts and on into my leg a quarter inch deep.

Which pretty much stayed me dry from further adventures in chemistry. So I've been there done that in the smallest way and it scares me in the biggest way and that's one reason the Green Rage dewd got my instant respect when I found out why he went to prison. Because my hat's off to all the go-boom boyz off even if they better wear it themselves to hide that hippie hair I swear.

Unless it's a disguise a brilliant disguise to blend in anonymous in places like Berkeley where they always look first for mad bombers. And the dewd must be pretty smart after all not just go-boom wise but otherwise too if he planned to take out a nuke without sending everybody on a road trip to the future and I mean road as in warrior and future as in no future. And though you can't help thinking smart yeah right the smart boyz doing shit like that don't get caught the truth is the FBI had him in their sights from genesis ground zero. Because he was such an in-your-face radical.

So maybe Roarke having no politics behind him might actually work in his favor.

As far as being suspected. As far as being caught.

Which is the first time I've thought of the words *suspected* and *caught* in connection with the words *burn up the place set it on fire* and I admit it they do make my blood run a little colder. But it's Jonnyboy who puts the big chill on.

hell boy, yr 2 young 2 rent a ryder truck. & i don't look hick enough 2 buy a ton of fertilizer w/o being remembered.

Not that big of bomb. I don't want to kill anybody.

well, there's a big diff between not wanting 2 & being willing 2. & i don't wanna rain on yr mad parade but anytime U start playing the go-boom game there's a risk yr gonna snuff some 1. starting w/ yrself. & if U don't wanna take the risk U better just 4get it.

After he finishes writing Jonnyboy looks up at me all *This is religion* and of course he's right. And am I glad he lays it on the line and forces me to think things through now instead of later. Because my first gut feeling about somebody dying even accidentally is *No way I couldn't have it on my conscience.* Besides it's playing God giving yourself life-or-death power over people even if you hope it never comes to that. And that game's crowded enough as it is.

Only it's crowded with the wrong players. Because all the selfish evil fucks are playing God on a daily basis for the worst possible reasons while the kewl people who want to change things and make life better for everyone now and in the future do nothing out of fear that somebody might get hurt.

I mean why should one innocent victim drag down the whole world. There's dead and dying people everywhere. Look how many in my own short life. My mom. My dad as soon as Tommy walks. Then Tommy probably for getting my dad. Ula's fiancé. Ula's sister. Critter's dad. Finn with a million prescriptions for an incurable disease. It's like seven people. I mean how many did the Mansonz get. Eight? And asking *What's one more?* or even a few more sounds harsh and definitely special circumstances in a court of law but there's only one right answer when you think about it. You take a million precautions but don't fool yourself there's no risk something goes wrong and somebody innocent pays for it and it's too bad but not exactly the first time in the history of the world it's ever happened now is it.

I don't want to hurt anybody except for maybe cops but what can a poor boy do. The only way to get serious attention is to rage so hard it might endanger somebody and us especially. But that shouldn't stop us just keep us smart and make us careful. So we just try to bomb the place enough to trash the office not blow up the building. Plus we do it at night and not just any night. Alice in B let me know when the cleaners are scheduled so we do it when they aren't.

rite on, i dunno about roarke tho. as in what would be the best way 2 take advantage of the connection. it's not like he's gonna snag us a set of keys. U already did the deed boy!

Put her there.

High-hand palm slap. Fingerpull. Wristlock.

Maybe it's best to just keep Roarke out of it. Even if he's not political. They might suspect he's in on it just from being a punk and all.

Jonnyboy doesn't even stop to think before he starts writing.

nah. not 2 save some trees. he's never been much of a nature boy. tho if it was 2 benefit a needle exchange program they'd probably smell a rat.

Not speaking of which. Hee hee. I saw Roarke's bro Heath at the office.

NFW! R U sure?

Oh most definitely. Alice in B had the hots for him and wrote out how he was Mr. Days of Thunder and the future big boss man and for seven seconds I thought maybe it was the wrong Tejon Holdings.

hmm. well 2 bad U didn't think 2 do a rolex romp cause he wears 1 with platinum & diamonds. or a wallet jostle & finance tickets 2 the islands on American Ex.

Screw the wallet just nab fashion boy himself for ransom and finance the rest of our lives in Hawaii like that great train robber down in Rio who hooked up with the Sex Pistols.

Jonnyboy reads it starting to laugh then stops and stares hard at the paper. After a couple of seconds he glances up at me all serious then back at the notebook but he doesn't write anything and I get this big chill knowing his mind is working over what I wrote.

Because it seems totally insane to me. Especially with someone who knows who you are.

I mean even the train robber boyz just stole a lot of money. They didn't take hostages or threaten any people.

I meant it as a joke.

Finally Jonnyboy starts writing.

yr a genius Radboy, i swear. it's patty hearst all over again.

I draw a question mark in the air. Jonnyboy holds one palm flat out as in *Wait* and the index finger of his other hand up as in *1* then reaches into his back jeans pocket for the Altoids tin. When he opens it on the mirror table I see the shiny glint of points and the dull milky plastic cylinder of a rig but he leaves them inside and just pulls out a junior Ziploc with about an eightball's worth of already crushed and powdered crack. And he doesn't use a key this time but a hacked-off Slurpee straw with a shovel end. Two full shovels in each nostril. He shudders and shakes his head then pinches his nose closed for a full minute afterwards. Then he takes my notebook and writes forever it seems. Stopping to think between sentences. Looking up at me with questions in his eyes sometimes. But he doesn't pass it back until he's written it all out.

How bombing Tejon Holdings is a good idea. But only a beginning. It's our insurance for when Roarke turns up missing.

Roarke.

Not Heath.

They'll know we mean business as in *We mean it man!*

When they get the ransom note demanding they sign over the Headwaters Forest to some nature group and flow us cash up front besides to get away. Or else we'll have our own little one-man chainsaw massacre.

You've seen one spoiled rich boy you've seen them all.

It's not really kidnapping though because Roarke's in on it from genesis ground zero. We just have to keep up appearances and take him someplace secret outside San Francisco and stash him there. Because with a family like Roarke's on their backs the cops are bound to search the city above and beyond. So we just have to chill someplace in the woods ourselves. Not those woods obviously. And then after the trees are safe and the ransom's collected we'll throw a bon voyage party.

Paper leis.

Tropical drinks.

Teach Ula the hula.

And the next morning Jonnyboy and me will rise and shine and we're talking high as heaven. Bright as gold. First stop Hawaii but only for refueling. Because our luggage tags read *RAR* which is airline-ese for Rarotonga. But might as well be *HEA*.

Happily Ever After.

I know I'm supposed to slap him high-hand double five and hug him hard as Gordo the Gorilla. Since after all he's turned my joke about nabbing Roarke's brother into history in the making and paradise for the taking. And I can tell he's disappointed when I don't. But it's like looking at a billboard from two feet away. The picture's so big it doesn't compute. All you see are the details. And some people say God is in the details and others say the devil. But whether I'm looking at heaven or hell all I know is I've got nothing but questions.

Starting with *Why would Roarke go along with it anywayz?* and moving right along to *How much ransom should we ask for?* and ending with *Do I need a passport for Rarotonga and if I do how can I get one since after all I'm underage?*

The first question's obviously the most important of all and Jonnyboy's solid on that one.

don't worry baby. i know roarke. he'll do it 4 kicks + he'll do it 4 me. he owes me bigtime. he said so himself.

The other thing Jonnyboy's certain as a fresh tattoo's hurtin' about is that Roarke's family will do the deal and in record time probably just to get it over with. Unlike the Patty Hearst kidnapping way back when. Which went on for years I guess even after her family gave a million bucks' worth of food to poor people meeting one of the ransom demands. Because she ended up joining the radicals herself and robbing banks with them toting a machine gun and in the world according to Jonnyboy that particular lesson of history would definitely be in the back of the Lovejoys' minds.

First because it was another newspaper family. Second because Roarke's personal history as a punk might make him a likely convert. And sure déjà vu all over again would sell a lot of newspapers but they sell plenty as it is. They're way too powerful to want publicity for themselves.

They want the opposite. And though I suspected Roarke was beyond the Mercedes roadster level as far as cash on hand goes it still drops my jaw to the bottom of the Marianas Trench when Jonnyboy's answer to my question about how much ransom we should ask for is a million bucks for each of us.

NFW!

YFW! but get this str8 Radboy, U don't ASK for ransom, U DEMAND it. cause we got em by the nards.

Five million bucks though?

five mill george washingtons 2 the lovejoys is maybe 1 week's interest on their investments or a decent day on wall street, take yr pick. i mean after roarke's mother dies he and heath will make the top top 20 yankee rich boyz list EZ even after divvying everything in 2.

So the afterparty looks pretty promising all right. Everything else is sketchy and Jonnyboy admits it but after all he just got the idea.

Like we have to find a place to take Roarke and figure out how to arrange the payoff of the ransom which seems the scariest part of all to me and those are definitely big-ticket items. Plus there's simpler stuff like getting a gun to hold to Roarke's head in the classic posed pictures with the newspaper headlines to show he's still alive after the nab but we mean business.

And then there's figuring out the passport situation.

But the main thing right now is whether I think Ula will enlist for the duration. Because I know her better than Jonnyboy and he's just guessing if she's up for bombing an office to show how much people care about saving redwood trees she's probably willing to stage a phony kidnapping to make sure the trees actually get saved.

Before I can write anything Jonnyboy's head snaps up and he turns toward one of the narrow windows beside the door.

My eyes follow his and there she is Miss Un-American Activities as in the Swedish Blond Communist. She's stoked seeing Jonnyboy and after he vaults over the back of the sofa to clear the deadbolt her smile's brighter than the Point Pinos lighthouse I swear. But up close it confuses me because after she kisses both my cheeks Euro style and messes my hair I look close into her eyes and I can tell she's been crying. She knows I know too and she's out with it before she finishes sitting down between Jonnyboy and me on the sofa.

Her sister died.

They pulled the plug.

At least she got to say goodbye.

We both go into shock ourselves holding on to her with Jonnyboy stroking her hair saying nothing and me just sitting there with one of her hands between both of mine again just like last night at her sister's apartment. Finally I sign to her that I wish there was something I could do.

—There's nothing you can do. There's nothing I can do. I wish there was.

She turns suddenly toward Jonnyboy looking startled. He looks me in the eye and nods kind of grimly and repeats what he said to Ula.

—There is something you can do.

And with his jaw set and his eyes determined and serious and his gestures angrier and more excited the longer he talks he says all the right things. I can't follow word for word he's speaking so fast and besides he mostly looks at Ula. But I know what he's saying.

Why send flowers when you can save some trees.

Inoculate with the poison to kill the disease.

A truth for a lie.

An eye for an eye.

A bomb for a bomb.

In memory of.

This is dedicated to the one I love.

And the change in Ula's eyes and the color rising in her cheeks and her quickening pulse that I can feel in my hands are all the reply Jonnyboy needs to the question he asked me right before she knocked on the door.

Asked and answered.

—There's only one thing that bothers me.

But it's not playing God or the chance of getting caught or any of my other usual suspects.

—The ransom.

And Jonnyboy's the first to start agreeing that collecting the cash is the sketchiest part of the whole plan but Ula stops him with a wave of her hand.

—I don't mean the practical details. I think we should trade Roarke for the Headwaters Forest and ask for nothing else.

When she explains why I second the emotion and I mean fully because by not asking for a penny even with someone so rich in our hot little hands we'd prove to everybody that what we care about is the trees and not just using them as an excuse to get rich quick ourselves. And that might give a little jolt to the mass of people who do nothing but work their nowhere jobs and pay their taxes and fall asleep drinking Bud Lite in front of *Monday Night Football*. Which could be the most important result of all.

I mean it's just like Ula says. She makes me realize this is about more than saving those redwoods. They're one example of a million other crimes against nature. Just think if thousands of people started taking it in their own hands to wage guerrilla war on the developers and the polluters. It would cost the big and glassies so much in losses they'd either clean up their act or just give up and put their money in the stock market instead.

And of course there's two main problems in making that happen and one is just getting attention in the first place by setting an example. So a few people and I mean a very few at first will start saying to themselves *Hey I hate this shit too and if those Tejon bombers are doing it and getting away with it then so could I*. And then it snowballs. But it also leads to problem two which is figuring out exactly what to do and how to go about it so you don't get caught.

Which Ula is ready to start solving as soon as Jonnyboy agrees to shine the ransom idea. At first he hesitates looking at me with a question in his eyes then picks up the notebook and tries to reassure me.

don't worry get happy i'll make it up 2 U kid. plan B is 2 get some $$ on the side directly from roarke. not millions or anything but enough 2 get us 2 the islands anywayz. i promise.

I'm all *whoever whatever have a nice day* because I just don't care all that much about the money and it was Jonnyboy's idea anywayz not mine. I mean what would a kid like me do with a million bucks. I couldn't put it in a bank or anyplace like that so I'd just have to carry it around with me wherever I went. And would that lag and I mean sooner not later and I mean hard.

So Ula's all *Let's get down to business* in full Mrs. Olsen mode and it kind of surprises me but not for long because after all this is kind of therapy for her. Doing something constructive instead of sinking deep as Death Valley into depression. Or destructive actually but it has the same effect. She looks at Jonnyboy and me kind of expectantly like she needs help choosing a sk8board deck or something and she's ready to pay close attention to our advice.

—So what do you two know about making bombs?

And Jonnyboy and me trade sly looks without busting up or anything though I'm sure we would have if her sister hadn't just died. But I have to plunge right in to keep from grinning big time so as innocently as I can I sign that actually I was just thinking she's probably more savvy go-boom wise than both of us put together. Which puts her on the offensive immediately with more than a little fire in her eyes.

—That's just the kind of thinking that led to misery for my sister.

I do feel pretty ashamed when she reminds me the reason people knew they could bomb her sister's car and not only get away with it but have most everyone assume that she made the bomb herself is that having radical ideas and not hiding them automatically makes you guilty of memorizing every recipe in *The Anarchist Cookbook* and turning out firebombs faster than Betty Crocker bakes brownies. So I apologize but I don't waste any time in grilling her on *The Anarchist Cookbook* either.

Which she hasn't seen in a long time but thinks you can mail-order from the back pages of magazines like *Soldier of Fortune* or else find in a few libraries. But either source is risky because you never know who put the ads in the magazines and you always know who the libraries cooperate with when it comes to investigating who reads what and is it the American Civil Liberties Union or is it not.

And does that suck because it needs to be a bomb all right. We're unanimous on that. Bombs get attention and they're hard to cover up afterwards with bullshit stories about frayed electric wires and gas leaks even though Ula says the targets always try and the law goes along with it as far as they can because the only thing worse than a bunch of mad bombers doing hit-and-runs against the big and glassies is word getting out and stirring up the copycats. Which makes it totally important to let the newsboyz know what's up. And right about the time it's going up or a little before. So credit goes where's credit's due and some PR slime can't say you're just stealing glory from an act of God or a slacker immigrant handyman.

But all Ula knows about are Molotov cocktails. Which I guess her dad was throwing at cop cars in Paris in May 1968 and the only reason her mom wasn't too is that she was back in Sweden giving birth to Ula. And which are pretty close to what I served up to that kid in fifth grade so they don't really translate into blowing up an office by remote control now do they. Because we need a bomb we can leave behind and let the fingers on the hands of a clock do the walking while one of us calls the media and does the talking.

Ula apologizes back for not knowing more than she does and shakes her head smiling kind of sadly.

—I wish Yuri was here. He'd know exactly what to do.

Meaning her boyfriend in the Russian army. Her late boyfriend. And is she right. Because the only hands-down-your-pants places to get the skinny on making bombs are in the military and in prison. And though I've got relatives in both it isn't something you just casually ask about because you get too many questions asked right back. Even from your own brothers.

Like I could ask Tommy under the cover of it being used against our dad. But I know his answer.

Just you wait. I'll handle it. You stay out of trouble.

And all Jonnyboy's ever done go-boom wise is twist the fuses of a bunch of M80 firecrackers together and light them inside a metal trash can and run like H E double L after putting the lid back on. Though I guess there's always pipe bombs. I've never made one myself but I knew some kids in Monterey who blew up a Goodwill collection station with one and scattered burning bits of secondhand clothes and pages of old magazines like confetti over two whole blocks. And they weren't the brightest porch lights on the block either. So it's not exactly rocket science.

We have to start somewherez.

Because repeat after me we're basically clueless.

But at least we're not listless. Ula's taking care of that. She's all *Sure we need a bomb but moving right along. That's not all we need.*

We need:

Reconnaissance.

Lookouts.

A run-through.

Disguises.

Maybe a diversion.

And that's just under TEJON HOLDINGS. Ula draws a vertical slash with a single bold stroke down the middle of the notepad page and writes ROARKE LOVEJOY at the top of column two. Then I feel a rush of air across my bare feet and seven seconds later warm hands around my neck moving down inside the front of my t-shirt and back up outside it to rest on my shoulders.

Finn. He smells so good. His hands feel so good.

But it's just my body talking.

I got me mixed up with somebody else.

And do I. Tilting my head and looking up at Finn he's all *Read my lips* so I turn around with my arms resting on the back of the sofa and he mouths:

—Jason said to say hi.

This time the knots inside are fisherman's knots sailor's knots bowlines sheet bends overhand splices. It's all I can do to keep from jumping up all *Later daze I'm outta here gotta date with my sk8* and making smoke for the Pit. My mouth gets dry and I can feel beads of sweat popping out on my upper lip. But Finn doesn't notice a thing and neither does Critter behind him. Mostly I guess because he's looking over Ula's shoulder and reading the list aloud to Critter and wondering WTF is up.

Which is my cue to let my fingers do the walking while Jonnyboy does the talking and fish the sketchpad out from under the mirror table then leaf through it to the drawings I did for *Greenheads vs. Greedheads*. I pass it to Finn and watch both boyz look them over to see if they recognize themselves as the models and I guess I'm a better artist than I thought because it takes less than seven seconds and I can tell they're pretty stoked about it even before Finn writes me a note saying:

You should keep this up! You've a proper gift. Though I'm not this handsome.

Which he runs by Critter who couldn't see what he wrote I guess. And then he adds a ps.

Critter says: Ditto ditto but I am this handsome & this built & I always wanted to be a super hero & wear tights to show it off. So let's do it Radboy, whatever you say.

At first I think they're just kidding but once Finn and Critter sit down in the chairs at the ends of the table I can tell from the way Jonnyboy and Ula suddenly turn all smiles and relax into the sofa cushions after just a few words of conversation that the Greenery boyz really are aboard and the train's

not only on the tracks it's pulling out of the station. Which
Jonnyboy confirms seven seconds later with a scribbled note
that reads:

Damn! Fuck! now we got an IRA bomb boy & a certified pyro
on the team. fuck this amateur hour shit. we're turnin pro w/ a vengeance. hee hee. only make that VENGEANCE.

Well not really all that pro. I mean Finn himself never had
anything to do with the IRA except to try and escape it by
being a skinhead. Though it turns out his mother went to
prison over there in a place called Armagh for refusing to talk
about people she supposedly knew who WERE go-boom boyz.
And she never got out because she died there. Then there's
back in the USA as in Pumpkin Center where Critter got even
with his parents for trashing all his punk rock stuff by taking
all the clothes from their bedroom closet one day when they
weren't home and piling them in the driveway and striking a
match after he doused them with gas. Which landed him in
juvee for a while but also hooked him up with another kweerboy for the first time ever while he was there. So he still feels
glad all over that he did it.

Which is exactly how I feel about everyone deciding to plan
and plot over pizza because am I hungry and whether Jonnyboy's hungry or not he looks like he could down a dozen jumbo
pepperonis without letting his belt out. When the pizza arrives
I'm practically drooling like a St. Bernard from the smell and
I guess my blood count still isn't up to what it should be because I almost feel faint. But there's a delay while Critter
whisks it back to the kitchen to serve it up like a white boy
and am I glad Ula goes in to help him since I know she'll speed
things up.

As in heh heh heh. Because when the pizza reappears and
Critter makes a little ceremony of centering it on the mirror

table every other slice is barely visible underneath a glittering blanket of snow-white powder. And though Ula's holding the can of protein powder that Finn warned her about adding to the pepperoni and mushrooms and cheese when she followed Critter into the kitchen I'm not fooled for a seventh of a second. Because I got pretty familiar with the stuff when I was spiking Finn and Critter's chocolate milk and it definitely doesn't come in crystals like that.

Finn realizes too when he picks up one of the pieces and he grimaces at Critter and holds his nose and sticks his tongue out as in *Yuck for days* so Critter follows up with a plastic straw and starts snorting the crack off the pizza while Finn stands there holding it in one hand and covering his eyes with the other. Then it's Jonnyboy's turn and he inhales half the topping I swear before Finn finally sets the slice back down and finishes vacuuming up the rest. Though there's plenty left melting into the tomato sauce and I'm a little surprised when Jonnyboy offers a bite of it to Ula and she takes a pretty big one. Not that she's all Ms. Just Say No or anything and if I was her right now I'd probably want my spirits lifted too. It just seems strange to watch a nurse doing crack.

Though not for some reason once it takes effect and she gets talkative to watch a nurse lay out the dangers of a bombing and kidnapping and ask each one of us if we're willing to say hello to San Quentin if something goes wrong and not turn against each other for a get-out-of-jail-free card because now is the time for the honest answer *No* and zero hard feelings about it.

Talk about heavy. The thought just hangs in the air like the gravity of Jupiter and those other big planets where a marble would weigh ten tons and bore a hole to hell if you dropped it from three feet high. And I look over at Jonnyboy who's usually Mr. Anti-Gloom Mr. Anti-Doom hoping to vibe him into one-man Joy Division mode but his eyes are somewhere else and I mean somewhere dark so the frequency's jammed and it's up to me to be Mr. Anti-Gravity and draw the smiley face that pulls the corners of our mouths back up. But the pencil's busted. The pen's outta ink. The chalk's been ground into powder and sold as drugs by my delinquent little brother.

All I can think to sign to Ula is more of the serious same as in *Just remember if we get caught it was all my idea.*

I'll admit it.

Blame it on me.

I won't even go to regular court just juvee.

Which turns out to be wisdom from the mouths I guess because it does the trick with Ula first and everyone else once she repeats it aloud. I mean we may still be on Jupiter but the atmosphere turns out to be straight nitrous oxide and we're all busting up.

Because even I see it as soon as she says it. The lawyers huddling on Court TV. The impatient minority or woman or preferably both judge. Then the disbelieving faces of the jury while the adult punk druggie radicals enter their goodgerman pleas.

Just following orders.

The kid was the mastermind.

We did everything he said.

And Jonnyboy looks back at me frequency locked at last then jumps up all *Eureka I have found it.* Because the best defense is a good offense and what's more offensive than kweer marriage. So just like that with an assist from Ula's stretchy white hairband around his neck for a collar he's transformed into Reverend Call the Doctor Jonnyboy performing the quadruple-ring ceremony.

And not air rings either thanks to a couple of cigar bands salvaged from yuppie scum litter at a sidewalk café and two quarter vending-machine rings from Critter's collection.

One Batman.

One Captain Marvel.

Plus the wire cork cage from a champagne bottle Ula found in the kitchen and snipped and twisted into a circle for Jonnyboy since he can't just officiate. He has to participate.

So dearly beloveds do you take these men including me and do you take this woman too for your unlawfully wedded partners in crime and if there's any objection especially from Radboy speak now goddammit or forever hold your peace amen.

We have to get married so the law can't make us testify against each other if we ever get caught. Plus we can say we're a family not a conspiracy. Just like the Mansonz did I guess though it didn't really help them too much because they went too far.

They took way too many drugs.

I mean from thinking things through earlier I can see how killing a few people could be ok if it led right off to a mass revolution that overthrew everything. But I saw that TV special and they didn't exactly pick the prime suspects now did they. Not judges generals senators bankers. Instead a movie star and a hairdresser and a bunch of Hollywood types plus some retired Mexican and his wife who owned a couple of grocery stores.

Real bigtime capitalist piggies all right.

But what do you expect from brain-dead hippies who thought they'd escape from L.A. by cruising out into the Mojave Desert in dune buggies.

I mean look at the map. L.A.'s big and the Mojave's bigger. As big as some states back east. And unfortunately count one dune buggies don't run on solar power and unfortunately count two there aren't any filling stations out in the Mojave because unfortunately count three there aren't any towns.

No people. Nothing. It may be pretty. But it's definitely vacant.

And they definitely didn't know what they were doing.

Ok I admit it so neither do we but at least we're not planning an all-out race war based on old Beatles songs now are we.

EIGHT

X marks the spot on the road map where according to the yellow pages we'll find all the go-boom supplies we need to carry off what we ARE planning. It's a place called Fremont. And in the world according to Finn it's basically beyond the valley of the fucktards. But what the hey. It's not like we're moving there. Just driving there. Across the Bay Bridge at sunset in the car Roarke gave Johnnyboy which is one of those old Plymouth Valiants with doors of real steel that clunk when they close instead of aluminum and plastic you can slam with your little finger. I'm squeezed in the middle of the backseat between Finn and Critter with Ula driving and Jonnyboy riding shotgun.

After we chowed the pizza we decided that pipe bombs are

the white boy's way to go and it can't be that hard to figure out how to light the fuses with a delay as in to be continued in our very next issue. The important thing now is to start collecting the raw materials as in *Right away* which is Ula's motto from some revolutionary group called the Situationists. I guess she's worried we'll all chief out or something. Because as soon as the discussion moved on to timers she started watching the clock and flowed me the yellow pages to look up gun stores.

We're not buying or stealing guns or anything like that. What we need is gunpowder. Which you can buy for loading into shotgun shells no questions asked. No ID required. And if you get enough of it you can load it into capped-off pipes too. Only as I found out fast when my fingers did the walking there really aren't any gun stores in San Francisco. Just a rifle range in a park and some pawnshops that specialize in firearms but more the Saturday Night Special types than guns for hunting. And there aren't even that many listings across the bay in Oakland which is supposedly populated mostly by black people killing each other and I mean with guns. It's more the suburbs to the south where the bullet boyz must hang their frontwards baseball caps and I mean in mass keeping the bottom line in the black for dozens of stores with names like *Code of the West Armory* and *Winchester Cathedral* and *White to Bear Arms*.

It's just as well if we get the goods outside of San Francisco anywayz. Finn and Critter swear up and down it's more like a small town than the big city it looks like and even though they base it on every new kweerboy they meet turning out to have shagged someone they already know and not anything to do with the police or politics I'm all for anonymous. I don't want to hop on the subway and sit across from some gun-store clerk reading front-page screaming headlines BOMB EXPLODES

DOWNTOWN who then looks up to see this sk8boarder he sold a case of black powder to a week before and starts thinking *Why would a kid with a skateboard need that much gunpowder anywayz?*

Not that any Fremont fucktard is going to lay eyes on a sk8boarder shopping for powder either. At least not this one. My sk8's stashed in the trunk. Before we left the Greenery Ula made this speech about trying not to look or act in ways that are memorable on our little shopping spree and I figure carrying around big signs saying ANARCHY and DESTROY while browsing the black-powder aisle probably ain't the way to go.

I'm lucky because at least it's something I can change. Unlike Ula and her measurements. Which is what she and Jonnyboy are arguing about in the front seat right now while Critter and Finn are busting up on either side of me. But every now and then Finn scribbles a line of dialog to keep me on the frequency.

As in **With your looks they'll be doing video captures off the surveillance cameras and posting them on the back of the men's room door.**

As in **Face it Ula you're the Hooters remix of Florence Nightingale.**

Which naturally gets her steaming like Mt. St. Helens. So she comes back with:

I'm no more memorable than you Mr. White Punk on Dope!

And my cap's off to Ula because though I've never been inside a gun store and don't know what the typical customers are like I bet they're nothing like Jonnyboy. Because nobody's like Jonnyboy.

Unlike Finn. In the world according to Ula anywayz. Though she doesn't mean it personally. What she means is that Finn's a skinhead and most skinheads are Nazis so he'll fit right in at *White to Bear Arms.* Which I don't get the details on till after Finn leans forward and argues bigtime with Ula all the way from the bridge toll plaza to the Oakland Coliseum BART Station then slumps back against the seats before taking my notepad in hand like it weighs a million tons.

I HATE feeding the stereotype. I might as well be black and going out in blackface.

What about Critter then?

Finn laughs.

The best place for him is waiting in the car park with Ula and Jonnyboy. He's not your everyday gunpowder customer, either. A bit too queer, that one.

You mean more than you? More than Jonnyboy? How?

Finn shakes his head back and forth and bites his lip with the pen hovering over the paper. I wonder if Critter's looking over my shoulder making Finn nervous about what to say but when I turn sideways a little to see Critter's not even looking our way. He's just staring out the window at what looks like toxic shock wasteland between the freeway and the bay. Finally Finn writes:

Since you can't hear him it's difficult to explain. The way Critter speaks is closer to the stereotype.

You mean he sounds like a girl?

Only sometimes, on purpose. There's a word for it. Camp, campy, camping. Have you seen it before?

And the truth is I have seen it and didn't understand it at all except that obviously it doesn't have anything to do with weenie roasts and Coleman lanterns. But I just play dumb and shake my head *No* and watch this trapped look building in Finn's eyes until Ula steers toward an off-ramp and Jonnyboy turns around to interrupt us saying:

—This is the story.

Before Jonnyboy and Ula convinced each other we need to be more cautious we just planned to hit one or two stores with each of us going in separately except for maybe me and buying a few cartons. Or whatever it is they sell gunpowder in. Now the revised standard version is for Finn and me to pose all mean and hard and pass ourselves off as a couple of bonehead skins. The idea is we're stepbrothers and Finn's taking me shooting for the first time ever. And we want to do it like white boyz from genesis ground zero as in loading our own shells and plucking the feathers with our teeth and all the other survivalist crap right down to roasting the birds over coals we get from rubbing two sticks together if anybody gets nosy.

The whole hunting thing does less than zero for me but I like the idea of being bros with Finn and start fantasizing about growing up with him in place of the brothers I have. Though instead of reliving Tommy's crimes with him except successfully and bigger like banks instead of AM-PMs I start seeing the two of us in the Old West on horses. Doing more of the Butch Cassidy and the Sundance Kid type deal by day then bedding down at night together beside the campfire with a million stars overhead and the smell of pinewood burning. Then falling asleep with our heads resting on each other's arms but no sex scenes more of a G-rated episode or PG actually for strong language and violence.

So why does the earth move. Then I realize it's not the earth moving me but Finn and my head's on his shoulder where it's been awhile I guess and I wonder if I'm coming down with that *Private Idaho* disease and then looking ahead through the windshield I forget Idaho and start thinking Kansas because I realize it's definitely time for a heart-to-heart with Toto.

Because this ain't the frontier anymore.

This ain't San Francisco.

This may be east of the bay but it's west of the west.

It's hot and muggy here without any breeze and in the twilight everything looks like old TV programs made before color like *Dragnet*. No one's hurrying around the way everyone does in the city and it's pretty obvious why looking out across miles of no places to go and nothing much to do. No big and glassies. No cool old buildings like City Hall in San Francisco. No narrow jammed streets. No wide streets with granite curbs and palm trees down the middle. No giant billboards. No fleets of dirty buses.

Just one- and two-story flat roof boxes.

Plastic signs hanging over empty sidewalks.

Half-built freeway ramps and spotlights on huge American flags flying over filling stations.

Plus the yellow pages didn't even tell half the story. Once we drive about a mile further there's suddenly mass gun stores and I mean one on every block like liquor stores in parts of San Francisco. So we just pick one out at random and park across the street at a Der Wienerschnitzel and I'm thinking this is too easy following Finn into the place because right in front of us is the aisle with the directional sign overhead saying Black Powder. Though I misread it at first and do double quad-ruple take WTF as in *Why Black Power?*

I write it down so Finn can laugh at me but he doesn't even crack a smile. He just stares back at the selection of gunpowder in foil-wrapped cardboard tubes the size tennis balls come in then glances nervously at the three-hundred-pound salesclerk with bushy black muttonchop sideburns and belly a mile over his belt rolling slowly toward us and fanning himself with one of those Indiana Jones men's magazines that have pictures of women in distress on the cover. And whether the distress is animal as in cornered by alligator or vegetable as in imprisoned in opium den or mineral as in buried alive in lost gold mine the women always look the same.

Big titties and long blond hair.

Just like Ula.

Score one for Jonnyboy.

Since I basically hide behind Finn to keep the deaf thing from coming up unless absolutely necessary I can't see the guy's lips and don't get any of either side of the conversation but I know from Finn's neck muscles tensing and the confusion in his face when he turns back to look at the tubes of gunpowder that someone switched reels on us and the movie doesn't match our script anymore and even worse has subtitles in a language we can't read.

Because it's obvious from there being seven or eight colors of foil on different tubes that gunpowder's more complicated than we guessed. And the labels are less than zero help in simplifying things with just numbers and meaningless words like 30 Grain and 10X2 Black.

Of course we weren't expecting the Emma Goldman Seal of Approval or helpful household hints with kewl old-fashioned curving arrows pointing toward pipe-bomb recipes on the sides of the tins but this is ridiculous. I mean who'd have thought gunpowder comes in colors and flavors like Ben & Jerry's.

So I'm watching sweat patches creep from Finn's armpits down the sides of his shirt while he's listening and talking and I'm vibing him as hard as I can.

Just go with the candy apple red Finnboy. It looks like the biggest bang for the buck. And get a couple while we're at it. They're only $9.99.

But he just shrugs bigtime and nods his head toward blubber boy like later daze and practically drags me out of the store. I've never seen him stressed like this I swear. And it gets worse too when we get back to the Valiant at the same time as Critter who went into Der Wienerschnitzel for Dr Peppers all round. Because while Finn is running down all the questions the guy asked and his own clueless responses he actually starts shaking and I realize it might not be stress or nervousness taking him over.

It might be the F word as in never make decisions based on.

Which is signed sealed and delivered when everybody's looking at me for backup and Finn scribbles out a note so I know what he said.

He was extremely suspicious, he knew I wasn't a shooter. He could be ringing Old Bill right now. We're all at sixes and sevens and nines. We don't know FA about this.

When I finish reading Jonnyboy catches my eye and mouths *Storytellers lie* while raising his eyebrows in a question though not real obviously so Finn doesn't notice anything. He doesn't notice me all slyboy nodding back at Jonnyboy either. And ok I admit it's easier to keep calm when I'm not the one doing the heavy lifting but all I can think of is Jonnyboy's rule to live by. I mean we can't let some fat-ass neanderthal derail everything just because he's pissed we interrupted his evening soft-core gun porn fest. Plus we've got two hundred bucks in our pockets to spend on gunpowder and this is America Finn-boy where the customer's always right and money doesn't talk it swears.

Still it's no good getting all aggro about it which is what Jonnyboy starts doing as soon as I nod my head by writing me a note that Finn can't help but see.

so the dewd in there's got 911 on the line 2 report what? a man & a boy came in 2 buy gunpowder & couldn't decide which kind 2 get so they left w/o buying any?

And is Jonnyboy right because even the cops in a town like

this wouldn't dunk a donut over that one. But his approach is wrong as in totally because I can feel Finn tense up beside me as soon as he reads it and the last thing we need is unhappy campers before we've even got wood for the bonfire. Which Ula doesn't need a help file to figure out either. She puts her hand on Jonnyboy's arm when he starts to open the car door all *Let me show you how it's done in the US of A* and shuts him up so she can ask Finn a few questions that I don't catch because of the angle of her head but result in Finn relaxing beside me and nodding his head back at her and even laughing after a couple minutes. Then he turns to me and mouths:

—I just got bloody paranoid. It's the crack catching up with me is what it is. And not speaking of which.

What Finn decides he needs before having another go at it isn't Dr Pepper but Dr. Go-Fast and since he thinks he's holding office hours in the gents he's sure we'll all excuse him. And while he's cracking on inside Der Wienerschnitzel Ula fills me in on the new strategy she figured out with Finn that puts our IQ as in ignorance quotient right on the table giving no food for thought to suspicious minds. It's simple. We just write down on a piece of paper the name of one kind of powder we saw across the street and two afterwards in brackets. And Finn shows it to the bullet boyz saying our older brother is taking us shooting and teaching us to load shells and he said to pick up a couple of these.

So wham bam thank you man two tins of powder comin right at ya.

Here's your change.

Love it or leave it.

Heh heh heh.

You boys tear up the tules.

Just don't shoot anybody I wouldn't.

Heh heh heh.

But you spot that yellow-bellied Clinton don't you worry none about Fish & Game.

It's open season.

Your secret's safe with me.

Which is exactly how the script goes at the Code of the West Armory on the next block where it takes like ninety seconds for us to pull the whole thing off and practically skip back to the Valiant with black powder in my backpack and grins on our faces. And are Jonnyboy and Ula stoked with high fives all around. But Critter who's been pretty quiet ever since we left the city just stares out the window after smiling at us kind of halfheartedly so while Finn's showing off the powder tins up front I climb in back and tap him on the shoulder and cock my head all quizzical with CARE package eyes as in *What's wrong?*

He grins a low-wattage sadface grin and mouths:

—I miss my bunny.

And I'm all *Awww* and pat his head but don't know what else to do because all I can think of is standing in that hot dirty alley with Finn thinking of dolphins on Mars and being sure as sugar shock on Easter morning that bunny is lost for keeps. So I don't know what makes me jab my thumb skyward with a cocky smile as in *She'll come back. Just you wait.* I mean talk about *Storytellers lie.* But then afterwards walking across the street to another gun store with Finn I remember how I actually kind of identified with that bunny myself standing there in that alley and I hope I'm right not just for Critter's sake but for mine too.

We hit three more stores in the next four blocks with pretty much the same smooth sailing. No questions asked. No strings attached.

Not yet anywayz.

Which reminds me to look around in the next place for fuses and I don't mean little glass ones.

The next place turns out to be this really big multilevel shop called *Don't Tread on We the People* with more stuffed bears and deer than the fucking Museum of Natural History and two good-looking boyz sitting at a card table next to the entrance with a hand-printed sign draped over the front reading MCVEIGH DEFENSE FUND and a Yuban coffee can with a slot chopped through the plastic lid sitting between them. They both smile at Finn and me and I realize they're brothers. Two blonds with almost identical patterns of freckles on their noses. Maybe two years apart. Say nineteen and twenty-one. They look so all-American. Like they should be changing into wet suits behind towels on Highway 1 instead of sitting here in Nowhere Town with about three bucks in change in their collection can after hours probably of waiting.

Instead of being all *Hey bros* with Finn and me because they think we're Nazis.

We're pros by now and seven seconds later we're through the checkout and out the door with Liberty bells on as in mission accomplished because this pair of powder tins makes lucky thirteen and we only planned on a dozen. And when we're back in the car cruising toward the twenty-four-hour Home Depot by the freeway on-ramp in search of plumbing supplies I notice a Swenson's ice cream parlor and get Ula to pull over so we can celebrate like white folks with what else but Five Alarm sundaes. Which leads to hella plenty pyromaniac humor while we're working on downing the whole things to earn free coupons for a return bout. None of us cross the finish line but it's Critter of all people who comes closest and he's almost as skinny as I am. Though it's mostly because he just keeps eating while Finn and Ula and Jonnyboy and I pass my notepad around playing *Can you top this?* with names for our little forestry society inspired by the likes of Winchester Cathedral and White to Bear Arms.

> *Don't Tread on Trees.*
> *Redwood Guard.*
> *Treedom Fighters.*
> *Strife and Limb.*
> *Tree Strikes.*
> *Anarchtree.*
> *Boston Tree Party.*
> *Wounded Tree.*
> *High Treeson.*

Then I come up with *Rust the Ax Ma'am* which finally gets Critter's attention when Ula repeats it out loud. He practically goes into convulsions and I bet Jonnyboy would too if he wasn't in the men's room cracking on but I guess Jack Webb never worked his magic in Sweden or the UK because Finn and Ula just look mystified even after Critter tries to translate.

In the Home Depot parking lot Ula and Jonnyboy decide they'll pose as newlyweds shopping for plumbing supplies and are back ten minutes later carrying long lengths of gray steel pipe and a heavy bag full of pipe caps but no hacksaw blade to cut the pipe because Ula freaked when she noticed an off-duty cop checking them out in the tools department and though in the world according to Jonnyboy the dewd was checking the contents of Ula's sweater and not the contents of their shopping cart better safe than sorry so Critter volunteers to go back in for the blades.

When he's in the checkout line we can see him through a plate-glass window and is he busting up and so are we afterwards when he shows us the birthday candles and candy cake decorations he slapped down on the cashier's conveyer belt along with the pack of hacksaw blades. Which was inspired by this prank he pulled in Pumpkin Center at a supermarket on Halloween when he went through the checkout line at the busiest time of day with nothing but a bag of apples and two packs of razor blades. And of course in a town that small the cops were already waiting when he got back home.

Jonnyboy's all *So much for not being noticed* but only *JK* as in *Just Kidding* and even those of us who aren't cracked on are in pretty high spirits driving across the Bay Bridge with the city skyline sparkling in the distance. It's not at all like the big and glassy evil empire. More like a dream city like Oz or someplace. And it lights the sky so the air itself seems to glow from within not so much reflecting San Francisco as extending it to Jupiter space.

Then right after we get through the tunnel on the island in the middle of the bay and start up the roadway of the suspension bridge section just before San Francisco there's this sudden jolt like we ran into something and Ula's steering for the guardrail.

Only she isn't really steering for the rail. It's more like the road itself is twisting us that way. And then I get it.

You always wonder if it's the big one and it never is.

But still.

This is the bridge that lost a whole section in the Loma Prieta earthquake.

They're still working on the repairs.

The roadway twists the other way.

I shift my eyes to the bright big and glassy ahead of us and just in time. Because in a blink that doesn't last a seventh of a second San Francisco goes dark.

All of it. All at once.

It takes our breath away. Finn and Critter and I just stare at each other eyes ocean wide. Then Jonnyboy turns around and is he grinning.

Not because the pavement isn't rippling like water in wind anymore.

Not because the sway of the cables is ebbing away.

He's grinning because he's remembering what I told him about the granite curbs on Market Street and if this ain't the night for four-wheeled fireworks that night will never come so am I with him.

And am I. Ula lets us out where the old elevated freeway they're tearing down crosses Market at Octavia and we grab our sk8s from the trunk and then it's let there be light and is there for Jonnyboy and is there for me.

Slaloming fast and switching the lead so we both get to see it and remember it always the sparks like stars shooting in the clear cold dark.

At the foot of Market Street the plaza I skated two days ago with the local boyz is crawling with tourists and business types from the big Hyatt hotel next door where there's a dim glow inside the windows on the first few floors but otherwise everything's black as night black as coal. There must be some kind of backup power for the restaurants and shopping and above all the cash registers but still it's a wasteland for Generators X jokes since there's nobody even close to young besides us.

Come to think of it the elevators must be plugged in too because most of the people hanging out couldn't handle more than two or three flights of stairs and I mean going down with God and gravity on their side. And that's not the only thing they couldn't handle either. It's what Jonnyboy calls an RR crowd which might or might not mean Rolls-Royce but definitely means Rolex Romp and it looks like pretty easy pickings from the purse-snatch patch too. But what Jonnyboy's looking for is a place to hide not a gravy train to ride and finally he jerks a thumb across the plaza toward one of the fancy new pay toilets that look like concession stands lifted from Main Street USA in Disneyland and does Johnny Rotten *Follow me!*

All the tweekers are real big on these toilets in the world according to Finn and it's the call of crack they're answering not nature. A quarter buys you twenty minutes of total privacy in a freestanding room sized to hold a game of five-card stud thanks to the handicapped laws and it's actually a kewl place to hang since it's kind of like being inside a big oval drum with everything down to the TP dispenser all space odyssey high-tech and not even smelly or dirty because it's fully autopilot with high-pressure jets of water and steam that do the Mr. Clean thing after every user. And users are the main clientele I guess and is it surprising. Because there's no better home away from home for running crack and talk about your tax dollars at work.

The trouble with space age self-cleaning bathrooms though is when the power's down it puts new spin on *Shit outta luck.* Which doesn't occur to either one of us until we're staring at the glass panel next to the coin slot where the digital readout telling you *Occupied* or *Vacant* or *Cleaning Cycle Please Wait* is MIA.

And there's no manual override. No Moonight Madness discount. No way to open the door at all since it's just a sliding curved panel on a motorized track. So Jonnyboy's all *Damn! Fuck!* and I'm wondering if somebody might be trapped inside or whether there's an escape hatch through the roof like an elevator when the little green computer letters suddenly shine back on before our eyes reading *Vacant* and Jonnyboy's pound-ing me on the back all *Signs and portents! Signs and portents!*

then spinning the quarter into the slot the way he lets pinball machines know who's CEO from genesis ground zero.

The readout flickers in sync with the mercury-vapor lights in the plaza zapping back to life above us but still challenges us with *Vacant* while the door slowly disappears into the curving metal sidewall. Once we're inside it's Jonnyboy who notices the orange syringe cap on the floor and the junk balloon plastered wet against the outside of the toilet bowl but I'm the one who spots the blood spatters on the pulled-out paper towels still joined to the roll and protected from the miracle of robot cleaning by an overhanging plastic shield. I point then reach to rip the sheets away but Jonnyboy knocks my hand aside a little harder than necessary considering I'm not exactly a stranger anymore to the literal poison in some human machines.

And I just shoot back a look as in *Warning! Caution! Merging buses!*

Which calms him down and he apologizes with his eyes and puts a hand on my shoulder then sits on the toilet seat and fixes up the highest voltage jolt of meth I've ever seen from a crystal big enough to tell a fortune from I swear.

Still rushing he holds the little blue Ziploc out to me and his eyes are slits so he doesn't see my autopilot head shake *No*. Then without really thinking about it I take the bag and pinch it open sly slick tweeker style between two fingers of one hand remembering the last time I squeezed a bindle of crack.

The envelope marked *Jason*.

And suddenly I'm all WTF not.

I'm hella tired and the night is young.

I push a few small rocks to the corner of the bag with my finger and flatten the corner on my belt buckle then grind it thumbnail down.

I reach over to Jonnyboy's inside chest pocket for last week seven this week eleven on the tweeker hit parade. As in a hacked-off Slurpee shovel straw.

I dip the shovel into the bag.

Scoop and raise it to my nostril.

Inhale deep.

Damn!

Fuck!

Jesus Mary and Joseph.

Oh heavens to Betsy oh suburban lawns oh kitchens of distinction.

Afterwards I wonder if Jonnyboy's surprised when I look into his eyes which are wide now staring. But though he's seeing me it's almost like he's staring at something else and even when I do *Earth to Jonnyboy* moving my hand in front of his face it takes more than seven seconds for the radio wave delay.

More than twice that before *Signal received*.

Let alone *Formulating response*.

Which turns out to be physical not verbal or written. Because Jonnyboy just kind of slides off the toilet down to the floor and slumps against the wall beside me with his legs straight out then slowly almost creepy slowly his left leg rises up. Not like he's lifting it with his muscles. More like it's levitating from an outside force.

Then it moves toward me and drops down heavy over mine. Which starts this movie in my head it must be the crack that makes it this way. Or more like a vision without words interrupting the regularly scheduled programming.

Or I know.

Instant replay.

But not of what just happened.

Instead what could have maybe should have happened. As

in Jonnyboy still ends up on the floor but that's because I push him aside when he hands me the crack and I throw the bag in the toilet and stand there reading the international symbols on the three big palm-sized buttons on the wall trying to figure out whichthefuck flushes the damn thing. Then it's not fade away but fade to black as Jupiter space. The power's off again but I'm too tweeked to care.

All I care about is.

Jason.

Jason said to say hi.

The movie ends when Johnnyboy presses his leg harder against mine. Just lightly clenching his muscles. Then un-clenching. And that's all it takes. Another movie starts.

Too late.

He's never tried anything with me.

Too long.

We've slept in the same room a million times.

No light.

It's just his body responding to the crack.

I can't see a thing tonight.

But wait. It's Johnnyboy isn't it.

Where are you now.

He wouldn't.

Where did you go.

Do anything to.

Now two things happen at once.

The lights come on and I know I'm gonna be sick. I jump up and move across to the door panel so fast I slam into the wall and smack my hip against the exit button without realizing it so when the door starts opening and the fresh air hits my face it doesn't seem real. More like I passed out imagining what I want.

But what's wrong with this picture.

For some reason my legs still work and they're taking me through the doorway and my eyes are open focused on a round concrete planter a few feet away and my feet work too and follow my eyes but my ears as usual are waiting in the unemployment line and that's what's wrong.

My dreams have audio.

I must be conscious.

This is real and is it ever.

Earth to Radboy Roger Copy.

I mean nobody pukes in the unconscious world it's a law of nature.

Seven seconds later Jonnyboy's beside me holding my head up and he stands there the whole long time it takes to know I'm finished and can move again without dry heave instant replay kicking in. Which happens twice so it's definitely a waiting game for both of us with Jonnyboy playing more than defense. He's towel boy too.

He pulls off his t-shirt.

Rolls it up to mop the sweat from my forehead then slowly gently wipes my face and lips while I watch the muscles rippling just underneath the skin of his flat brown belly and wish we could lay down somewhere warm with my head pillowed there wish I could circle the little raised ring of flesh around his navel with the tip of my tongue wish everything was different wish we weren't in complicated San Francisco wish it was just the two of us far away in a simple place like Rarotonga living on fruit from the trees fish from the seas.

When you wish.

I may.

Wish I might.

How many sparks did I see tonight.

I can't say.

I can't see.

I can't stand up for falling down.

He catches me as soon as my knees buckle and lowers me down to the pavement turning me around so the planter makes a backrest but my head still lolls to the side like my neck muscles turned to beach kelp and my eyes are opening and closing though I don't know which I don't know when. Because either way I just see stars and confuse them with sparks.

Or sparks and confuse them with stars. I don't see Jonnyboy anymore but I know he's there. I know my lips are moving. I know the words I'm trying to say.

Help me.

Jonnyboy's kneeling in front of me holding my hand to his lips which are moving too. Moving nonstop. Moving meaningless. Until I pick it up. A rhythm I can follow. Repeat to the beat. Whatever he's saying he's saying it over and over he's saying it fast and something makes me wonder is he praying is he promising always to be good and then I wonder who it is kneeling beside him whose warm wet breath blowing on my face and the last thing I remember is the breeze in Rarotonga I can feel it.

NINE

The next thing on the screen I'm sitting bolt upright triple time like the corpse in *Night of the Living Dead* but my eyelids aren't quite in sync with the rest of me yet so I'm sitting here seeing nothing in a room I don't know remembering an old Hellen Killer joke.

Q. How did her parents punish her?

A. They rearranged the furniture.

Then I realize I'm not blind after all. I just have to open my eyes. And talk about wish I may. I mean do I wish ears worked that way too.

I thought Finn and Critter's place was jammed with stuff but this living room is the size of two king-size beds plus a twin and just checking off furniture there's a plaid sofa I'm laying on with my legs draped over one end and a low table almost as wide as the room in front of it and on the other side a ratty vinyl recliner facing a TV on a stand in the corner with a big ugly thrift store lamp on top of it. Except for a path just wide enough to walk sideways connecting the sofa and chair there's no clear space anywherez just milk crates filled with records floor to ceiling and wall to wall. Plus interesting-looking junk like this old gunmetal Hallicrafters shortwave radio teetering above me on top of a stack of *Encyclopaedia Britannica*s with bindings that used to be maroon now speckled gray and green with mold or mildew I never know the difference.

That's the setting but you know what they say about the details and it's the devil this time hands down your pants no doubt about it.

As in Door number one.

The scene on the TV screen.

Two burly guys screwing a third guy laying on his back on a kitchen table with his head hanging down over the edge and his legs up in the air.

One big dick pumping his mouth.

The other plowing his butt and I mean hella hard so the whole table shakes and the guy getting reamed is holding white-knuckled onto the sides to keep centered in the frame and prove he's a pro.

I mean if you look close you can see his marks.

Parallel strips of masking tape stuck butt-to-shoulder distance apart on the tabletop.

Moving right along.

Door number two.

A bleach-blond crop top just visible over the back of the

recliner. One thin pale upper arm and elbow jut out from the side.

And finally.

Door number three.

On the table in front of me a carved wooden tray holding rigs and points and dozens of little Ziplocs. Clear ones filled with crack and blue ones filled with something else more powdery. Plus a big amber Ovaltine jar on its side with capsules spilling out Pilgrim style. Thanksgiving style. WTF the word is. I never remember the ones I don't learn to spell.

But the colors aren't apple corn squash fall. They're neon blue. Hottest pink. Hornet yellow.

There's fifteen Franklins on the tray beside them fanned just far enough apart to count. So where am I besides not in Kansas anymore.

And who's the crop top.

I could probably think of twenty questions easy if my head didn't ache so hard and that's it Radboy lay back down.

Close your eyes.

Out of nowhere I remember my sister Rita holding a damp cool wrung-out washrag to my forehead after I had my tonsils out. And maybe Jonnyboy will do the same. He's here someplace. I can feel it. He wouldn't sell me for a sex slave. Not for fifteen hundred bucks.

He'd drive a harder bargain.

Even with a drugged and passed-out discount. Then kidnap me back first chance he got.

Which reminds me.

Jonnyboy.

Roarke.

we're turnin pro w/ a vengeance. hee hee. only make that VENGEANCE.

I have to sit up or I'll puke I swear.

With my head upright again my stomach settles and I open my eyes and for the first time I wonder if those bathroom bumps were cut with something weird that made me sick then kept me hallucinating right up till now. Because there's no sign of crop top anymore. And the air is filling my nose with the scent of my all-time favorite food in the whole wide wonderful world of beautiful people. And I don't mean Snickers. I mean cream puffs. And I mean totally homemade. As in nothing says loving like something from the oven. Which definitely does not compute because from the look of this room a likelier prospect for specialty of the house would be something more along the lines of Kellogg's Pop-Tarts and that's on holidays and Sundays.

Still I can feel a warm draft from behind ruffling the hair on the back of my arm dangling over the end of the sofa and the smell gets fuller and richer and there's no mistake about it. Because the first thing I ever learned to cook was cream puffs from *The Joy of Cooking* when I was ten and the just-baked eggy butter smell is like the spicy strong incense they burn in church at midnight mass on Christmas Eve. It always takes you back to who you were and how you felt there breathing air you'd never breathed before and couldn't wait to breathe again.

With promises in it. And not the usual stale Catholic ones either as in kept in some golden hazy hereafter. More like promises kept right here and now.

Eggnog.

Angel hair.

Which makes me think of Ula.

I wonder if she's here and do I wish she is. I'm not sure

why. But it suddenly seems like the most important thing in my life to talk to her.

Whoa.

l actually tell myself to talk to Ula.

And I never do that.

Duh right.

I mean I think in different terms. As in let people know. As in write. As in sign.

I don't talk.

I told you so at the very beginning.

When that word flickers by on the grayscale screen upstairs my heart starts racing.

Is it possible.

Signs and portents.

Could it be.

Is getting sick really my body getting ready to talk?

I swallow hard moving my tongue around inside my mouth and stretch my dry lips wide and narrow rubber-band style.

It definitely isn't ready yet.

But somehow nothing's ridiculous about the idea that it might be soon. And I don't panic or anything but suddenly there's a dread about shooting all my words out into the room instead of holding them inside and I don't mean Natty I mean scary. I mean shaky.

Like the first time you ride a bike without training wheels when you're a kid.

Because I do not pass Go I do not collect $200 I immediately start thinking *What will I say?*

And *Watson come in here I need you* is already taken.

So I have to come up with something original. Something for the grandkids. And not only come up with something but turn it over and over in my mind so I don't blow it big time when the moment comes. Though I wouldn't be the first or the worst.

I mean in the world according to the Internet they spent a year probably and no doubt a million bucks figuring out what the first guy on the moon was supposed to say.

That's one small step for a man.

One giant leap for mankind.

But when he touched down on good old luna firma he left out the word *a*. Which basically made the whole thing meaningless and left everyone wondering WTF difference there was between *man* and *mankind*.

I smell the cream puffs getting closer. I can almost taste them on my tongue. And though I don't know what to say to Ula when she carries them in I do know this.

It's strictly an accept-no-substitutes deal. If the first person bearing cream puffs isn't Ula all bets are off. The kid don't talk. Don't ask me why. I just know that's the way it is and it makes me almost overly calm. No more non-Jah dread. I fold my hands together in my lap and wait uncaring like 40 million other Americans who already called the doctor and call him back like clockwork for a refill.

A Prozac a day keeps the demons away.

Makes the waiting ok.

Even waiting for the news of a lifetime.

The end of the world.

AIDS diagnosis.

Plutonium poisoning.

I saw your mommy and your mommy's dead.

I turn my head slowly when I feel footsteps through the floor and who do I see.

Nobody but me.

All of a sudden I'm out of myself and watching myself like a skycam on the ceiling in the corner of the room. Or a floating angel. And maybe I am still drugged. But at least I get to watch myself talking for the first time ever.

Then the cream puffs appear. And it's a first time ever all right. Or make that all wrong.

It's the first time ever I'm disappointed to see Jonnyboy.

He kneels down beside me balancing the plate of cream puffs on the arm of the sofa and puts one hand on my forehead checking for fever while he looks away checking out the porno on the TV screen. His hands are cold from drugs or else I'm hot or maybe both since after I look close into his eyes when he finally turns back toward me I know drugs are definitely in the mix. Because the blues only get that shiny and the whites that bloodshot when he does a needle hit.

But they only stay that way a few minutes. Which I hope means he only did a hit once the cream puffs went into the oven and not before. Since the last time he ran speed then ran into the kitchen he came back out with a plateful of perfect chocolate-chip-and-blue-M&M cookies that smelled even better than they looked but didn't exactly pass the taste test now did they since he used two cups of salt and one teaspoon of sugar instead of the opposite.

He holds two cream puffs out for me one in each hand and mouths *Taste both* and moves one toward my lips and when I close my eyes and take a bite the warm crust outside and cool Reddi Wip inside combine like matches and gasoline no more like matches and rocket fuel to blast me back to being five years old and eating cream puffs in the bakery at Fisherman's Wharf in Monterey with my mom and sisters and brothers while the Coast Guard searched for my grandpa's boat with my dad aboard during that year's hundred-year storm. Then with my eyes still closed I bite the other hand that feeds me and it's smooth slippery chocolate this time. Rich instant pudding. The way they made it at deaf school.

Topped with big blobby peaks of sweet condensed milk that quivered above the compartments of our lunch trays like the Matterhorn overlooking Disneyland during a really bad earthquake.

Which reminds me.

Part 2.

I still don't know if what we felt on the Bay Bridge was just a minor-league quake centered here or the outer limits of the Big One somewhere far away.

Other things I still don't know:

Why I got sick.

What happened afterwards.

Where we are.

Who he is.

Meaning bleach-blond crop top.

I open my eyes.

Asked and answered.

I close my eyes.

Jason.

All those records. This must be his place.

I open them again and catch him watching me and smiling to himself before he looks away. And I do know one thing anywayz.

He likes me.

I'm sure of it and it gives me a shiver of excitement and just like that I'm cured. Recovered. Ready for action. Your own Private Radboy reporting for duty SIR!

Once I take a leak anywayz. I do Lewis and Clark seeking a route up the misery river and they both gesture behind me where a short hallway leads past a door to a kitchen about the size of a walk-in closet. There's no more real estate in sight so I guess the sofa must be Jason's bed. The door opens outwards into the hall and it's obvious why because the bathroom is also closet-sized as in broom closet with a toilet right next to a shower stall. When I finish Jonnyboy's waiting for me in the hall.

—Are you ok?

I fish my notepad out of my pocket.

I think so. Kinda woozy. How'd we end up here anywayz?

fuck dewd, ole Jason saved us bigtime. he was doing a crack delivery to some 1 who works @ that big hotel there when the lights went out. & he was heading towards home across the plaza after finally finding 'em in the dark when he saw me all wall-eyed panicked bending over U all white-faced and going in2 convulsions-like on the pavement. & was i freeked cause people around us were starting 2 notice & there were cops & security everywhere. but Jason cruised up saying i'm Finn & Critter's friend & lemme help & 7 seconds later he was helping me carry U thru the crowd 2 a taxi on market st talking nonstop the whole way & i mean loud about FIRST a banana split THEN fish tacos @ fisherman's wharf THEN three cones of cotton candy @ pier 39 & the most appetizing flavors of course purple pink and green & FINALLY those virgin kamikazes in the Hyatt lobby when the lights went out. so we got by all the concerned citizens no prob then back here he tasted my stash to figure out what went wrong w/you. & am I pissed at my connect down south Bcause that cream of the crack bag i bought in L.A. turned out 2 B Special K mixed w/ junk.

No wonder I got sick. I mean Special K is like a cat tranquilizer and everybody knows you get sick the first time you try junk. It's like with cigarettes. Your body's trying to tell you something.

Same wayz mine's telling me something right now. I'm just not sure what part of my body's giving me this feeling about

Jason that started spreading inside me while I was reading what
Jonnyboy wrote. It's partly in my head and my thoughts I guess
but there's more to it than that and it's not the tight-tied knots
in my guts like before. It's like this new sweet warmth everywhere that I've never felt before.

So when Jonnyboy's asks if I'm SURE I'm ok I'm all *Am I
ever* and make eating gestures like the cream puffs cured me.
Which gets him smiling and he takes the pen and writes:

*kewl with a k. Bcause we gotta get back 2 F & C's & move ahead
with U know what. i guess they been pretty busy overnite there & now
we gotta plan some more + i gotta figure out how 2 break the news 2
roarke. so i'm taking a shower here & then we'll bail but w/ J in a taxi
on his way 2 the Pit, not sk8ing. i want you taking it EZ boy so save yr
strength 4 showtime.*

Back in the living room Jason's sitting on the sofa now and
I don't know what gets into me because what I want to do is
thank him but instead as soon as I sit beside him I point toward
the rigs on the table and back at him with a question in my
eyes.

He shudders and I mean bigtime then does a genuine *No
way never nohow* and with gestures manages to get across that
pretty soon he'll have a hole inside his nose big enough for a
Ubangi-style bone but he'd rather have that any day than holes
in his arms.

The feeling gets stronger.

Deeper.

Like a river grows.

I reach for my notepad to follow through on thank you but
I don't write two words I write four.

Can I kiss you?

We lean toward each other at the same time same slo-mo
speed and somehow I knew already.

How perfectly our lips.

How soft his are.

How melting the warmth how sweet the taste the touch the time together lasts forever.

Even when we leave him all I can think about is.

This.

Is.

It.

What all the poems and all the stories and all the books from in the beginning. What all the duels and fights and even wars.

As soon as we walk through the outside door on Sumner Street Jonnyboy claps his hands over both ears and even before he starts fingerspelling I'm dead sure on the audio algebra as in A plus B equals B plus A. But whatever Abba sounds like there's NFW their songs are the white boy accompaniment to what we see once Finn opens the inside door. In the center of the mirror table and spilling over the edges onto newspapers spread on the floor is a volcano of black powder. Sections of gray steel and shiny black PVC pipe lay scattered on the newspapers every which way like pickup sticks. Ula has a hacksaw in her hand and waves it over her head when she sees me. Critter picks up two threaded steel disks from the tabletop and holds them in front of his eyes doing *See no evil* until Finn takes charge and repositions them on either side of his chest like robot nipples.

Next to Critter on the floor is a heavy cardboard spindle of dark green waxy-looking cord. The big cone of powder has a waxy shine too. It doesn't look like powder at all. More like tiny chunks of charred wood from a beach fire that went out from the damp in the air before it could burn to ashes. The smell is partly sulfur partly tar partly something weird and oily almost peppery. I take a handful and let it sift back down between my fingers. It looks so much heavier than it feels. I stare at a couple of pieces still sticking to my palm and think *Somebody Chinese invented this stuff a long time ago*.

In the world according to *True Facts* on the back of Instant Quaker Oats anywayz.

Then my eyes focus past my hand on maybe a dozen sheets of paper covered with small print fanned across the seat of the chair at the far end of the table. And the strangest thing happens when I walk over and pick one up and start reading. I get this craving for a cigarette and look around for a pack on autopilot until it hits me and I mean right between the eyes that I don't smoke and never have.

To the Ownership, Management
and Staff of Tejon Holdings
You have waged war on Planet Earth.
You have killed.

You have destroyed life of age and enormity beyond your comprehension. Your nominal support of environmental protection has been without substance and effect. In refusing to recognize the gravity and immorality of your actions, you have lent your tacit support to all crimes against Nature. You have not acted, communicated, or proved in any other way the validity or sincerity of your statements that the Headwaters Forest of Coastal Redwoods deserves care and concern.

We are aware of your crimes.

You have helped construct the killing machine of our economy. To those of you who consider yourselves to be environmentalists, working for change from within, we say this: We will not respect you. You have shown none for the life your organization is now killing. In refusing opposition, you have legitimized that which you claim to oppose. You too will feel the war you have conspired in creating.

You have perhaps defended those who will not be inconvenienced and co-opted those who care, but you will no longer control our rage.

HERE IS YOUR WAR
THIS IS REAL
THIS IS OUR FUCKING RAGE

I've got goose bumps afterwards I swear. It's so hard-core. It reads so scary. Which is perfect. Because you can't write something like that unless you believe it in a place inside that nothing can touch. Nothing can change. Not even fear. And Ula's probably the only one of us who has that place. It's weird because at first I tell myself it's like a stranger wrote this. A scary stranger but a hella strong one. Then I realize it's really the opposite. It's totally Ula one thousand percent. And I know one thing after seeing the evidence on paper like this. I want to be the same. I want to be that pure. I never want to be a stranger to myself.

Like most people are.

And I know something else. It wasn't all a dream last night having Finn for a brother in the old Wild West. Because I've got him for a brother now. And Critter too. And Ula for a sister. And I made it happen.

All of this was my idea.

We're putting the pipe bombs in the Hobart Building tonight.

In the world according to Ula.

Because the cleaners won't be there.

Because timing isn't everything when it comes to bombs.

It's the only thing. And the timer on ours is a Mrs. Olsen special. As in Finn and Critter's coffeemaker. Which has a clock you can set so you're not waiting for your morning java like the rest of the wonderful modern world. Instead it's fresh and hot delight before your eyes as soon as they're open. And the wires that make it happen get hot enough to fire fuses.

Fifteen fuses.

Two BC and thirteen AP.

As in *Before Chronicle*. As in *After Plastic*. Because what happened last night once they dropped Jonnyboy and me off and came back here is that Finn and Critter went to work filling pipes with powder and capping them off while Ula started cutting letters out of the newspaper for the Roarke ransom note. Then she suddenly threw down the *Chronicle* and totally flipped out screaming *Stop! Don't Move!* and in the world according to Finn her face went white as a goth's in line outside Death Guild at the Terminator.

It was a story about a pipe bomb found on some playground in Japantown and Ula hit the panic button when she got to a quote from a cop about how they suspected juveniles.

Since whoever made it used steel pipe.

Which is hella dangerous from genesis ground zero let alone underneath the slide where they found it since just screwing on the end caps could squeeze out sparks inside the pipe and make any snot-nosed junior anarchists in the vicinity go boom boom permanent bye bye.

So Ula looked over at Critter who just happened to be threading the second steel end cap onto a length of pipe that was already drilled for a fuse and filled with powder and talk about *Shock! Horror!*

Still they took it in stride and just looked up the nearest twenty-four-hour Home Depot out in South San Francisco and went on a night-owl run for PVC pipe. And are we all laughing now about getting safety tips on building bombs from the boyz in am I blue.

Or are we. I glance over at Jonnyboy and realize I'm wrong. His lips are making a closed-mouth rubber-band shaped smile but his eyes aren't in it.

In the world according to Jonnyboy tonight's not necessarily the night.

In the world according to Jonnyboy this is all so sudden.

What about reconnaissance.

What about the run-through.

What about.

Disguises.

A diversion.

Ula starts waving her hands in the air but she isn't slinging sign. The color rises in her cheeks and she tosses her long loose blond hair from side to side and does she look like St. Joan in the color painting in the back of my grandpa's Bible. Or wait I know she looks ready for the bow of a Viking ship. And no not the cruise line.

She.

Also.

Looks.

Tweeked.

I catch Critter's eye and press my thumb against one nostril and inhale nodding in Ula's direction. And he's all *Oh yeah bigtime* grinning and doing the talk talk talk thing beating four cupped fingers against his thumb. While Ula tears into the talk talk talk thing in real time aimed at Jonnyboy who serves it right back while her lips are still moving until pretty soon Finn and Critter are watching them Wimbledon style with their heads pivoting back and forth in unison.

It would be pretty funny if they didn't both look so serious and if it weren't for the black bombs stacked up like Lincoln Logs between two milk crates full of records behind Ula. Because there's nothing funny and nothing pretty about bombs.

They're ugly.

This is real.

They're scary.

This is our fucking rage.

All of this was my idea.

It's not second thoughts I'm having so much as different thoughts.

I wish I wasn't here right now watching Jonnyboy and Ula argue.

I hate family arguments.

I wish I was with Jason.

Kissing him.

And more.

My foot kicks something heavy under the mirror table and at first I figure it's one of the abandoned steel pipes. But it turns out to be *Webster's Unabridged.* And that reminds me. The word that Finn couldn't explain for me.

Camp.

I hoist the dictionary up onto my lap and remember how my grandpa who never learned English too well bought a section of *Webster's* every week for like two years at Safeway and joined them in this rad fake leather binder a foot thick I swear and gave it to me the year I started deaf school when I was too little to even pick it up and had my mom write on the title page I'd find everything I needed in life inside I just had to look for it. But it turns out he was wrong because though some of the definitions are pretty kewl with a k like *To strive with others in doing anything, e.g. drinking* and *To kick (a per-*

son) like a football none of them come anywherez close to explaining how Critter could seem more kweer than Finn.

Which is definitely something I need to know in life and it's missing in action. But which also turns into yesterday's news as soon as I notice another definition right above camp and is it the consolation prize in the Cracker Jacks box.

Camorra. A secret society of lawless malcontents in Naples and Neopolitan cities. Hence Camorrism, the principles or practice of this society; lawlessness, anarchy. Camorrist, a member of a camorra.

It hits me like a bolt of lightning. Makes the hair on the back of my neck stand up like a mohawk and my heart drop deep in my stomach and roll around useless like the silver ball when you tilt the table. Because here it is. The missing piece that fits below *This is our fucking rage.*

The Camorrist International.

I letter it at the bottom and show it to Finn then point to the definition in the dictionary. And in less time than it takes a supercomputer to add two and two he says something that stops both Jonnyboy and Ula. They look at me then at each other and finally come around the table and check out the dictionary and what I wrote at the bottom of the flyer. Then the next thing you know everyone's pounding me on the back and rubbing my head and we're huddled over *Webster's* trying to figure out if our unanimous vote to found the Band of Five Cell of the Camorrist International means we've done it by acclamation or exclamation.

Which isn't all we voted on though I didn't know it at the time. We all decided to cut off debate and let me decide.

About tonight.

Since Finn's with Jonnyboy.

And Critter's with Ula.

Two against two.

So I break the tie and vote to put the bombs in Tejon Holdings tonight. Or try anywayz even if we fail. Not because Ula's already cracked on and won't be able to sleep tonight so hey ho let's go. And not because her sister's funeral is two days from now and she wants to nab Roarke that day.

Because the bombs are already made. And you don't keep pipe bombs sitting around the house any longer than necessary. Especially when you're a drug dealer with all sorts of people coming and going. All sorts of people coming and going and getting careless with butane mini-torches.

Plus because the sooner we do it the less time for second thoughts. Which means the sooner we do it the more likely we actually WILL do it.

And because even if Jonnyboy's fears come true and the keys I snagged don't work or there's witnesses we don't expect or some emergency 2:00 A.M. board meeting in Tejon Holdings it won't hold us back from what matters most. Which is saving the redwoods. And which is what the plan with Roarke is all about. This is really just laying a foundation. So when the ransom note comes along followed a couple days later by a photo of Roarke with a newspaper in front of him proving we really did nab him all right they'll snap to attention in the Hobart Building as in Yes SIR how high SIR.

They'll have to. Even if Tejon Holdings doesn't go boom tonight. So we don't need any delays. What we need is a place to hide Roarke and a gun to hold to his head for the ransom photo. But those things can wait. A least a little. What we need that can't wait if we're Hobart Building–bound tonight are walkie-talkies. Because we do need lookouts. Once we get up to the fifteenth floor we'll need somebody to hold the elevator there while the deed is done. Partly to make a fast get-away to the second or third floor where we'll switch to the stairs down to Montgomery Street. And partly to make sure nobody gets off the elevator on the fifteenth floor while we're brewing up the Mrs. Olsen special wake-up blend inside Tejon Holdings. That person needs to be in contact with whoever's inside the office.

And also with who isn't. Because even though the Hobart Building's an office not apartment building and it's long after business hours it only makes sense to have someone watching for unexpected trouble.

As in police cars converging or helicopters approaching in case there's a silent alarm.

And what better place to watch from than the same place on the roof where Alice takes her lunch breaks.

The Promenade.

I remember looking up there. And you can bet it's got the kill view of every street on every side of the building.

Plus Jonnyboy's sure the roof has to be accessible 24/7. As in unlocked. As in required by law.

In case of fire.

Heh heh heh.

Say Ula's on the roof. Finn's in the elevator. Critter's watching the fire stairs on the long shot somebody gets tired of waiting for the stalled elevator and starts up on foot. Jonnyboy and me are in Tejon Holdings attaching the fuses to the coffeemaker heating element and setting the timer to go off two hours later and reminding each other to plug the damn thing in before we leave.

That means four walkie-talkies.

Ula can stop at G.I. Joe's on Market Street on her way back to her sister's apartment. She pulls her black beret on and signs that she has to leave to spend the rest of the day working on funeral arrangements.

Jonnyboy has to leave to try and connect the dot dot dots with Roarke.

Finn and Critter have to leave to work at the Pit.

That leaves your boy Radboy on his own until the Camorrist International reconvenes at 2400 hours.

To hold the fort.

Baby-sit the bombs.

Which suddenly look even scarier.

But not to worry in the world according to Finn. Because I have nothing to fear but fear itself.

Ten points if I know who said it first.

I don't.

Hint: President ———.

Soundz like one of the dead Kennedys I guess.

Wrong. More like one of the dead ———.

I give up.

Roosevelts.

And I'm all kewl with a k. Because though I didn't know the second President Roosevelt said that I know a lot about him. I've even been to his house. Not the White House though. Last year this dewd Rob in the Big Brother program in Monterey took me to the secret hideout they built for Roosevelt down in Big Sur during the war in case the Germans invaded the East Coast and took over Washington I guess. And though the house was basically finished right down to draperies being hung there isn't any carpet or furniture or appliances because they just stopped working on it and never came back and the reason they stopped was that Roosevelt died.

Hardly anyone knows about the house today. It's high up in the hills overlooking the ocean inside a state park but it's hidden away closed to the public and far from any roads so it's never been trashed. Plus the outside's all steel from scrapped car bodies so it's lasted just like new and basically everything's still the way it was the day he died with just some water damage from the flat roof leaking and mouse and rat shit here and there but not even much of that.

Rob found out about the place because he was an environmental planner and worked on the master plan for the park which meant he had to see everything. Jonnyboy found out about it because I ran it all by him and we always planned to check it out together but we never had a way to get there. And Finn and Critter and Ula find out about it because when I write a note to Finn describing the place Jonnyboy starts reading it over my shoulder and then he's grabbing me hard nodding *Yes Yes Yes* at least triple quadruple time when I look up at him with his eyes questioning mine to be sure I understand him and do I.

A place to hide Roarke.

A gun to hold to his head for the ransom photo.

One down. One to go. Put 'er there Radboy.

Only when I hold my hands out palms up Critter grabs my wrists from behind and wrestles me to the floor. I'm about to keep him from tickling me which I figure is the next item on the agenda when Finn's hands enter the picture holding the spindle of fuse cord. Then Jonnyboy's hands follow unreeling it and wrapping it around my chest again and again with my arms pinned behind me throw-him-in-the-trunk-and-dump-him-in-the-woods style.

So I go into kiddie tantrum mode pounding my heels on the floor until Critter gets my ankles bound and the three of them drag me over to the front door and prop me up against it with Ula standing in front of us laughing and fumbling with

Finn's Polaroid. But when she holds it up to her eye Jonnyboy jumps up with his palm flat out like a traffic cop and races back toward the bedroom while Finn writes something with a marker on the back of a pizza box.

I know Jonnyboy isn't moving in slo-mo when he comes back into the room but it definitely seems that way. Maybe it's the toy gun in his hand and the way he stands there a second frozen next to Ula with her blond hair spilling out from her black beret.

It's another movie.

Ultra slo-mo.

She's Bonnie.

He's Clyde.

Suddenly I go Alaska inside imagining really being kidnapped by people who might hurt or even kill me. But of course it won't be real.

Roarke's kidnapping I mean.

It's those words on the flyer confusing me. They're giving me goose bumps. I can't get them out of my mind.

This is real.

This is our fucking rage.

And seeing it this way I'm looking at the picture developing even before it's taken with the details emerging like events in dense fog and the first detail is how words have been cut out from headlines of the newspaper Jonnyboy holds in his other hand and the second detail is what Finn wrote on the pizza cardboard.

Save those trees or we'll shoot this boy.

TEN

I fall asleep on Finn and Critter's bed after everybody bails and it's almost midnight when I wake up. I know they're back from feeling different kinds of vibrations from different parts of the apartment. And I just lay here thinking about *Save Those Trees or We'll Shoot This Boy* and wondering what's in it for Roarke and I keep coming up with less than zero. I mean maybe he does owe Jonnyboy but does he owe him that much? Because afterwards he'll have to lie like a MF to the boyz in blue and maybe even take a polygraph test. Leastwayz he would in the world according to *Dragnet*. And talk about no fun.

It just doesn't add up. But what do I know.

Asked and answered.

I know tweekers are unpredictable.

The first rule is There are no rules.

Anything can happen.

Only Roarke's not a tweeker. Not anymore. He's about the only person I know right now who isn't doing speed. I wonder how long Jason.

I get to his name and I go back into that kiss. I close my eyes and the kiss goes on. It's funny how it doesn't seem new and exciting though but like something that's always been part of me since genesis ground zero. Something old.

Maybe it's me that's getting old.

Old enough I mean.

Though still not old enough to buy a Magic Marker.

Use a pen go to juvee.

Which is the moral of the story on Jonnyboy's lips that I start reading as soon as he comes in with orders to rise and shine. What happened is he bought this kewl pistol off a black dewd on the street in the Tenderloin who pointed him toward a corner liquor store when he asked him where he could score some ammo and was he stoked when he walked up to the register first to find a waterproof Magic Marker to black in the gouges on his boots from those granite curbs on Market Street and second when the cashier behind the bulletproof glass just looked I'm so bored and slid the ammunition toward the pass-through.

But then he asked for ID.

And was Jonnyboy spooked and ready to bail until he saw a sign taped to the glass and realized they were proofing him for the pen.

Ula can't believe it. She comes in with Critter and they stand on either side of Jonnyboy next to the bed. They're both wearing rubber gloves. She's all *Talk about the pen is mightier than*. It makes her want to learn the words to "God Bless America." Which Critter starts to teach her since it's permanently anchored like a sailor's tattoo to the hit parade in Pumpkin Center.

But Critter and Jonnyboy start arguing over the lyrics when he gets to *Stand beside her and guide her with the light from a bulb*.

Because Jonnyboy thinks the song was written before electricity and it's supposed to be *light from above*.

Which makes me sit up in bed with my own lightbulb switching on hella bright. As in the virtual one floating in comic-book space above my head. The one as in one-and-only that doesn't depend on electricity.

Unlike our plan for bombing Tejon Holdings using an ELECTRIC coffeemaker for a timer. Which we coincidentally drew up after the longest power outage since Loma Prieta. And I mean right after.

But I figure what the hey and just get up and get dressed and help wrap the bombs in newspaper and load them into two backpacks. While we're doing it I notice everyone keeps looking at the kitchen clock with identical unmoving expressions as in jaws set and mouths closed. And I catch myself doing it too. Like we're all waiting on dentist appointments and the sweaty little folded and refolded cards in our pockets don't read *Teeth Cleaning* either. They read *Root Canal*.

So I try to get the don't worry get happy vibe on the frequency by taking out my notepad and calling for a run-through of "God Bless America" while we're loading the coffeemaker and flashlights and walkie-talkies into backpack number three. And I mean the light from a bulb version because three words are all I don't have to say about that coffeemaker.

Batteries not included.

As in tonight's definitely not the night for another power outage so we better pray there's lightbulbs burning bright till the dawn's early light or else the Electrical Parade is canceled on Main Street USA.

And we do a killer version of it too. As in Hellen Killer. As in how does she sing and play the piano at once.

She plays with one hand.

Sings with the other.

Ula starts signing along with me and the boyz join in too and why not. Sure they don't know sign but they don't know the words to the song either. Leastwayz not all of them. Still it looks pretty funny and for some reason it reminds me of learning "This Land Is Your Land" in sign in fourth grade and performing it on Parents' Day with my deaf friend Shredder who later moved away to Texas.

All of it. Every verse. The teacher played the piano so our parents knew the tune. But they didn't know all the words. That song has a lot of words. Some pretty radical ones I found out later.

But that was then. And this is now. And what's happening now is the music stops for everyone but me. Though relax your mind it isn't the power going off.

This isn't Memorex.

This is real.

What's going off is the made-in-China panda timer in the kitchen telling us it's time to do the same. And do we. With Ula at the wheel and the keys to Tejon Holdings on a chain around my neck. With the heavy backpacks filled with pipe bombs on the backseat floor in front of Jonnyboy and Ula and the lighter one with the Mrs. Olsen special on my lap between them.

With the stamped addressed envelopes with the flyers for

the media stashed under the passenger seat up front inside a plastic bag.

With plastic in our pockets too. As in enough pairs of disposable gloves for a manic panic party on Poly Styrene's birthday.

This is real.

Before we left we sponged every square inch of the bombs and coffeemaker with soapy water to ruin any fingerprints we might have accidentally made and that's when it started getting very real. It got more real afterwards moistening the flaps of the envelopes and the backs of the stamps with the corner of the sponge instead of licking them and leaving traces of DNA.

But now it seems less real for some reason. Maybe it's all of us riding in the car together again. It feels like leaving on a family vacation which is definitely unreal. Or maybe it's just that I'm sitting in the middle and can't really see where we are so I'm deprived of two senses and basically running on empty as far as reality anywayz.

Still I can't shake it even after we park and walk two blocks in the fresh night air to the Hobart Building and don't see a soul on the way there. The *Mtgmry entr* clamgun key works just fine 'cause it's all mine and forget crack it's adrenaline alone that powers us past fourteen count 'em landings in the dim concrete-walled stairwell. When we get to the door marked *15* we all kind of hold our breath then I pull on gloves and open the pack and hand walkie-talkies to Ula and Critter and Finn and Finn hands me his heavy pack in return. Then Ula starts climbing on toward the roof and Critter opens the door for Jonnyboy and Finn and me.

And does it look creepy on the other side like something out of *The X-Files* with the corridor barely lit by cold gray-green light seeping through the venetian blinds on all the windowed office doors. But I'm not even worried and suddenly realize why it doesn't seem real.

Because it's so easy.

Which makes me want to smack myself upside thinking *Signs and portents* and *Why am I surprised?* I mean remember how I got the keys. If there's somebody up there he either likes you or strikes you and I know one thing he's smiling at me.

So even though I can feel Jonnyboy tensing up beside me after we leave Finn stationed at the elevator and walk to the unmarked Tejon Holdings door I'm all *whoever whatever have a nice day*. I know in seven seconds we'll walk right in and do we.

Once we're inside I feel ten feet tall and proud of it. Like that general in the Civil War I think who said *I shall return* and did. But when I shine the light back on Jonnyboy he's kind of hunched over like he's trying to look as small as possible. It must be the crack. The paranoia I mean.

I lead the way swinging my flashlight from side to side just above floor level looking for an outlet. One thing Finn learned in Northern Ireland I guess and reminded us a couple of times in the car as in repeat after me is *The more confined the area the more forceful the blast* so instead of out in the reception area we decide to put the bombs back here in the hallway by the private offices.

They're all locked of course though I hold the light while Jonnyboy tries the outer door key in every lock just in case. His hand is shaking and I can't help thinking *Are you that scared*. So to put him more at ease I act out that a hubcap told me tomorrow morning the suits won't need keys to get into their offices because the word on the street is Tejon Holdings is switching to the open plan.

But no sale. He just mouths —Hurry.

The outlet's conveniently located at the far end of the corridor between the big corner office and the conference room Roarke's brother Heath walked out of with all those redwood-killer yes-men. And talk about so far so good. There's walls and doors on three sides. The ceiling's pretty low.

Compression.

Expansion.

Explosion.

I'm thinking like a radical now all right.

This is real.

This is our fucking rage.

And this is when I start getting scared. Combining Ula's words in my head with the bombs on the floor. They looked gnarly enough back at the Greenery but somehow the other surroundings like the aquarium and the Abba records and all the crack paraphernalia sort of took away from the full impact. Here on the soft peach carpet the bombs look black and menacing as Darth Vader's mask. In the captioned *Star Wars* it always reads *[heavy breathing]* whenever he's talking. And that's what I'm doing while I lay them out in two neat rows and tiptoe back between them to hold the fuse ends for Jonnyboy while he wraps them one by one around the bared wire of the coffeemaker heating element.

Wearing the gloves makes it no fun at all and *Damn! Fuck!* is flying and now beads of sweat off Jonnyboy's upper lip are actually dripping into the guts of the machine which makes me think of *We're the poison* but also makes me wonder if DNA survives explosions and fire. The reason Jonnyboy's hyperventilating practically is because he can't figure out how to set the mode switch on the digital readout to *am* or *pm* and I guess this is what they mean by black comedy with the deconstructed Mr. Coffee and the homemade bombs and raggedy fuses and Jonnyboy almost in tears because he can't work the little rubber buttons on the back of the machine that must be designed for elf fingers I swear.

But I wouldn't laugh out loud even if I could it isn't that kind of funny.

I just kneel down and gently move Jonnyboy's hand away and press the buttons until both the time display and the brew-master readout show *am* instead of *pm* with coffee set to brew at 4:30 which is five minutes less than two hours from now. And Jonnyboy looks at me all *Isn't that amazing it slices it dices* like I'm the kindergarten kid who programs the VCR his parents can't get past flashing high noon 24/7.

But it turns out to be what Finn calls a premature ejaculation of congratulation because the red *Set* light is blinking instead of staying lit continuously and that usually means something needs attention. Just like your typical user-unfriendly flashing VCR. At least to me anywayz because to Jonnyboy it means mission accomplished boy we're ready to bail.

I explain why I'm worried with gestures and face moves and it takes longer than it would to write it out but Jonnyboy finally gets it and just looks disgusted and nervous and impatient and then starts pacing so I know I'm on my own. I look over all the setting buttons and double press a couple but nothing happens. And it's my turn to be all *D* as in *Damn!* and *F* as in *Fuck!* because we made coffee using the timer back at the Greenery so I know the sucker works.

I wonder if some wires that we stripped the insulation from are touching which is actually a scary thought and scary turns to terrifying when I pick the coffeemaker up by the base where the carafe sits and the *Set* light stops blinking and just glows defcon 3 red alert red. It seems like the brightest thing this side of a Coleman lantern on a dark and stormy night and for a second I wish I had shades and then I set it back down as gently as I can considering my hands are shaking harder than a politician's at a county fair. Harder than Ole Fatman's finger moving slo-mo to raise his ragtop. And now the joke's on me for thinking he'd be shopping for Attends after his close encounter of the Jonnyboy kind because I was one-seventh of a second away from defiling my own drawers when that light flashed on like one of those giant red suns out past Alpha Centauri somewherez.

But when I let go of it the blinking starts up again. At first I think it's some kind of levelling device so the coffeemaker won't start heating if there's been an earthquake and it's tilted back against the wall or something. But that isn't it. I go through the same motions twice more with the same results and I can feel the vibrations from Jonnyboy's pacing getting stronger and stronger and my own sweat flowing faster and faster but nowhere near as fast as my blood. Plus my tongue is hanging out and I realize I'm panting.

With fear.

And forget about rules to live by it's fight or flight taking over now and it hits me and feels like the greatest kiss in the world like the Jason kiss I swear that if I turn to Jonnyboy all *Shine let's bail* he'll race me to the door.

The door.

The cool fresh air in the soft gray-green light.

I tense the muscles in my calves to spring up from my knees.

Flight.

If only I could stay just a little bit longer.

Fight.

One last cigarette with Dad.

Too much pressure.

No.

Not enough pressure.

There's a pressure switch under the base so you don't get hot coffee spewing all over if you forget to put the carafe in place before you go to bed. You don't get any coffee period. Which is not what the doctor ordered for the Camorrist International even though we left the carafe behind as excess baggage. And neither is disconnecting the wires to the pressure switch not at this late hour with possible unforeseen consequences and I mean major ones.

I look around for some substitute weight to put on the base. Nothing with us or on us would be safe to leave though Jonnyboy's crack pipe would definitely muddy the headwaters if there was anything left of it. Then God bless America as in the light from a brain bulb because I remember the Garfield paperweight on Alice's desk.

I signal wait one minute to Jonnyboy who's wound tighter than Joan of Arc around the stake with the flames licking closer and sure enough it's right where I saw it last and I run it back like it's a baton in a relay for Olympic gold.

And now it's a virtual carafe.

And the red light's glowing in the dark at the end of the corridor tunnel and I mean by its lonesome.

Because Jonnyboy and me are already out the door and I'm turning the keys while Jonnyboy runs toward Finn who's standing in the open elevator and already on the walkie-talkie to Ula and Critter. And seven seconds later Critter's running out the fire-stair door and then toward the rest of us waiting in the elevator.

Which seems slower than Grandma's molasses on sandpaper going up to the twenty-second floor to pick up Ula. Jonnyboy stands with his legs spread apart and his forehead

pressed against the fake woodgrain back wall which he's drum-
ming with his knuckles. Finn gives me a big wink and a
thumbs-up and I try to smile back but it doesn't even work
because I feel like Jonnyboy I guess like I'm trapped in a cell
or something. And when the fluorescent light inside the plastic
ceiling panel gives the tiniest flicker it pushes my power-outage
panic button and I mean totally turning my sweat glands on
like faucets again thinking of being stuck in here while the city
sleeps and the timer's not ticking then nabbed like fish in a
barrel when security makes the early-morning rounds. It freeks
me so much that when we finally see Ula I'm all *Can we talk?*
as in *Maybe we should take the stairs down just in case and I
don't mean the last two flights I mean all twenty-two.*

Which Ula translates looking all WTF and Finn and Jonnyboy just veto thumbs-down *NFW.* Finn rubs my head with
one hand while he stabs the 3 button with the other and the
elevator starts the long crawl down. He keeps his head-rubbing
hand on the back of my neck and is it cold as in Nanook of
the North by Northwest cold as in Mickey's daddy cryogenic
cold and I want to take it in my own hand and one stop it
from sending chills down my spine and two warm it up but
hello in there I realize my own blood's running just slightly
warmer than the Yukon River in ice-fishing season so I just
stand here doing nothing and waiting for the lights on the buttons to change.

Then we're all running feet pounding through the third-
floor hallway in the creepy light and barreling though the doorway to the fire stairs and hurtling down three at a time until
we stop short at the bottom and catch our breath before.

Slowly carefully calmly.

Walking out into the damp cool night air that.

Tastes like freedom.

Once we're on Montgomery Street a few taxis cruise by but no cop cars or bomb squad units or anything to get our pulses going and when we get to the Valiant Ula motions for me to ride shotgun while the boyz all climb into the back and kind of collapse against each other with their eyes closed without saying anything. Ula looks in the rearview mirror then glances over at me and winks. She doesn't even look tired herself. And I can tell it doesn't have anything to do with crack either. I guess she's high on rebellion like that Patti Smith song.

I feel high too but in a different way than Ula. At first while we're driving to the post office to drop off the media letters I'm not exactly sure what the difference is but I know it's there because I don't have all her beliefs or someone to get revenge for like her sister. But then I realize I do have someone.

Period.

Jason.

Which is really why I feel high. Not because we just bombed the Hobart Building.

And I can't get him off my mind once Jonnyboy mails the letters and Ula drops us off at the Greenery on her way back to her sister's where she'll be anonymously calling TV and newspapers in a couple of hours and playing the deliberately distorted microcassette tape message she made while I was sleeping earlier. So after Finn and Critter go to bed and Jonnyboy's sawing logs on the sofa I almost think I'm hallucinating when I see Jason's name on a flyer for the Endup on the refrigerator door. But it's Jason all right and tonight's the night or this morning's the morning actually because he's spinning from two to six.

So he's only four or five blocks away. Right now. And even though I know I can't get in I'm outta here.

The streets are deserted except for a couple of middle-aged guys like my dad on the corner of Seventh and Folsom with no shirts on and those leather chaps that show your butt if you're not wearing underwear which fortunately they are. They check me out all hubba hubba when I skate by and one of them says something too which makes me thank Jesus Mary and Joseph I'm deaf so I don't even have to pretend to ignore it. I just push off harder than usual from the curb at the light and speed up until I turn right from Folsom onto Sixth Street and there's the Endup two blocks away with a knot of people standing on the corner and taxis parked with lights on waiting.

At first I convince myself it's kewl with a k even if I can't go inside. Because one at least I'm close to Jason and two I can check out all the people coming and going which is hella better than lots of entertainment you have to pay money to see. So for what seems like at least an hour I just lean against a parking meter on the other side of Sixth Street watching pairs of boyz walking out the Endup side door and down the sidewalk then ducking into an alley and coming back out five minutes later arranging their clothes. But finally it gets to me and I decide to check out the escape route stairs that zigzag down one of the huge concrete pillars supporting the freeway deck right next to the solid wood fence around the Endup patio.

I mean I can't take a cold shower so cold air will have to do.

So I cross the street and monkey-climb the ten-foot-high chain-link fence guarding *State Highway Property Trespassing Punishable by Law* and start up the stairs which are steep and narrow with a rusty cable handrail. Plus everything's hella fore-shortened from below because the freeway is seriously higher than I thought and by the time I clear the top of the billboard blocking my view of the Endup patio I'm a little dizzy and don't really want to go any farther. It's so far down I can't identify anyone let alone see into the DJ booth inside like I hoped. Plus there's so many people moving around on the patio I couldn't keep track of anyone very long if I did see somebody I recognize.

It's like another world down there. All these people wide-awake and partying nonstop while the city sleeps. From here I can see it's just a tiny world. A postage stamp of flashing lights and moving bodies surrounded all sides every direction with old dark dead wood brick concrete steel glass. All the lights out there are stationary. Nothing moves except the rarest car lights on distant empty streets.

But inside that world down below everything's in motion and it must seem big enough to live your whole life there because so many people do I swear. It's never-never land really. The way you think it will be when you grow up someday and can do whatever you want eat ice cream for breakfast Lucky Charms for dinner stay up all night every night so you don't miss anything. And maybe that's why the only thing standing still down there is time. Because however old they are and some are even forty they're all waiting to grow up and putting off everything until they do and what do they call themselves.

Club kids.

It spooks me. It seemed so kewl with a k that first time at the Pit. I think it would bore me though. I know it would without the drugs. Because it's so small and the real world is so big.

And just when I'm looking at the buildings downtown and thinking even if it's big and glassy you can always try to find a bloody rock I see moving lights out of the corner of my eye and look back down but they're not flashing white strobes from the dance floor inside the Endup.

They're not flashing white strobes in time to the music Jason's spinning.

They're flashing red lights on the wide street in front of it.

Fire engine lights. Three fast sets of them rocketing toward downtown. Toward Market Street. Toward the Hobart Building.

And do I wish I could hear the sirens. Do I wish I could ride along like I've wished ever since I was a kid and never have.

And I don't know.

I wish.

I may.

I wish.

I might.

But I know one thing.

I'm not just wishing.

I'm not just hoping.

I'm not waiting till I grow up.

Not even to get into the Endup. Because when the fog suddenly starts swirling in so thick I can barely see the other side of Sixth Street and my teeth are chattering faster than the tweekers sitting on the benches around the patio below I head back down the stairs and there he is five feet in front of me standing alone on the sidewalk smoking a cigarette in front of a door I didn't even know was there.

Jason flashes me this wide little-boy grin with the green sparks in his eyes dancing two hundred beats per minute before he looks away like he always does but even though he looks away he doesn't move away and I mean no not even. Instead he comes over and takes my hand in his and warms it inside the front pocket of his baggy brown corduroys. I'm not embarrassed or anything but that doesn't mean I'm not shaking inside. I like Jason so much. There's something about him. I squeeze his hand hard and try not to make him self-conscious by catching his eye or anything so I'm just looking straight ahead with my own Grand Canyon–wide grin and then he takes our hands out of his pocket but doesn't let go and leads me though the door.

It's so dark inside at first it makes the Pit look like high noon in *Death Valley Days*. I have to stop moving as soon as the door closes behind me. I can't see anything at all except a galaxy of flashing red and green mini-lights at eye level a few feet ahead. Then Jason puts his hands on my shoulders all *stay where you are* and bit by bit my eyes adjust enough to see we're in the DJ booth which is just above the heads of the dancers on the floor below and lit only by the level meters on what looks like a whole low wall of electronics. I can see the dark outline of Jason's hands putting headphones over his ears then he kneels down rummaging in a box on the floor for something that fits in one hand when he finds it. He stands back up and moves toward the wall with his body blocking out most of the meters so I'm basically blind again and that plus the thump of the bass vibrating every molecule of air around me keeps me from realizing he's coming back toward me until his eyes and his lips are six inches from mine.

Jason pulls his stocking cap off with one hand and takes my hand with the other and rests it on his fresh-shaved head. It's not what stops us from kissing though when we lean our heads toward one another. We're forehead to forehead looking into each other's eyes and reading dictionaries full of words in this private language nobody else could translate and then at the exact same moment we're not just forehead to forehead we're all-head to all-head rubbing each other up down turnaround please don't let me hit the ground neck to ear to throat to chin the hollows curves the grain of hair against it with it over under sideways down. Like silk like bristles feathers velvet new-mown grass.

Eyes closed. Each single hair a distant star a warming sun a thousand million points of light.

And heat.

His heat. This heat. Our heat.

There's a high bench attached to the wall behind us by the door and still nuzzling each other we boost ourselves up with our legs dangling down feet off the floor. Only our heads are touching and the only skin showing below our necks is on our hands gripping the edge of the benches while our necks and shoulders dip and arc and rotate rolling side to side. But are we naked making love and there's no need to make it last it lasts on its own like the tide of the ocean like the beating of our hearts. It goes on and on and I mean for like an hour because that's how long the tape is. The tape of himself spinning somewhere else that he cued as soon as we got here. The tape with rhythms I'll remember for the rest of my life. The tape that teaches me something I never knew before.

Shows me something,

As in I'm not waiting till I grow up but I know what I want to be when I do.

A DJ.

Like Jason.

I.

Like.

Jason.

He likes me.

Nothing else really matters. Not even the early-bird news complete with captions that I watch on the monitor hanging over the bar below while Jason collects his records. I lean over the wall at the end of the booth just in time to catch the last few close-up seconds of firemen in yellow moon-man suits running into the lobby of the Hobart Building. Then a long shot with the camera aiming high and pulling back to show clouds of smoke pumping out of broken upper-floor windows.

Clouds so thick and black even against the nighttime sky that the dull orange glow inside only shows when a gust of wind whips them suddenly away. Then another billow of smoke repaints the picture black and the reversed-out caption scrolls across the screen in white.

A five-alarm blaze early this morning gutted an entire floor of the historic Hobart Building in downtown San Francisco. No one was hurt in the fire, which spread through offices on the building's 15th floor and caused extensive smoke damage above and below before it was extinguished by firefighters using high-pressure hoses. Fire investigators said faulty wiring was the probable cause.

My eyes stay lid-locked on the screen and when the announcer reappears I'm mentally writing my own caption before the real one starts to scroll.

But telephone calls made to news media including this station while firefighters were still arriving on the scene said the blaze was set by a radical environmental group protesting the impending logging of giant redwoods in Northern California's Headwaters Forest . . .

And does reality bite and I mean literally and I mean never harder because what Mr. Blowdry Gelmousse is actually saying kicks off with:

There's a new plan to catch that pesky alligator who escaped from San Francisco Zoo to put the fear of jaws in boaters on Stowe Lake in Golden Gate Park.

And talk about jaws. If I wasn't deaf already I would be now from the sound of mine slamming to the floor like a pile driver bound for China the hard way. But then I realize that Ula probably fell asleep and didn't make the calls so the question authorities won't get the word until the post office delivers *This Is Real*. Which I saw Jonnyboy drop into the mailbox with my very own eyes. So Ula screwing up just delays everything a little and that's fine with me. Because instead of spending the day getting supplies ready for our little holiday in the Big Sur sun with Roarke like we decided last night I now have other plans.

Though once we're inside a taxi on the way to Jason's apartment on Ellis Street in the Tenderloin I realize maybe we should detour by the Greenery so I can leave a note letting everybody know I haven't flipped out and gone over to the dark side or something. But when I write Jason a note he just points to himself then holds an air phone up to his ear and moves his lips. And the first thing he does after he unlocks his door and puts down his records is leave a message on Critter's voice mail.

The second thing he does is draw the curtains to dim the light.

He stands grinning looking at his shoes not touching me at all until I reach out and rub my hand across his head and does he shoot me a sly seventh of a second's worth of eye contact. And do we bust up both of us and fall to the sofa with our arms around each other and our legs wrapped tight.

At last.

He's so shy.

His skin is so soft.

It's like I'm the older one. Like I have to lead the way. Kissing him. Undressing him. When he's down to his snow-white tube socks and I reach to pull them off he waves my hand away. He's all *You don't even wanna see my feet*. And I just grin and shrug and rest my head on his cool flat stomach sighting down his legs and I want to speak out loud the most I've ever wanted anything and what I want to say isn't all that original now is it.

You are so beautiful.

Could these feelings flooding over me be the same those boyz had looking at me.

NFW. It doesn't seem possible.

That anybody anywhere ever felt like this about anybody.

Any.

Body.

His legs.

The trail of hair from his belly button down.

His body so beautiful and he doesn't know. Not built from muscle like Jonnyboy or Roarke not extra big where it's supposed to count like Finn but.

Perfect. The lines the curves the hollows swells. Like waves. That's it. This feeling.

It's so much like surfing. Like fighting your way outside at a monster surf break. Where suddenly you're not struggling anymore and the waves you thought were mountains trying to kill you turn out to be bumps that gently rock you with a deep slow cradle rhythm.

The truth is he's just a boy. And he knows I know.

It makes him even more self-conscious. I take him gently in my hand then gently in my mouth and gentle are his hands running over my head and the back of my neck and everything's gentle with Jason it seems except the racing of his heart and the force of what's inside him rushing fast inside of me.

After we lay clinging and sweating together catching our breath and holding one another like we'll never let go he kisses me and sits up with one hand always touching me and makes a line for himself on a jagged-edged slab of marble on the table in front of the sofa. It's the biggest line I've ever seen and have you heard the news I'm no virgin when it comes to speed either. But he doesn't offer me any and after he inhales it he settles back against me naked and he's still gentle Jason there's no difference like Jonnyboy no difference like Critter no difference like Finn. And when I try to make a joke doing praying hands beddy bye next to my head as in *You'll never get any sleep now* he misunderstands and makes it loud and kweer he's not planning on sleeping anytime soon which leads me to asking what day he's on just making conversation but that confuses him too and he thinks I want to know the longest he's gone without sleeping and the answer's two fingers.

Though not two days not two weeks not two months but.

Two years.

NFW.

YFW. As in a full night's sleep. Not counting naps. When he didn't have a place to stay and mostly just cracked on and walked the streets and alleys till dawn on the nights there weren't clubs that would let him inside. Which was most nights back then since he was.

Sixteen.

Seventeen.

It turns out Jason wasn't much older than me when he started hanging out at the Pit. He lived down in Santa Cruz then but he had something going with this older guy up here and his parents knew and they gave him a choice of stay or go when they moved up to Idaho. So he voted stay and they said later daze and basically signed him over to the guy. Who split for New York after a while leaving Jason on his own.

I hold him tight against me spoon style hugging my arms around his narrow chest and kiss the back of his neck over and over while his fingers reach back tracing figure eights up and down my face and neck. I run my hands over his head I part my lips they feel different heavy it's like slo-mo but no popcorn no previews no movie though talk about coming attractions talk about *This is real*.

We all fall down like dominoes.

I want him piled on me covering me up and I mean completely. I want every inch of my skin touching his skin. We're rolling on the carpet laughing kissing touching licking sucking lightly pulling everywhere there's hair. We're giving off this incredible heat. The temperature's rising in the air around us thick and humid and the hotter it gets the slicker our bodies the smoother we slide over one another under one another into one another.

This.

I have to close my eyes to make it last.

Is.

I have to open them to know just when to hold him back.

Our.

I have to know to show him what I really want.

This.

What I crave what I want.

Is.

What I want want.
Our.
Oh I wait.
This.
I'm a time bomb.
Is.
Facedown.
Our.
My head on my arm on the floor.
This.
My lashes make cell bars.
Is.
I look out from inside.
Our.
See crumbs of cream puffs.
This.
Flakes of crystal meth.
Is.
No wait I'm a fuse.
Our.
My lips make words.
This.
Burn it down.
Is.
It's so hot.
Our.
It's so hot hot.
Fucking.

ELEVEN

Every breath Jason takes afterwards seems to relax his body more muscle by muscle until it's melting into mine spoon style on the sofa again and then he's asleep. I don't know how long it takes. It could be minutes or hours or even a day though it's still light outside.

Sometimes I sleep too. Mostly I'm awake. I never let go of Jason and I stare at his shoulders till I've memorized every pore every freckle every curve of muscle over arcing bone. My hot breath moistens his clear pale skin and blows back toward me in invisible clouds. I guess I'm kind of hypnotized by the rhythm of our breathing and the beat of his pulse. I don't know what time it is when I first feel the vibration in the air from his pager moving on the wooden tabletop but somehow I know whoever's paging Jason really wants me and it scares me.

But why does it scare me. It was my idea in the first place.

Actually no. Not the kidnapping. That was Jonnyboy. Only it isn't a kidnapping. We just have to make it look that way. For Roarke's protection. In the world according to Jonnyboy.

Because even though Roarke's the victim he's sure to be grilled about every detail once we set him free and if he tells the cops one thing and some filling-station attendant on Highway 1 who remembered his face after he saw it in the paper contradicts him they'll be hauling out the old polygraph before you can say Frank Sinatra Jr.

In other words Jonnyboy wants Roarke to take some heavy tranks and then we haul him down there in the trunk.

Why does it scare me.

Is it Jonnyboy protecting Roarke when really now he hates him?

I know he does. I can see it in his eyes.

Is it Ula and the way she believes in this now more than ever more than anything?

Or is it me and the way I believe.

In.

This.

Now.

As in Jason.

And who knows why we believe in things or why we believe in people. There's no bigger why in the large-type dictionary or anyplace else.

Because we're scared.

Because we're stupid.

Because we're confused.

Because we're human.

Whatever the reason sometimes we believe the way I believe right now. We believe in our hearts. And it can be for better. It can be for worse. But either way it can also be like a disease. With no immunity. No inoculation. No isolation ward.

And when I finally reach over for the pager and look at the display and see Finn and Critter's number with a dash and 911 I just think kill the can be and call the doctor.

Because have I got it and I mean bad.

I don't shut down the pager but I push the reset button so it won't vibrate anymore. Leastwayz until another call comes in.

Which it does.

I kiss Jason's neck and hold on tighter. Waking sleeping twilight dark. The calls keep buzzing in. Finn and Critter's number. Ula's sister's number. 911. 811. 411. Emergency. Semi-emergency. Where are you?

Lost.

Dreaming.

Found.

Waking.

The light in the sky. The spark in my heart. I try to squint and realize my eyes are closed. Then I know something and know it like my name. If I leave Jason now my life will be different and I mean different as in worse and this is religion I feel it bone and blood. And I don't have to leave. The pager stopped. It's getting bright outside.

Heart attack.

Hit and run.

I roll away from Jason and stand up shivering naked in the cold.

Jonnyboy needs me. No news is bad news. A promise is a promise.

I pull on my camo pants and my flannel and look down on his neck and his shoulders that I know by.

Heart.

I cover him. He doesn't move. I sit down beside him tying my Van's then stock-still staring at the mound of crack heaped glittering on the marble slab in front of me. I reach for the keys to the Greenery in my pocket but then tell myself *Shine*.

I'll do it like a white boy. There's a butane mini-torch under the table and a glass rod next to the marble.

Hot rails.

One for each nostril.

I do as much as Finn or Critter would. Not as much as Jonnyboy. Not as much as Jason.

I don't see anything to write with so I shape letters on the marble out of crack.

I Love You.

Good night my baby.

Sleep tight my baby.

I reach into the cargo pocket of my camos for the lyric sheet and unwrap the Polaroid of me skating at the bridge overlook and prop it up against the mini-torch.

Heart attack.

Hit and run.

When I'm out on Ellis Street I feel like I could walk all the way to Big Sur if I had to and still be ready for a marathon when I got there so I don't even think about taking the subway or a bus to the Greenery even though it's like a mile away. But when I get to Market Street one of those oldschool streetcars is pulling up to the stop across from the adult movie theater and I figure WTF it's foggy as SFA in the world according to Finn and I might as well. It's weird though because it isn't even six yet and I'm the only passenger and all the other traffic is empty buses and street-cleaning trucks. I feel like I'm being chauffeured in this hella long stretch limo up a street that's been totally cleared for me and me alone. I guess it's the way the President must feel.

As in permanently cracked on.

I like speed.

For about fifteen minutes anywayz. Until I get to the outside door at 99 Sumner Street where I first met Jason a long time ago in a galaxy far far away. The key goes into the lock and behind my eyes I see the key going to Jonnyboy's nostrils again and again in Alamo Square when Roarke went back to the limo for the phone call.

The day Roarke sang the song where Jonnyboy was dead.

And though Jonnyboy isn't dead he's definitely a casualty. He looks up startled and scared when I open the inside door and his whole left ear's a mass of dried blood with blood spots speckling the shoulders and chest of his white v-neck t-shirt. Walking toward him I can see a big red-and-yellow bruise swelling underneath the hair above his ear.

We stare at each other. It must be as obvious I'm tweeking like a trooper as it's obvious he's wounded like a war boy. His eyes go from mad for a seventh of a second to understanding for maybe twice as long and then they're just same old same old Jonnyboy and we're hugging each other with my head on his shoulder and his hand running through the stubble on my head.

His heart beats double-quadruple time. He smells like a chemistry set. He pulls the notepad from my back pocket and steers me to the sofa and we both sit down while he's pulling the pencil stub out of his undamaged ear.

so U got yrself a boyfriend.

Yeah.

He puts both hands on my shoulders and leans back a little kind of taking me in and smiling but more sadfaced than happy.

ahhh Radboy i'll never bring it up again but U can't B w/ a tweeker w/out turnin in2 1 yrself.

I guess so.

it just don't work.

I can tell he wants to write more but what I want is to change the subject which isn't too difficult under the circumstances.

What happened?

Ula!!!

NFW!

YFW. The bitch whapped me upside w/ the toe of my boot.

I just shake my head back and forth. It's like the last thing I would have expected. Though maybe she's been cracking on more than I thought.

i couldn't Blieve it either. & was i pissed, she don't know how lucky she is i didn't rearrange her facial design. i mean, ok, so i fucked up, but still.

What happened?

know what i did, i mailed the RANSOM notes the other night 2. not just the Tejon Holdings 1's. so now the pedal's 2 the metal, Radboy. PEOPLE ARE GETTING THOSE LETTERS IN TODAY'S MAIL. we're rats in a corner. if we don't pull the roarke nab off this morning we'll never B able 2.

Don't you want to? What about Roarke?

fuck, i dunno. it's so sketchy. it ain't the same Btween him & me anymore. not @ all. he wants us 2 make it look so much like a real nab that if anything goes wrong we'll all B hanging w/ yr brother Tommy after he gets life 4 snuffin yr dad.

And I admit it I feel kind of relieved that Jonnyboy's having second thoughts even if it does go against *Never make decisions based on fear.* So I write back:

At least we toasted Tejon Holdings. Too bad Ula didn't make the phone calls though.

But Jonnyboy just looks at me all WTF and finally writes:

waddaya mean? she DID make the calls. i guess the boyz in blue hushed up the newz boyz. that's Y she got so pissed. she wants revenge 4 her sister & she wants it bad & anything/anybody that gets in the way, watch out. she's all WE'LL SHOW THEM. THEY CAN'T KEEP THIS OFF THE SCREEN.

And for seven seconds I'm all *Damn! Fuck!* But when I think about it why am I surprised. And why should Ula especially be surprised since she's the bigtime radical. No wonder all the bombings that get on *World News Tonight* come with body bags included. Usually a lot of them. It's not the only kind of bombings there are. It's just the only kind they can't cover up. Which amounts to encouraging people to do it messy instead of do it clean.

I mean how did we ever think the question authorities would be all *Extra! Extra! Read all about it!* over the Hobart Building. NFW. As long as nobody gets hurt they've got a whole Kellogg's Variety Pack of white-boy explanations.

Faulty wiring.

Flammable cleaning fluids and pilot lights.

Bare bulbs on dry Christmas trees.

Storytellers lie.

I look up at Jonnyboy and there's beads of sweat like a rosary all across his forehead right above the eyebrows. Even though it's cold in here. I've no way never seen him so nervous. So I try to change the subject.

Where is everybody?

F & C are workin early @ the Pit cause they're takin time off. &

Ula's @ FoodCo buying candles & water & food & shit. she should B back by now. i'm s'posed 2 hook up w/ roarke at 7 & she's s'posed 2 drive me.

Really? Where?

i'm pickin him up 2 go surfin @ ft. point, this break by the GG bridge. he's all cracked off & wants 2 do healthy stuff or so he says. he's got an xtra board, an old Cheyne Horan thruster. + he don't want 2 cut me off, just doesn't have much in common anymore 4 hangin out purposes. or so he says. so i got him by the nards w/ that fone call, he had 2 say yes or talk about storytellers lie.

Jonnyboy takes both my hands in his and squeezes hard. Partly I guess to stop his own hands shaking. His eyes are glassy as a Pyrex factory. I wonder what he's seeing when he looks at me but not for long once I read what he writes.

rite now it's down 2 U & me again. just the way we started. we can carry everything we own. we still got the coin collection. let's hit it, Radboy, split sf, learn or burn, bail or fail. there's nobody stopping us.

Wrong.

There is somebody stopping us.

Stopping me.

Jason.

I bite my lip looking back up at him and he knows. I can see it in his eyes.

Waves again. Mountains trying to kill you. The waves between the drowning man and the life preserver.

I can't.

Something passes behind his eyes for a seventh of a second. Something dark and cold. Then it's gone and he's nodding his head and taking my hands again. Sweat trickles down the dried blood splotches on his neck but his hands are ice.

I think he hated me then.

He looks up and I turn around.

Ula.

Holding the car keys in her hand and nodding back toward the door. She barely even looks at me. Jonnyboy kneels down and pulls the crack paraphernalia box out from under the mirror table. He starts to open it then stops and stands up and says something to Ula. Then he walks away with the box in his hands.

Ula signs to me that she's going out to the car to get her purse. She's so businesslike. It's almost like a different person. Same wayz her and Johnnyboy together look.

Different.

Somehow.

It's hard to explain but it creeps me out. Then I remember *Bonnie and Clyde* again and the way that movie ended. Which sends a shiver through me like the first winter wave slapping my face on the paddle-out at Asilomar where's it's always foggy and cold and there's sharks in the kelp beds. But when Ula's halfway through the door she turns around and mouths —Congratulations.

It throws me for a seventh of a second and I sign *About what?* so she adds —Jason.

Which gets both of us smiling and she even takes a step back toward me and I step toward her too thinking a hug would probably do us both good. But then she stops and asks if I know where a wrench is in here so she can loosen the bolts holding the backseat in place while she's out there. And I'm all *Why?*

—The trunk. It isn't big enough.

She pauses.

—To hold the surfboards.

I sign for her to look under the sink in the kitchen and

when she walks back out with the wrench in her hand she flexes her bicep as in *It's a woman's job* and smiles bigtime. Then signs for me to let Jonnyboy know she's waiting in the car and watching her leave I remember the book in her sister's apartment.

The Monkey Wrench Gang.

By the big and glassy dewd.

Now I remember something else.

The question he asked.

What do you have to lose?

I shiver again.

Jonnyboy comes back out with the paraphernalia box in his hands and a look on his face and a welt on his arm and talk about different.

The look says *World don't fuck with me now.*

Not to mention deaf boyz who might think of getting in the way.

He does waiter check please kind of impatiently like *WTF don't you have the pad out already anywayz.*

ok boy, it's showtime comin up & i gotta count on U. F&C are s'posed 2 B back here @ 10 sharp. & if they're not U sk8 not walk 2 the Pit & drag em back here. i ain't playin' no waitin game w/ roarke in the trunk & besides those tranks only last so long & we got a long drive. & make sure they don't bring any extra shit cause it's already crowded w/ 5 of us + roarke & food & water in back. but make sure they DO bring hella plenty crack cause we all got our work cut out 4 us 2day & especially U boyz cause U gotta walk that old road up 2 the house & clear it so we can drive up after dark. we'll take the hacksaw 2 cut the chain. but we can't do it till late cause it's rite on hiway 1 & we'll dead sure get noticed there's so much traffic. so the plan is, we're gonna drop U boyz off @ the road & U go up clearing rocks & branches & shit then fix up a couple rooms in the house 4 hidin out. Ula and me will drive 2 the pullout for the Fuller's surf break where we can park w/o gettin attention + Ula's buying surf racks while we're out this morning & the boards'll be on the roof so it'll look fully casual. we'll give roarke some crack 2 get him wide awake & put some shades & a hat on him & mayB even go surfin there 2 pass the time. tho it's a long wayz down & especially back up that steep cliff trail 4 some1 who just tranked out. hee hee. anywayz, it starts getting dark & we bail Fullers & cut the chain & cruise up. then U gotta meet us where that road ends 2 lead the way 2 the house. U got that? Radboy, this has gotta go orange as in clockwork 2day & U gotta keep these tweekerboyz in line & do whatever i say & don't get all dreamy over Jason & 4get anything, ok?

I just nod my head.

Still the whole thing kind of takes my breath away. Jonnyboy puts on Finn's Fred Perry hoodie to cover his ear and he's out the door and all I can think of is everything that could go wrong starting with what if somebody sees us in Monterey and recognizes me or worse Jonnyboy who the boyz in blue must be after for stomping my dad. And maybe more. Because leave it to my sisters to tell the cops Jonnyboy kidnapped me for immoral purposes. So we get pulled over and the next thing you know the cops are opening the trunk and wham bam what do we have here a double kidnapping not to mention enough crack to addict the minority population of a medium-size inner city.

But not speaking of which. Maybe it's the crack that's got my braces in a twist as Finn would put it. Though here I am getting paranoid about speed and speed makes you paranoid and I've been doing speed myself so pay your money and take your choice.

Either call the doctor or let's call the whole thing off.

I could just go back to Jason's.

They'd never find that house without me.

They'd just take Roarke someplace else.

Ula's sister's place.

Yeah right.

I could have stayed at Jason's.

Jonnyboy needs me.

All of this was my idea.

Never make decisions based on fear.

I can't sit still so I just wander around the Greenery feeling cold and lost and lonesome. Now I know why tweekers always seem to want other people around. You've got to bounce the energy off somebody else or it eats you up inside. It's awful being alone right now.

Except I'm not.

Jonnyboy didn't close the door behind him and sitting on the sill nosing between the bars of the side window on the aluminum bunny carrier is Critter's bunny. Looking a little thin and definitely off-white now but not too much the worse for wear.

I remember there's still this dried grassy bunny food in a cupboard in the kitchen so I start backing up as slow as I can on tiptoes so the bunny doesn't freek and bail for the street life again. She flicks her head in my direction a couple of times so I know she notices me but stays right where she is by the carrier. Then when I start breaking up the food on the carpet in front of the breakfast bar she starts hopping toward me in fits and starts but stops just out of arm's reach twitching her nose and kind of panting. So I decide to shove a pile of the grass into the kitchen itself and back away through the curtain walling off the bedroom. And sure enough the bunny makes a couple of long hops into the kitchen as soon as I'm out of sight and starts munching away. Which is my cue to pull apart the curtains and take a couple of running leaps myself to slam the door closed.

I decide to reward myself for mission accomplished with a shower but I write a note to Finn and Critter first and tack it to the outside of the door so they won't leave it open long enough for her to escape if they show up while I'm in the bathroom.

I Have Seen Your Lost Bunny
She's in the kitchen but she might run back out the door if you're not careful.

Then when I get my clothes off a shower doesn't seem like such a good idea anymore. I still smell like Jason. And I don't want to wash him away. I don't know how long we'll be down there. Long enough leastwayz for the paperwork to go through turning the redwoods over to Earth First! Which is who Ula decided could be trusted the most not to make some kind of secret deal behind our backs.

I know I'll miss him however long it is. And I don't have a picture of Jason. All I have is part of him as close as my own skin.

When I go back out into the kitchen the bunny's nowhere in sight and am I glad I took precautions. As in she can hide but she can't run. But it turns out she's not even hiding. She's in the living room checking out the bunny cube again. I slowly walk over and she doesn't take off or even look at me really. And when I lean forward and unlatch the door she hops inside as soon as it swings open.

I gently push the door closed with the toe of my shoe and it must be the crack zapping connections in my brain that instant replays it into something else.

My little brother Timmy kicking my dad in the leg after

Jonnyboy took him down in our living room on Grace Street in New Monterey.

Home sweet home.

Not for Timmy it isn't. Talk about lost bunnies. I sit on the sofa wondering what I could do to help Timmy escape my sisters let alone my dad and I admit it I start feeling pretty ashamed. I mean I'm all set to risk my life practically or at least my freedom to save a few redwood trees I've never even seen but it didn't occur to me till now to lift a finger to help my own little brother from a fate worse than. Which puts me in full-on fantasyland mode and I mean for days imagining that Jason and me somehow adopt Timmy and live happily ever after yeah right until I look up at the clock on the VCR and realize I'm doing exactly what I promised Jonnyboy I wouldn't. Going all dreamy over Jason and forgetting I should be on my way to the Pit with liberty bells on since it's 10:18.

I jump up at the same moment Critter pushes the door open just far enough to slide through sideways and runs toward the kitchen without even seeing me. I run after him and we hit each other head-on when he wheels around in front of the breakfast bar all *Where is she? Where is she?* I lead him by the hand back to living room and point to the carrier and seven seconds later he's kneeling on the floor with his eyes closed and the rest of his face buried in bunny fur.

I wonder if his eyes are closed to keep tears from spilling out and then I feel a draft and look up at Finn peeking through the barely cracked door. He's smiling and gives me two thumbs-up but then he jerks one of them back over his shoulder and points to his wrist then does both hands on a steering wheel followed by a couple of hubba-hubba air curves.

I don't need a help file to figure that one out. I leave Critter with the bunny and make smoke for the kitchen where I toss the bricks of bunny food into a plastic grocery bag and double-time it back to the door where Finn's already standing over Critter trying to hurry the bunny back into captivity. Finn looks up at me and draws Jonnyboy-style sideburns on his face and goes all hard and mean and am I two for two at Easter Parades which is Finn's rhyming slang for charades. Because a promise is a promise and I know what Jonnyboy's like when somebody breaks one. The way he sees it he gets back to the Greenery at 10:18 and if Finn and Critter are just showing up too they better be stepping lively with me cracking a whip behind them.

So I grit my teeth and lead the way out expecting dark clouds in the forecast but nothing like the black as night black as coal look in Jonnyboy's eyes staring out the open passenger-side window. And that's before he sees the bunny carrier. When he realizes we're not only late for check-in but loaded down with excess carry-on baggage he swings the door open hard enough to bend the hinges I swear and jumps out standing in front of it with his arms folded across his chest all *Read my lips.*

—No.

—No fucking way.

He's still got salt powdering his eyebrows from surfing and a bulged-out vein like a jagged lightning bolt standing out in the middle of his forehead. He jerks his head around and snaps two or three words back at Ula who must have said something. I look at Finn and Critter standing on either side of me and they're all *WTF?* though I can tell they're also getting pissed at being yelled at like this and for the first time ever it hits me that I'm a lot better friends with them than Jonnyboy is.

And what are friends for. Jonnyboy turns back to us saying nothing with his lips but his body language says *No compromise No bunny* loud and clear so I take a walk around the back of the Valiant without meeting his eyes again and sign to Ula that it's all my fault and I know it's gonna be crowded in back but it's us three riding in back anywayz not her and Jonnyboy and the bottom line is the bunny goes or none of us go. And in seven seconds flat she's out of the car all *I understand. But please please don't put it that way to Jonnyboy. You can see he's very upset. He's not himself right now. Partly it's my fault. I'm so ashamed I struck him. I didn't know the toe was steel. So let me talk to him. But promise you'll smooth things out with Finn and Critter after we drop you off today. We can't have trouble among us. Not now. Not with a body in the trunk.*

And talk about *Damn!* Talk about *Fuck!* She might as well have whapped me too.

PARTLY it's her fault.

A BODY in the trunk.

WTF is going on here anywayz.

Which I don't sign or anything but I guess the look on my face gives me away because Ula reaches for my wrist and mouths —Don't worry. Roarke's all right.

And am I all good day sunshine once that's cleared up. Because for seven seconds there I was thinking we're real kidnappers. Or worse.

As in *This is real.*

Which looks pretty scary on paper but is it a joke when you look at the crew in question standing shivering in the fog on Sumner Street. A kweer skinhead. A club kid holding on to his bunny like a little kid welded to his lunch box on the first day of kindergarten. A fourteen-year-old deaf sk8boarder. The Hooters remix of Florence Nightingale.

Some kidnappers.

But then there's Jonnyboy.

Who looks like he means business. And I mean dirty business. But somehow Ula talks him first into sitting back down inside the car and then after a couple of minutes into waving us into the back *All aboard* and *Get in if you can fit in* before he slumps down in the seat with his head in his hands and stays that way.

Past the dark spooky skeleton of the Santa Cruz roller coaster and the monster stack of the Moss Landing power plant poking up through the summer fog bank. Past the Giant Artichoke in Castroville and Dennis the Menace Park by the El Estero off-ramp in Monterey and on over Carmel Hill to the mouth of Carmel Valley and the hot sun seeping through the mist around Point Lobos. Every now and then I look out for a seventh of a second at landmarks I've known all my life then settle back with my eyes closed between Finn and Critter and go back to what started in Jason's apartment just minutes ago but seems like something that was always part of me since genesis ground zero. It's the world outside the window that seems new and strange somehow and finally not very important.

Until we cross the Camel River Bridge which is where I always start getting the Big Sur feeling that grows and grows the windier the highway gets and the steeper the cliffs and the sharper the ocean smell from waves smashing rocks and I mean smashing hard.

The bluer the sky and in it the hawks. The eagles soaring higher and higher.

But something's wrong. I breathe in the salt air through the open window and it charges me up like it always does but the feeling's not the same. The thrill is gone.

And I don't get it at Garrapata Creek or Andrew Molera or Pfeiffer Beach or Little Sur River or even Nepenthe where we stop for hamburgers and you can see a hundred miles. Just like you can from the metal house. Which isn't that much farther down the coast so I ride in the front seat with Ula after Nepenthe on the lookout for the place to start hiking. It's on a bend in the road a little past Partington Canyon but hella tricky to find. And it takes a couple of false starts but finally I recognize the rusty chain and oldschool brass padlock across the overgrown road disguised as a cow path complete with dried cow pies.

We have to do the drop-off fast because one there's only about six inches of shoulder on the inside of the bend in the highway where the old road takes off and two there's Winnebago after Winnebago barreling into the turn at high velocity in both directions. So Ula does a rolling California stop and Finn and Critter and I pile out double time with Jonnyboy flowing backpacks and bunny carrier onto the gravel behind us then climbing in up front and holding all ten fingers up palms inward looking at me and nodding as they drive away.

As in *I'm counting on you.*

As soon as we're up the hill a ways and Highway 1's out of sight I get the Big Sur feeling I was missing earlier and do I with a vengeance. Because the air never seemed clearer and the line where the dark blue of the ocean meets the light blue of the sky never seemed sharper and the breeze never seemed to touch my skin the way it does now like it wants to undress me and make me feel the way I made Jason feel. Maybe the crack has something to do with it. But there's another part of the feeling from the size of the mountains dropping sheer into the water and the water forever to mother China and the world beyond and nothing moving but the faraway swells and the wind-rippled golden grass. It's the part that's like God watching you and it's nothing to do with drugs.

Not that I'm Mr. Just Say No under the circumstances and

actually I'm glad we're all cracked on because it does a lot more to power us up the road in the hot sun than those hamburgers at Nepenthe. Which they call ambrosia burgers on account of using blue instead of ordinary cheese I guess but still work your guts like greasebombs from the old In and Out In and Out when you're sweating your way up a mountain with water as far as you can see in one direction anywayz but not a drop to drink thanks to tweekerboy hiking partners who remembered to pack a wide selection of pipes points and syringes not to mention five canteens but forgot to fill them up. Though it's really Finn and Critter who suffer most since they're switching off carrying the bunny cube as well as their backpacks. Plus I drank three Dr Peppers at Nepenthe so I feel like Joe Camel anywayz. I just keep it to myself to squelch the hump jokes.

At first all the roadwork we have to do is move rocks to keep the Valiant from high-centering and most of them are just sitting on top of the roadbed so it's easy it's easy it's easy to pick them up or roll them over to the edge. But the higher we get the more of them turn out to be like icebergs with two-thirds of them out of sight out of mind until we try to lever them out. Sometimes we have to dig foot-deep trenches all the way around the rocks to even move them at all. Fortunately though as we keep climbing up to the big tree level where the pines and cypress take over from the scrubby live oaks and open slopes of tall golden grass we also have to clear away a lot of overhanging branches so we have plenty of digging sticks. Still it's hard work and we're all sweaty and dirty by the time we're under the cool leafy shade at the top of the mountain. I'm a little dizzy from dehydration I guess and I have to sit down. I feel like I just hiked the entire John Muir Trail with the Sahara Club.

Finn and Critter sit down too a few feet away with Critter

on the bunny carrier and Finn beside him in the dirt. But after a couple minutes Critter stands back up and walks over to some bushes to take a leak. As soon as Critter's gone Finn wraps his arms around his knees and rocks sideways to lean against a tree trunk and pushes his sunglasses tight over his eyes. He frowns the way he does when he says he's feeling indisposed and I realize how much more tired he is than he ever lets on and probably how much sicker. And I jump up like a reflex without thinking because the only important thing in the world to me right now is putting my arm around Finn and smoothing his soft sawed-off hair with my fingers.

Then I stop and play statues when I see Critter's walking tall and fast back toward Finn like he's meeting someone at an airport or something and I mean someone he's been missing and I mean missing hard. But he doesn't call out his name and sweep him into his arms like some cheesy American Express commercial. Instead the closer he gets the slower he walks until he's perfectly still an arm's length away.

Then he bends downs to barely touch Finn's shoulder with a motion so gentle so filled with a million deep things no one else will ever know it makes me want to cry I swear.

But leave it to Critter to get me laughing instead. After stroking Finn's head he looks up at me watching and mouths:

—It's so hot and dry it reminds me of my dad.

Which gets Finn smiling fast and I mean smiling wikked. But since the only thing I know about Critter's dad is that I met those boyz on the way back from his funeral I'm totally clueless. So I'm all wide-eyed innocent Radboy drawing a Y in the dirt with the tip of my shoe.

—Because of how he died.

I can tell from the gleam in Critter's eyes that he's setting me up. Plus Finn's about ready to bust out laughing I can tell.

But what can a poor boy do but play along. So I kick away the Y and replace it with *How*.

—He killed himself.

Back to *Y*.

—The drought. It ruined his business. He was a windshield-wiper salesman. To auto-parts stores. And nobody's wearing out their wiper blades anymore.

At first I'm all WTF while they're both whooping it up and I decide it must be a joke and trace out *NFW*. But I guess it's true since Critter puts a serious face back on and swears on a stack of imaginary Abba records and Finn nods all *Right-o mate*. Which gets me thinking about how there's been droughts most of my life it seems and wondering why Critter's dad got in that line of work in the first place. In Oregon maybe but why the fuck here.

Though my grandpa came to California to fish for sardines when they were already pretty much gone. I guess something draws people and they just stick around and hope for the best.

But still.

He could have switched to air conditioners or something.

So I just look disgusted and spell out *What an asshole* which gets them both laughing again and with our spirits back up we're practically good as new on the last leg of our hike. Which doesn't require any more road clearing because the actual road part ends where we stopped and narrows into a trail before it starts dropping down to the south side of Partington Canyon. And if you're clued in enough to notice the change you definitely wonder why the road stops right here since you can't see out and there's nothing visible to make it an obvious destination.

Unless you're a tree-surgeon intern looking for a place to get some practice. Because then there's definitely something to make you shout *Eureka!* Namely about a hundred eucalyptus trees growing closer together than Mother Nature ever intended. Not that she intended them to grow here at all since they're originally from Australia. And I'm not real big on eucalyptus because of the way the leaves fall to the ground and move in the wind like snakes and startle you sometimes when you see them out of the corner of your eyes. Plus they smell so strong they short-circuit your other senses. But you have to admit they're hella good camo. Like right now. If I didn't already know it was here I wouldn't even see it. The person wide pathway covered and I mean deep and I mean completely with leaves and curving curling strips of dry eucalyptus bark.

I guess it crunches under our feet. I know that word from Cap'n Crunch cereal and how it feels when you bite into a spoonful before the pieces soak up the milk.

I lead the way and I'm walking a lot faster than Finn and Critter and scanning ahead for the wooden water tank behind the metal house and when I see the lines of its shingles standing out through a covering of vines I do my own *Eureka!* thing and break into a run. The tank's as big as a swimming pool and there isn't any cover. Steel ladder rungs go up the side. I climb to the top and the water looks clean but cold and dark. I feel like jumping in but it's five feet down to the surface and I'd never make it out. So I go back down and do Johnny Rotten *Follow me!* and start circling the tank looking for the water pipe leading to the house. Which is right where it was last spring with Rob and so is the big peeling sign five minutes down the hill.

U.S. GOVERNMENT PROPERTY
PUBLIC HEALTH HAZARD
KEEP OUT

Finn lets out the whoop I feel and claps me on the back. We push through about twenty feet of tangled willows whipping our bare legs and here we are.

It's green to match the trees though faded by the sun to almost gray green like the powdery underside of all the eucalyptus leaves. And it's not dignified and oldschool official looking. Just spooky and modern. All straight lines and boxy with nothing but stamped-in geometric shapes for trim. Overgrown rosebushes everywhere around. The front porch looking out down a gentle grassy oval hill as big as Laguna Seca Raceway. A grove of trees lining up with the front of the house at the bottom of the hill so you don't see anything else looking west straight on but the rest of the whole horizon is ocean. Blue sky over sky blue water. It feels like the top of the world.

And are Finn and Critter stoked. It isn't even like we're here to hide out with a hostage after bombing a building. It's more like Disneyland and we just landed on Tom Sawyer's Island.

As in *Welcome to the Wild Western White House.*

Squelch Frontierland though this is more along the lines of Adventureland and I go into safari guide mode as soon as we're inside. When I came here with Rob we circled the place trying every one of like a dozen doors and finally I broke a window with a cypress branch and we climbed through into the kitchen. This time I head that way right off and the window's just the way we left it so history repeats and we're inside holding our noses. Because there's mouse shit everywhere and I mean fresh and I mean smelly. I guess the mice eat the wallpaper for the glue. Plus there's pools of black water on the floor and the linoleum's rotting.

Just like Rob did with me I point to the low-down counters and light switches and the spaces for specially sized stoves and other appliances then do a wheelchair impersonation which they both get easy. But Finn still has to explain that Roosevelt was crippled because at first Critter thinks it must have been affirmative action for a disabled cook.

For some reason the kitchen and the big pantry next to it are the major mouse bathrooms and the air clears when we walk into the presidential parlor. It seems bigger than San Carlos Cathedral and the ceiling's at least twenty-five feet high with once-white curtains over the windows rotting away and thick black blinds behind them for blackouts so enemy planes couldn't find the place. I have trouble playing charades with that one and finally have to write it down which also helps explain the big map of the world on one wall with a rolled-up movie screen behind it. Part of the map is ruined but you can see how Germany takes up most of Europe and even part of Africa and Japan has all China. But North and South America are just the same as now.

We check out the rest of the house and all the quirky little devil details like the way every hallway zigs and zags as part of the strategy for holding off invaders and how all the closets are L-shaped with hiding spaces at the back. Two walls of one big room with no windows are covered with weird-looking metal tiles that must be lead judging from the weight of the dusty spares stacked in a corner. And the other two are filled completely floor to ceiling with rows of empty file drawers lined with concrete two inches thick. There's a wooden library step-ladder on wheels to help you reach the high rows and it runs on miniature railroad tracks around a full-length counter in the middle of the room with about a dozen old stand-up telephones in a row tin-soldier style.

We decide this must be the War Room and play around with the phones awhile and decide it's the Command HQ of

the Camorrist International hands down your pants no doubt
about it. Then we cruise on into Roosevelt's bedroom close by
which is in kind of a wing of its own and the nicest of all. The
ceiling doesn't leak and the mice haven't got in yet so the
wallpaper's still untouched. The ends of the curtain rods are
capped with eagles that look like they're made of gold. Plus
there's a double Dutch sailor's door leading outside and lots of
louvered glass windows you can crank open for ventilation. I
write a note about how good a field HQ this room would make
and they're both *Amen brother you're the bomb Radboy or make
that bombs heh heh heh.* So we dump our packs out on the
floor and use the whisk brooms Ula bought to sweep out most
of the dust.

Which gets us dirtier and drier than ever and when Finn
and Critter spread out the thin airline blankets we brought with
us and kick back leaning against the bedroom wall they both
look so beat I volunteer to head back uphill to the water tank
and figure out a way to fill our canteens so we don't all pass
out and never wake up. Because I know from the health department *Take a Tweaker to Lunch* posters you see everywhere
in San Francisco that using speed makes you need more H_2O
than normal people anywayz and we've been doing nothing but
sweat for the last five hours at least.

Along with the canteens I take the claw hammer we
brought to pry off the big wooden X brace across the kitchen
door so I won't have to climb back in through the broken window on the return trip. And after I clear the wood away and
glance through the window at my sunburned reflection in a
long wide mirror behind what probably was meant to be a liquor cabinet I walk about ten feet away from the house and
notice something creepy when I catch a whiff of dead smell
on the breeze and turn around to check the source.

I don't see anything dead. But I'm still directly in line with the liquor cabinet in the kitchen and I don't see myself either. I don't even see the trees behind me. I stand on tiptoe and I'm still not in the mirror. I walk back toward the kitchen windows slowly step-by-step watching the mirror. Two steps before the doorway I'm a blur. One step back I'm gone. Two steps forward I'm less of a blur and one more forward in the doorway itself I finally look sharp. Though not exactly. Even this close I have kind of a ghostly look.

Where have I seen a mirror like this?

I can't remember but maybe it's because I'm dehydrated. Which reminds me.

Water.

Lucky for me the canteens have plastic loops connecting the unscrewed tops to the bottles themselves and back near the water tank I find a long forked branch I can hook through the loops and use to lower the bottles from the top of the ladder. But after I fill the first three my foot slips while I'm lowering the fourth and I pitch forward a little and it all happens in a lot less time than it takes to tell. As I reach forward on autopilot to grab the rim of the tank to steady myself I look down at my reflection in the cool clear water and imagine the splash I would make if I didn't stop myself and the way the water would feel on my skin and the way the light below the surface would filter down dappled through leaves and for a seventh of a second I see my arms outstretched my body a cross and this angel looks down at me and says:

Ah pretty boy can't you show me nothing but surrender.

And then he's gone.

And I grip the rim of the tank with both hands so hard I end up with splinters in eight out of eight fingers and just stand there with my legs shaking until I figure out what I need to do is down all three bottles and do I. Then I fill them up again plus the two remaining empties and pour all the water over my head and repeat rewind twice before I fill them all one last time and get the H E double L back to the metal house.

Back to that mirror.

Where HAVE I seen a mirror like this?

In the Monterey County Hall of Justice in Salinas. That room where they took me through it again and again.

You saw him chase her through the open door at the top of the stairs.

You ran toward the door yourself.

You saw them scuffling and then she fell.

You did not see them scuffling. You saw him push her.

You did not see him push her.

Try to remember. You must have seen him push her.

It was an interrogation room. Usually reserved for the bad guys. But I was a good guy. I was being interviewed. Not interrogated. I got Ben & Jerry's cookie dough ice cream before the interview started and they showed me how the two-way mirror worked with the observation area on the other side.

The other side. I walk through the door into the kitchen and hang my backpack filled with water bottles on the crank of this industrial-strength can opener that's mounted on the wall next to the liquor cabinet. I open the cabinet door and pull on the shelves inside. Solid. I look underneath the shelves for latches or hinges and in the wooden drawers below the glassed-in part for panels that move. Nothing.

I step back and look through the doorway to the right of the cabinet that opens onto a zigzag corridor. The cabinet's built into a wall that runs right angle to the wall on one side of the corridor. I walk into the corridor and tap the wall. It vibrates like metal. I tap the wall on the other side of the corridor. It thuds like wood. I walk down the corridor counting my steps to the first doorway on the left. Fifteen. It leads into a square room with one barred frosted window and a walk-in closet and another door leading to a small bathroom. The fixtures and light switches are all at the regular height so it definitely wasn't meant for Roosevelt. Probably the cook's bedroom. I pace off the length of the inside wall parallel to the corridor.

Nine.

I tap the back wall of the bedroom.

Metal.

I tap the wall on the corridor side.

Wood.

Back out in the corridor I walk toward the kitchen tapping the wall and counting my steps. Just past nine the wall changes from wood to metal.

In the kitchen I look everywhere and I mean over under sideways down for a way into the secret room. I could always break the glass inside the cabinet to see what's on the other side. But then it wouldn't be secret anymore. And I still might not be able to go inside.

I look at my backpack hanging from the can opener and think *Busted again.*

As in sketch-o-rama.

Those boyz are dying of thirst. Not to mention that bunny.

When I lift my backpack the crank snaps back up to twelve o'clock high so hard and fast it makes me jump. And the beveled edges of the mirrored wall behind the liquor cabinet multiply and magnify the movement kaleidoscope style. I stare into my own startled eyes.

Oh heavens to Betsy. Oh suburban lawns. This truly is a kitchen of distinction.

They disguised it pretty well but riddle me this. What does a can opener do?

It opens metal things.

But a crank this stiff. What does it do?

Opens big metal things.

As in rooms.

It isn't even a crank. More like a ratchet under tension. Connected to a cable. Disappearing into the wall. It has to be. Which means there also has to be a ratchet lock to stiffen the cable. As in button button who's got the button. And the closest thing to a button is the cap on the outer end of the crank spindle. But it doesn't move. At first. Then I find the thumbnail groove on the underside of the handle and line it up precisely with the tiny braille dot at 8:00 pm on the spindle cap. I push in the end cap. I turn the handle.

The ratchet clicks. The cable's stiff. I crank it once and the rusty cable tenses. Jolts. Jerks on unseen ungreased wheels. It's just like reeling in shark chum. The four-foot-wide floor-to-ceiling panel of mouse-chewed cork bulletin board next to the liquor cabinet slides back an inch into the wall.

I crank it again. And again. The panel clears the edge of the inner wallframe. It moves a foot each turn three more times and I walk into the unsealed room.

In the dim light filtering through the two-way mirror and the gaps in the wall I see a folding wooden chair with a wrinkled magazine on the seat. Metal lockers line the inside walls. A railing of painted pipe makes an L around a stairwell. Narrow shallow concrete steps drop down into the dark. It's just like the fucking Hardy Boys. I used to read those old books when I was little and dream of shit like this happening to me. But this isn't a dream.

This is real.

I know we've got flashlights in Roosevelt's bedroom so I cruise back out into the kitchen and down the hallway to score one and share the news with Finn and Critter. When I crack the door open in case the bunny's loose the light almost blinds me because it isn't dim and cool and dark in here like all the interior rooms it's bright and hot as sun from the curtainless windows floor to ceiling on two whole walls.

They're asleep naked on the airline blankets. They look like a couple of kids. Not kids really because after all they're naked and kids don't have bodies like that. Plus there's a crack pipe alongside Critter's cigarettes at the top of the blanket. Still somehow they look so innocent. So carefree. It must be nature that does it. Being out in nature I mean. I felt that way on my dad's boat on the bay.

The lines are gone from Finn and Critter's faces and there's no tension in their muscles at all. They don't twitch all suddenly at random the way they do sleeping in the city. Their bodies are arranged like a giant letter *P*. Critter's the upright part laying on his back head toward me with his arms at his sides and his legs straight out. Finn's laying on his side with his back toward me and his head tucked into the curve above Critter's waist. He's bent at the hips and his legs curve around so his toes touch Critter's. His right arm wraps around Critter's thigh with his hand somewhere underneath between his legs. The barest ripple movement of the skin on Finn's broad back matches the rising falling inhale exhale rhythm of Critter's chest.

Everything else is perfectly still. The louvered windows by the door that leads outside are open for air but there's no breeze or even draft through the doorway where I stand. I guess because the hallway zigs and zags.

Which reminds me to shut the door behind me even

though there's no sign of the bunny. I just figure she's in the carrier in the corner and pour some water in a plastic cup and kneel down to open the door and push it inside. But she's not in there either and for seven seconds I panic then notice the bathroom door is closed. So I head thatawayz with the cup of water and almost jump out of my skin when I open the door because is that bunny running the Indy 500 in here.

She's racing around the length of the bathtub and hopping out for a circuit of the toilet then up onto the countertop around both sinks followed by flying leaps back into the bathtub again. It's like a Roadrunner cartoon minus the beep beep sound effects which I know about from my little brother Timmy. And when I see the chewed-through corner of the Ziploc bag protruding from Finn's kit bag next to one of the sinks it's definitely no further questions your boner.

She doesn't even seem to notice me she's so fixed on chasing around. Which is definitely un-bunnylike behavior. I guess what saved her from OD'ing is she got so amped so fast she couldn't sit still to eat anymore.

I stand here watching her like the first time I watched all the tweekers on the dance floor at the Pit.

It was Jason making the music they moved to.

But he's so different than they all are.

I can't explain it but I can feel it.

Still.

U can't B w/ a tweeker w/out turnin in2 1 yrself.

Maybe he just keeps doing it because everyone around him does. Maybe I can change all that.

I wish.

I may.

I wish.

I might.

TWELVE

Some of the crack effects must be wearing off a little finally because I'm starting to feel more like myself again instead of a stranger in a strange land. Though what am I but when I think of that room. When I think of why we're here in the first place. When I think of what we've already done.

Bombed a building.

This is real.

I take a flashlight with me back to the kitchen but I don't use it to explore any more of the secret room. I've seen all I need to see. I just crank the panel back into place so nobody's the wiser. Because I'm keeping it a secret. It's like my ace in the hole.

In case of trouble.

In case things don't work out.

This is our fucking rage.

A gust of wind blows through the open window and I smell something dead again and decide to go outside and investigate like a white boy this time. Though it's not what you'd call a job for Sergeant Friday because it takes all of two minutes to follow my nose to some bushes twenty feet behind the house. And there it is. A coyote. Old looking with scraggly fur and yellow stubby teeth bared by tight bloated skin. It stinks so bad I cover my mouth and nose in the crook of my arm and run all the way to the front of the house where the church-sized parlor opens onto the main front porch.

Which is bigger than both floors of my family's house on Grace Street in New Monterey. And supported by solid cement walls with riveted steel reinforcing panels. So it's actually the roof of a bunker or bomb shelter. I'm not sure which. Or even if there is any difference. I know Hitler died in a bunker and if they had one for him it's dead sure we had one for Roosevelt. I mean that was what the war was all about. Keeping pace with the Germans. And beating them finally to rule the world with atom bombs instead of storm troopers.

Though all I really know about politics is from punk rock zines and song lyrics and stuff on the Internet. Plus what I've picked up from Ula and a few books like the bloody rock one by the desert dewd. And from my dad I guess too since with a lot of things I just figure that whatever's the opposite of his beliefs has gotta be the way to go.

Then there's what I know because of Finn.

Who's dying.

Whose mom died in a prison over there and all because of.

Politics.

The sun's going down but the chill I feel comes from inside not outside. I could have thought *We're all dying* because we are and it's closer every day and my world wouldn't have gone Greenland all buried under ice. Not now anywayz and probably never because the blood and the clippers and what Finn told me in the Pit and even the medicine cabinet seem like dates in ancient history that you learn in school and forget about after the test and I mean right after. No wonder he's calm about what happened to his mom. She's dead. He's alive. For now.

Same with my mom. She's dead. I'm alive. So what can a poor boy do.

Good things.

Starting right now. I know it'll be a while before I need to be back at the eucalyptus grove to meet Jonnyboy and Ula and Roarke because even if Jonnyboy starts hacksawing the chain at the bottom of the mountain the moment the sun sinks into the ocean it's still going to be a long slo-mo drive up here in that old low-slung car. But I decide to head for the trees now anywayz. At least if I fall asleep it'll be where I'm supposed to be in the world according to Jonnyboy. And when I lean back against the same live oak where Finn rested earlier while Critter took a leak I do close my eyes. I don't sleep though. I just wait.

I feel the car move the ground before the headlights make monster tree shadows all around me and I stand up shading my eyes with one hand and waving with the other. As soon as she sees me Ula kills the lights and rolls to a stop. I walk over to the driver's side and at first all I can see inside the car are her pale hands still gripping the steering wheel at ten and two. Then her hair. Then a white lump of something at the other end of the backseat.

Jonnyboy opens his door and the interior lights come on.

Ula stares straight ahead out the windshield into the dark. The white lump in the backseat is the back of Roarke's head almost completely wrapped in bandages. With bloodstains showing through.

He's alive at least because I can see his chest rise and fall underneath a plaid flannel draped over him like a blanket. I'm all *What happened?* but Ula doesn't answer back. Instead Jonnyboy walks around the hood of the car and takes the flashlight out of my hand and shines it up so I can read his lips.

—Where's Finn and Critter?

The angle of the light makes Jonnyboy look hella creepy with his eyes lost in dark sockets and the skin on both sides of his nostrils lit all the way through glowing pink while the rest of his skin looks china white only dirty with stubble like coffee grounds.

I do praying hands beddy-bye next to one ear and he lets his breath out. I point back to Roarke and draw a *?* in the air.

—He hit his head surfing.

Jonnyboy justs stands there.

Ula just sits there.

Finally Jonnyboy moves his lips again.

—On a rock.

Inside the car Ula leans forward resting her head on the steering wheel.

—How far is it to the house? Can we carry him? Just the three of us?

I shrug my shoulders then nod my head and Jonnyboy hands back the flashlight. His fingers brush mine and I almost pull away they're so cold. He motions for me to hold the light while he opens his Altoids tin and dips a key into a mini Ziploc bulging with crack. His hand shakes so hard that most of the powder's gone by the time he gets the key to his nostril. He's all *Damn! Fuck!* and motions for me to hold my palm out and shine the light down on it. After he dumps about half the bag in a mound on my palm he spreads it into a line with the tip of his finger and takes a dollar bill out of his wallet and rolls it into a tube. He bends over my hand and vacuums up the crack in two long inhales.

Afterwards his neck stiffens and a shiver runs through him head to toe. Then he raises his head and points to his lips and I shine the light back up.

—Let's do it.

Roarke's unconscious but his skin's a lot warmer to the touch than Jonnyboy's so I guess he can't be hurt too bad. Plus we're moving him which Ula wouldn't stand for if there was a medical reason not to. Especially since the way we have to carry him is by making a tripod seat with our hands gripping each other's wrists so we're basically stumbling down the hill to the house in the dark like an awkward six-legged animal with Roarke's body pitching back and forth up down turnaround please don't let him hit the ground.

Which he does a couple of times though when we all three simultaneously slip on eucalyptus leaves. At least we manage to keep his head up anywayz. I don't know how long it takes until we're finally carrying him down the zigzag hallway to the War Room but it seems like hours. Then as soon as we lay him down on the table with the stand-up telephones and Ula folds Jonnyboy's jacket up for a pillow we have to head back up to the car to fetch supplies.

Leastwayz Jonnyboy and I do. We leave Ula to look after Roarke. And seven seconds after we're out the door Jonnyboy starts getting nervous. He stops and asks me if I'm sure that Finn and Critter are asleep. If they're very heavy sleepers. If I remember when the last time they slept was. And then to explain himself I guess he reminds me that Roarke doesn't want to have any contact with the rest of us now so he won't have to lie so much to the question authorities.

I'm all *Don't worry get happy they'll sleep through the Big One* and *Yes boss whatever you say boss* because the last thing I want is Jonnyboy worrying more than he already is. Though I wonder if Ula's included in the rest of us or not. I guess Roarke could have taken the tranks yesterday and crawled into the trunk on his own while Ula was out buying the surf racks. I never asked about it.

Jonnyboy double-times it up to the car and I can barely keep up. When he opens the trunk and we start stuffing our backpacks with food and drinks from grocery bags it's pretty obvious it's going to take at least one more trip to haul everything down and I figure maybe he was asking about Finn and Critter because he realized it then and wanted to roust them to help out. He probably decided Critter would insist on bringing the bunny along and it'd be more trouble than it was worth.

Jonnyboy fills his pack first and walks around the car to the front passenger door while I'm wedging the last couple packages of HoHos into mine. When I lean my pack on the bumper for a better grip on zipping it closed an orange rolls down into the trunk and I shoot my hand out to stop it from rolling to the back. Only instead of digging into orange peel my fingernails practically split in pieces ramming into something hard and solid underneath the folds of a surfing towel. Something hard and solid and cross-shaped.

A tire iron.

With two cupped ends that look like they were dipped in rust.

No. Not rust. Even in the dim yellow light of the trunk

lamp I can tell it's too red to be rust. Rust has more orange in it. Plus rust never looks like it flowed in streams like liquid.

Like blood.

On autopilot I crumple the towel back over it and shine the orange and slam the trunk. I can feel Jonnyboy's steps coming back and I don't want him seeing how bad my hands are shaking. How bad all of me's shaking.

Less than a minute after we start back Jonnyboy stops in his tracks and puts his hand on my shoulder all *Wait right here*. He starts running back toward the car which isn't visible anymore in the total dark under the trees and I kneel down and put my palm on the ground. I can feel the rhythmic vibrations of his feet for about thirty seconds then nothing for maybe five seconds and then a single deep thud before the rhythm of his running again getting closer and closer. It kind of hypnotizes me into staying bent over and Jonnyboy almost knocks himself out on a tree branch veering to the side when he sees me too late. But instead of getting all aggro which is what I expect and makes me start shaking even harder he just wants to know if I'm ok.

I nod my head.

Storytellers lie.

Back in the War Room Roarke's still out and Ula's sitting in one of the wooden swivel chairs staring at a candle flame. She must have gone into the bedroom and found it inside Critter's pack. Which Jonnyboy realizes too and starts grilling her on what's up with the boyz in back. I know because I can read the answers on her lips. After a while she's just listening to Jonnyboy and nodding and then she turns to me and starts to sign but Jonnyboy cuts her off and instead she mouths:

—Jonnyboy wants to stay here now and wants me here

too. So will you please make as many more trips to the car as you need to bring everything down.

I'm all Kewl with a k and Jonnyboy hands me the keys. He doesn't look me in the eye and am I glad. Because if he did I'm sure he'd know.

That I know.

That he shouldn't trust me.

But he does.

More than Ula or Finn or Critter anywayz. Which means I scored. I've got the car keys. I don't have that much experience driving but I've got enough to get down to Highway 1.

And what.

Call the cops. On Jonnyboy. Which would mean calling them on Finn and Critter and Ula too.

Yeah right.

Go home. To my family. But my family's not in Monterey anymore. My family's right here.

Except for Jason.

I could go to Jason's. But what would I do. What would Finn and Critter and Ula and Jonnyboy do. And what about Roarke.

Most of this was my idea.

Back at the car the first thing I do is look for the tire iron in the trunk. It's gone. But the towel's still there. And it's definitely got bloodstains on it.

I wonder if he ever even asked Roarke about ransoming the redwoods.

we're turnin pro w/ a vengeance. hee hee. only make that VEN-GEANCE.

I wonder how much Ula knew and when did she know it.

I don't think she knew till sometime yesterday after they dropped us off. She was just too calm.

And now she's freeked. But she wants vengeance too. For her sister. And Roarke doesn't mean anything to her. No wait. Actually he does. He's a symbol. Of everything she's against. The forces of control. The society of the spectacle. Which she tried to explain to me is the way we live our lives based on images of things instead of real things. The way Jonnyboy based his idea of Roarke on a picture of Lou Reed. The way Jonnyboy based his life on being like Roarke.

Who he didn't even really know.

And the way Roarke let him.

That's why she's going along with it. Or maybe she's going along with it because Jonnyboy's got.

A gun.

Tucked into the waistband of his jeans. I saw the outline through his shirt.

Thinking of the gun makes me decide to make smoke back to the house with the first load anywayz because the last thing I want is Jonnyboy suddenly getting paranoid and deciding I've been gone too long and chasing up here after me with live ammo. I mean I've still got at least one more trip's worth of stuff and just because I don't bail now doesn't mean I'm ruling it out later. Though I have second thoughts as soon as I get close to the house again and smell the dead coyote which puts the Reaper front and center in my mind so the house fully creeps me out as soon as I get inside and I mean hard as in gripped with fear and dripping stinky sour sweat. And I realize why when I'm halfway down the hallway to the War Room. It's the flashlight beam skittering high and low on the blank gray maze of walls and what it reminds me of.

Which is those two boyz in that movie *In Cold Blood* going into that farmer's house in Kansas in the middle of the night and just like me they aren't exactly sure what the future holds but they know it won't be pretty and suddenly do I wish I jumped behind the wheel of the car when I had my sure chance and burned rubber all the way to Monterey. Because Jonnyboy's planning on killing Roarke. After the redwood ransom goes through. I'm sure of it. It's the only way to keep him quiet.

Or is it.

Jonnyboy's got the gun. But I've got the secret room. If I could make a diversion I could hide Roarke in there and make it look like he somehow got away and headed down the mountain. And while Jonnyboy went chasing after him I could lead him down the trail to Partington Canyon.

If he promised not to tell.

Anybody.

Anything.

The trouble is what would Jonnyboy do then. And it's pretty obvious he'd totally flip out. He'd figure the boyz in blue were on their way and no telling what might happen. He might hurt Ula. Or Finn. Or Critter. Or all of them.

I hate Jonnyboy.

But not like Jonnyboy hates Roarke.

Not like Ula hates Roarke.

The only way to stop this cold is to get Roarke completely out of the picture. Make Jonnyboy think he's already dead.

Oh heavens to Betsy.

Oh suburban lawns.

Oh kitchens of distinction.

I practically tread air like Roadrunner turning around and then run back through the kitchen and out the door to the bushes where the coyote is. I crouch down as far away as I can and still grab the tip of the tail. I bury my mouth and nose in the crook of my other arm but the smell and the touch of the greasy prickly fur get me dry-heaving halfway back to the patio behind the kitchen.

I'm holding my breath and dripping with sweat. I grit my teeth running doubled over the rest of the way to the huge brick barbecue on the edge of the patio and swing the coyote into the open firebox which is big enough to crawl inside. I slam the cast-iron door so hard I feel the vibrations in the hot still air.

Which is weird. I mean it's dark and it's hotter now than it was before sundown.

When I get to the doorway of the War Room Jonnyboy's facing me holding Roarke upright in one of the wooden chairs while Ula's got her back turned getting ready to shoot Roarke up with a syringe full of crack. Which she doesn't look too happy about and I'm dead sure it's against the nurse's code or whatever it is. But I guess Jonnyboy wants to do *Save Those Trees or We'll Shoot This Boy* and do it now because the Polaroid's out on the table and so are the gun and today's newspaper. And does that rock my world because I realize that either Jonnyboy or Ula will have to take that picture to the nearest mailbox or maybe if they're smart not even the nearest one and since Jonnyboy's so paranoid from crack he probably won't let Ula do it alone. Which means they'll have to leave for at least a couple hours and probably more like three or four.

When Jonnyboy sees me he points toward Roarke and draws his hands across his eyes like a blindfold and gestures for me to move along down the hallway out of sight at the same time he's saying something to Ula. So I start to head on but pause when I see Ula's whole body stiffen as she answers him back and I can read Jonnyboy's lips snarling with rage in the hellish light from the red beeswax candle.

—You forgot!

—You forgot to buy the fucking film!

Jonnyboy hauls his arm back then breaks her nose with the flat of his hand.

Ula runs past me out the door holding her face with blood streaming through her fingers. Jonnyboy starts to follow her then pivots looking at Roarke who's coming to.

—Fuck!

He runs back to Roarke and winds a cocoon of parachute cord around him and the chair. Then he stares me hard in the eyes his face two inches from mine on his way out the door and mouths —Don't move.

I count to five then rush over to Roarke pulling out my notepad and scribbling as fast as I can in the weird red jumping candlelight.

U gotta trust me. I'm not part of this. I found a place 2 hide U. L8er. I'll divert J somehow. U'll get outa here. U won't get hurt any more I swear.

He reads it and stares into my eyes. I realize I sketched out words just like Jonnyboy. Bad move. Why should he trust me. I mean I am part of this.

Or am I.

Yes.

I was wrong. I don't hate Jonnyboy. I love him. Which is why I have to stop this.

Roarke starts to move his lips and I bend close over the candle.

—He's going to kill me.

I just nod my head. Then Roarke's whole body stiffens and I jump back away from him and rip the page from my notebook and stuff it in my mouth. In the seventh of a second before Jonnyboy comes charging back in Roarke shoots me a look and I know what it means.

He trusts me.

Jonnyboy's wild-eyed panicked. He stops beside me and looks over at Roarke whose eyes are closed now. He turns to me fullface and moves his lips.

—I have to trust you. I can't trust her.

I draw a question mark in the air and he reaches for my notepad. I freeze. It's not in my left pocket as usual but my right. Because my left hand is on the door side and I couldn't chance him seeing me put it away.

He doesn't even notice and just reaches into my other pocket and leads me over to the table by the candle.

we gotta get film @ Nepenthe & we have 2 leave now while it's dark. it takes 2, 1 2 drive & 1 2 see if the coast is clear before driving on2 the highway, then put the chain back. & we can't come back till after dark so nobody sees us leave the road. it's up 2 U Radboy, i gotta count on U, i'm so fuckin stressed & all this is fallin apart. it's gotta B me and her goin down the mountain, i wouldn't trust her alone anywayz, she might chief out, she's way pissed at me now. tho she wants 2 save those trees 4 her sister. so U gotta watch roarke, keep him blindfolded, keep F & C away if they wake up, keep the door closed, if any fuckin hikers show up scare em the fuck away. R U W/ ME???

He holds both of my hands in his and I stare back and nod my head slowly and surely. Then I give him the car keys.

He ties a bandanna around Roarke's head for a blindfold and rubs his palm across my head and he's gone like a song.

I wait a long time before I untie the bandanna and write down for Roarke the basics of the way it has to be.

As in he can't just run away.

As in he can't ever say anything to the question authorities and I mean who what where when how or why.

As in he has to trust me.

He nods after reading it and picks up the pen.

He trusts me.

He hesitates.

He trusts me not.

I motion for the pad.

I believe you that Jonnyboy said he'd kill you. But I don't know it for a fact. That he said it. That he'd do it.

Which I don't. Which makes me think of my dad and my mom. My sisters. All those lawyers. But they're all out of the picture. That was then and this is now. It's just between the two of us.

I stare into his eyes. He stares into mine. Somehow it's settled without more words. We trust each other. I don't know why.

I untie him from the chair and help him stand up. He's pretty wobbly. But before I take him into the secret room I walk him outside toward the eucalyptus trees and get him to fake a scuffle with me so the leaves and bark on the ground are all disturbed. Then I wrap my arms around him from behind and try to drag him back toward the house with his legs limp.

But I'm seeing stars after the first ten feet and I mean in addition to the endless skyway above our heads because it isn't even dawn yet. So Roarke tries dragging me for like three seconds and then it's him all wasted. We end up trading off with me doing most of the heavy lifting until we get to the edge of the brick patio. Which takes about an hour it seems and the sky in the east is definitely lightening up.

I show Roarke how the can opener works and he's fully not maybe I'm amazed. In the secret room he picks the magazine up from the chair and I aim the flashlight while he blows a mushroom cloud of dust off the cover.

Collier's.

March 1945.

The Coming World Without War.

After the wall is back in place with Roarke inside I walk out across the patio and stare at the barbecue. Now all there is to do is wait.

Well not quite all.

I have to stay awake which isn't too difficult considering all the crack in my system. Not to mention all the thoughts in my head of everything I've done and could have done and might have done and should have done but didn't. The sun gets high and hotter than ever and a few flies buzz around the barbecue trying to get inside. I run my fingers over the first signs I've ever noticed of stubble on my chin. I wander back inside and stare at Finn and Critter sleeping naked again and for some reason I'm so lonesome I could cry. Then like magic Finn's fluttering his eyelids and yawning and grinning and asking where is everybody.

For seven seconds I want to tell him everything. But I'm afraid to. He might want to wake up Critter and just bail down the hill and hitchhike home. I know I probably would if I was him. And then what would Jonnyboy do. All in all I think it's safer for everybody if Finn and Critter stay in the dark. So I just answer back with whole truth and nothing but as in Jonnyboy and Ula went to get film and Roarke's kicking back somewherez else in the house but we're supposed to keep our distance.

Finn just nods and stretches and takes a drink from the water bottle I left beside them earlier. He asks if I need any help with anything. With kind of a sly look in his eyes. Which along with him being stark raving naked makes me blush while

I shake my head. But I guess it doesn't show through my sun-
burn because he just gives me a satisfied smile and starts to
settle back down beside Critter.

—Well then. It's a right holiday. Innit. In the Presidential
Suite no less.

He yawns bigtime.

—Only in America.

He's asleep again by the time his head hits the blanket. I
look at them for a while longer then take Finn's knife and
Critter's butane mini-torch for later and end up sitting by my
lonesome in the War Room in the same chair where Roarke
was tied. I don't really sleep or anything but I kind of blank
out counting the lead plates on the walls the way some people
count sheep I guess and the next thing I know the cool draft
through the ventilation slits tells me it's getting dark again.

I walk out through the kitchen to the patio and cover my
mouth and nose with my t-shirt and use the mini-torch to light
the barbecue. I walk back over to the eucalyptus leaves by the
door where Roarke and I started making the drag marks and
unbutton my pants and pull them off after I take Finn's knife
out of the pocket. I stare at the shiny blade and draw my breath
and squat cutting the skin on the insides of my legs until the
blood from the cuts makes shimmering dark pools in the hollows of the eucalyptus leaves and soaks the ground.

I walk around the corner of the house and stop the bleeding with cold water from a canteen and my balled-up boxers
clutched between my legs. I barely make it back to the blanket
in Roosevelt's bedroom next to Finn and Critter before I'm
really seeing stars this time and I mean constellations. I mean
the fucking Milky Way.

At first I think it's the smell that wakes me but even before
I open my eyes I realize it's a voice and one loud enough to

move the air and shake the windowpanes in the split second before two hands under my arms like steel claws are shaking me and I mean Richter 9.

I don't want to look at him. I don't want to remember his eyes. His screaming mouth.

—Where is he?

Drops of spit so hot they burn my skin.

Ula's face behind him frantic distorted witchlike in the weird blue torchlight.

I struggle to raise one hand to fingerspell.

I killed him.

She stares.

Her lips move.

—No. No. No.

Jonnyboy turns and screams at her then lets go and pushes me so hard my back slams into the bedroom wall ten feet behind me. He reaches into his jeans pocket and moves toward me yelling but there's no way near enough light for me to read his lips. I can see the bare-skin silhouettes of Finn and Critter standing still as statues in front of the open double door holding on to one another like the shell-shocked refugees you see in war photos but no hint of their faces. Ula's behind Jonnyboy holding the butane torch. Following him. Afraid of him.

Without taking his eyes off me and with one hand still in his jeans he stops and reaches inside his jacket with his other hand. He yells at me again and Ula's hand over his shoulder makes a Y.

I see a glint of silver in Jonnyboy's hand.

It doubles in size.

A switchblade.

Ula's fingers move down to his shoulder.

He whirls standing and screams something at her and she

drops the torch. Either Finn or Critter picks it up. I can't tell with the shadows. Jonnyboy turns back toward me lunges forward leaping and pins my head with his fist on one side of my throat and the blade stuck solid in the wall on the other. He holds another knife to my throat. An eight-inch Buck. My brother Terry's knife.

I never knew he kept it.

Déjà vu all over again.

Only my dad won't come running in. Jason won't come running in. I'm on my own.

Suddenly it hits me why he's like this. He wanted to kill Roarke himself.

I slowly palms out and up raise a finger to my ear then make a scribble move.

Jonnyboy reaches for the pencil stub in his piercing on autopilot then pauses. He doesn't look me in the eyes. He's breathing in gasps. His hand is shaking when it puts the stub between my fingers. I turn halfway so I can write on the wall and it's weird. My hand isn't shaking at all.

I did it because I love you. Because I knew you were going to do it. And I didn't want you to have to pay for it. They'll let me off EZ.

He reads it and shudders. Shakes his head in a wide arc back and forth.

Does he believe me.

He takes the pencil stub back and writes on the wall in big shaky letters that carve across the necks of a row of eagles on the wallpaper.

SHOW ME.

It was Finn who picked up the torch when Ula dropped it and with a gesture from Jonnyboy he leads the way down the corridor past the War Room to the kitchen. He's wearing nothing but a mummy sleeping bag wrapped around him with the fitted foot section over his head and walking in front of us with the torch held high his shadow looks like the Reaper and I mean fully.

He kept his eyes on Jonnyboy when we first walked toward him. I wonder if he's afraid of me. Afraid of Jonnyboy. Afraid of both of us.

I would be.

At least Critter looked at me. He just stared like somebody at the scene of an accident. But he looked right into my eyes and didn't even glance at Jonnyboy.

Jonnyboy holds my upper arm in a grip that hurts. We walk past the liquor cabinet and I hold my breath. I suddenly realize I don't know if Roarke can hear what's going on from inside the secret room. I never even thought of that. I never even thought about whether the magic can-opener system makes any noise.

What a little criminal.

We walk outside and everybody holds their breath. The burned flesh smell is awful. Which is just what I wanted to discourage close inspection of the firebox.

Jonnyboy pushes me ahead to guide but Finn doesn't need any directions. The torch is a lot brighter than any flashlight. It definitely looks like somebody did a lot of bleeding here. I gesture toward my front jeans pocket and Jonnyboy pulls out the knife. Which I smeared heavily of course even though only the tip got bloody when I cut myself.

Finn bends over getting sick and drops the torch. The dry leaves flare up like a bonfire in the hot wind blowing hard now and for a second we're all frozen in bright hot light like on a movie set. Then everyone else even Finn springs into action stamping out the flames while I just stand here. I barely even notice Jonnyboy isn't holding me anymore. It's all sort of just hitting me for the first time.

What I did.

What I'm doing.

I look up to the stars then east hoping for a hint of gray but it's black as night black as coal. The boyz smother the fire completely by stretching out the corners of the sleeping bag and rolling their bodies over the embers one by one. Ula sits huddled on the ground crying. I take a step toward her and Jonnyboy grabs my arm again. His hand is gritty with dirt. His grip is a thousand percent weaker but I still flinch and I mean hard I'm already so bruised.

Then the strangest thing happens. He lets go. And messes my hair.

But he grabs me again and harder too. Tips my head up roughly with his other hand. Puts his face inches from mine so I can read his lips in the starlight.

—Lead the way little man.

Ula has a little penlight on her key chain. It actually fucks up your night vision so you see less. Except in the little circle underneath the light. Where you see the drag marks of heels in the dirt and the occasional bloody leaf that I scattered from my pocket.

Until you get to the bricks of the patio. Where you can't see anything because your eyes are watering from the acrid smoke still leaking from the barbecue and you don't want to anyway because your stomach is churning like a Tilt-A-Whirl from the smell.

Jonnyboy nods toward the dark brick tower and looks at me expectantly. Everyone else looks down holding their faces in their hands. I nod *Yes*.

—Really.

I double-nod squinting my eyes from the smoke.

Yes I did yes.

—Jesus.

—Fucking.

—Christ.

Jonnyboy draws each word out looking me hard in the eyes. He believes me.

A gust of wind practically knocks us over.

Jonnyboy's scream scares everyone but me.

Flames shoot into the dark beyond the patio.

There must have been embers left from Finn dropping the torch.

The wind. The sparks. All those drought-dry leaves. All those drought-dry trees.

Jonnyboy charges toward the flames arms flailing. Ula follows him hobbling barefoot and yelling. I stand still. Finn and Critter start running too but away from the house not toward it. Then they slow down and I can see them talking all wild-eyed and scared. Suddenly they veer left and head for the kitchen door.

I'm behind them like the Wheaties boy but I turn my head before I run inside. The line of eucalyptus trees flames up like a screen of fire all the way to the stars. I can't see Jonnyboy or Ula anymore just shapes and shadows in the smoke where they were.

Or maybe it's flames where they were.

In the kitchen the cork panel's already opening. Roarke squeezes out as soon as he can. He grabs me and starts talking a mile a minute. I touch his arm with my hand and he's vibrating. Finally he slows the flow enough for me to figure out by holding my eyes an inch in front of his lips that he heard voices yelling about clothes and car keys and something about a bunny.

And do I thank Jesus Mary and Joseph that bunny came home. One more little delay. At this end of the house we're a little closer to the car but Finn and Critter have a head start. Plus I saw the keys on top of Ula's red backpack when Finn led us out of Roosevelt's bedroom so I know they won't be searching more than seven seconds. But rounding up that cracked-on rabbit may take long enough for Roarke and me to race them to the Valiant and slide the back seat forward and hide in the trunk. So I shut Roarke up and do fast and dirty Johnny Rotten *Follow me!* and he huffs and puffs and barely keeps up but once we get past the fire which must be ten stories high now he gets second wind and we're through the car doors and squeezing into the trunk so fast it's like we tele-ported. I mean I don't remember anything except the raging fire so hot it crisped the hair on my arms from fifty feet away and my brain shouting relief when the car doors weren't locked.

I just wish I didn't remember the ride back either. The almost suffocating heat from our bodies jammed together and the stomach-turning smells of dirty wet towels and our sour scared sweat and Roarke's blood-soaked bandages. Plus exhaust fumes seeping in through a little rust window below the passenger-side back-panel light from a hole in the muffler I guess and aching bruises everywhere first from Jonnyboy grab-bing me and second from the head- and body-banging descent of the rough old road. And that was just the physical side. Inside my brain was this endless loop movie of Jonnyboy and Ula and Roarke and me. Complete with endless loop sound-track *Why oh why oh why oh why.*

The dawn light was coming through the cracks around the

trunk lid when we could tell we were back in San Francisco from the stops and starts and also by the wheels of the shopping carts of homeless people on the sidewalk that somehow seemed to be at the perfect angle and distance to be framed in the rust window. Since it was Monday but still too early for people to be on their way to work it took forever to find a parking place and then forever to the tenth while we waited inside after Finn and Critter left. We held out about a minute max and it seemed longer than the whole trip. And during that minute's when claustrophobia set in. I started twitching and gasping for air like a drowning man I swear.

So was I all cartwheels and parking meter hurdles out on the sidewalk gulping fresh damp air. But reality bit as always and did it hard and I almost started crying. Then I found out Roarke just wanted to bail by himself since he didn't really know Finn and Critter and he figured it was better if he never did based on what he heard them saying on the ride back up. And I did start crying. Because the only way they'd believe me was to see him in the flesh and immediately as in right then and there. Otherwise they'd just figure I did kill him and was doing the only sensible thing under the circumstances as in flee undercover and deny everything.

Standing there on the sidewalk by the motorcycle store at the corner of Eighth and Sumner with tears running down my cheeks I felt alone and scared like I did the night of the concert in the park before Ula took me back to Finn and Critter's. Only worse because not only was Jonnyboy gone and this time maybe for good but Ula was gone with him and Finn and Critter thought I was a killer. It made me want to end it all I swear and I didn't even think of Jason.

Roarke just stood there looking at me like he was seeing a

stranger or I know a ghost. But then I guess it all came back to him.

Jonnyboy. The War Room. The horrible fear.

Because he put both his arms around me and started crying too and we stood there shaking in each other's arms for the longest time until he broke one arm free and motioned for me to lead the way down Sumner Street and did I.

I still had my keys but I figured it was better to knock on the inside door and when Critter answered he almost slammed it in our faces thinking he was hallucinating on crack and is it surprising. But Roarke yelled at him and Finn came up behind Critter and with one long look in my eyes I think he understood everything. They hustled both of us inside and sat us on the sofa and Roarke started talking a mile a minute about how Jonnyboy attacked him I guess and how I came to the rescue and naturally they were asking him a million questions and forgetting I was even there until suddenly it hit me what happened and I mean REALLY hit me as in that fire burned the hair off my arms from fifty feet away. And I could feel my eyes bug out and this choking sensation in my throat and I threw my head back and opened my mouth and out came a long loud howling scream of a sound that made Finn shiver and press his fists against his eyes just remembering it two weeks later.

Then I blacked out. It wasn't sleep because I don't think I dreamed one-seventh of a second in the next thirty-six hours. And when I came to I remembered everything like it all just happened and my head was still numb and my bruises still ached so it wasn't like I got any rest. I was laying on the sofa and Finn and Critter were sitting on the floor in front of me making crack cards. They both turned toward me when they heard me move and pulled themselves up on either side of me and between the two of them held all of me tight in their arms until finally I did sleep. Then they carried me to their bed without waking me up and they slept too.

It was early morning when I woke up between them thirsty and hungry and wandered into the kitchen where all I found to eat was Pop-Tarts and chocolate pudding. So I stuck the Pop-Tarts into a bowl of pudding like saltines into chili and carried it out to the living room. The bunny was playing statues in the middle of a folded newspaper on the floor and I shooed her away when I saw the huge black headline.

BIG SUR BURNS

Firefighters from six western states are in the air and on the ground battling the 15,000-acre Partington Ridge blaze in Big Sur that threatens to surpass the 1982 Ventana Cone fire as the scenic region's most destructive this century. With efforts to contain the rapidly spreading fire hampered by 100-degree heat and gale-force Santa Ana winds, Los Padres National Forest officials refused to predict where and when the flames may be stopped.

Officials did announce, however, that arson has been ruled out as the fire's cause. According to a Forest Service spokes-person, smokejumpers have traced the fire's flash point to a clandestine methamphetamine lab located in an abandoned World War II–era defense facility high atop Partington Ridge, 20 miles south of the town of Big Sur. The spokesperson de-clined to confirm that human remains have been airlifted from the site by helicopter for examination by forensic pathologists. But in a bizarre twist, he revealed that on-site personnel dis-covered evidence pointing to ritual animal sacrifice and possible satanic worship.

I stopped reading and the newspaper slipped through my fingers and fell back to the floor.

I knew I was going to be sick.

I knew what a murderer must feel like. Even though I saved a life.

I doubled over clutching my stomach and started to fall but warm arms caught me and held me from behind.

Finn.

He turned me around and raised my chin up with his thumb so I could see him fullface.

—It's not your fault.

I answered back with my eyes.

Yes it is.

—It was me who dropped the bloody torch.

Because you saw the blood I spread around.

—You were trying to do good.

I didn't know WTF I was doing.

—If you want to blame somebody blame your dear old dad. Blame whoever posted the handbill for the Green Tortoise bus. Don't blame yourself.

I just nodded my head back and forth as in *No way can I not blame myself.* And Finn looked disgusted with sparks of anger in his eyes and he unwrapped one arm from my shoulder and pointed down at the newspaper.

—Blame drugs then. They did.

Then he turned away and stomped back toward the bedroom.

I looked up at the clock showing 7:29. The remote was on the mirror table and I punched the mute button on autopilot and then the channel for the captioned news. The announcer was an Asian woman doing the morning wrap-up in front of a video screen showing the trunks of trees bursting into flames.

Huge trees.

The caption scrolled.

In today's top California story, firefighters in Big Sur aban-doned efforts to save the Willow Creek grove of thousand-year-old coastal redwoods as the 25,000-acre Partington Ridge Fire jumped Highway 1 and burned its way to the sea.

I turned around. Finn was standing there with tears run-ning down his cheeks and two candles in his hands reading the caption out loud to Critter behind him in boxer shorts.

And I wondered why. Because Critter was staring right at the screen. Then it hit me.

All that time and he'd never written me a single note. Or fingerspelled anything except that very first morning here.

W-O-R-K.

The universal four-letter word.

Later he held his fingers in a cross when I nicked Finn's scalp with the clippers.

But it was Ula fingerspelling *A-I-D-S.*

And I thought I was handicapped.

Critter scratched the dog's-paw tattoo on his chest and rubbed Finn's head then came over and put his arms around me and we hugged each other tight. Afterwards he raised the dustcover on the turntable and while Finn lit the candles he cued up an Abba record.

I watched it spinning.

Stared at my reflection in the grooves.

I saw horses.

The green light at the bottom of the hill.

The heart drop into the water sunset and the fog bank sitting on Monterey Bay.

Like the lid of a coffin closing forever.

Why do good things never wanna stay.

I didn't know what to do. So I didn't do anything. Just sat

there. Took no action. Tapped my foot to the unheard music. All day long and through the night. Slept a few hours and did the same. Like punch the clock. Like welcome to the working week. Like good morning America how are ya.

Asked and answered.

I'm tired.

I'm hurt.

I'm fine.

It was never the same with Finn and Critter and me again. But it's not like they put me out on the street or anything. They got me a job at the Pit. And now I'm staying with Jason.

It was his idea I really could be a DJ. As in fuck that weak deaf-boy shit. As in you don't just hear songs with your ears you hear them in your head. And if you can hear them any which way you can play them for people.

As in I can play them for people.

My favorite songs.

Or at least I can try. And do I have to. Because almost everything's good between Jason and me and we spend most all our time together when he's not spinning in clubs and that means he's living in the slow lane these days when it comes to go-fast. But there's one thing wrong and it's all my fault.

He doesn't know.

What happened.

And I don't know how to tell him.

He doesn't know.

How much I love him.

So I'm counting on the songs.

To help me.

And I'm not waiting. I mean I got a pretty good track record already for a deaf boy. Starting in fourth grade when we rocked everybody's world performing that song in sign on Parents' Day.

This land is your land.
This land is my land.
This land was made for you and me.

And for California Jonnyboy and foreigner Ula and my Portuguese dad and my US male brothers who I need to see before too long because I ain't no Rodney King but why can't we all just get along. I mean amongst ourselves. So the big and glassies have to worry a little more about their foundations. Especially here in earthquake country. You know what I'm saying? Let's have a few more rocks and a little more roll. Shine them bloody rocks though. That's what got us where we are today.

Which is nowhere.

There is no land but the land.

From the redwood forest to the gulf war waters.

This land is.

Some things you lose.

This land was.

Some things you give away.

Oct. 7, 1997
San Francisco
Jason sleeping